A LIVING HOPE

Also by E. C. Jackson

A Gateway to Hope
Pajama Party: The Story

A LIVING HOPE

a novel

E. C. Jackson

ISBN: 978-0-9961812-5-9

Editing: amberbarryeditor.com and angela.trent@sbcglobal.net
Cover design: FormattingExperts.com
Typesetting: FormattingExperts.com
Book blurb: standoutbooks.com

The Write Way – A Real Slice of Life: ecjacksonauthor.wordpress.com
Author Page: facebook.com/ecjacksonauthor
Designed by Standoutbooks

Acknowledgments

A Living Hope, the second book in the hope-themed series, is a reality. I sat down at the computer one day and the story practically wrote itself. But not without the help of key people along the way.

As always, my family and friends supported me throughout the process with prayers and encouragement. Editors Amber Barry and Angela Trent helped to polish my tome. Alex, with Standoutbooks, wrote the perfect book blurb. And Rafal, along with the team at Formatting Experts, furnished the book cover, formatted the copy, and did everything else needed to present this book to the reader.

Also, the good reviews for the first book, *A Gateway to Hope*, propelled me forward.

Through God's grace this book was written, polished, and formatted, with Him giving the increase of a published novel.

Thank you all for your prayers, support, and good wishes.

Praised be God, Father of our Lord Yeshua the Messiah, who, in keeping with his great mercy, has caused us, through the resurrection of Yeshua the Messiah from the dead, to be born again to a living hope, to an inheritance that cannot decay, spoil or fade, kept safe for you in heaven.

1 Peter 1:3-4
The Complete Jewish Bible

Chapter One

Restless, twenty-one-year-old Sadie Cummings wiped down the counter space in her small kitchen nook. It was eleven o'clock. Five minutes had passed since the last time she'd checked. Sighing, she fretted about her boyfriend's visit that morning.

"Why does he agree to come over, then not show up?"

In no time, morning had slipped into early afternoon. The breakfast she'd hoped would receive raves from Lincoln congealed on the stovetop. So much for using her cooking skills to entice him. With several swift movements, she scraped the masterpiece into the garbage disposal, fighting to control the uneasiness she couldn't dismiss.

She was an expert at fooling herself and others, but today her mind refused to be pacified. One could only pretend for so long before the bottom dropped out completely. Truth had a bad habit of intruding into fairy tales. Especially when the make-believe stories were about real-life events.

The ringing cell phone grabbed Sadie's attention. That her mother was on the other end was a forgone conclusion. Except for an occasional chat with her younger sister and older brother, the cell phone never rang. These days only her mother contacted Sadie on a regular basis. She peeked at the caller ID.

A moment before the call transferred to voicemail, Sadie snatched up the cell phone, held it against her chest, then gave a cheery greeting. Minutes later, she sauntered through the studio apartment thinking up reasonable excuses to end the call early. Jeanette Cummings expected a good deal more than her middle child was able to give.

Still stumped about finding an excuse to satisfy her mother, Sadie walked around in circles.

"Mother, I'm not trying to hurry you off the phone. I recognize your concern for the Franklins. Our families have been friends for years. It's just ... look ... it's ... mother, I don't have time to talk now."

Sadie picked up twine from the counter and wove it between her fingers. Pulling it too tight, she winced, then unwound it from around her fingers and wrapped it around her thumb.

"I made plans for the day."

Lincoln could arrive any moment. Somehow, she had to quickly end this conversation without hurting the only person who regularly called. Friendships were difficult to maintain these days. And her brother and sister only gave duty calls, then ended the conversation in a snap.

Jeanette sighed loudly. "I would offer to call back at a better time, but there isn't one, is there, Sadie?"

"Mom ..."

Sadie slowly shook her head. Guilt surfaced each time she talked to her mother. Raised in an orphanage, her mother wasn't a clingy parent. She believed loneliness caused people to accept unhealthy conditions that a person who felt treasured might avoid.

"Of course, you're removed from the lives of the families in Shiatown," said Jeanette.

Blowing breath through her lips, Sadie laid her head on the cabinet with more force than intended. Wincing in pain, she rubbed the sore spot. The lull in the conversation helped gather her thoughts as her fingers massaged the painful area on her forehead. She parted her lips, then she shut them in hopes that her mother would continue speaking.

After a long pause, Jeanette spoke with a harsher tone than any she'd ever used with her daughter. "Listen to me. The Franklin family supported us through your father's illness and death. We are burying Pastor Franklin this afternoon. His wife deserves a phone call from you."

She paused before continuing. "Don't forget, Sarah treated you like a daughter. You and Pastor Franklin shared the same birthday. September twelfth is four days away. My friend is burying her husband four days before his fifty-eighth birthday. And ... what about Kyle? He lost his father and inherited a ton of responsibility on top of it. Honey, be the friend that I know you are. Time is slipping away. The funeral starts in two hours."

Sadie stretched her neck from side to side, hanging her head in despair. Lately, her mother had begun to accept her decisions without fussing. However, today she seemed determined for Sadie to send well wishes to a man she'd rather forget. Feeling faint, she squeezed her eyelids together, but all she could see was Kyle's sad gaze begging, pleading with her to choose him over the man Sadie picked.

Instantly, anger rose as Sadie justified that choice. She couldn't back down now. There was too much lost ground and no way to regain her footing. The future she'd hoped for was gone. Somehow the leftovers had to be salvaged into a win or, at least, a tolerable solution.

Eyes darting around the room, she braced against the wall. "Friend? Kyle and I didn't break up as friends. He acted like a judgmental pig; his last remarks were cruel."

Sadie fumed. With one look Kyle had made her feel like trash. Less than the muck beneath his shoes. Disposable at best, and at worse ...

"Sadie—"

"Don't excuse him, Mom. Kyle humiliated me in front of Lincoln." She glanced at her shoes.

And the truth is, I didn't deserve any better.

"Oh yes, Lincoln. The wonder man who is far from wonderful. I hate the way he treats you, honey. All women deserve respect." Jeanette continued when Sadie failed to respond. "So Kyle, the man we expected to welcome into our family, means nothing to you? You can just ignore the difficulties he's facing?"

Sadie rested her forehead in her palm. A magic wand could wave all her troubles away. Too bad real life didn't offer fantasy solutions. No one moved forward without blood, sweat, and tears. But where would she begin? Her mistakes had obscured her direction. She felt like a rudderless ship adrift on an endless sea.

Closing her eyes, Sadie brushed teardrops from her cheeks. "Mother, you don't understand."

"More than you can imagine my dear." She paused. "I admit life was difficult while your father was alive. For too many years, his illness handicapped the entire household. Nevertheless, we raised our children using godly values. Principles I'd hoped would follow you throughout your life."

Her mother's appeal fell on deaf ears. Reason came too late. Values? Sadie had surrendered those beliefs to the unpredictable man who could arrive any moment. Somehow Lincoln had worn down her defenses from the moment she met him. His mercurial personality had kept her off balance from the start. First, he'd downplayed her views, and then he stole her innocence, until finally her conscience hung in the balance.

Wavering, Sadie stared off into space, lowering her voice to a whisper. "No promises, but let me think about it, okay?"

"What more can I ask than for you to do the right thing? I love you, honey. We'll talk later."

Saying goodbye, Sadie made her way to the alcove she used as a bedroom. Her gaze went straight to the high school senior picture she'd once cherished. The one that showed a bright-eyed young adult bent on living out her dreams. The photographer had captured a smiling face that exuded hope for a happy future. The ecstatic senior had been on top of the world. About to embark on a new life, knowing the man she loved adored her in return.

Sadie sat on the floor, studying the photo. Her anticipation rose each time she recalled her life before college. Could it be possible? Might there be a second chance with her childhood sweetheart?

Remorse replaced her anger. Teardrops plopped over her neck and chest. In one regretful conversation two years ago, her relationship with Kyle had ended. Slowly, she shook her head at the self-created havoc. Her foolish decisions had destroyed the relationship with the man she'd never stopped loving.

Since then, multiple bad choices had taken her life in a different direction. But the obsession with Lincoln Miller increased in fervor. All Sadie knew was that she had to marry the man who'd single-handedly wrecked her life.

Her college graduation had offered a chance to walk away from the relationship that should've never begun. Instead of saying goodbye to Burgundy, Missouri, Sadie stayed on. She was determined to make a life for herself until Lincoln finished his senior year at the university. After that, who knew where a pro-football career might take them? Unable to find a job in her chosen profession, she was waiting tables at three restaurants to pay the bills.

But last June, Sadie had invited her mother and eighteen-year-old sister for a two-week visit. She'd had big plans for their arrival, revamping the space she rented from the Sloanes into a cozy home with a cottage feel. And after accepting the invitation, the duo drove three hundred fifty miles for a two-week visit.

Sadie had ticked off the hours until their arrival, happy for the first time in two years. But three days into the visit, they repacked their bags and left the following morning. And all because Lincoln's boorish behavior had finally pushed them beyond endurance.

At first, the surprised Sadie had been happy when he showed up to meet her family. However, ten minutes after arriving he'd revealed the real purpose for coming. Lincoln wanted her completely separated from everyone who loved her. He behaved horribly, sowing discord while smilingly shaking hands. He casually insulted her mother and sister whenever the opportunity rose.

So, Sadie had suggested touring the state to enjoy her family alone. But those plans ended once Lincoln invited himself along on the trip. In three days flat, he'd ruined the relationships she'd hope to rebuild, plus tarnished his reputation in her mother's and sister's eyes.

Although they had left her apartment in a rush, her mother and sister's spring vacation hadn't been an entire bust. After bailing out on Sadie, they took the scenic view home, spending eight days touring Missouri before driving back to Shiatown, Oklahoma.

Sadie remembered her sister's outburst as her mother climbed into the car to leave. Sadie had asked her why they were running out on her so quickly.

"No one's running out on you, Sadie," she said, frowning at her. "Trying to like your boyfriend is exhausting. You chose that piece of filth over Kyle; we didn't."

Sadie's spirit died as she observed the tears in her sister's eyes.

The younger woman grimaced in disgust. "How can you let him touch you?" Rolling her eyes, she stomped to the car, then spun around at the door. "Keep him," she whispered, "but don't inflict him on your family." And then, as if they'd just ended a pleasant discussion, her sister entered the car, swiveled in the passenger's seat, and waved goodbye.

Standing at the curb, Sadie had cried openly. Another lifeline had driven off, leaving her with Lincoln. Her family had brought the only happiness she'd experienced since breaking up with Kyle, and then they deserted her three days later. She was alone again, and it was her fault.

After her family drove off, Sadie saw less of Lincoln than ever before. His usual once-a-week stopover dwindled to the occasional Wednesday evening. Isolated from family and friends who had all stopped calling by now, Sadie depended on Lincoln's company more than ever.

Today, reliving the past depleted her energy. Sadie was already anxious before the conversation with her mother had begun, Jeanette's phone call had unsettled her even more. She walked to the bathroom and took a long look at herself in the vanity mirror, trying to bolster her flagging courage.

Moaning, Sadie tilted her head from side to side. Her sleepless nights had become quite noticeable in bright lighting. Troubled, dark-brown eyes, surrounded by blemish-free toffee skin, stared back at her. What did it matter anyway? Looking her best didn't count anymore. At least not to the man who was late showing up. Nowadays when he paid a rare visit, his gaze flickered across the room instead of centering on her.

Ever since she'd broken up with Kyle, she'd tried convincing herself that she was loved and appreciated. A persistent question hammered her mind day and night: Why had Lincoln stopped even pretending to care? The last time she saw him, her wonder man had smiled into her eyes, and then disappeared for three weeks.

While scouring the city, Sadie had realized he'd covered his tracks because no one knew his whereabouts. In fact, most people she'd contacted denied having seen him around at all. Refusing to search for Lincoln anywhere on campus, exploring off-campus hangouts had turned up nothing. Even his running buddy claimed that he hadn't seen Lincoln in weeks.

When things went wrong, the word lunatic surged through her mind as usual. Her hands trembled as she rested her face in her palms. An intense fear of hearing that word flung at herself always paralyzed Sadie. The fact that no one in her hometown had ever hurled that accusation at her father, at least not that Sadie heard, didn't matter. Young ears often heard words no one spoke out loud. *Sadie Cummings's father is a crazy man, and maybe his daughter is crazy too.*

Oh, Lincoln, please cooperate with me just this once.

She sank to her knees in front of the vanity cabinet. Could two years of servitude end with her prayers unanswered? Had she forfeited the man she loved only to lose the man she left him for as well?

Standing, her gaze darted around the room. She refused to give up. There must be a reasonable explanation for his three-week absence. At least one that she could live with.

Resting her chin on her chest, she considered her options. There was no easy way out of the mess she'd created. Following her heart meant facing Kyle, a man who might hate her. Anyway, her ex-fiancé had left Shiatown for California, moving himself light-years away from past burdens. Available females had flocked around Kyle since his thirteenth birthday. How much more would they swarm the man as he continued to live out his dreams?

God, I won't be able to rise above a rejection from him.

Mind made up, she took a deep breath. Call Kyle? The disgust in his eyes the last time she saw him still haunted her dreams at night. And Miss Sarah, the woman she'd always considered a second mother, must loathe her too. Gasping for breath, Sadie wiped a warm towel across her face. How could she contact the woman she'd ignored since breaking up with her son? It would be much better to express her regrets through a floral arrangement sent to their home.

She stared unblinkingly into space. Unless her suspicions concerning Lincoln were confirmed, she would forgive and forget as usual. How could she give him up? Too much had been lost. Her whole way of life had changed since their first introduction. No other viable avenue existed since she'd burned her bridges behind her.

Staring at her reflection, Sadie frowned at the shadows beneath her eyes. There must be a way to keep Lincoln. She snapped the lid shut on her makeup kit and squeezed her eyelids together. Why delude herself? Somehow, the man she lived for was slipping farther away.

But how do I fix a relationship I simply want to end?

She jumped when the doorbell rang. Should she ignore the person or shoo them away before Lincoln arrived? Walking slowly to the door, she peeked through the blinds.

"Lincoln?" Why hadn't he used the spare key he'd talked her into giving him?

Sadie took a deep breath. Mumbling to herself, "I won't be a pushover," she swung open the door and slammed into a brick wall of resistance from Lincoln.

Chapter Two

He refused to enter the apartment once Sadie stepped aside. Without speaking a word, his challenging gaze raked over her body until he turned around, staring at the woman climbing the steps behind him.

Sadie almost gasped out loud. She hadn't noticed someone was with him. The woman wearing shorts and sandals with ties strapped just below her knees stepped close to Lincoln. The woman's hostile gaze revealed her low regard for a person she'd never met.

Breathing deeply, Sadie nipped her tongue between her teeth to keep silent. What was the deal? Had she somehow failed to live up to the stranger's expectations? Or did this woman expect to find a rival ready to fight for her man?

Forget those thoughts, lady. Who are you? Free entertainment isn't written in my script.

Sadie's heartbeat accelerated. While trembling inside, her hand dropped from the doorknob as she glanced at Lincoln's amused face. Instead of speaking to Sadie, he puckered his lips at the woman, then walked into the house.

Sadie swiftly closed the door and snapped the lock. Leaning against it, she surveyed the man staring at her. His smug expression said it all. Contempt highlighted the gaze that never left her face. The self-satisfied smirk sunk Sadie's last hope of a permanent bond.

Willing herself to remain calm, she matched his silence as her stomach muscles throbbed feverishly. Another humiliating confrontation awaited. Only this time, Kyle wouldn't have a ringside seat for the spectacle.

Suppressing thoughts of defeat, Sadie overcame the urge to scream. She refused to plead, beg or give in to the desolation that threatened to overpower her. That last debasing incident with Kyle flashed in her mind. In that scene, he'd advised her—in front of the man now glaring at her with narrowed eyes—to prepare for the day Lincoln Miller walked away. And two years later, that day had arrived.

Instantly, a haze seemed to cover the room that swayed before Sadie's eyes. She'd never felt such despair in her life. Not even on that horrific night when she'd witnessed a rookie police officer gun down her unarmed father. What had begun as a routine disturbance call (which usually resulted in a prolonged stay in the hospital's psychiatric ward), had ended in her father's untimely death.

Not even the self-inflicted pain of fingernails boring into her palm stopped the agony. A man who never deserved her affection was dumping her. But Lincoln's cockiness enabled her to just let him walk away without a fight. His disregard for her feelings supplied the fortitude needed to retain her self-respect and not beg him to stay with her.

But why doesn't he speak? Is he remaining quiet because I refused to grovel at his feet?

And then she remembered. Lincoln had never spoken when she'd talked to Kyle in her dorm room; he had stood behind her the entire time with his hands touching her arms.

The irony penetrated her sadness. Two years later, Sadie stood in the same position she'd forced on Kyle in her dorm room. Full of regrets, she hoped Lincoln failed to detect the deathblow he'd dealt her.

Drawing on new reserves, Sadie straightened her spine. Smiling into his eyes, she reached behind her back for the doorknob. Abruptly reopening the door, she stepped aside. The uncertainty on the man's startled face was priceless and emboldened her further. Her hand ushered him out the door as the woman jumped up from the porch swing where Sadie loved to sit in the evenings.

In the midst of closing the door, she tossed the woman her version of an *I feel sorry for you, too* smile.

Tears rolled down her cheeks after she closed the door, and a beaten Sadie crumpled to the floor.

* * *

The phone rang just as Kyle Franklin placed a blanket over his sleeping mother. Ignoring the call, he stared at the smooth skin that still defied age. A week ago today, Sarah had awakened next to the cold body of her husband of thirty-five years. No sickness had alerted her to any health issues that could cause a problem. And even though all appeared well when his father went to bed that night, William Franklin's life had ended suddenly. He stared at the empty space beside his mother, remembering the call that woke him up that morning.

Kyle had sat up in bed and turned on the light while comforting the one person who kept his life centered. As his mind reorganized the day, he'd talked to his mother until his aunt and uncle arrived at the house to help her.

Climbing out of bed, his mind went on autopilot. Fifteen hundred miles separated him from the mother who needed his support. All of his life, Sarah labored night and day, blessing anyone within her reach. She always helped out wherever she was needed. Now his mother required the comfort she'd willingly given to others. Pulling a suitcase from the closet, Kyle prepared himself for taking the journey back in time.

An hour later, fully dressed, packed, and his flight booked, twenty-three-year-old Kyle descended the stairs to the living room, mentally ticking off his checklist. He'd been serving as youth pastor at Hope in His Word Church for twenty-two months. The senior pastor and Kyle's staff had been alerted that he was leaving town until further notice. He'd already contacted the friend who was more like a sister, asking her to house-sit the condo until his return. Before hanging up, he'd decided to give her use of the car as well.

Primary duties accomplished, he stared out the living room window, watching for the taxicab, still staggered by his father's death. Kyle had welcomed the sunrays warming his body as he waited. They reminded him that God's love never failed, even during trials. Almost two years ago, father and son had healed their troubled relationship. Before his father passed away, the Franklin men had cemented an unbreakable bond. Still, Kyle regretted not being able to say goodbye to the father he loved.

His mind created a checklist for settling his father's estate while riding to the airport. Kingdom Life Church's five hundred members deserved another good pastor to take his place. Ready to retire, Minister Dawkins might take the job until Kyle installed someone else into the position. Plus, relocating Sarah to California meant selling the bookstore that she loved. And even though Kyle missed the college town's art and theater culture in the midst of the heartlands, he planned to stay in California. At least for now. Too many memories bound him to the past in Shiatown. A past that included Sadie Cummings.

At home, his mother's hope for them to reconcile reminded him of the good times before Sadie ended their engagement. The two of them had worked well together, often anticipating one another's wants and needs in advance. All of his expectations to live a happy life had included her. But those dreams were over. Now Kyle wanted to maintain his lifestyle in California for a few more years. New doors of opportunity opened daily. Projects he'd expected to develop in his father's church thrived under his tutelage here. God-ordained ideas never failed. And those ideas had included his ex-fiancée until she threw him away.

But Kyle had rebuilt his life without her in another city. He assembled dedicated volunteers who impacted multiple lives seven days a week. Young people experienced real problems ranging from depression and terminal illnesses to losing their families. Now the church possessed a vast network of professionals and lay people equipped to minister to those needs.

The ringing phone brought him back to the present. Time never stood still. His father was buried. And now he felt the full force of his parents' wish for him to pastor the church. On the flight home, he'd underplayed the tug their desire would exert on his conscience. But wisdom demanded that he seek God before making a final decision. Especially since his mother refused to leave her home and expected him relocate to Shiatown. Last June, he'd begun a promising relationship and preferred not to test the waters long distance. Kyle took another glance around the bedroom before gently closing the door.

Sadie popped into his mind again as he headed downstairs. Before lying down, Sarah had placed the white calla lily Sadie had sent on top of the mantel in the living room. The florist had left the bloom on the porch of their house. Sadie's simple message had touched his mother's heart.

Please accept my regrets. I miss being there today. So sorry ...
Sadie Mae Cummings.

As always, when he thought of her, a replay of their last meeting filled his memory. That agonizing confrontation had grown him up in a hurry. Kyle had gone to bed that night with a different mindset than the one he'd awakened with that morning.

Truth be told, a change in his life had come quickly after that meeting with her and Lincoln. Undeniable blessings had lessened the shock of losing his fiancée to another man. In fact, many past nemeses fled in the aftermath of his fighting for her. He'd tried hard to save Sadie from herself in spite of Lincoln laughing in his face.

Every aspect of the day filled his mind. Kyle had just taken a shower when Sadie called, crying hysterically. Although she was difficult to understand, one thing was clear. His fiancée had booted him for another man, and he'd known the relationship wouldn't last while she sobbed.

Years of drying Sadie's tears told him her remorse was genuine. Her impulsive nature had landed her into a situation beyond her control. Cleaning up her messes in the past had been a mistake. He should've let her solve her problems on her own. Now, Sadie had trapped herself into a meaningless relationship. She needed him.

Kyle raced from his home, speeding to Burgundy, certain she required a lifeline he was more than willing to toss. As he drove to see her, a tiny voice in his head told him he was crazy. What if he arrived only to find her and the new guy laughing at his expense? But he'd been right that the new guy was the wrong man for Sadie and was glad he went to rescue her.

Sadie and her two best friends since preschool were inseparable, and she roomed with one of them in college. When Kate opened the door, Sadie burst into tears and clung to his arms until Lincoln pulled her away. And Sadie let him. But, the teardrops rolling down her cheeks begged Kyle to help her. And even though Lincoln's hands rested lightly on Sadie's arms, to Kyle, they were a death grip around her throat.

Stranger still, Lincoln didn't speak a word throughout the ordeal. Yet the smug gaze directed at him and Kate held a challenge that drove Kyle into battle.

Lincoln won. Sadie had stopped crying long enough to ask Kyle to leave.

Even so, Kyle had won a personal victory despite the loss. Pleasing his peers against his better judgment vanished for good that afternoon. He liked staying true to his convictions as he had done in Sadie's dorm room. Kyle had ignored the man laughing at him, and he had fought for Sadie. He'd repeatedly forgiven the time with Lincoln, and he'd begged her to marry him as planned.

But it didn't work, he reminded himself. *She left you anyway.*

Now he shook his head, whistling softly. Remorse at being rejected never gained a foothold in his life. Kyle had felt liberated on the drive home to Shiatown. Standing his ground with Lincoln made a difference in Kyle's outlook.

Later, he experienced total freedom from his peer's opinions—they no longer defined his life.

Many bondages disappeared after the face off with Lincoln. Including protecting Sadie from real and imaginary foes. Never one to run away from a fight, Kyle had remained calm while he contended with the man eager to destroy her life. And it wasn't the quiet that preceded a storm, but the stillness that led to a life worth living. From that day forward, God strengthened him to weather the unexpected. Psalms 112 soon became a prized chapter in his scripture reading.

Instead of mourning losing his fiancée, he marveled as previous roadblocks disappeared in remarkable ways. Once Sadie said goodbye, breakthroughs in his personal life achieved what wishful thinking had never accomplished. He and his father became friends. They finally achieved the solidarity Kyle craved.

Both father and son savored the newfound rapport, releasing Sarah from straddling the fence between them. The relationship had become so bad at one point that Kyle moved into an apartment after graduating from college. But overnight, the rancor that developed during high school ran its course.

Kyle prayed every day that Sadie would land on her feet again. Their relationship wasn't the only one she'd ended that day. She refused to visit her family, and until last June she didn't allow them to visit her. Her best friends, Kate and Dee, claimed she'd avoided their company in Burgundy. Except for Lincoln, school, and tutoring, she spent all her time alone.

His father had shed light on her strange behavior while eating dinner at Kyle's apartment one evening. Far from surprised that Sadie had chosen another man over his son, William believed low self-esteem made the decision for her. "Sadie projected a false confidence that fooled most people" he said. "Because of the intimacies they shared, she tried to keep Lincoln. Marrying him became her number one goal."

His father's comment stayed with Kyle long after his parents went home. He considered making another trip to Burgundy to see Sadie, but wavered back and forth.

Would a visit make a difference to a woman he hadn't spoken to in weeks? Could a phone call suffice? If Sadie had ignored his pleas in person, would she take advice from him long distance?

He called her cell phone in a weak moment and Lincoln answered the call, flippantly stating he would give Sadie the message when she got out of the shower. Disgusted with the lie, Kyle hung up. The background noise confirmed they were in a public place. Perhaps Sadie had walked away, leaving her cell phone unattended on a table. Would she notice that he'd called and then return it?

Evidently not. Kyle had waited days to hear from Sadie. He wanted her safe but felt unable to provide the protection she badly needed.

Before long, one of his father's longtime friends convinced Kyle to accept his current position. The senior pastor considered him the perfect candidate for the newly created job. Kyle accepted the offer, believing it was the godsend he needed to shift his life into a new direction.

Still, loving Sadie had presented a problem. He'd wanted her to get her life back before he moved to California. To be the vibrant woman he'd adored, and to make her mark in life. Sadie had awesome dreams to touch lives through theater, and he wanted her vision to become a reality.

Unsure why he was making another trip, Kyle had set out for Burgundy the afternoon before his flight to Los Angeles. It took a while to find Sadie, but he did. Her shoulders drooping, she looked lonely as she sat on the grass in the quad, trying to blend in with the scenery. Less than two feet away, the big man on campus caroused with several women.

Kyle had silently fumed as heat rose up his neck. She wasn't in a good place at all. Her uncertainty and discontent cried out to him from the distance. Sadie was miserable. The valiant smile plastered on her face brought back memories. She always displayed a brave grin when weeping inside. Years ago, she'd mastered the art of looking more confident than she felt. Although shaking in her boots, she appeared in complete control of whatever obstacle she faced.

The quasi-sophistication on display from Lincoln and his entourage confirmed for him that she wasn't in a good place. Sadie battled in an arena where everyone knew the rules but her. And the noisy gang ignored her presence until a guy wearing glasses sat down beside her.

Hidden behind a canopy, Kyle argued to himself. *Why drive over three hundred miles without saying hello?*

Suddenly Lincoln grew tired of the mating games. He waved his little finger at his playmates, then beckoned Sadie with it. And like a trained poodle, Sadie leaped to her feet and trotted off behind him.

About to dash after them, Kyle spun around when a voice spoke beside him.

A close friend, Matthew Sweeney, shook his head. "Let her go, man. Making a scene is his specialty. She's stuck here long after you drive away."

Resisting the urge to sprint after Sadie, Kyle massaged his neck muscles until noticing that Dee and Kate stood nearby. Fury dominated Kate's features, but moisture pooled inside Dee's sad eyes.

He stared at Sadie following behind Lincoln. Nothing mattered more than leaving her some measure of peace. Kyle accepted his limitations, gripped Matt's hand in a firm handshake, and then waved goodbye to Sadie's best friends before walking off.

There's nothing more for me to do here. Jesus loves Sadie more than I do. The Holy Spirit will make the difference in her life if she lets Him.

At the airport the next day, wise words spoken by his father carried Kyle through those first few months of releasing Sadie into God's care. While saying goodbye inside the airport terminal, William had laid a hand on Kyle's shoulder, but instead of speaking, he cleared his throat, glancing at Sarah. His father's serious expression caused Kyle to grab his mother's hand. Smiling up at him, she rested her cheek on his arm.

The movement caught his father's eye, and William glanced at his wife before centering his gaze back on Kyle. He cleared his throat again. "Son, we know you drove up to Burgundy yesterday. Did you see Sadie?"

He nodded, watching his mother's expression. "I saw her, but she didn't know I was there."

"Son, always remember that love doesn't tear people apart but strengthens them for greater works. I'm proud of you. It takes courage to believe that saying goodbye to Sadie didn't end the story but began a new chapter."

The humility his father displayed encouraged Kyle. A rite of passage took place that moment. Kyle knew that his father trusted God with the family he loved. That simple faith made him feel better about moving away from home.

As usual, the older man had been right. Away from his support system, Kyle obtained a self-assurance that had evaded him while living in Shiatown. Glendale had treated him well. The woman he dated bore no resemblance to Sadie. Tiny in stature, her low-maintenance personality ranked with his.

An image of Sadie flooded his mind at the thought. The way she looked before Lincoln. Kyle closed his eyes to retain the vision. Even though their relationship had ended, his conscience carried one tremendous burden: Somehow, he'd failed the woman he loved.

Chapter Three

Several hours later, Kyle mindlessly set the porch glider into motion, pre-occupied with the privilege he'd received. His father's personal writings touched him. The man who'd shaped his life for the better wrote about personal observations concerning his son. And Kyle had devoured every word written about his high school years. Although many artists had sung about wasted years they could never restore, his missed chances seemed to surpass them all.

Immaturity fed by stubbornness had allowed hostilities to fester until he'd lost control of reality. Now his father's private thoughts revealed the true story. William had understood his son better than anyone other than Sarah.

In high school, Kyle had stoked the fire, letting people believe the worst about his character. But now, he realized that his father had understood his son's real nature. And although William had punished the misleading actions, he'd known the truth all along. One significant section written on his seventeenth birthday revealed why his father had piled punishments on him as a teenager.

Kyle slipped into the house tonight, smelling like a drunk in a gutter. He reeked of alcohol as if his mother and I had never punished him for drinking. I grounded him from attending Nate's party this Friday. The boys planned this birthday celebration because their friend won his bout with cancer. But Kyle will stay home.

Father, it's so difficult to punish him for wanting to fit in. No scent of alcohol is on his breath. Did he deliberately pour it on his clothing to fool his friends? Couldn't they see he wasn't drinking along with them?

This punishment is deserved. He refused to stand on his personal convictions. Lord, Sarah disagrees with what she calls my heavy-handed methods. But I believe this is the correct way to teach my son integrity.

I decree this day that Kyle Michael Franklin will answer Your call in his life. Though misguided, my son is a good young man. Give him the strength to walk alone if necessary.

The facts showed the depth of his father's love. Kyle had wasted his youth, warring against the man who labored to grow him up. Pride had trapped him into making senseless errors in judgment. Many mistakes dotted his past. And it was too late to thank the man who'd prayed for his maturity. By donning the mantle of a father, William had taught his son to become a man.

Cracking his knuckles, Kyle surveyed the church building next door that sat on three acres of land. It had ministered to countless people for decades. His parents had sunk their life savings into the abandoned building on their second wedding anniversary. He turned his attention to the house his grandparents built. Kyle loved his home. One day this place would become a haven for his wife and children, too.

Sarah planned to enjoy her home for years to come. And so did Kyle. He would accept the job his parents had groomed him for since his birth.

Eyes half-closed, he nodded at the church building his father founded thirty-three years ago. As if in answer to his lightened spirit, a gentle breeze swirled leaves haphazardly across the lawn. Then, just as suddenly as it had begun, the wind died down, and Kyle could almost hear the old building say "welcome home."

* * *

The next morning, Sadie sat up in bed, blinking at her surroundings. Once the blurry images cleared, she rested her back against the headboard.

"It was just a dream," she whispered, her gaze roving across the room.

She had finally drifted to sleep before dawn and dreamed of a game-changing pajama party. Each girl attending had touched her heart as if she'd known them personally. "It was a book," she said out loud. God gave her a novel from beginning to end while sleeping. She leaped from the bed and then paused in amazement, touching her fingertips to her lips.

It was my mother's house. I'm going home.

Then she could become Sadie again … if she could remember who she really was. Still, she wrapped her arms around her body, reveling in the newfound freedom.

It's over! I can rebuild the life I almost destroyed.

Reality hit her before the thought gained traction. The letdown came quickly, and Sadie crawled back underneath the covers, her mind full of yesterday's drama. Lincoln dumped her. All the mistakes she'd made had become evident after he left. "People probably wondered if I have a brain at all," she mumbled to herself.

Just a little over two years ago, her junior year had started off perfectly. At least until the campus buzzed with gossip about the football team. The head coach dropped a bombshell on the players after practice one evening. The news had everyone on campus shouting for joy. Last week, Rutledge College's sophomore phenom, Lincoln Miller, had transferred to Burgundy University.

No one knew why he switched schools three weeks into the term. But the coup shot adrenaline into the football season. Running backs of his caliber only came by once in a lifetime.

Sadie was only on the fringe of the excitement, but suddenly everyone was talking about her. The talented player was deficient in several subjects, and the head of the tutoring lab chose Sadie to keep him from failing. When she asked the scheduler why she was picked, he joking said that "she drew the short straw." It seemed the notoriety mattered in some circles. Tutoring the newcomer in five subjects catapulted a bewildered Sadie into the limelight.

Every place she went on campus, people treated her like a pop star. It was like graduating to the inner circle overnight. But as the hoopla increased, congratulations wore thin, and she questioned the pointless status. She wanted the new guy to become someone else's headache. Experience had taught her to run away from unearned praise. Sadie hated basking in another person's fame.

The star football player's arrival on campus had females young and old clamoring for his attention. Those in the know broadcasted that the running back oozed physical appeal. Too bad his partying reputation had preceded the introduction with Sadie.

On his first visit to The Mentor Lab, every tutor on campus stopped by to take a peek. The massive turnout left Sadie speechless. Even tutors who blew off their assignments on a regular basis showed up to gawk that day.

It put Sadie off completely. The man's off-field exploits didn't warrant admiration. But even though she disliked him on sight, he did exude a mysterious appeal she couldn't explain. Her heart actually fluttered when he touched her hand while looking into her eyes.

Stunned, Sadie hid out in an empty room until the instructor drafted a schedule between her and Lincoln. Contract signed, she gathered her belongings while the new guy worked his way around the room. People gossiped in every corner. From all accounts, her failure to swoon had offended the man as he tried to win over everyone present.

What a prima donna. Did he expect to captivate everyone he met?

Sadie headed for the exit. But before she could leave the building, he sneaked up behind her and kissed her neck. The raucous laughter provided cover as Sadie shook off the warmth flowing throughout her body. But Lincoln's half-closed eyes had noticed her reaction.

Too late, Sadie recognized that as the moment he resolved to bring her to her knees. The big man on campus used every trick in his playbook to date her. Although she resisted getting friendly with him, bit by bit she changed her habits to accommodate his whims.

One evening Lincoln suggested meeting at Sadie's dorm instead of studying at The Mentor Lab. She agreed since the common area was always quiet. Football practice usually ended late. The location shift kept her from walking across campus alone at night.

Looking back, nothing had alerted her to stop tutoring Lincoln. He was a party guy. That made him safe to be around, because she could never fall for a man like him. Lincoln was just like the other men she tutored who constantly asked her out; necessary baggage until she graduated from college. Besides, Sadie didn't like him. She only had to tutor him five days a week. But agreeing to add the sixth day to the schedule had undone her.

Sadie had almost canceled the spur-of-the-moment meeting. Weekends were the time she tackled her own workload. That morning, Lincoln had called asking for help. He'd just remembered he had a term paper due on Monday, but he couldn't meet her until after the game. Another student had pulled a similar stunt the day before.

Instead of meeting her in the lobby at six as agreed, he dropped by her room at nine-thirty. By then, they were having a birthday party for the resident assistant in the lobby, so they headed to his dorm. The mayhem in his common area made writing a paper there impossible. His room was the only option, unless she wanted to walk two miles back and forth to The Mentor Lab. She climbed the stairs to the second floor without really thinking about it. Lincoln talked nonstop, and she just wanted him to be quiet.

Sadie gasped when Lincoln opened the door to his room. It was pathetic. No wonder he couldn't concentrate on his studies. Every available space was filled with junk. Moldy food laying on the desk made her skin crawl. Ready to leave, Sadie sat down and wrote the paper herself. Instead of being grateful she saved his hide, his campaign to wear her down went into overdrive. Even though the Don Juan antics annoyed her, Sadie submitted to one kiss.

But Lincoln's response to the kiss still puzzled her, even now. It wasn't even a real kiss. He'd only brushed his lips across hers. She still couldn't explain why it had ended in intimacy. Sometimes she hated herself. Would she ever forget the indignity of losing her self-respect?

Afterward, Sadie had run back to her dorm at twelve-fifteen in the morning. She couldn't stop crying. The engagement to Kyle was over. He would never forgive her. And how could she explain actions she didn't understand herself? Being nice had backfired. She'd destroyed her life with a self-absorbed jerk. Lincoln had barely said goodbye when she left his room. He'd muttered something at her, then turned his back to the door.

It was over at last. Hopefully, memories of ever knowing the man would soon disappear, too.

Yesterday after Lincoln left, she'd sent flowers special delivery to Sarah and Kyle, and then knocked on her landlord's door, explaining the duplicate key was missing. And the kind man promised to change the tumbler within the hour. And a good thing too.

Last night, a weight pressed against the door. Instead of leaving when his key didn't work, Lincoln kept trying to get in. Sadie lay in bed, ignoring the taps against the window. Then her cell phone rang. Back to the window again, he called her name several times until he finally left her alone.

Did he think I was stupid enough to let him in?

Fighting back tears, Sadie left the bed to get ready for work. Now she had a chance to make a new start. She felt in control of her life for the first time since meeting Lincoln. Standing in the middle of the floor, she combed fingers through her hair; happy to be alive. Acting like a doormat for two years had ceased with one visit.

Thinking about her mistakes, she assigned herself the "what was she thinking" award.

It was time to leave Burgundy.

Chapter Four

Sadie bit into a cupcake, then dipped her spoon into a bowl of chocolate ripple ice cream. She seldom ate dessert—and usually pigged out when she did—which is why she normally didn't. But it was her birthday, and she celebrated it alone. Just like last year. But that was okay; she was going home. And soon. But not soon enough. She was anxious to get on with her life.

All day, she'd wondered what Kate and Dee were doing in Shiatown. Kate had worked in an advertising firm during school breaks from college. She had planned to go full time after graduating last May. She was a talented illustrator who could sell anything. What about Dee? Deanna dreamed of being a homemaker. Engaged to Matt Sweeney since her sophomore year in college, she'd planned to get married last June. Just like Sadie and Kyle.

In fact, she and Dee had wanted a double ceremony. Even though she wouldn't attend the wedding, Sadie had bought a gift, waiting for an invitation that never came. She wondered what had caused them to change the date.

Should she call her friends before going home? Best friends before kindergarten, the triplets shrunk to the twins after the showdown with Kyle in her dorm room. Perched on the top bunk, Kate had watched the confrontation from the beginning. After Kyle had walked out, Kate slid to the floor in one motion. But before following behind him, she shot Lincoln a look of hatred that had shocked Sadie.

The following morning, Sadie had gone to breakfast alone, returning to the room forty minutes later. Except for her stuff, the room was empty. All of Kate's belongings were gone. Somehow her friend had managed the impossible: swapping rooms overnight.

Even though Kate moved out, no outward hostilities existed between the friends. She and Dee greeted Sadie whenever they came face-to-face. Still, neither girl sought avenues to rekindle their friendship. And Sadie, numb with shame, avoided contact as much as possible. Merely existing quickly became the new normal. Her unteachable spirit had sealed her fate.

Getting advice from other people usually irked Sadie. Kate had warned her not to blow off Kyle for a loser. Dee had compared Lincoln to quicksand; dangerous and difficult to escape its pull.

Matt, Dee's boyfriend and a close friend of Kyle, played tight end on the varsity team and knew Lincoln well. One day, he'd cautioned Sadie not to match wits with a gamester. Intrigued by the comparison, she listened until he said Kyle deserved better than a cheating fiancée.

Sadie exploded. There was nothing between her and Lincoln. She'd been inoculated against jerks in middle school. Much later, Sadie understood Matt's reasonable advice. Lincoln craved female devotion. He knew about her engagement and wanted Sadie lying at his feet.

Even though she'd burned her bridges, she couldn't wait to go home. But would her friends welcome her back? And would she be able to work in theater as she'd always intended? It was the ideal life she'd planned with Kyle. The man who had encouraged Sadie to pursue her dreams. Five years ago, the couple drew up plans to restructure Kingdom Life Church and the surrounding grounds. The finished design expanded the fellowship hall next door to the church, plus added three buildings serving dual purposes. One of them would house a learning center, with a dinner theater on the main floor.

Her mother said Pastor Franklin had stayed true to the blueprint Kyle had given him. The renovations were completed last March. And although the daycare center thrived with a six-month waiting list, the other two buildings remained empty. She still hoped she and Kyle might work together. The career she craved would be icing on the cake of a perfect life: A lifetime spent building happy memories with him.

Sadie set her bowl and plate into the sink and padded into the bathroom. Troubled eyes stared back at her from the vanity mirror. Like the prodigal son, she refused to remain in Burgundy licking self-inflicted wounds. There would always be a place for her in Shiatown. She felt free to live in her mother's house until striking out on her own.

She sighed, looking at her hands. Tremendous changes had taken place since her last visit home. Her grandparents had sold all of their rental properties last year. Then they passed The Main Street Diner and the duplex next door to the restaurant to Sadie's mother. It had been seven years since their son's death.

Jeanette transformed the large cafeteria into a four-star restaurant that filled to capacity daily. Today the restaurant consisted of four distinct dining areas joined by a connecting door. Soon Sadie realized viewing pictures on her cell phone didn't work. She needed to see the place in person.

Earlier that year, her brother had received her grandfather's heating and cooling business, plus the family home. It was a unique present for her then twenty-three-year-old brother. But Roland had apprenticed at the company since turning thirteen, and he now owned one of three heating and cooling businesses within a thirty-mile radius of Shiatown.

Her grandparents joined their daughter's family in Naples, Florida, feeling secure that their son's family was financially independent. They loved Shiatown, but couldn't move past their only son's brutal death.

Sadie got into bed while imagining the buzz around Shiatown. Gossips probably had a field day asking the question on everyone's mind: Would Kyle remain in Oklahoma or return to California? She already knew he wouldn't leave his mother alone. Kyle was home for good.

But even if everyone else welcomed her arrival, would he be happy she moved back home?

* * *

When Kyle opened the door, a small boy with crumbs on his lips jumped into his arms. Then the fatigued woman staring at him pointed to suitcases at the curb. "I hope you still think of me as a sister," she said. But the brave smile vanished when he didn't respond.

He tousled the youngster's bright-red hair. Seeing Cindy and Brian was a pleasant surprise. Two of his favorite people had safely landed on his doorstep. Besides, nothing shocked him anymore. He'd settled back into his old routine the first day he parked the rental car in the driveway. Now Cindy and Brian arrived all the way from California.

He hugged her with his free arm. "Moving in, Cindy? Or did you bring clothes for the yard sale this weekend?"

Cindy broke free of the bear hug, then poked his chest with a finger. "Don't even joke about selling our things. Sorry we're four days late for the funeral." Cindy stared at their luggage. "See, I knew you wouldn't leave your mother alone. The day you left, I made arrangements for Brian and me to follow you here. The bus trip was awful, Kyle."

"What happened to your granny's keepsakes?"

A light in the green eyes twinkled. "Stored in your living room with our other stuff for safekeeping. Kyle, please haul our bits and pieces with your things. I took the plants to the office so your secretary could water them. And left your car parked in the garage." She patted her shoulder bag. "The keys are in my purse. See, big brother? I covered all our bases." Suddenly, she turned away. "Did I assume too much this time?"

Little Brian squirmed to get down, and Kyle set the boy on his feet. "Come on, little helper, let's do the heavy lifting while your mom holds the door open wide."

The visible relief on Cindy's face tugged at his heart. She lived a quiet but busy life. She volunteered her free time at the church he pastored. Kyle met the single mother the day he moved to California. The following Sunday, she joined the youth ministry the senior pastor hoped to build. She was a natural with teenage girls and worked hard to help them. She once told him, "teaching them to make better choices for their lives keeps me happy."

That comment sealed the deal with Kyle. Her willingness to help teens with problems that had troubled her registered big with him. Would Sadie do likewise once she came to her senses? Or would she try to convince the world that all was well? The choices people made during trials highlighted their personal strengths and weaknesses. Cindy had fled the lifestyle that left her an unwed mother at nineteen. But Sadie tried to stage-manage circumstances that were uncontrollable.

After Kyle settled the family into the guest bedroom, he went into the kitchen to tell his mother about their visitors. He was happy to assist two people he'd grown to love.

Sarah spun around with soapsuds dripping from her hands before he finished speaking. "You mean she followed you here without your knowledge?"

"I was surprised, too. But showing up unannounced is vintage Cindy." Chuckling, he held up a hand. "Don't jump to conclusions. She sees me as a big brother. She and Brian are all alone. Her granny passed away six weeks after we met." Laughing as he talked, Kyle tweaked his mother's nose. "But they're not alone anymore. Now they have us." He walked away, turning around at the door. "Cindy worked as a waitress. Do you think Miss Jeanette has an opening at the diner? I'd better head over there to ask."

Sarah rinsed the suds off her hands and dried them on a towel lying on the counter. "First you'll introduce me to my guest. Then you can run off on your mercy mission." She paused, smiling. "FYI, both sides of the duplex next-door to the restaurant are empty."

"That's the spirit."

Wrapping an arm around his mother's waist, he led the way down the hall, whispering nonsense into her ear. It worked, because his mother warmed to both mother and son immediately. A laughing Sarah fully embraced her visitors, showing off her home before Kyle had even left the house.

* * *

Ten days after her twenty-second birthday, Sadie snapped the lid on the trunk, scooting it across the floor. Her fingers stroked her chin as she looked around the room. Her brother, Roland, would arrive any moment. And a good thing, too. Sadie wanted to leave town without seeing Lincoln. Not that she expected him to show up at the last minute, begging forgiveness. The message he'd texted four days ago claimed Sadie didn't merit a second chance.

"Hurry up, brother dear. Sadie Cummings is going home."

She hoped Dee and Kate would be happy to see her. She accepted the blame for the standoff, but how could she hang around people who were blasting the man she prayed to marry?

Teary-eyed, she stared out the window, coming to terms with her losses. Kyle had predicted Lincoln would drop her. Her closest friends couldn't stand him. He purposely ruined her family's visit. How did she close the gap with the people she loved after pushing them away?

On graduation day, Sadie had refused to walk with her peers because she was too embarrassed to see her family again. So her family and Sarah, who would never miss an important event in Sadie's life, didn't make the trip. As her friends graduated, Sadie had emptied a tissue box while watching a comedy matinee in a theater.

Well, at least Amy still loved her. The sisters had enjoyed a pleasant chat just that morning. "I'm on it," said Amy before hanging up. "I've never let Kyle forget about you, Sadie. And he won't as long as I'm around."

Sadie's mouth had dropped open. "Are you serious?"

Amy laughed. "Of course. I reminisced about you whenever he visited his parents. What sister wouldn't?"

Warmth flooded Sadie's body from head to toe. Long ago, she'd lost faith in the romance, yet her younger sister still believed. And then Sadie remembered, hanging her head in shame. She'd failed to ask Kyle to forgive her. She hadn't repented to God either. Oh, she'd begged Him to bless her outside His will. But not to forgive the sin that had ruined her relationship with Kyle. The sin she repeated for two years. Thank God Lincoln had never proposed.

Jesus, I foolishly asked you to bless me while sinning against Your word.

Sadie stumbled into the bathroom, asking God to forgive her. Dabbing a wet paper towel over her face, she sat on the floor, leaning her head against the vanity.

* * *

Sadie jumped to her feet when a car door slammed outside. Hearing footsteps on the porch, she sped across the room just as the doorbell rang.

She threw the door open wide. "Roland, I'm glad you're here."

Her brother looked at her then pushed inside the door, surveying the room. The tall, handsome man with the trimmed mustache glanced at Sadie. "You look done in, sis. Did Lincoln stop by?"

"No, I haven't seen him since we broke up." Sadie grabbed his hand. "Roland, I never asked Kyle to forgive me for cheating on him." With her tears flowing freely, Sadie thrust herself into her brother's open arms.

He draped an arm across her shoulders, leading her to the couch. It reminded her of the times the ambulance had driven off with their father. Sadie nestled closer. After breaking up with Kyle, she'd resisted the urge to dump her problems on him. One night she'd dreamed about the outcome. In the dream, her brother put Lincoln on notice. Lincoln mouthed off. Roland decked him. And both the university and Lincoln pressed charges against the man who was only trying to help her.

Roland began training as a boxer in the neighborhood boys club at eleven. For years, he won every fight in his weight division. Weekly, he taught kids and young adults in the same facility where he trained. So Sadie had refused to involve her brother but knew he would've helped her if she'd asked him.

She glanced at him when he pulled away. "You have a strange expression on your face. What are you thinking about?"

"Your mindset. Why didn't you ask Kyle to forgive you?"

Sad eyes stared at her brother. "I can't explain my actions," she said, shrugging.

"Stop searching for a single motive," said Roland. "I'm sure there are many." He hesitated, watching her closely. "You fell into a moment with the wrong man. Lacking the proper response, you winged it. Asking forgiveness is difficult if you don't believe you deserve it. You didn't expect Kyle to forgive you because you couldn't forgive yourself."

Sadie nibbled a fingernail. "I had no one to talk to."

"Really?" he asked. "Sadie, you called me the Sunday after it happened. I left home ten minutes later. I asked you to tell The Mentor Lab that you were dropping Lincoln, and to let me take you home for a week. Leaving would've distanced you from him while letting you talk to your fiancé in person. You blew me off. You doused the fire with gasoline." He brushed the hair off Sadie's face when she turned away. "I suppose a life sentence with Lincoln seemed adequate punishment at the time."

Sadie dried her eyes with her fingertips. While talking to Roland, several puzzle pieces fell into place.

"Kate blasted me for calling Kyle that Saturday morning. She said my mistake with Lincoln had just taken place a week ago. To just let it die out. But calling him seemed the right thing to do. Miss Sarah had called the day before, inviting me to his surprise birthday party the following week." Sadie winced when Roland just looked at her. "Kyle had accepted the associate pastor position at Kingdom Life. I can still hear the excitement in her voice. 'Dear, let's make it a triple celebration for Kyle. Announce your engagement at the party.'"

Sadie glanced down. "When I said I couldn't make it, she explained Kyle planned to surprise me with my engagement ring on my next visit." Her eyes pleaded with Roland to understand her position. "I had to end it quickly."

"All Kyle deserved was a phone call? Sadie, you dashed the hopes of the man who loved you long distance."

Teardrops rolled down her cheeks. "I couldn't face him in person."

"So, are you justifying inviting Lincoln over before he arrived at your dorm?"

Sadie shook her head. "Lincoln stopped by unannounced. Besides, I didn't know Kyle was coming to Burgundy."

"Of course you knew Kyle would show up after you called him. Sadie, you should have talked to him alone. You asked Kate to leave the room after he arrived, why not Lincoln?"

Sadie relived one poor judgment after another. In front of an audience, Kyle had handed her his heart, and she had trampled on it. She'd stared at Lincoln after Kate ran behind Kyle. His smug expression almost caused her to scream out loud. Sadie had forfeited the man she loved for a man she never wanted to see again.

Incapable of meeting her brother's eyes, she stood up. "But Kate didn't leave, Roland. She stayed. Do you think I have a second chance with Kyle?"

Taking her lead, he opened the door, then picked up two boxes. "Time will tell," said Roland, and he headed outside with his load.

Sadie followed him out the door, stopping on the porch as he loaded the van. "Kyle's your best friend. Be truthful. Can I make amends with him?"

The speculation in his gaze spoke volumes. "Today or tomorrow? No." His expression softened when she rested her head on the doorframe. "Please—don't worry about getting Kyle back. If a happy reunion isn't in the cards, ask God what He has in store for Sadie."

On the way back into the house for another load, he kissed her damp cheek. "Sis, don't relive the past; build on it." His brown eyes filled with compassion. Bending over, he picked up several items, handing them to Sadie.

"Carry the smaller boxes. We'll have this place cleared out in record time."

Chapter Five

Kyle watched Cindy head toward his table carrying a tray with two cups before he placed his order. He'd had a busy morning and was happy to sit for a while.

"Are you hungry?" Cindy set a cup of ginger tea in front of Kyle, then claimed the seat beside him.

Without looking up, he shook his head, reaching for the drink.

"Are you okay?" she asked, touching his hand.

He held the steaming cup inches from his lips. "Now that's a strange question, even from you. What gives?"

She burst into laughter, causing several customers to glance their way. The place was packed. The Cummings family's restaurant was a popular place. The college crowd congregated in The Teapot. High schoolers preferred Burger Barn, and young families ate in the kid-friendly atmosphere of Bon Appetit. But Kyle preferred eating in the original restaurant, The Main Street Diner. Miss Jeanette had turned a cafeteria into a dining experience.

He glanced at Cindy's soft palm covering his hand. Kyle worked out his problems alone but understood her concern. Even his mother was treading lightly since learning Sadie was coming home. And everywhere people talked about her return to Shiatown. Individuals chatting with him dropped her name into the conversation while searching his face for a reaction. Regardless of speculations, his morning began as usual: on his knees before the Lord. And night would find him meditating on scriptures before dropping off to sleep—a proven recipe he'd learned to live by. Every day, numerous decisions begged his attention, and unnecessary drama never crossed his mind.

Roland had stopped by his house that morning on his way to pick up Sadie. And both men were candid about her coming home. But his friend's last comment kept creeping into his thoughts. "Sadie refused to see me when

I dropped by her dorm. And she wouldn't level with me over the phone. But my sister will always find me there when she reaches out to me."

It seemed that Sadie had traveled a rocky road with Lincoln. Now she needed to rebuild her life on a firm foundation. He studied the woman holding his hand. Time to offer a little brotherly advice. "Ready to fess up? Or will you continue to keep secrets from me?"

Cindy coughed, almost choking on her drink. Her eyelids blinked rapidly. Clearing her throat, she studied Kyle. "What do you mean?" she asked while stirring her tea.

"I know you love me like a brother. But how about discussing the other reason you followed me here." She sipped her drink without answering. It appeared the discussion was long overdue. "Where is the relationship heading with Roland?"

"Relationship?" Cindy asked with a wide-eyed stare. Her expression resembled a person playing for time.

"Judging by the reports I receive, you two are an item. Cindy, don't hand him your heart on a silver platter. Make him earn it." Kyle pushed forward when she nipped her lip between her teeth. "Sometimes a listening ear can work wonders."

"Do you have an objection to us dating?"

"Far from it. Roland is a good, though hard, man. Growing up in an unstable household took its toll on him and Sadie. Amy's too young to remember the turbulent years. The family lived in a war zone. Mental illness plagued Russell Cummings for years before his life ended."

Unwilling to tell his friend's story, he paused, thinking about what to say. "While taking his medications Mr. Russell was the perfect husband and father. Off the meds, his family often fought for their lives. Roland has few happy childhood memories. Until meeting you, he kept a bevy of women on hand but didn't allow anyone close enough to affect his life."

Her eyes shone brightly. "I'm certain he only dates me now." Her face took on that dreamy quality of happy memories. "Roland treated Brian and me like royalty when he visited you in Glendale. I thought he liked us enough to add two additional weeks to his vacation." Her gaze searched Kyle's face for confirmation.

"So you admit liking Roland brought you to Oklahoma?"

She nodded, but her smile seemed forced.

"Stop assigning motives to other people's actions. Only God knows the heart. Roland's always upfront. You would know if he wasn't serious about you."

Cindy grasped his arm when Kyle stood up. "What about you? Sadie's coming home today."

Kyle drained his drink, replacing the cup on the counter. He winked at her, then walked off humming. His ex-fiancée needed rallying around; he didn't.

* * *

"Roland! You're home. Wanna play catch?" a small boy yelled, dashing out of the Franklins' house. He ran to Roland and wrapped his tiny arms around his leg. Sadie froze when a woman hurried out the door behind him. She wore jeans and a green T-shirt, and red curls framed her face in a pleasing way. Makeup-free, she had a fresh look that would appeal to quite a few men. A soapy scent filled the air when she stopped on the sidewalk beside them.

Then a loud crash sounded as Amy slammed the door to their house and raced across the lawn. She gave Sadie a bone-breaking squeeze, then stooped to hug the boy, who struggled to evade her grasp. Giggling, he freed himself, then clung to the woman shyly smiling at Roland.

"Sorry, Brian flew out the door before I could stop him. He's watched for your van all afternoon." Cindy shrugged, glancing at Sadie. "I explained you might be too tired to play ball today."

Except for Sadie, everyone watched Roland. Outwardly calm, her mind raced ahead of the introductions. The strangers came out of the Franklins' house, but where was Kyle and his mother? Who was this woman and boy? It seemed that her brother and sister knew them well. Her face almost cracked from the unnatural smile plastered on it.

Okay, family, hurry up with the introductions.

Amy pointed to the strangers as if she'd heard the thought. "Sadie, Cindy and Brian relocated to Shiatown with Kyle. Cindy works at The Main Street Diner. They live in one of the duplexes next door to the restaurant."

About to speak, Sadie backed up when Cindy glanced away. Amy looked puzzled when the woman sidled closer to Roland. "We're celebrating today," she said. "My big sister is finally home where she belongs." When neither of the women spoke, she gazed at her brother's expressionless face.

Roland pulled out a small paper bag from the van, handing it to Brian. "Hey, buddy, I picked up a snack for you at a gas station on the way home." He winked at Cindy. "We'll toss the ball after dinner if your mother approves."

Sadie's eyes darted from her brother to Cindy. *Are they dating? No one had mentioned the woman to her.* She watched as Cindy took the treat from her son's fingers.

"Brian," she said, laughing, "this cookie is bigger than your hand. Do you want to eat half of it after dinner? Or after playing catch later?"

Brian jumped up and down, giggling. "After dinner, after dinner."

Roland laughed when Brian decided to eat the cookie before they played ball. "Beat by the sweets again," he said. Then he pointed to the van. "I have work to do before calling it a day. We can knock out this job in ten minutes."

Picking up two large boxes, he directed Brian to hold open the door. Both Amy and Cindy grabbed a box then trailed Brian into the house, leaving a mystified Sadie more confused than ever. Cindy and Brian came out of Kyle's house. Legs buckling, her body swayed as she covered her mouth with her fingers. Breathing deeply, she tried to relax.

Get a grip. My sister likes the woman and adores the son but wants Kyle for me. There can't be anything romantic between him and Cindy. Cindy never took her eyes off of Roland.

Sighing, she surveyed the familiar surroundings until the church grounds caught her attention. "Wow!" The photos her mother had texted failed in comparison to what she saw. Five structures lining the west side of the square were connected by hallways. The grounds buzzed with activity. Numerous cars were parked in the large lot, and several workers trimmed bushes and mowed the lawn.

Sadie headed into the house carrying two lamps while the others came back for another load. Neither Kyle nor his mother had welcomed her home.

* * *

Roland blessed their food while the family joined hands around the table. So many changes had taken place in just two years. Her sometimes-sulky brother had turned into a family man, while her awkward little sister had grown into a beautiful young woman. Their laughter, along with Amy's hodgepodge of community news, made her feel at home. And mimicking a sponge, Sadie soaked up every detail until saturated.

A car horn sounded outside. Amy jumped up from the table, grabbing her purse from the counter yet forgetting to give the punchline to the joke she'd been telling. Instead, she headed to the kitchen door, but she turned around when Roland stopped her.

"I thought you had a date for the movies this evening," he said, strolling toward her.

"Please, Mom," Amy mouthed to Jeanette before answering. "I do. That's why I'm leaving."

Roland turned to the lady eating ice cream. "Mother, have you met him?"

Sadie grinned when Jeanette shook her head without looking up.

Sucking on her lower lip, Amy extended her hand in appeal. "Goodness, Roland. It's our first date. I'll be home by eight. He works the night shift on weekends. Mom!" said Amy as Roland left the room. "Please … don't let him embarrass me."

Sadie glanced at her mother after Amy ran out the kitchen behind him.

Jeanette pushed her bowl away. She stopped at the door. "Welcome home, Sadie. Do you think you can tolerate the drama?"

Laughing to herself, Sadie listened to the voices talking in the foyer. Thank God, He'd brought her home. She needed these family interactions to keep her sanity.

Roland and Jeanette returned to the table after Amy and her date went to the movies. While scarfing down two banana cupcakes and a bowl of choco-late ripple ice cream, her brother suggested adding a separate eating space to the restaurant. A private oasis only for couples. Intrigued by the idea, mother and daughter debated the concept after Roland left. They cleaned up the kitchen together until a neighbor dropped by for a visit. Sadie finished tidying up the room, half-listening to the animated conversation on the back deck.

After storing leftovers in the refrigerator, she climbed the stairs to her bedroom, thinking about her siblings. What movie was Amy watching? Was Roland tossing the ball to Brian? Did the boy's mother watch them play? It was fun knowing her family chilled out with friends, but it was a bummer to be left alone on her first day home. Their packed schedules exposed her need to renew old friendships. To get on with her life.

That afternoon, she and Amy had unpacked and put away her things. And then Sadie placed her trinkets throughout the house. The crystal vase, a gift from her grandmother, sat on the end table. The Parisian café print from

Aunt Yolanda hung on the dining room wall. And a laminated family portrait snapped by Miss Sarah sat on the mantel above the fireplace. Personal items tucked here and there made her feel like she belonged.

Sadie opened the window. She was alone and ready to move forward with Kyle. Seeing the complex next door convinced her that God wanted them to work together. Kingdom Life Church beckoned, and Sadie knew she must answer its call.

Would Kyle accept her help? They'd always worked well together. His best interest had filled her mind every day of her life. That fact alone made her time with Lincoln irrational. Her excitement about starting over left in a hurry. Sometimes painful circumstances altered lives beyond recovery.

One day, her father's sickness had done that to their family. Even her best girlfriends didn't know the full story. That her brother's alert responses to their father's paranoia episodes had saved his family's life on a regular basis. Russell Cummings had become a ticking time bomb waiting to explode. And Roland bore the brunt of his father's wrath whenever it happened. He sprang into action if the man's illness threatened anyone's safety.

The first episode had shocked them all. Russell thundered through the house threatening his bewildered wife. Roland secretly called his grandparents and the police. After that, he hid potential weapons and unlocked the exterior doors. Those swift actions probably prevented a tragedy, plus allowed Pastor Franklin and Kyle to help him restrain the violent man. Pastor Franklin assisted Roland, and Kyle picked up the sleeping Amy, taking her and Sadie next door where Sarah waited on the porch. Once they entered the house, he rushed back to help the others.

Minutes later, Sadie heard sirens wailing as the ambulance arrived with a police escort. She peeked out the living room window, watching neighbors on their lawns whispering and pointing fingers. Eleven-year-old Sadie prayed on her own for the first time, asking God to help her father. Unfortunately, that awful night set the precedent for the future. Russell's paranoia episodes escalated daily.

Three long years of living in fear tormented everyone in the house. After her father died, Jeanette held the family together, which wasn't easy. The shattered woman had lost the only man she had ever loved. Little by little the sad memories faded. And then Sadie only recalled the good times they'd shared before his illness disrupted their lives.

She took a deep breath, exhaling slowly. Her nightmare with Lincoln would disappear too. In Shiatown, she was free. She'd stopped blaming God for her problems. He brought her home to live the life He'd planned for her.

Her lips parted in amazement as the truth sank in. Lincoln had tormented her for two years, but now she was able to pursue life as it should be lived. Accepting love from others and returning love to them; agreeing with sound advice and imparting what she learned. She thought about her mother. Jeanette had set up a full physical for Sadie at the doctor's office next week. She said it was because Sadie hadn't had an exam in over two years. But Sadie knew better. New knowledge of Lincoln's lifestyle worried her mother. And Sadie consenting to the visit was a small thing if it allayed her fears.

Sadie peeked at the church again. She wanted Kyle back. Her childhood friend had truly loved her. He knew secrets never shared with Dee, Kate, or anyone else.

Unanswered questions flooded her mind. Whatever happened to her engagement ring? What did it look like? Did Kyle return it to the jeweler? Or did he store it away to give to some other woman? If Kyle and she had stayed together, they would've been married by now and living in the guest house over his mother's garage.

Maybe she'd invited her family to visit in June to salvage a small part of her old self.

I'm home, and so is Kyle. We're in the same place for the first time in two years.

But his success in California proved losing her hadn't mattered much. His life thrived because he trusted God. Kyle had maintained the lifestyle he'd eagerly embraced in his youth. The job in California prepared the way for his current position: senior pastor of Kingdom Life Church. He had expected to serve as associate pastor until his father stepped down. But he left Shiatown because she broke off their engagement. Maybe it was right that neither he nor Miss Sarah showed up today. Even though they'd shared every precious moment in her life, Sadie failed to truly contact them when Pastor Franklin passed away.

Still standing at the window, she pressed her forehead against the screen. There were two cars parked outside the church building that weren't there earlier. Did one of them belong to Kyle?

Thoughts of Queen Esther's yearlong preparation before meeting the Persian King ran through her mind. Her mind made-up, she stepped into the shower, praying for a breakthrough with Kyle.

* * *

Thirty minutes later, Sadie opened the outer door to the fellowship hall, awed by the renovations. Once a large dining room, the area resembled the outline Kyle had sketched at his kitchen table. Sadie tiptoed across the lobby and down the passageway along the west wall.

No map was required to find his office. A woman's high-pitched snicker led the way to a room with chairs and a sofa set on one side. She peeked through a crack in the door and there was Kyle, talking to a woman Sadie didn't know. Her heart fluttered as his face came into focus. Just like Roland, her ex-fiancé had matured since the last time they'd seen each other.

The handsome man looked incredible. His broad shoulders strained against a light-blue shirt. So the fitness fanatic had maintained his workout schedule while living in California. Her knees trembled just listening to the deep voice that fielded questions from the woman leaning across the desk.

Sadie peered down the hallway then stared into the room. The woman flirted with him. When Kyle glanced at the door, Sadie stepped backward, refusing to reveal her presence. Instead, she stared at the attractive woman demanding his attention. Then the conversation switched to food, and they danced around the topic until the woman stopped the pretense and invited Kyle to dinner. Fed up, Sadie knocked on the door and breezed into the office.

"I'm home!" She moved farther into the room, smiling at the startled woman. Calm filtered through her nervousness. "Sorry to barge in, but I'm ready to check out Burger Barn." The ball was in Kyle's court now. In the Old Testament, King Ahasuerus held out the golden scepter to Queen Esther, sparing her life. Would Kyle call her out as a fraud or play along with the ruse?

He grasped Sadie's hand without looking at her, pulling her closer as the stranger rose to her feet.

"Liz, Sadie Cummings is the girl next door and is home after living in another state." He faced Sadie without looking at her. "Sadie, Liz joined our congregation last week. I provided her a rundown of upcoming programs."

Sadie hoped Kyle wouldn't call her bluff. "Okay, tell me on Sunday which group will work best for your family."

Holding on to Kyle's hand, Sadie retraced her steps to the front door, forcing them to follow her. Making small talk the entire way, she marveled at her boldness and his willingness to play along. In the past, he chided her to think before acting. Thank God, Kyle didn't make her sound like an idiot.

Stepping outside, Sadie stopped in front of the silver sedan. The woman opened the car door, glaring at the silent man, allowing Sadie to take control.

"It seems the rumor mill got it wrong," she said. Slamming the car door, she drove off in a rush.

Chapter Six

Suddenly anxious, Sadie turned to Kyle. The man had practically ignored her while Liz was present. Now his blank expression worried her. "Whew … thank you for not embarrassing me, Kyle." She studied the ground when he failed to reply, and then she glanced up with a half-smile. "I didn't intend to interfere, but Liz was making a play for you."

Kyle dropped her hand as if it was fire. "And you supposed I needed rescuing?"

Her mouth hung open when he walked off, leaving her standing outside. Sadie didn't know if she should go home or follow behind him. Even though she probably should've waited until the next day, she refused to give up. Kyle would probably be in a worse mood tomorrow. She laid her head against the glass then marched backed inside. Although she couldn't see him, Sadie listened as he rattled doorknobs and closed doors in the hallway near his office. Finally, his footsteps sounded closer until he reappeared in the lobby, moving toward her.

She tried thinking of something to say, but Kyle spoke when he reached her.

"Welcome home, Sadie," he said with a lazy grin. "By the way, I liked your impulsiveness better when you were younger."

She hated his remark, but laughed, hoping to lighten his mood. "You must admit I've finessed my game big time since then."

"Was that a joke?" Kyle studied her expression then switched out the lights on a side wall.

Sadie moved closer, then stood still, forcing him to look at her. The recessed lights revealed the doubt in his eyes about her being there. Was that because she'd showed up? Or because he distrusted anything she might say? This was more difficult than she'd imagined it would be. "Please, Kyle." His muscles tensed when she touched his arm as if he prepared for an attack.

She licked her lips, summoning up courage she didn't feel. "I'm ... nervous, and have important things to say." She wrung her hands. "I don't know where to begin." Pausing, she tried to smile. "How about grabbing that meal at Burger Barn? But give me the grand tour around the complex first."

Sadie twiddled her thumbs when he gave her a "have you lost your mind" look. It took him several minutes to speak. But she waited on him to continue, praying he would change his mind. Or at least soften his voice.

"Look, I'm tired. My mother will have dinner on the table in fifteen minutes." He paused when she backed up. "It's been a long day, Sadie. Say your piece so I can go home and rest."

That wasn't the response she'd hoped to hear. But, it was late. Perhaps she should've waited until tomorrow after all. Although the harsh tone startled her, it hurt less than his suspicious expression. Heartbroken, tears pooled in her eyes. For the first time in her life, the man who'd acted as a buffer in every trial refused to cooperate. And it wasn't a pretend indifference. Kyle had detached himself from anything Sadie.

At least he'd refused to humiliate her in front of a stranger; which really mattered if she considered their last meeting. Whatever his response, she must set the record straight. She reached out her hand, then dropped it to her side.

"You're right. It's too late to visit. I—I just wanted to apologize for acting like an imbecile when you came to Burgundy." She pursed her lips to stop them from quivering. The impassive expression on his face undid her. "I love you, Kyle. So very, very much. You know ... I wanted to leave Burgundy with you when you left my dorm room. But you tied my hands, saying things your heart didn't feel. That you forgave me and wanted us to continue our plans." Closing her eyes, she opened them quickly, then took a deep breath. "I waited, Kyle. Not once did you say, I love you."

Sadie's head shook in agony at the narrowed eyes and tilted head. "I was happy when Kate opened the door and I saw you standing there. I'd thought the nightmare was over. But you cringed and almost batted my fingers away when I touched you." Tears overflowed as she closed her eyes, placing her fingers over her lips. She laid her face on her palms before facing Kyle again. "You didn't want me to touch you, and yet you expected me to reach out to you?"

A sad smile spread across her lips. "I understood the body language. You were relieved when I asked you to leave. You did your duty; you could start over without me."

The derisive gaze Kyle had shot Lincoln while leaving her dorm room resurfaced. The truth hurt so much that she wanted to yell. "In your mind, Lincoln was trash. And that mindset branded me as soiled goods. It's okay to admit the truth. You never mentioned love because, at that moment, you didn't love me."

Tears blinded her eyes that filled with grief. She fled from the building, tripping over her feet. She kept running even though Kyle called her name several times. She fumbled in her pocket for the key, but she never slowed down until she closed her bedroom door. Lying across the bed, she sobbed for herself and the man who failed to pursue her, even though she'd initially pushed him away.

* * *

She thought the nightmare was over when she saw him? More riddles from the woman out of answers.

Kyle watched the Cummings home until a light appeared in Sadie's bedroom window. Satisfied, he returned to the fellowship hall long enough to secure the exterior doors. Then thinking about Sadie's flight across the parking lot, he slid into the car. He only drove to work if he came from a destination other than his house.

More thoughts of Sadie ran through his mind as he pulled into the driveway. Numerous times he'd imagined meeting her again. But the real-life episode contrasted with the fantasy he'd created in his mind. In his version, Sadie admitted that she'd treated him badly and moved on with her life. But he was pleased with his change of attitude concerning her. The old Kyle would've run after Sadie, confirming she was okay in person. Not anymore.

Still, the confrontation sapped his energy. He'd expected to see Sadie at church Sunday morning. But it appeared some things never changed. She was still too impatient. The woman sprang the first evening home. Nevertheless, her breakdown solved the mystery that had plagued him for two years. How he'd failed her in the dorm room that day.

I neglected to declare my undying love for her. Evidently, driving three hundred fifty miles at short notice meant nothing special.

No longer in the dark, he now understood the problem with Sadie's *confession*. The phone call she'd made on the day he drove to Burgundy had hurt him badly. He'd focused on eight words as she cried out her story that morning.

"Kyle, I slept with Lincoln more than once."

Multiple infractions didn't constitute a mistake. Even he could concede a slip-up. Anything more than one time was willfully undertaken.

How could she continually break a promise? What did it matter if it occurred twice or twenty times? One fact remained. Sadie couldn't stay away from Lincoln.

He went into his bedroom, tossing his keys onto the nightstand. How had Sadie sensed the relief he'd only realized on the drive back to Shiatown? Could she possibly be as in tune with his feelings as he was with hers? Perhaps their connection had been more even-handed than he'd ever imagined.

Even though Kyle didn't want her back, her tears had undone him before she spoke. She'd confessed loving him with such ease. As if she'd been practicing a role. He settled into a loveseat by the window. At least she'd severed the destructive tie to Lincoln. In time, she would land on her feet … if she learned from her mistakes and pursued godly choices that excluded Kyle.

She'd sauntered into the office as if she owned the place. He'd known she stood in the hallway long before she'd entered the room. Sadie still wore the subtle fragrance her mother supplied on her thirteenth birthday. And while talking to Liz, Kyle smelled the scent for the first time in two years.

He stood up when a knock sounded on the bedroom door.

"Dinner's on the table, dear."

"I'll be there in a minute, Mother."

Shifting to the bed, Kyle untied his shoelaces, then slid his feet into sneakers. His mind filled with Sadie, he left the room and remained preoccupied with thoughts of her during dinner. Finished eating, he wrapped an arm around Sarah's waist, kissing her cheek when she closed the refrigerator door.

"Mother, as always, dinner was superb," he said, trying to make amends for his silence during the meal.

Sarah patted his hand absentmindedly, busying herself at the counter. Kyle lounged against the wall, watching her wipe the same spot on the stove three times. His mother engaged in mindless tasks when troubled. Did Sadie stop by the house before visiting him?

"What's troubling you, Mother?" Kyle asked after Sarah hung the towel on a rack. He led them into the den.

"Sadie ran into her house minutes before you arrived home. I saw you, watching her from the parking lot." A sad smile parted her lips. "What happened, son? Didn't the reunion go well?"

Kyle clasped her hand in his, settling them on the sofa. Sarah loved her neighbor's children as if they were her own. Especially Sadie. Her friend's middle child occupied a special spot in his mother's heart.

Surely she no longer hoped for a marriage between us? Better let her down gently.

"Sadie dropped by to say hello, and we chatted awhile."

"No one runs home in tears after a chat. What happened?"

"Tell secrets?" he asked, grinning.

She leaned back on the cushion, staring at him.

"Okay, I'd hoped to avoid talking about Sadie, but ... she apologized for taking up with Lincoln."

"Why was she crying?" asked Sarah when he hesitated.

"Don't let those tears concern you. Experts agree, crying is cathartic."

"Did she receive the forgiveness she sought?" Sarah pressed.

Kyle shook his head. "I forgave her on the phone and in person two years ago."

"Forgive her, Kyle. Then you both can move forward."

He put an arm around her shoulder. Three weeks ago, his mother had suffered a tremendous loss. He refused to disrupt any peace she'd managed to find. However, marrying to please anyone was a bridge too far. She must accept that that her son refused to live in the past. "Please don't worry about Sadie and me. This time, our discussion cleared the air for good."

Doubt entered her eyes. "Does she want to rekindle the relationship, Kyle?"

"Does it matter if she does?"

Sarah's sigh sounded more like a moan. "I'm sure it will to Sadie if she wants you back."

"Well, the topic never came up, so she probably doesn't."

"It's hard raising serious subjects without encouragement. But … Sadie won't remain silent for long. You know, forgiving Sadie means taking her back."

One eyebrow rose as he chuckled. "Really? Say that again. I want to make sure that I heard you correctly."

Laughing, Sarah threw up both hands. "That was not a rule of thumb, dear. But seriously, forgiveness goes beyond forgetting the injury; it embraces the person who hurt you."

Kyle shook his head in disbelief. *Was this the same woman who'd warned that if a person tricked him the second time it was his fault?* "Just let it go, Mother. It isn't a matter of forgetting but of understanding *why.*"

Sarah's eyes brightened. "Why she strayed?"

Going to bed early looked pretty good at this point, but he loved his mother enough to stick it out. They both needed closure. Why not unwind on the wise lady who respected his confidences. Hitching up his pants leg, he crossed his leg over his knee then glanced at Sarah. "More like why she continued to stray."

"Your father believed Sadie's strict upbringing bound her to the man."

Throwing back his head, Kyle laughed. "That same upbringing teaches against sin, yet that truth didn't stop her."

"Sometimes Sadie reaches hasty conclusions without considering all the facts. She was a victim of wrong thinking, and you know it. She felt terrible after it happened."

He stroked fingers over his chin. "So, you continue sinning to feel better about yourself?"

"Stop making fun. Trust me. For lots of people wisdom comes too late. All I have to do is look at my own life to figure that out."

Kyle ran his hand down the back of his head, squeezing his neck. At the moment, why Sadie moved back mattered more than having her home. She always adapted coping strategies as needed. Was she running away from Burgundy? If so, how long might she remain in Shiatown?

"What are you thinking?" asked Sarah.

"About why Sadie moved back here. Is she wiser? Or did Lincoln kick her to the curb, and she bolted?"

Sarah gripped his arm. "Does it matter at this point?"

"I thank God it does. I forgave her for punching me in the face, but it still hurts. That's what it felt like. Mother, the promise of marrying the woman I loved kept me from cheating. I can't trust her at all."

He'd let his mother down, but the empathy on her face proved she understood his position. Kyle wanted her to accept that it was over between Sadie and him.

Sarah smiled up at him. "I agree; trust is the foundation of good relationships."

* * *

Sadie crossed her fingers underneath the table when the doorbell rang. Did Kyle stop by to see her? She held her breath as footsteps clicked across the floor. Then her mother's voice came within hearing range.

"I knew you would drop by tonight," Jeanette said, leading the way to the kitchen.

Sadie leaped from the chair when Sarah stepped into the room, flinging both arms around the older woman's neck.

Pulling Sadie closer, Sarah returned the hug, kissing Sadie's forehead.

Tension lifted from Sadie's limbs. Her family and Kyle's mother were making a place in their lives for her. Loneliness had fled the moment she'd opened the door to Roland. Sadie was loved, missed, and welcomed home.

"Thanks for stopping by, Miss Sarah. I know that you work with the auxiliary team every Friday. I pictured you in bed and planned to visit you tomorrow."

Sarah laughed. "In bed at eight thirty? I'll prepare your favorite breakfast if you drop over in the morning."

Sadie's eyes lit up. "You remembered. Every Saturday, you cooked breakfast while I worked on a puzzle in the den."

Amy glanced up from peeling an orange. "I'm coming, too. Think Roland and Kyle will join us?"

Sadie marveled at the effortless conversation around the table. She belonged. They acted as if she'd never brushed them aside. That was the difference between living in Shiatown and Burgundy. At home, she counted as a person. None of them would make fun of her dreams. She spoke before she could change her mind. "I have big news to share."

Sadie hesitated then plunged ahead. "God gave me a complete novel in a dream the night Lincoln and I broke up. Nine teenage girls woke up to life and each other at a sleepover." She licked her lips, stiffening her muscles for their reactions.

"My goodness," said Amy. "The entire story from beginning to end?"

"Uh-huh, it all came together before I woke up."

"Adapt the book into a play and produce it for your dinner theater." Jeanette opened her arms when Sadie dashed around the table before she finished speaking.

"Thanks for remembering, Mom," She brushed fingers across her eyelids. "I guess my sometimes forgetting makes it easier to believe someone else could too."

Jeanette grasped Sadie's chin between her fingers. "Honey, deep down, you never lost sight of the promise. Now shape the desire into reality. We'll talk more about it later."

Her mother's love surrounded her. And she knew that coming home was the best decision she'd made in two years. Grabbing an orange slice from Amy's plate, she stuck it into her mouth, soaking up the peaceful silence. There was no need to chatter. Everything important had already been said. And not just with words. "Goodnight, everyone," said Sadie, blinking back tears. "It's been a long day. I'll take a bath and pop into bed."

"Don't forget breakfast in the morning. You and Amy stop by at eight-thirty. I'll give Cindy a call tonight." Sarah glanced at her friend. "You're welcome to join us."

Laugh lines formed around Jeanette's mouth. "I remember the old days well. I scooted the children next door, then took a nap."

The ringing doorbell pulled Sadie out of the room. *Kyle!*

Zipping down the hallway, she opened the door to her beautiful smiling friend. The dark-skinned beauty with the hazel eyes looked prettier than ever.

"Dee!" Sadie touched Dee's arm before hurriedly stepping aside. "Please come in! I'm so happy to see you." Before closing the door, she peered outside. "Where's Kate?"

"Babysitting, and sorry she couldn't come." Dee paused as laughter erupted from the kitchen. "Company?"

Sadie's gaze followed hers. "Mom, Amy, and Miss Sarah."

"Let's talk in your bedroom," said Dee, climbing the steps.

Sadie noticed the baby bump for the first time. "Deanna, oh my goodness, you're pregnant!"

Dee stared over her shoulder at Sadie. "Wait—did you know Matt and I got married in June?"

Sadie tried not to look disappointed. "I guess the invitation got lost in the mail. Out of sight, out of mind. Can you climb steps?"

Dee hooked Sadie's arm underneath hers. "I'm pregnant, Sadie, not ill. We'll talk in private upstairs."

The silent women sprawled across the bed like teenagers. They were comfortable just being together. The camaraderie was still there even though the friends had fallen out of touch. Sadie thought about the conversation with Kyle. Groaning, she covered her face with her hands. Where to begin?

Dee scooted closer. "Straight talk is never easy, even among best friends." She paused when Sadie's fingers shook. "Hey," said Dee, "did you doubt my friendship? Oh, Sadie, I had to stay clear of the madness. You were free to contact me at any time."

"It wasn't that easy. It seemed like a part of me died when anyone criticized Lincoln. I couldn't take any more."

The door sprang open, catching them both off guard. Kate breezed into the room in high spirits. Her bubbly personality attracted men like a magnet. She kicked off her shoes, then claimed the middle spot on the bed.

"Welcome home, Sadie. My brother-in-law sprang me early," she paused, looking at them. "Did I come at a bad time?"

Sadie's lips curved into a smile. "Hello, friend," she said, hugging Kate's neck. "Perfect timing, as usual."

Kate sat up straight once Sadie released her. "Finish your comment. You couldn't take any more of what? Our butting in to your business?"

"Advice I refused to act on." Sadie clasped her fingers together. "I ruined my relationships with friends and family. And I didn't know how to escape from Lincoln's hold."

Kate made a sound like a hissing snake. "Lincoln Miller is one of those people the Bible says lies awake at night plotting evil. He isolated you from people who cared about you."

Dee nodded. "I overheard what he told you at the coffee shop. That your preacher boy would dump you in a minute. He dared you to tell Kyle. And he almost broke his face laughing when you ran out."

The memory made Sadie shiver. "I didn't know you were there. Why didn't you tell me?"

"Adding embarrassment on top of everything else? You were my friend."

Kate sighed. "Sadie, you cried when anyone joked that little miss Christian cheated on her fiancé."

Dee passed Sadie the tissue box. "We figured you were with him to stop the rumors. You expected the chatter to stop if you dated him, but it gave him an advantage."

Kate's fingers tapped a rhythm on her thigh. "I gave you bad advice to tutor Lincoln at The Mentor Lab again. I didn't think he'd embarrass you in front of everyone there."

Sadie burst into tears, and both girls wept with her. "I should've handed him off to a male tutor," she said in between sobs. Real freedom seemed impossible at the moment. Each time she made peace with the past, something else roped her back in. And all because she'd sided with the enemy against her friends.

Sadie tried to smile as Dee slung an arm around her shoulder. "I went to his room the day you saw me run out of the coffee shop. I'd thought he might understand how much his lies were hurting me. But ... I ... ended up sleeping with him."

"Why, Sadie?" asked Kate. "You didn't like Lincoln. You were in love with Kyle."

Chapter Seven

Sadie stared at her friends. How did she explain one ignorant mistake after another? "Because … he said my relationship with Kyle was over, and he would walk away, too, if I didn't do what he wanted me to."

Dee buried her face on her lap. "Why didn't you take us with you, Sadie? Why did you go alone?"

"Because he would've talked about our first night together if you'd ticked him off. I couldn't chance that happening. I thought I could reason with him."

"I know you have to forgive people, but ooh that man makes it difficult to do," said Kate. "I don't ever want to hear his name again."

Sadie dried her eyes. "Me neither. I didn't even know Dee and Matt got married. Dee, I'll give you your gift before you leave tonight. Tell Matt I said congratulations."

"I didn't send an invitation because I knew you wouldn't come. What were you going to do? Mail the gift?"

Sadie nodded without looking at Dee.

"Don't be mad at Dee or blame your family," said Kate. "Remember the friends marrying friends thing? You guys always joked about having a double ceremony."

Dee nodded. "It was kinder not to say a word."

At least they had a good reason for leaving her out. Besides, no one asked her to buy a gift without receiving an invitation. "Did Kyle come?"

"He and Roland were groomsmen," Dee admitted.

Sadie threw up her hands. "I can't believe neither Amy nor Roland told me one of my best friends was getting married. Everyone kept it a secret including you two. Humph. It's okay. I'll get over it. Earlier, Kyle and I talked at the fellowship hall until I ran home bawling." She told them about the reunion.

"You want Kyle back," said Kate when Sadie finished speaking.

"Can you tell I'm miserable without him?"

"Maybe this will make you feel better. Kyle visited Burgundy the day before he moved to California," said Dee, explaining what happened when he came.

Stunned, Sadie rushed to the window, thinking. None of this made sense. Why would Kyle drive to Burgundy without talking to her even if Matt had warned him off? Had he come to win her back or say goodbye for good? No wonder he barely talked to her at the fellowship hall. The man had caught her making too many dumb mistakes. He'd probably left the campus thanking God she'd refused to marry him.

Kate and Dee joined Sadie at the window. "Don't be sad," said Kate. "Kyle only has good things to say about you."

Dee pointed toward the church. "I'll tell you the latest happenings, Sadie. Let me finish before asking questions. Okay?"

An hour later, Sadie stood at that same window, peering into the night. Kyle drove three hundred fifty miles to see her before moving away from Shiatown. Dare she believe that he still cared?

I won't let him go easily. I'll fight for his love and earn his respect.

Sadie practically cooed when she slid underneath the covers of her bed. Stretching her limbs, she rubbed her feet together. Her mind was overloaded. But having it stuffed with information about home felt wonderful.

She thought about what Dee had told her. That at a meeting last Saturday, Kyle had outlined the church's agenda for the year. He planned to answer questions and concerns at another meeting tomorrow. Then he would finalize the plans after Sunday's service. He'd made a lot of changes. Matt was the new associate pastor, and Kyle had added a youth and children's pastor as well. Still serving as a pastor, Minister Dawkins limited his duties to seniors within the congregation. Kyle left the elders and deacons board intact. Pastor Franklin had utilized volunteers for outreach ministry, and Kyle left them all in place.

And just like his father, he refused to separate the youth and children from the adult service on Sundays. But he implemented a Wednesday service that would begin next week, allowing children, teens, and young adults to congregate with their peers.

Her friends also said that morning prayers Monday through Friday began last week, along with a Friday evening service highlighting praise, worship, and personal testimonies that Matt serviced. Plus, all Sunday and Friday services were recorded now. The itinerary bulged with the programs Sadie and Kyle had designed together. Only the learning lab and dinner theater, programs featuring Sadie, were cast aside.

I never lost sight of the vision, Kyle. I'll bring it up at the meeting tomorrow.

* * *

The next morning, breakfast at the Franklins' brought Sadie face-to-face with Cindy again. This time, the women were friendlier and joined Amy in working a five-hundred-piece puzzle Sarah had discovered in storage. Overstuffed with her favorite meal, Sadie walked beside her sister to the fellowship hall. Kyle had already left the house before she and Amy came over. Yet, Roland, who dropped off Cindy and Brian, ate breakfast with them before going to the boy's club where Roland volunteered.

Sadie's eyes darted everywhere as she and Amy followed the paved walkway to the fellowship hall. The well-designed grounds looked magnificent. Even the lawn and shrubbery were beautifully maintained. Cars lined up on the road, waiting to enter the parking lot. And the sidewalk teemed with people laughing and chatting as they strolled along. Members who lived in the neighborhood made the trek to the meeting by foot. At least two hundred people poured into the building. Apparently, the congregation wanted a voice at the table before the final rollout tomorrow.

Sadie looked behind her at Jeanette walking to the church with Cindy, Brian, and Miss Sarah. Her mother laughed at something Cindy said, and suddenly, Sadie felt like an outsider instead of a family member. Glancing behind her again, she vowed to visit the diner and the new additions to the church as soon as possible. "Amy, Roland drove by the restaurant yesterday so I could see it. Let's go there after the meeting. Or do you have other plans?"

Amy agreed just as someone spotted Sadie and blew a car horn at her. After the first greeting, she happily waved at every person she knew. When they reached the door she opened it wide, letting a group of seniors stroll inside the building ahead of her.

"Well, Sadie Cummings finally came home," said a gray-haired man with a mole beside his nose. "Ann is babysitting our first grandchild today. I'll tell her you're back."

Then Sadie's second-grade teacher hugged her. "I'm so happy to see you. Jeanette shared the news two weeks ago at the diner." She lowered her voice. "Don't fret over Pastor Kyle walking out on you, Sadie. He'll come around. Good men always do."

Sadie's smile froze in place. *Kyle walking out on me ... What is she talking about?*

A woman wearing a red polka-dot dress who lived across town chimed in as well. "Sometimes men get wanderlust, but I knew he would mend his ways someday. Take him back quickly," she advised before walking away.

"That's right, dear. Don't make him suffer too long. Pastor Kyle will make an excellent husband for you," advised an unknown woman with a gap between her teeth.

Sadie felt foolish just standing there, smiling at them, but she didn't know what to say. She guessed that her cluelessness didn't escape their notice when another stranger patted her arm. "You haven't spoken a word, dear. You look confused." Eyebrows raised almost to her hairline, the woman trailed off behind the others.

Seeing friends, Amy scurried away, while Sadie stood alongside a wall, interpreting what they had said. And the comments didn't change when other people stopped by to chat. Somehow, they thought she was the injured party and not their pastor. It baffled her. She felt everyone knew the punchline to the joke except for her.

"You're deep in thought," said Kate, appearing beside her. Locking Sadie's arm, she headed them toward the auditorium. "Dee's saving seats for us."

"What's going on?" Sadie whispered. "I'm on sympathy overload. People think Kyle broke off our engagement."

"They think Kyle chose the youth pastor job over marrying you. And don't correct them, Sadie. As my granny always says, so far, they only think they know."

The friends claimed the seats beside Dee in the auditorium. The meeting was called to order while Sadie digested the news.

* * *

Kyle returned to the podium after Minister Dawkins handed him the mike. The vast turnout this morning truly encouraged him. It proved that most of the congregation took an interest in Kingdom Life's future. And many members appeared to be on board with the new direction they were taking. The naysayers only questioned the short time span before the launch.

That morning, he had crafted a plan that addressed valid concerns after last week's meeting. From the comments given during the earlier Q&A session, people assumed key players were already in place. But final selections would be made that evening. Of course, Sadie had upped the ante by asking what the plans were for the fifth building. The simple question forced him to address the issue today. Kyle silently prayed for wisdom. He couldn't afford to make any mistakes going forward.

"Let's wrap it up," he said, bringing everyone to attention. "The building project invested in our futures and not our wallets." Kyle walked from the stage until he stood directly in front of Sarah on the front row. "Last week, we repaid the loan my father took out to overhaul the grounds. That makes us debt-free. And the Bible says we should owe no man but to love him. Everyone knew the plans in their pastor's heart before he passed away. He set the stage. His part is completed. It's up to us to transform the dream into a reality by touching this city for God's glory."

Applause erupted throughout the six-hundred-seat auditorium. Spotting Sadie sitting between Dee and Kate, Kyle strolled to their row. "Some people think I'm moving too fast with these new projects. But I feel confident about the programs we'll put in place tomorrow. Before we took a break, Sadie Cummings kicked me out of the comfort zone with specific ideas to increase our visibility in Shiatown. Using those methods will impact our city." Kyle studied the eyes glowing with tears. "Expect to hear the layout of the learning center tomorrow. It'll house our learning lab and dinner theater."

Private conversations erupted throughout the room. Eyes stared at the woman leaning on Dee for support. Her innocent expression justified his decision. Tearing his gaze away, Kyle glanced around the auditorium. "Tomorrow we'll meet here after the morning service." He glanced at Sadie. "Please meet me in my office at three thirty today." He turned to his associate pastor. "Matt."

While Matt concluded the meeting, Kyle stood at the door waiting to thank everyone for coming out. His mind reorganized his afternoon appointments. The unscheduled meeting with Sadie disrupted his itinerary for the rest of the day.

Multiple voices speaking inside the auditorium alerted him that the meeting was over. The first person to leave asked questions about the transition, and other people followed his example. Kyle answered each question until the last couple said goodbye. After their SUV had driven off, he locked the door and headed down the hall, humming.

Minutes later, he ushered Matt and Minister Dawkins to the conversation area inside his office. The older man commended Kyle and Matt for including the congregation in the discussion.

"Joe, you and Dad worked together at Kingdom Life for thirty-three years," Kyle began. "Thanks for keeping us on the straight and narrow. Will you start us off with prayer?"

After praying, Minister Dawkins stared at the younger men. "I think you should know people are questioning you and Sadie's relationship more than ever."

Kyle chuckled. "Is it the who broke off with whom thing again?"

Minister Dawkins laughed so hard he began to cough. "Or something like that." Still laughing, he poured water into a glass.

"Why do people assume they're no longer a couple?" asked Matt, stretching out his legs. "I don't recall either one of them saying they broke up at all."

The amazement on the older man's face surprised Kyle. Matt was right. Only ten people knew the truth about what happened. He twisted a pen in his fingers, then, tapping it on the table, he brought the meeting to order. "Let's review the financial layout for the new programs first. Reserving thirty percent of the budget in a contingency fund should eliminate future deficits."

* * *

Kyle was lounging on a bench in the square in front of the church when Sadie parked her mother's car in their driveway. Instead of heading over to the fellowship hall, she sat down on the top step of her porch, resting her face on her lap. Then, hugging her arms around her legs, she peered down the street in the opposite direction.

Something's upset her. Where did she go after the meeting?

Kyle rose to his feet and then sat down again. Once Minister Dawkins left, Matt told him that Dee and Kate had visited Sadie last night. Except for a few relatives, no one else in town merited a next-day visit. Her time was better spent mending fences with the family she'd neglected for two years.

Kyle thought about the talk he'd had with Matt after Minister Dawkins left. His friend had shed light on Sadie's relationship with Lincoln. Once Sadie broke up with Kyle, she resisted becoming part of the entourage. She mostly saw Lincoln at tutoring sessions or not at all. Three months after Kyle's last visit to Burgundy, Lincoln replaced Sadie with four other tutors, leaving Sadie with one subject. Senior year, he cut her off entirely, choosing another female to take her place.

Matt said they had maintained an association of some sort. He'd seen them talking from time to time in the quad. Lincoln had females falling over him, and Sadie was no longer a part of the crowd. He also said that before Lincoln and Sadie became an item, the locker room was rife with gossip about the man's sexual exploits. He dropped names to anyone within hearing distance. Even though Lincoln never lied that he'd slept with Sadie before it had happened, he didn't deny it either.

One day after the locker-room scene, and before she got together with Lincoln, Matt took Sadie aside and tried to shock her into reality. Instead, the accusation hurt her feelings. She exploded, saying she was immune to Lincoln's immature tactics. The man didn't believe in God, and she detested him. Those last words had been flung over her shoulder as she stomped off down the hall. That same haughty attitude afflicted most people before a fall. Life changing mistakes often take the person by surprise. Had her outlook matured any?

Kyle checked his watch; it was three forty-five. Fifteen minutes late and the woman still stared off into space. He'd better go over there before he changed his mind about interviewing her for a job.

Sadie jerked around when he reached where she sat. There was no mistaking the hope in her eyes as she rose, reaching out her hand to him. The intense stare caught Kyle off guard. "You're late," he said, seeking a peaceful way to deal with the wearisome woman. "Were you waiting for me to come get you?"

Her smile disappeared in an instant. Sitting down again, she nodded. Her eyes never left his face. Taken aback, he stepped closer to her. "Were you that sure I would come?"

"I only knew that I needed you to." She lowered her head for several seconds. Tears glistened in her eyes when she looked up again. Kyle moved nearer, brushing teardrops from her cheeks. Then Sadie stood up, squeezing the hand he held out to her before falling into step beside him.

Chapter Eight

Touring the grounds she helped design with the man she loved was amazing. Her toes tingled whenever Kyle released her hand to unlock or relock a door and then grabbed it again. Seeing her dreams come alive made her heady.

Except for a few insignificant alterations, it looked just like the blueprint Kyle had submitted to his father. The workmanship was well-crafted. And the three additional buildings blended right in with the original setup. Kingdom Life Church, fittingly named "The William Franklin Memorial Expansion," put the complex into focus. Sadie wanted a rundown on every operation, even the daycare center, and Kyle answered her questions concerning each building's function.

Sadie eagerly listened as he explained the intricacies involved in operating the daycare seven to seven. The Little Jewels Daycare was filled to capacity with both children and seniors. The center had to turn away applicants weekly. As planned, the fourth building housed areas dedicated to children, teens, and college students, along with a wing for adults.

The children's space was fantastic. A large room resembling a cave included a merry-go-round and occupied the front wing. The teen's hangout resembled a coffee shop. They could enter their getaway from the square as well as from inside the building. Upstairs, the young adult's space resembled a ski resort. Outfitted with a wood-burning fireplace, it occupied half the second floor. The other portion contained various sizes of meeting rooms available for group discussions.

As of Pastor Franklin's death, two buildings remained unused. How had Kyle convinced the prudent man to build for the future? No doubt the father had envisioned his son in an active role in the very near future. The thought saddened Sadie. Kyle had accepted an associate pastor's position and then left town because of her rejection. Many lives suffered because she chose the wrong man.

Still, she got goose bumps as they entered into the hallway leading to the last building. If the original draft was adapted, the learning lab occupied the second floor, with a dinner theater on the main level. It was the space she thought of as her own private domain.

Once inside the lobby, Sadie screamed in delight and her voice echoed throughout the space. Running ahead of her tour guide, she jerked open the heavy doors leading into the theater. "Wow! This place is unbelievable!" The professional auditorium was equipped with a full-size stage. Sadie studied the huge space at length; then she pulled on Kyle's arm as he stood beside her. "We didn't pass a stairway. How do we get upstairs?"

Silently, he retraced their steps through the thick doors and went down a narrow passageway on the lobby's far side. Upstairs, the ecstatic Sadie spent ten minutes opening and closing doors before racing to a landing that led to the lower level. Downstairs, she grabbed Kyle's hand. "Okay, how do we reach the dressing rooms?"

Done pouring over every inch behind the stage, she grinned at the man walking patiently behind her. The only drawback to the design was the eating facility. Sadie had wanted to serve meals inside the auditorium, but Kyle admitted it was more cost effective to set up a dining area in a separate room.

But that didn't matter. She could overlook one tiny hitch in the vision. Now, the blank canvas demanded an excellent designer. She knew without asking that Kyle would never hire a professional to stage the place. Busy viewing the area with half-closed eyes, her mind sketched out the perfect layout. Before long, Sadie forgot the silent man surveying her movements. Finally satisfied with the drawings inside her head, she hurried to Kyle, who was standing exactly where she had left him.

"Let's add a platform and set up tables surrounding one side in a semi-circle," she said, pointing to the area. "I think inviting local authors to read the first chapter of their books to dining patrons will help fund the live productions." Scratching her head, she surveyed the area again. "Maybe we can keep it going once the plays begin. Giving our customers double for their money is a good idea. What do you think, Kyle? Do you like my ideas?" asked Sadie, turning toward him.

"I agree, if expenses remain unchanged. A platform is doable."

Sadie blinked at the quiet delivery until she noticed the disbelief in his eyes. Kyle had detached himself from their discussion. Her spirit waned as if someone had doused her with cold water. Too late, Sadie remembered the once-in-sync couple no longer operated as a team.

Chewing a thumbnail, she re-examined the space from all angles. But her heart sought out ways to bridge the gap that had surfaced between her and Kyle. While concentrating on the dining room, she'd missed Kyle's pulling away from her. She had hoped they would visit Burger Barn together after the tour. The teen hideout was the perfect place to tell him about her book, plus pick up pointers about teenage girls.

Back in his office, Kyle sat in the chair behind the desk instead of on the couch. The question in his eyes alerted Sadie that she'd missed whatever he'd said. "Sorry. I was thinking about Burger Barn ..." she hesitated when Kyle sighed, slightly shaking his head.

"Let's try it again," he said after she apologized. "I asked what were your thoughts. Do you see yourself working here? If so, in what capacity?"

We're not strangers, Kyle. Why are you doing this? It appeared their earlier camaraderie was lost. Unable to straddle the fence any longer, Sadie rested her chin on clasped hands. He would hear the truth whether he believed it or not. "These are my thoughts. I love you, Kyle. Please, let me back into your life."

Kyle leaned back in the seat. "Sadie, you can't show up two years later expecting to pick up where we left off."

"Why not? We were good together, and you know it's true."

"Because ..." He paused, obviously choosing the exact words to say. "The engagement ended when you chose another man over me."

Her heart broke in half. God, wasn't there some way around the chaos she'd created? Could one regrettable error ruin her whole life? Unshed tears stung her eyes. "Thoughts of you gave me hope through it all. The Bible clearly states love never fails."

"Keep the scripture in context, Sadie. Jesus's love never fails," said Kyle, checking the clock on the wall.

Sadie combed fingers through her hair. Somehow, he had to understand that hard lessons had finally grown her up. She was happier with Kyle than without him. They'd been separated long enough. It was time to make their relationship work. She held out her hands to him. "I love you, Kyle."

He fingered a pen before replying. "What does love mean to you, Sadie?"

Her hand plopped onto her lap. And then hope rose again. Although Kyle failed to offer an olive branch, he never denied loving her.

Pushing file folders to the side, he rounded the desk and sat down beside her, clasping her hands in his palms. The compassionate expression on his face showed his affection more than words. Sadie wanted nothing more than to lose herself in his kindness. Then, the heat from his hands infused her body with warmth, and she almost crawled onto his lap and cried.

"When did you begin loving me again?" he asked. "Yesterday, last month, a year ago?"

Tears flowed as she acknowledged the injustice she'd dealt him. A lesser man might've detested her by now. Sadie hesitated, licking her lips. They always dried out when she was upset. "I never stopped loving you."

Kyle dropped her hands, returning to his seat before speaking. "You never stopped loving me, yet you rejected me for someone else. Can you even explain that statement? I would like to hear it, if you can." He tilted the chair backwards, staring at her.

His words and body language confounded Sadie. Of course she loved him. How could she not love the man who had always treated her special? Yet how could she profess undying love for a man she walked away from? She shuffled in her seat, but what she really wanted to do was cover her face in shame. Kyle expected more than she could give to him. How do you make someone understand when you can't grasp it yourself?

The words stuck in her throat as she tried to speak. "I—I was very con-fused," said Sadie, her voice barely above a whisper. She prayed for Kyle to understand until his doubt-filled eyes hit her like a physical blow. Obviously, her words meant nothing to him.

"Are you less confused now?" he asked, grinning at her.

Nodding, she attempted a smile. "Please trust that I am."

When curiosity replaced the skeptical expression, her stomached flip-flopped against her ribs. And then it hit her: Did he question her intent or doubt her ability to be truthful?

Chuckling lightly, Kyle stared at her. "Might you become confused again?"

Powerless to sit still, Sadie sat beside him on the desk even though she disliked his teasing her. Today may be the last time to plead her case; to somehow explain the unexplainable in a logical manner.

"Kyle, I'm a different person altogether now. I'm fighting for the man I don't want to live without." She felt cornered when he studied her with half-closed eyes. And although her answer seemed to surprise him, his lack of response almost made her give up.

He sat up straighter. "That response suggests that living without me two years ago didn't matter."

Sadie closed her eyes then opened them quickly. "I thought I had lost you two years ago," she said in a soft voice.

His slow grin depleted her hope supply. The glowing promise now resembled an ash pile. At least their conversation confirmed his willingness to listen. The battle was far from being over. Maybe he required more time before starting over.

Sadie focused on the expressionless face. "Why won't you talk to me?"

"I'm unraveling your comment. You sent me packing because you supposed you had already lost me?"

Sadie closed the gap between them. Her logic sounded ridiculous even to her. Who built futures with irrational partners? "My thoughts were chaotic, Kyle. I couldn't grasp basic concepts at the time."

He studied the pen in his hand. "There wasn't one person you could confide in? An individual wise enough to guide you through it?"

"As they say, hindsight is always twenty-twenty."

Kyle briefly closed his eyes. Her reply appeared to settle some issue deep within him and Sadie realized he didn't like her answer. As her stomach churned against her ribcage, Sadie wished she could retract the insane response to a reasonable question.

"Kyle—"

"So hindsight is always twenty-twenty. Too bad we live in the here and now."

Sadie crouched on her knees in front of him, resting her hand on his knee. "I didn't say that correctly. Together we can make it work."

"Too late," he said, pointing to her chair. "I don't know about you, but I refuse to live a life controlled by errors and good intentions."

"Please ... let me explain what I meant to say."

"Sadie, I missed two important meetings talking to you. The third one starts in twenty minutes. If you take a seat, we can finish up quickly."

Kyle rushed Sadie out of the fellowship hall fifteen minutes later. Nursing her wounds, she settled into a corner table at Burger Barn. But in no time, the playfulness in the restaurant eased her anxiety a little. Life hurt. Her grandmother used to say, "Smooth the covers when you make the bed you're sure to sleep in later." Remaking her bed would hardly suffice at this point; Sadie wished for a total redo. Would God grant her a second chance with Kyle?

Earlier, he'd conducted the meeting as if they'd never met. The one-on-one went purely by the book after her remark put him off, and Kyle escorted Sadie to the main entrance as soon as it ended. Instead of going home, she drove to Burger Barn, pledging to use any free time to research her book. Teenage girls. Not too many years ago Sadie numbered among that crowd.

Pulling the wrapper off of her straw, she rethought her strategy regarding Kyle. Just letting him know she loved him fell flat. In her heart, she longed to pick up where she left off before leaving home. But that was impossible. Too much living had happened since then. She couldn't make light of past events, and neither would Kyle. Getting him back appeared to be a long shot at the moment. But each day offered a ray of hope. And today dropped four useful nuggets into her heart. Kyle never denied loving her. He willingly listened to her appeal. His personal rebuke was gentle. And although he physically separated himself from Sadie, he had continued the conversation from a distance.

However, something in her remark "hindsight is always twenty-twenty," had angered him. He'd dropped her hand like it had scorched his fingers. Somehow, being close to her triggered pain. No wonder Kyle refused to forgive Sadie. She'd broken faith with him in the worst way possible. Memories of herself with Lincoln still haunted her.

Instead of giving him platitudes, she should've confessed the truth. But even Sadie didn't grasp how an unwanted kiss led to intimacy with a man she disliked. She broke off the engagement because both Kate and Dee agreed that Kyle hated sexual sins just like his father. And Lincoln convinced Sadie she'd already lost Kyle because of their time together; that no man who shared her godly convictions would ever want her. And she'd believed him until two weeks ago. She cringed at her pathetic response to Kyle's question. Of course she had a wise person to talk to. He knew that her mother kept an open-door policy with her children, making herself available whenever needed.

Handing Kyle clichés won't turn the page in our relationship. Even though it will break my heart, I must be honest with him. I can't give up now. Even though I'm fighting for us, Kyle, I can't wage a battle alone. You have to stay engaged. Help me, help us.

Deep in thought, Sadie jumped when someone sat beside her.

"Wow! What were you thinking about? Wish I could read minds."

Seeing her sister's smiling face was exactly what she needed. Sighing loudly, she watched four boys and three girls eyeing one another across the room.

"What's up with you?" asked Amy, sipping her sister's lemonade. She shook Sadie's arm when she didn't respond.

"My botched talk with our neighbor. I wanted him to take me back."

"Really? After your second day home?" Amy's eyes opened wider. "As if the two years you spent apart didn't matter?" She paused when tears entered Sadie's eyes. "It's too soon for that, but I think he'll make you a part of the team at church," Amy said, slurping the last of Sadie's drink.

"I was hopeful until the meeting. Anyway, he'll make the final decision tonight. I think he touched base with everyone in the running to gauge our interest."

"Then what's the problem? You're interested ... and in the running ... and know Kyle's plan for Kingdom Life. I like those odds."

"May I borrow your perspective?" asked Sadie, smiling for the first time since the meeting. "Working with him will fulfill part of my dreams. I want our lives to connect in every way possible."

Amy scooted her chair closer. "Did you truly expect for Kyle to take you back overnight? Don't you prefer a man with strong convictions?"

Sadie immediately hugged Amy against her side. "Thank God for little sisters. Where were you two years ago when I needed sound advice?"

"People watching. Look around you, Sadie. Bet you'll pick up loads of information for your book tonight," said Amy, pointing out a couple sitting down at the next table.

Chapter Nine

The sanctuary was quiet as Kyle delivered the message that Sunday morning. This was the first time Sadie had ever heard him teach. She sat in awe, marveling at the practiced delivery and peaceful air. It was a skill he must have learned while working in California. Yet, the timely message really spoke to her heart, hitting her right where she lived. She closed her eyes as his words sunk deep into her spirit.

"Spiritual growth is essential to the life of every believer. It enables us to choose correctly in each arena where we live. Maturity develops as we actively seek His presence throughout each day. Without the proper fellowship with God, our attitude will become complacent toward godly things. And that is the state of many believers in Jesus today.

"You see, there are subtle games we play to stay within our comfort zone. That place where we feel emotionally secure. The list of reasons is endless. One favorite ploy is to surround ourselves with other Christians who think like us. Then we have no reason to change; our agreement makes us right. Or we keep as friends Christians who disobey His teachings more than we do, so we feel pretty good about our own obedience. Or non-believers who make no claim to knowing Jesus at all. Then we really feel great about our behavior.

"These and similar tricks allow us to think that we're being obedient, even in the act of disobeying. But Christians are instructed to observe His entire counsel, not just the ones easiest for us to achieve. For there are obvious acts of disobedience that most of us accept as sinful. And then there are those subtle sins of character we often overlook. Those culprits allow us to escape conviction of our rebellion against God.

"This one failure lets us feel spiritually alive, when in reality, we are quite dead to some godly principles."

Sadie squirmed in the chair when Kyle described individuals who listened without hearing much and then diluted whatever they heard. Not Sadie. At least, not today. She felt thoroughly convicted and sifted her past through the message, appalled at the self-delusion that had kept her in bondage for so long. Over breakfast yesterday, Miss Sarah had said Kyle prepared his sermons at least a week in advance. Yet, this morning, the message hit home as if he'd aimed it straight at her.

It proved she should've opened up to him yesterday when she had the chance. The pastor who just finished speaking might've understood her past dilemma—even if the man wronged remained unmoved by what she said. Even though she'd come home, the fallout from her errors still remained. Sadie couldn't move forward unless she opened up to the man she desired to marry. There was still a mountain to climb without a foreseeable way to come back down. What if Kyle left her stranded?

Jeanette's lips grazed her daughter's temple, interrupting her thoughts. "Cheer up, love. I see the look on your face; we've all experienced it. The first time Kyle spoke, I just knew he'd overhead my conversation with Millie Wagner the day before." She lowered her voice. "The lady got on my last nerve, and I reacted *quite* inappropriately."

Sadie, feeling disoriented, was thankful when Amy joined in. "My come-uppance happened last Sunday," her sister said in a sing-song voice. "Now, how did Kyle know I'd fudged on my calculus assignment on Thursday?"

Sadie laughed along with Amy, but Jeanette didn't crack a smile. "Sweet-heart, it's time you took your education seriously. You're no longer in high school where you easily breezed through every subject."

"I am serious, Mom." She whispered in Sadie's ear, "Be thankful you at-tended college in another state. But," she said in a louder voice, "I could live on campus if Mom would spring for a dorm room next term."

"And deny you the chance to live at home with me? I love you too much to push you away like that," her mother countered, watching the crowd enter the hallway to the fellowship hall. "Let's go before they start the meeting without us."

* * *

After the meeting, a dazed Sadie walked alone until Sarah fell in step beside her. "Congratulations, love," said the woman with the steady gaze. "Our church will thrive with you and Kyle at the helm. I can't wait for you to get started."

Sadie had almost fainted during the meeting. Kyle actually set her in charge of the learning lab and dinner theater. He had put the church's interest ahead of his personal feelings. That was Kyle. He seldom allowed pettiness to cloud his judgment. It seemed that her zeal had won out while the experience factor would follow later. She beamed at the lady who always supported her efforts even when they failed.

"Since the position is part-time starting off, working in the bookstore could supplement your income," Miss Sarah continued. "We can work you in between the learning center's schedule if you agree to help us out."

Stunned, Sadie touched her chest. Miss Sarah sounded as if Sadie had to be talked into working for her. "That's another job offer I don't have to think about," she said in a hurry. "I definitely want the job. On Friday, I told Mom I'm taking a hiatus from working in restaurants. Juggling three waitressing jobs the last four months ruined it for me."

Miss Sarah chuckled. Sadie loved Miss Sarah's laugh. It held an earthy tone that no one else could mimic.

"Jeanette told me after you left us in the kitchen on Friday. Come to the bookstore tomorrow afternoon. I'm eating lunch with friends today."

Sadie planned the upcoming week on the spot while she searched the room for Kyle. Tomorrow, she would set up the learning lab using the Mentor Lab as a model. She would also secure volunteers for the tutoring sessions that would begin the following week. She knew a slew of retired teachers who should be willing to lend a hand.

There were key people who could assist with the live productions as well. The drama teacher at Shiatown University had offered to jump in to help her when the time came. In fact, the town was full of people experienced in theater, both professional and semi-professional. And Sadie planned to contract The Main Street Diner to cater the meals. Her grandmother had promised a substantial discount if Sadie was the recurring customer. She hoped her mother remembered the conversation they'd had.

She tuned in to the crowd still talking in the foyer. Anticipation was everywhere she looked. People refused to leave the building. Still searching for Kyle, she spun around when Roland called her name. And there was Kyle, talking to Cindy and her brother, who held a whiny Brian in his arms.

He's probably tired and hungry like me. I wish everyone would go home so I could talk to Kyle in private.

"Hi, Sadie," Cindy said when Sadie reached them. "Congratulations. I'm beating out the crowd: Take me on as your personal assistant."

"I like the idea," said Kyle, studying Sadie's reaction.

Sadie fumed. Of course he did. And he stated the fact even before she could reply. The random comment didn't fool her, though. Kyle wanted her and Cindy to work together.

"Do you have theater or tutoring experience?" she asked to buy time.

"No tutoring experience," Cindy admitted. "But I reigned as the drama queen in high school. Kyle told me you had a passion for theater, too."

"All behind the scenes," said Sadie, studying the redheaded pixie. Kyle and Cindy plotted against her, but why? Jealousy wasn't an issue. Cindy hardly took her eyes off Roland while they talked. Then the child rested his head on her brother's shoulder, asking when were they leaving. "Soon," said Roland, turning to Sadie. "I can't think of a better team to whip the new program into shape."

"Then it's a done deal," she said, smiling at him. Her brother was happy for the first time that she could remember. His expression was lighter around the boy. Did he intend to become a father figure in the child's life? Well, he'd better tread softly. It seemed mother and son were a package deal. Amy had told her last night that Roland met them when he visited Kyle last spring. Cindy began writing to him, and her brother answered each letter. So be it, if the young family made him happy.

Sadie blinked at the couple then stood on her tiptoes, whispering into Kyle's ear, "Run away with me … okay? We need to talk honestly, Kyle." She plopped a wet kiss on his cheek. "Please say yes."

The sudden hush in the lobby sounded louder than the previous conversations had. Their small group was now the center of attention. Sadie ignored the stares. It seemed as if she and Kyle were alone in the room, even though the lobby was full of people. And she couldn't have been happier. Her eyes sparkled with unshed tears. "I promise not to disappoint you this time." Watching him carefully, Sadie pinpointed the exact moment he relented and decided to go with her.

"We'll give it another shot," he said in a way that sounded as if it was the last thing he wanted to do. He checked his watch, then glanced at her, but this time Sadie failed to read his expression. "Meet me in front of your house in ninety minutes." The remark was made in the same toneless voice he'd used before. Saying goodbye to the others, Kyle walked across the lobby, greeting parishioners as he headed to his office.

Sadie waited, but he never looked back, which was the very thing she'd wanted him to do. To look back as if he couldn't bear to be without her. Feeling deflated, and questioning her own judgment, she smiled shyly at the couple still looking at her. Roland started to speak but apparently changed his mind. Cindy looked stunned, until she suddenly smiled, mouthing the words, "I'm praying for you." She scooted closer to Roland before Sadie waved goodbye.

Moving swiftly to the door, she slipped quietly away.

* * *

Sadie strolled into the house, locking the door behind her. Abandoning her heels beside the stairs, she padded down the hallway on her bare feet. "Mom, I'm home! Something smells delicious." Sniffing the air, she followed the scent into the kitchen, laying her purse on the counter. "Ooh, hot chocolate. How did you get a pot ready so fast?"

Carrying two steaming cups, her mother sat down at the table. "Practice." A shining light in her eyes, she pushed a cup and saucer to Sadie. "Have a seat. What are your plans for today?"

Sadie pulled out the chair across from her mother. "Pleading my case to Kyle. Don't worry; I won't become anyone's doormat again," she said when her mother frowned. "Fighting for the man I love feels right. Finally seeking God's plans instead of calling the shots myself. Oh Mom, I've acted silly." She hung her head. "Look at my stupid mistakes."

Jeanette grasped Sadie's fingers in her hands, squeezing them gently. "Who hasn't behaved foolishly at some point in their life?" she asked when Sadie refused to look at her.

"I know I'm not the only one, but most people come to their senses instead of being forced into sanity. Seeing that woman on my porch woke me up in a hurry."

"Honey, from what you've told me, Lincoln usually paraded other women in front of you. Only this time, you walked away. And we both know that staying in Burgundy was much easier than moving back home. Yet, you came home anyway."

Sadie left her seat and knelt at her mother's side. Laying her head in Jeanette's lap, she sobbed as soft fingers stroked her hair. This is exactly what she'd expected from her mother last summer. But Lincoln had denied her those comforting embraces. She apologized to the woman who loved her in spite of their ruined vacation. Loving unconditionally was a tremendous responsibility on the person bestowing that love.

After a few minutes, Jeanette scooted back the chair and pulled Sadie to her feet. "What time are you meeting, Kyle? I need twenty minutes of your time," she said when Sadie glanced at her watch.

"In forty-five minutes. Why? Do you need help with something?" asked Sadie, her curiosity engaged.

"Follow me. We have just enough time for a private talk before your sister comes home." Jeanette led the way to her own bedroom, and she laughed when Sadie sprawled on the bed, patting the space beside her like she did as a child. She crawled next to Sadie, throwing her arms over her giggling daughter. Then she rested her head on her palm; her expression grew serious.

"Let's talk about my relationship with your father, Sadie. There are a lot of things we've never discussed but I think you'll find interesting. You know, I met Russell while waiting for the interview with your grandmother. Well, he drove me home afterwards, hooking me into his world before he dropped me off. He asked me out, and I quickly accepted. Once he found out I had no family, the Cummings family adopted me as their own.

"I knew in advance that I needed to leave the orphanage two weeks after my eighteenth birthday, so I started working at the diner the day it opened. I moved into the same duplex Cindy and Brian are living in a week after I turned eighteen. Your Aunt Yolanda soon became the best friend I'd never had. Suddenly, my life had a purpose. I dated a man who cared about me, his family encouraged our relationship, and I loved my job."

Sadie sat up, smiling. "You fell in love with Dad at first sight."

"Yes, he was handsome, thoughtful, and so full of grand ideas. No one could paint a beautiful word picture like Russell did. Honey, you definitely inherited that gift."

Staring at Sadie, she shifted positions. "Then circumstances gradually altered, and I noticed undeniable changes in Russell's personality. His conversations became guarded, and I began to feel uncomfortable being around him. But, we'd already been intimate, and I was pregnant with Roland."

She hesitated as Sadie's eyebrows reached her hairline. "I've learned wisdom, honey, I wasn't born with it. Obeying God-given rules protect us from life's trials and unnecessary hardships. Sure, problems will come, but it's worse when our disobedience brings on the trouble."

Then sadness entered into the eyes that studied her daughter. "I'd never felt so alone in my life, Sadie. And I couldn't share my condition or fears with your aunt and grandparents. Perhaps a wiser person would've quietly moved away and raised her son alone. But then I wouldn't have had my two lovely daughters." Her eyes clouded over as if she were reliving the confusion. "Instead of leaving, I married him. And since he was later diagnosed with paranoid schizophrenia, I subjected my children to a broken home life that could've proven fatal."

Instantly, Sadie wrapped both arms around Jeanette. Her mother understood how difficult it was to make the right decision. No wonder she never gave up on Sadie even as Sadie pushed her away. At one time, her mother had felt trapped in self-made errors just like she had. Thank God her own ordeal had only lasted two years. Although, when a person is miserable, one day can feel like an eternity.

Sadie snuggled against her mother until she dressed to meet Kyle.

* * *

Ten minutes later, she held out her hands for the keys even before Kyle reached his car. He passed her, opening the passenger door for her, but paused when her bottom lip drooped.

"Are you asking me to let you drive?" he asked when she refused to get in.

"I know where we're going, and you don't, Kyle. So let me drive."

"No way. Frankly, I'm amazed Miss Jeanette let you borrow her car yesterday. Have your driving skills improved since the last time I rode with you?"

She rolled her eyes. "Of course. That was years ago."

"How many times have you driven since then?"

"Yesterday ..." Sadie stared at him when he held his side, laughing. "Hey, stop teasing me. I drove while Amy gave me the tour around town."

He laughed harder. "Have you ever ridden with your sister? Her driving skills are worse than yours were. You both have two speeds: fast and faster. I think about you every time she shoots away from the curb."

Good. What other situations remind you of me? I hope they're all pleasant blasts from the past.

* * *

Sadie stopped the car in front of the teen hangout. This was the third time in three days she'd tried to get him to that particular restaurant. What was the attraction there? "Burger Barn?"

Sadie glanced at him before getting out of the car. "Before you ask, it's all about teenage girls. I'll explain inside."

Here we go again. Sadie was changing tactics like most people changed socks.

Kyle studied her troubled face while waiting in line to place their order. Although she gazed around the room, her mind was clearly somewhere else. He laid the receipt on the table before sitting down. "We have a twenty-minute wait. This place is packed as usual."

"And I can see why. I enjoyed watching them mingle together yesterday. It felt like I was in another world altogether."

"Six years ago, you were one of them," he told her when she stared at him.

Sadie turned away, shaking her head, then she bridged her fingers in front of her nose. "Just six years, huh? It feels like I've lived fifteen in the last two."

As he thought about her remark, she filled him in on the eye-opening dream from God. When Sadie finished speaking, she stared at him, visibly holding her breath.

"Do you know the thoughts, words, and deeds of each character?" he asked.

"No, but I know the sequence of events from beginning to end. I basically know what they do and how they do it. Only the why is missing. For now, their motivation is still a mystery—" Suddenly, she laughed, then pulled a finger and thumb across her lips in a zipping motion. Scooting her chair closer to him, she watched him with twinkling eyes. "Imagine God trusting me to help teenagers mature in a godly way."

"Why not? Spiritual maturity is the plan for every Christian. You know that. God uses our hardships to grow us up. Our trials will bless many people if we learn from them." He noticed the server bringing food to their table. "Jesus is the gift that gives," he said, ending the discussion.

While eating, Sadie asked him about his plans for the learning center. And then she explained her own agenda. It seemed she was hoping to have it up and running within the week. His eyebrow raised at her time projection. He reminded her that sleeping was required to sustain life. After that, he asked questions until she'd answered each one to his satisfaction. But Sadie was full of surprises that day, and she supplied details for the dinner theater's first author reading. Miss Jeanette had guaranteed they would receive a discount for each event. The target date was set for the first Saturday in November, only six weeks away.

"Who did you select to start us off?" he asked, thinking of ways to slow her down.

"I'll ask your mom's advice when we meet tomorrow. Her owning a bookstore will come in handy."

As Sadie was speaking, several teenage boys converged on the couple, asking for the teen's schedule starting Wednesday. Kyle referred them to the youth pastor, then requested ideas for future meetings.

"Don't forget, field trips will give us hands-on experience in lots of areas," said a husky kid as the boys left the table.

Sadie got up when Kyle set down his glass. "The words 'field trip' caught my attention. Let's go."

Inside the car, Kyle watched Sadie pop in a favorite jazz CD. He noted the subtle changes in her personality as well. The old Sadie had talked nonstop. But unlike Friday and Saturday, she appeared more peaceful today. Perhaps she'd given up on them getting back together.

Slowing down, she made a right turn at the corner then entered the ramp to the highway that led out of town. What did she want to talk about that couldn't be said at the restaurant or in one of their houses? A typical Sunday found him in rest mode. After service, he relaxed in his bedroom, thanking God for His many blessings throughout the week. Although Kyle thanked Him every day, he'd discovered that a special day of solitude strengthened him for the week ahead. And Sunday was his day of choice.

He paid attention once Sadie exited the highway in Silverton. And then Kyle knew her destination. He groaned inwardly as she stopped the car at the exact spot where he had proposed four years ago.

* * *

She removed the key from the ignition. "I still love Indian summers. Looking at fall foliage really relaxes me." Her gaze roved over the vividly colored trees and shrubbery. A heaviness hit her that she couldn't shake off. Unwinding in the countryside usually worked, but it didn't this trip. It was time to be real with Kyle, and with herself. Optimism had propelled her through the last two days, but now the past couldn't be swept aside. Kyle wasn't being open with her, either. Sadie had been the only woman he'd ever dated before her rejection opened the door to other women. Was another female a part of his life?

Finally, she turned to him. "Please tell me about her, Kyle. Where did you meet and how long have you dated?"

Chapter Ten

Sadie touched his hand when he stared at a patch of wildflowers growing on the hillside. She'd guessed accurately. He was involved with someone else. Kyle had failed to put his life on hold until she returned home. Had she really expected him to. Now, many unanswered questions created a gap between them.

"I'll go first." Sadie sat up straighter. Somehow the rigid posture boosted her courage. But subjecting herself to further rejection made her nervous. Her lips quivering, she faced Kyle again.

She covered her mouth, exhaling into her hands. "This isn't an easy topic for me to discuss. It's so hard to begin." She blew into her hands again before clasping her fingers on her lap. "Lincoln intimidated me into submission after the first night." Kyle parted his lips, and she paused, thinking he was about to speak, but he didn't. "He kept taunting me that you would never forgive me for being intimate with him." Looking down, she hesitated. "I believed he was right." Trying to smile, she glanced at him with tear-filled eyes. "Leave it to me to pick the one sin you hated above anything else."

Tears rolled down her cheeks as she cleared her throat. "I didn't go to his room on a date, but to walk him through a late assignment. Earlier that day, Lincoln had called, begging for help. He had a term paper due the following Monday."

Sadie hesitated when Kyle glanced out the window. "Unforeseen events placed me in his dorm room that night. The coach held the team over after the game, and Lincoln arrived at my dorm at nine-thirty instead of six. The resident assistant was celebrating her birthday in the common area, so we couldn't study there. We went to his lobby, but students were partying there too. It was either write the paper in his room or walk two miles across campus from The Mentor Lab alone at night."

"Lincoln wouldn't have walked you to your dorm?" he questioned.

She had stopped crying, but now tears filled her eyes before he finished asking. "He never had in the past. That's why I began tutoring him at my common area." Sadie wrung her fingers, sighing. "Kyle, I didn't like Lincoln, and he knew it. In most instances, he worked hard to gain my acceptance. But nothing worked. I simply didn't like the man."

"Please continue," Kyle said when she paused.

"I got a negative feeling when I saw his room for the first time and wanted to escape so badly that I wrote the paper myself." She attempted a smile. "A definite mentoring no-no." Then tears rolled down her cheeks again as she gasped for breath. "Kyle, he refused to let me leave until I let him kiss me. He gave me a light smack on the lips at the door, but instead of being free to go, I ended up flat on my back."

Sadie stared at Kyle in amazement. He was angry. Outrage dominated his facial expression.

"Explain that statement," he said through clenched teeth.

Sadie watched his jaw muscles pulsate. Lying her head on the glass, she stared at him, twiddling her thumbs. "Lincoln picked me up, dropped me on the bed, and his body penned me down."

"He attacked you?"

"Two years ago, I said it was unstoppable because I couldn't break free, and not because I had reached some point of no return. I begged him to stop, to leave me alone, and when he didn't, I just lay there, crying. I allowed the situation to get out of hand. I didn't scream or crack him over the head with a lamp. I just lay there humiliated and despising myself for going into his room."

"Sadie!" Kyle moved closer, caressing her cheek, then he dropped his hand. "I need time to think." After staring at her for a moment, he rushed from the car.

Sadie sniffled into a tissue. Relief flooded her body as never before. Each time she owned up to the past, a purging purified her soul. She dabbed her eyes with another tissue, then stepped outside the car. Kyle was leaning against the car trunk with his hands in his pockets, gazing at Sadie as she stood beside him. And then he pulled her into his arms, resting his chin on her hair.

"Your honesty settles several loose ends for me, Sadie. It also explains some of your mind-boggling behavior lately. Until now, I couldn't make sense of any of your actions. Even since you've come home."

She hung her head. "I still can't understand why Lincoln hurt me or why I began a relationship with him after he did."

Kyle sighed into her hair. "Why did he leave Rutledge three weeks into the term? It's odd the school just let him go after investing heavily into his being there."

"Who knows?" she said, brushing a tissue below her eyes. "Wild rumors were everywhere, but no one knew for sure."

Kyle held her at arm's length. "Did you know that experts say traumatized individuals can develop an affinity for their abuser?"

Sadie shook her head. "I only know I felt trapped by my mistakes. And each effort to undo the previous dumb error dug me in deeper. I ate breakfast alone the next morning until Lincoln found me at a coffee shop. He never gets up early if he doesn't have a class, but he found me before nine. At first, I thought he'd come to apologize." Tears glistened in her eyes. "He came to gloat and make fun of me. I left him there and called Roland. I told him about Lincoln when he arrived."

Kyle's eyebrow rose. He clearly didn't believe her. And she knew why. Had he known the truth, Roland would've never left the campus without confronting Lincoln. "You told him what you just revealed to me in the car?" he finally asked.

"No," Sadie stared at the ground. "I gave him the watered-down version I originally gave you."

"Sadie, why would you hide it from Roland? The tie with Lincoln would've been severed had he known the truth." A light dawned in his eyes. "How do you think your brother would've responded to the truth?"

"He might've killed him. How could I ruin my brother's life along with my own?"

Kyle shook his head. "No. He would've strictly gone by the book—ensuring Lincoln never touched you again. Why didn't you confide in Dee and Kate?"

"And have them both betray my confidence? Dee would've told Matt. I was so confused; I actually envisioned Matt confronting the team's star player. It would've landed Matt either on probation or off the team. And Kate would've alerted the authorities, making it my word against Lincoln's."

"What was wrong with making a police report?" asked Kyle.

Sadie hoped she looked more confident than she felt. The truth was simple enough. She'd been afraid no one would believe her. "I'd played into

Lincoln's hands, Kyle. He made the move after I let him kiss me. To some people, agreeing to one kiss to exit his room would constitute consent for whatever followed. It allowed him to overpower me without consequences. My word against his. The louse covered his bases."

Kyle tilted her face toward his. "He understood how to muddle the facts, which probably makes him a repeat offender. But other people become needless prey when crimes aren't reported. Criminals should be stopped before they strike again."

Her eyes widened. "Do you think he harmed anyone else? I can't believe that I never thought it might happen to another woman."

"Perhaps, but we'll deal with the fallout going forward. Sadie, you have many supporters. Your family, friends, and a host of other individuals would've backed you, including me and my mother. And through God's grace, truth *will* prevail in the end."

Teardrops splattered onto her collar. "Looking back, I fumbled the ball big time. I felt worthless and undeserving of anything good; even from God."

His calm eyes caressed her heart, filling up the empty places. Her earlier thought was correct. Pastor Kyle Franklin sympathized with the illtreatment. But would her ex-fiancé forgive her for staying with the abuser for two years after it happened? When Kyle failed to say more, Sadie watched the scenery, feeling miserable. She'd actually prayed to marry the man who forced her into submission. At the time, it seemed better to just forget how it happened and move on with her life. What did it matter if she'd already lost Kyle? Cringing, she moved away from him.

God, how could I ever see that position as reasonable? Or believe Lincoln and I had anything worth fighting for? Especially since I didn't want to win. I'm too embarrassed to even look at Kyle.

"Sadie," said Kyle as she stared at her shoes. "You ran to me crying when I walked into the dorm room. You then let Lincoln pull you away from me. The tears bothered me. You always projected a fearless front. I repeatedly asked why you were upset."

She glanced away. "I was still trying to process what had happened. It was like I was in a fog and couldn't see my way out."

"If you'd leveled with me I would've dealt with Lincoln on the spot."

Her gaze met his. "I couldn't, Kyle. You looked from me to Lincoln, hating what you saw."

"What you said at the fellowship hall Friday was incorrect. I didn't view you as soiled goods but as the woman who threw me away. Why was he there?"

"He just dropped by, which is something he never did," said Sadie, spreading out her hands. "Since then, I learned to expect him whenever something good was about to break for me."

"That realization should have sent you running for cover," said Kyle.

"I'm afraid it held me captive. I didn't think you could forgive me. So, I believed that staying with Lincoln would make it all go away somehow. At the time, those irrational ideas appeared quite valid to me."

Drying her eyes, Sadie studied the man examining the landscape. Unlike her, Kyle enjoyed spending time alone. She had once jokingly labeled it as only-child syndrome. Still, it felt right surveying the beautiful countryside together, just like they used to before she left home for college.

Suddenly, Kyle pointed to foliage about thirty feet away. She knew he hoped to lighten her mood and restart their day.

"Think you can beat me to the first goldenrod patch?" asked Kyle, breaking into a sprint as Sadie raced ahead. Laughing, he touched the tree trunk just as she puffed to a stop beside him.

"Okay, you won." Sadie panted to catch her breath. "Bet I can reach the Chinese pistache before you do." She reached behind her back, patting the tree with the beautiful fall colors.

Then they traipsed through the fields while Sadie picked various shades of pink and magenta leaves. The vast open space seemed endless. Time stood still in unpopulated areas. Feeling more lighthearted than before the walk began, Sadie marveled at their soundless communication. Somehow she just knew Kyle wished to talk about the other woman in his life. As they walked in the direction of the car, he smiled down at Sadie's upturned face.

"I met Leanne at a dinner party my first week in Glendale. She was easy to spend time with. I eagerly sought new experiences, and Leanne was happy to provide them." He hesitated as the parked car came into view. "She's a few years older than me, and her self-confidence paved the road for a stress-free relationship. Not only did we click right away, but we shared similar viewpoints on many subjects. We began dating last June."

Sadie sighed within herself. Although her heart shouted that Kyle still loved her, it didn't mean that he wanted her back in his personal life. Especially if Leanne came maintenance-free. Her stomach somersaulted against her ribcage. While she had been busy going nowhere, Kyle was rebuilding his life on a firm foundation. By never losing sight of working in full-time ministry, he rose above their troubles and pressed forward to the goal.

Stooping down, he picked up a goldenrod leaf for her collection, handing it to her. "Leanne's roots are established in California, and my base is in Oklahoma. I'm a hands-on person, Sadie. A long-distance relationship won't suit me for long. She's equally dedicated to her family's consulting firm."

Any pastor worth his position didn't casually date anyone. He had known Leanne over a year before asking her out. To Sadie, that meant he was serious about the woman. *What happened Kyle? Did the nostalgia from Matt and Dee's wedding push you into action? After all, June was the month we had planned to walk down the aisle together. You selected Leanne for your bride once you returned home.*

"How serious is the relationship?" she asked while wishing she hadn't.

"Before my father died, I was probably six months away from proposing. But then I relocated to Shiatown."

"Is it over?" asked Sadie, bracing herself for what was coming. Was he happy about the separation? Or was he thinking of ways to bring Leanne here?

Kyle appeared to consider his response before speaking. Finally, he glanced at Sadie with a blank expression. "That's a good question."

Sadie had always hated when he responded to her questions without giving anything away. It meant he truly didn't know the answer. Whistling softly, Kyle opened the car door on the driver's side, gesturing her inside. For Sadie, the next seconds played out in slow motion. It took him forever to get into the car and snap his seatbelt into place.

On the drive home, she prayed for godly wisdom going forward. Her pent-up tension had evaporated during their hike. And now she had a name plus insight into the courtship that might keep her from building a future with Kyle. What was the current state of the relationship that, at least to Sadie, should've never begun?

Her only option was to wait and see what happened next between him and Leanne. Dishing out mea culpas to an uninterested person would only lead to heartbreak. Kyle contrasted favorably when compared to Lincoln. But how did she stack up to the woman who seemed to possess all the traits she lacked? Keywords hammered her brain as she drove them home: maintenance-free, self-confident, and enjoyed similar viewpoints to his. Those comments hurt. It suggested he found her lacking in all those qualities. She guessed her second chance was over before it had begun.

* * *

Several hours later, Sadie sat underneath the apple tree in her backyard, kicking leaves swirling around her shoes. She'd just returned home from a gathering in Kyle's office. The love everyone had lavished on her there had left her speechless. An event that could've crushed her spirit had overwhelmed her with joy. The support from the people she loved alleviated the feeling that only her mother truly loved her.

Right after dinner, her mother poked her head in the family room with an interesting summons. Kyle had requested the family come to his church office in thirty minutes. Equally puzzled, Amy stared at Sadie until she shrugged her shoulders, and then both girls questioned their mother. But they stopped when Jeanette appeared just as clueless as they were.

Alone in her bedroom, Sadie vacillated back and forth about going. It was evident Kyle had news to deliver, but was it good, indifferent, or none of the above? Then her heart skipped a beat. Leanne. Had he decided to marry her?

Sadie pooh-poohed the thought while changing clothes for the third time that day. Kyle would never subject her to endless pity by squashing her hopes in front of an audience. Lost in speculation, she mechanically applied lip gloss to her already-glistening lips.

I don't have to show up. Amy will feed me tidbits later on. Will he be surprised if I stay at home? Or is it wiser to hear the news firsthand?

Undecided, Sadie surfed the net, still attempting to predict the future.

* * *

Ten minutes later, the trio hurried across the square as three vehicles turned into the parking lot, one behind the other. While the car occupants went inside the building, Roland and Cindy exited the truck, then waited for his family to reach them. Sadie's mouth dried instantly when she didn't see Brian. Did Kyle set up an adults-only meeting?

Then Amy skipped ahead, grabbing Roland's arm. "What's going on? Why are we here?" Her eyes darted from one person to the other.

Cindy glanced at the man, studying Sadie. "Kyle called Roland while we were buying movie tickets. He said we'll be glad we came, so here we are."

At the door, Dee and Kate converged on Sadie, separating her from the others.

Kate whispered in Sadie's ear just loud enough for Dee to hear. "What gives, Sadie? Why are we here?"

"I have no idea. I hate mysteries that may involve me," said Sadie, disliking the whine in her voice.

"Hmm," said Dee, "have you seen Kyle since church this morning?"

"We went hiking earlier," said Sadie, "and I haven't seen him since."

But the truth unfolded quickly. Kyle had invited the people who knew that Sadie had left him for another man. Since he considered Cindy a younger sister, he may have confided in her about the broken engagement. And then Sadie shook her head.

I can't be right. Miss Sarah isn't here. Kyle would have his mother here if he intended to set the record straight.

Following the queue to his office, Sadie moaned when an obviously perplexed Sarah greeted them at the door. Ushering everyone into the room, she pointed to tea cakes atop a serving tray on the sofa table. But Sadie avoided the tempting sweets. Her mouth quivered too much to chew.

Once they sat down in the conversation area, Kyle dragged a chair across the floor to join them. "Thanks for interrupting your evening to come over," he said in a low voice. "I know you'll appreciate the call after our talk." Then he made eye contact with Sadie's mother. "I prayed long and hard before making the calls, Miss Jeanette. Everyone, please allow me to reveal everything before commenting."

Sadie wanted to disappear. Since no one looked her way, she imagined that they thought the meeting was about her. Why else would Kyle summons them all at the same time? He'd never done it before. Her body quaking inside, she leaned against her mother for support.

Kyle movingly repeated his and Sadie's earlier conversation. Minutes later, each person rallied around her with love and good wishes. Her family was very quiet, though, telling Sadie they would talk to her in private, later.

Dee said, "Sadie, no wonder you said that you couldn't take any more in your bedroom yesterday. No one could've under the circumstances."

A teary-eyed Kate nodded in agreement. And then Matt dropped a bombshell.

Several teammates had cornered him after Lincoln bragged that Sadie dropped her fiancé for him. Four guys, out after curfew, had seen her running across campus one night, crying and shouting something. But they were hurrying to sneak into the dorm without getting caught and apologized for not stopping to help her out. Also, Matt's friends openly questioned that Sadie was in love with Lincoln. One buddy stated, "Sadie and Lincoln? There's something wrong with that picture."

Then Kyle dropped his own bombshell. He insisted that Sadie lodge a formal complaint against Lincoln at the university the following day. Before she could decline to go, Jeanette and Miss Sarah promised to accompany Kyle and Sadie on the trip.

Thinking about Lincoln abusing other women prompted Sadie to agree. But now, alone in her backyard, her knees literally knocked together. Her body trembled at the thought of actually going to Burgundy. If she went, her fears would become her reality. She would become the target of anyone attempting to redeem Lincoln's questionable reputation. Two years later, the outcome of reporting the attack frightened her more now than when it first happened.

God, please don't let Lincoln get off scot-free. I should have reported him at the time it happened. I hope no one else suffered because I was too afraid to speak up.

Sadie's emotions ran from hot to cold the rest of the evening, until she finally took a warm bath and watched mystery movies with Amy.

* * *

The following night, she climbed into bed, thankful she'd made the trip to Burgundy after all. Their prayers were answered beyond her wildest dreams. What started out as hush-hush and "we'll contact you later," ended with them speaking to several administration officials before leaving the university. And all because one special lady in the Dean of Students office cut through the red tape.

Another staffer said the woman pushed the complaint forward to finally get somewhere with pressing charges. The school had already dismissed several grievances against Lincoln—even those that trailed his steps from Rutledge College. The news encouraged Sadie to supply a detailed written account, including that four football players had witnessed her flight across campus after the incident occurred.

A receptionist had stepped into the room while they waited, handing Sadie a sealed manila envelope with her name written on it. Splitting the seal, she extracted two folded sheets of paper, reading each one twice. Then, smiling at Kyle, she passed the notes to Jeanette. The one marked "Sadie" was sweet and to the point.

"I saw you go into the administrative building, Sadie. If you're here to right a wrong, count us in."

The one designated "office" detailed the occurrence and included the witnesses' names and cell phone numbers. Sadie recognized the name of each person willing to back up her account. Two of the men were already graduated and established in their professions. The two remaining players were still seniors.

It had worked out well. The mission was accomplished. She left Burgundy wondering if God had used Matt to intervene with the men on her behalf. Sadie would never ask him, and Matt would never tell her.

Too keyed up to sleep, she stared at the streetlight outside her bedroom window. Her mind was consumed with losses—numerous precious moments that were impossible to recover. Earlier, Kyle had accused her of discarding people who had proven their love throughout her life. And though her denial had come swiftly, lying in bed, she accepted the truth. She'd failed to trust her loved ones when it counted the most. Lincoln's assault had landed her on a road to self-destruction. It made her avoid individuals she'd always trusted.

Kyle had willingly made sacrifices for her whenever possible. Her mother had demonstrated exceptional coping skills during family struggles. Kate and Dee had safeguarded her secrets from everyone since preschool. Both Roland and Matt had earned spotless reputations for avoiding unnecessary trouble. And Amy had neither been too young nor Miss Sarah too old to share in the confidences along with the others.

Too bad she couldn't wave a magic wand to restore the lost time with her family and friends. Sadie's mistrust of people she should've confided in had thrust Kyle into Leanne's arms. Now, she understood the trauma had allowed Lincoln to undermine those time-tested bonds.

Her fiancé would've defended her through the ordeal with Lincoln. But did Kyle help Sadie today because he wanted a life with her or because he wanted to help a congregation member overcome her abuse?

Chapter Eleven

Sadie's first week working at Kingdom Life Church exceeded her expectations. Her priority was getting the learning center up and running while remaining faithful to her and Kyle's original plans. Not just for their church members, the vision incorporated students of all ages throughout the city and surrounding areas.

Both Kate and Dee provided tremendous support in Sadie's efforts, helping her set up the tutoring program the day after her visit to Burgundy. It was just in time for a newspaper article showcasing local churches.

In Wednesday's early-morning edition, *The Shiatown Star* featured a front-page article about Kingdom Life Church and its newest programs. Also, it highlighted the multipurpose center's opening that very evening. Plus, it included information about the author reads, with dinner set to begin the first Saturday in November. There were also details regarding the tutoring program taking applications on Monday the following week.

The all-day mentoring service included ten free thirty-minute group sessions every afternoon from eleven to two. One-on-one sessions for individuals would be held throughout the day and evening, offered at minimal cost.

The free advertisement paid off within the week. Thirty-five people outside the congregation immediately agreed to volunteer their services weekly, and schools and students across the city quickly took advantage of the classes offered. Closed on weekends and Friday evenings, the program was full unless God added more hours to the day.

During the board meeting Friday morning, a surprised Sadie beamed with pleasure as Kyle commended her rapid response to the challenge.

Sadie was in her element setting up tutoring programs, but opening the dinner theater proved intimidating. Miss Sarah had already provided her with a lengthy list of local authors. Each night before going to bed, she sampled various writing styles as she sought future candidates. All the while, she searched for a play to produce before Christmas.

* * *

The following Monday, Sadie lay in bed wide awake. The learning center had debuted without a hitch, and she was completely drained from wearing multiple hats that day. Thank God, Amy filled the spot that afternoon, allowing her time off to work at the bookstore. But after leaving that job, Sadie rushed back to the learning center to oversee the evening sessions.

While at the bookstore, Miss Sarah had invited her to a birthday party for Kyle on Friday.

"Nothing elaborate," she said. "It'll be a small gathering to celebrate his twenty-fourth birthday."

Sadie grinned. "How small is small?"

Finished cataloging new books, she turned to Sadie, laughing softly. "About thirty people for a lawn party. It's still warm enough to hold an outdoor bash."

"Is there a special theme?" Sadie asked, running ideas through her mind. What would Kyle appreciate the most? Probably being left on his own, but Sadie rejected the thought.

"It's an early Thanksgiving celebration," she said, obviously delighted. "My son is pastoring the church just like his father wanted him to." Miss Sarah glanced at the door when a customer entered the store. "It's a surprise, Sadie. And I'm tasking you with keeping him away from the house and church until eight. Everyone will park their cars in the lot behind the daycare center. Come in from Adam Street instead of Apache Lane."

Now Sadie lay in bed abandoning one idea after another. How could she lure Kyle away from home on a Friday evening without asking for a date?

* * *

For once, a nagging problem disappeared without her manipulating behind the scenes. An unplanned meeting solved the problem of keeping Kyle away from home Friday evening. It just happened to work out that way without her forcing the outcome for her own benefit. Yesterday, Sadie found out that a fifteen-year-old tutoring student was being bullied at school. Five girls continually mocked her and her friends, spreading malicious rumors about them daily. The girl skipped school as much as possible. And she was afraid to tell her parents, fearing that reporting the girls might make it worse than before.

Shocked that three of the girls attended Kingdom Life, Sadie immediately set a plan in motion. The three students that she knew, the girl being bullied, and all of their parents, would dine together today in a meeting room at The Main Street Diner.

She was happy with the speedy results but suffered a setback when Kyle rejected her plans in that morning's meeting. He said she wasn't trained to facilitate bullying problems and forbade her to spend personal funds on projects the church should arbitrate. To him, a group discussion at the fellowship hall worked better than sitting down to a restaurant meal. Kyle called her forty-five minutes after she reached her office to update his thoughts. He said it was too late to change the location, but Kingdom Life would cover the tab. A professional counselor, who attended their church, agreed to facilitate the meeting on short notice.

So while Sadie and Kyle gorged on deli sandwiches and drank apple cider at The Tea Pot, a meeting occurred simultaneously in a private dining room in The Main Street Diner.

Kyle glanced at Sadie, chuckling. "That's the fifth time you've looked at your watch in ten minutes. Relax. Meetings of the mind seldom end quickly."

Sighing loudly, Sadie set down her mug. "It's already seven. They've talked for over two hours."

"How long has the bullying gone on? There's probably a lot to talk about. Look, so far no one has run from the room in anger. Or thrown their cutlery against the wall."

"Stop laughing at me being concerned. Why would they pick on a shy girl who doesn't bother anyone?"

"Come on, Sadie. Did you expect them to pick on someone who might fight back? Now, I don't know the student you tutor, but the three girls from our church understand bad behavior. Their parents will deal with them. I promise. Besides, we prayed for God to bless them. Right?"

Sadie finished her drink then smiled when she looked at her watch again. "I know trusting God means believing He will keep His promises," she said when Kyle caught her.

"Exactly. It's a truth we often forget."

She wondered how far should she go with opening up to him. "I'm learning to trust Him more and reading the Bible again. And praying according to His will." She leaned closer to Kyle, then hesitated.

"What are you thinking about?"

"How blessed I am," she responded. Sadie felt better when the smile on his lips reached his eyes. "God never stopped loving me, Kyle. I can feel His warmth surrounding me again. I was very lonely."

He covered her hand with his. "Yet never alone, Sadie."

She cupped his hand between her palms. "I wanted to help those girls. Too bad I didn't know the other students or their parents."

"I know your heart is in the right place. However, bullying can turn lethal. Next time, communicate with me before branching out on your own."

About to reply, Sadie looked up when a shadow fell across the table. The female counselor stood beside them, with a huge grin.

"It went well from the onset. My hubby holds workshops about bullying for school administrators and teachers several times a year, so I brought him with me. Now the parents want to thank you and Kyle for caring enough to make a difference. I'll give you a heads-up on the way over."

The aftermath left Sadie marveling. God responded swiftly to right the wrong. The counselor and her psychologist husband agreed to host a support group ministering to bullies and their victims. The girls who attended her church promised to attend, and they agreed to invite their friends after prompting from their parents. Once they agreed to come, the victim said she would do likewise.

Walking to the car, Kyle winked at Sadie when a bully invited the victim to the movies the next day. Although the startled girl declined the offer, she suggested going the following Saturday, saying she would bring her friends. It seemed the willingness seed was planted in good soil.

While Sadie drove home, Kyle relayed highlights from his tenure at Hope in His Word Church. An unknown load lifted off her as he recounted the success of projects he and Sadie had developed jointly. Had he thought of her while implementing the programs in California? Or ignored her input completely? The success stories showed how well they worked together. Earlier that morning, Kyle had tweaked the bullying plan to his liking, but fell into step with the overall idea.

At home, Sadie turned into the driveway and sprung from the car before Kyle shut the door to his side of the car. Hooking her arm through his, she laughed at the alarmed expression on his face.

"No, I'm not hitting on you. I promised your mom I would stop by for a visit after the meeting was over."

He glanced at her with hooded eyes, then averted his gaze. Once Kyle opened up the door, thirty eager people yelled, "Surprise!"

Glancing at the woman whose arm was still entwined with his, Kyle stepped into the foyer. After closing the door, he gazed at Sadie again. "So, you didn't forget my birthday after all." His eyes roved over the happy faces. "You saved the good wishes for the celebration tonight."

His comment filled Sadie with excitement. Kyle had wondered why she'd failed to wish him happy birthday. That he expected her to care about his birthday was good to know. "Kyle—"

"Are you two on again?" his older cousin interrupted. "If not, you should be. You two remind me of Lil Abner and Daisy Mae."

"Who?" asked Amy, frowning.

The older man shook his head, laughing. "I forgot about you under-twenty-somethings being here. Comic strip characters. He refused to let her catch him." Laughing, he stared at Kyle. "Are you on again?"

Kyle kissed Sadie's cheek. "Whoever said we were off?" He moved away from the group, pulling Sadie with him through the crowd.

Smiling at him, Sadie removed his hand from her arm, beckoning him into the living room. Kneeling beside the sofa, she pulled a sizeable gift-wrapped package from underneath, offering it to him. Everyone gathered around the couple as Kyle slowly peeled away the paper.

Talk about precious moments. Kyle stared unblinkingly at the present, then removed it from the wrapping. Walking across the room, he placed it on the mantel over the fireplace. Now the birthday gift Sadie gave him set in a place of honor, right beside the plant she'd sent the day he buried his father.

Drawing together, the guests oohed and aahed over the picture professionally framed and matted. A local artist had created a mosaic featuring the beautiful leaves she and Kyle had gathered while hiking through the countryside.

Time stood still for Sadie when Kyle reached out, stroking her cheek. Although her surprise made him drop his hand quickly, nothing could erase the warmth in his eyes before he looked away. Sadie had seen the reaction he sought to hide. It was a look she remembered well. Shrouded in happiness for the first time since arriving home, Sadie felt at peace with life. Indeed, it seemed like the old days were rekindled.

Holding her hand, Kyle took the party outdoors, greeting each person until his granny called him over.

All night, story after story recounted the birthday man's happiest moments, and Sadie costarred in many of them. No one mentioned the two-year separation when they'd lived in different states.

The party ended well after midnight. Sadie was the last person to leave, and Kyle walked her to her house next door. But instead of saying goodnight, he sat on the porch swing and pulled Sadie down beside him. Tired from an exhausting day, she laid her head on his shoulder, surrendering to the peaceful night.

She yawned, covering her mouth with her fingers. "It's been a full day."

He looked down at her. "A very different birthday than the one I anticipated."

Raising her head a little, Sadie glanced at him, then laid her head back onto his shoulder.

"How so?" she asked.

But instead of answering the question, he changed the topic. And then jumped to another subject once that one was exhausted. Critiquing the day's events took some time. There was a lot to recap, from the weekly meeting at work that morning to Kyle's fantastic birthday celebration that night. But mainly, they discussed the dinner meeting with the youths and their parents at the restaurant. Despite the late hour, they took their time, dissecting details the counselor provided before they left.

Sadie realized Kyle was being kind, and she refused to read more into their talk than he intended to convey. Just as tired as she, he could've easily said goodnight and gone home to bed. Maybe he sensed she needed a quiet chat before ending the night. But she couldn't help wondering about him and Leanne. Were they still talking? Or did she give up a man willing to share his life with her? Sadie had made that foolish mistake once, but never again. Kyle was worth the fight to win him back. Sighing, she closed her eyes, drifting to sleep.

Gently shaking Sadie awake, Kyle rose, pulling her to her feet. Rubbing her eyes, she stumbled the few steps to the door, giggling as she stabbed blindly for the lock. He removed the key from her limp fingers, turned it in the lock, and then placed the key into her outstretched palm.

"See you Sunday," Kyle said, giving her time to go inside.

Sadie desperately wanted him to stay. It felt right to sit outside talking in the moonlight. He looked tired but happy, as if he'd recalled the good times they'd shared just as much as she had. Exhaustion kept her from thinking of a reasonable excuse to stay out longer.

"Goodnight," said Sadie. Shutting the door quickly, she secured the lock to keep from running after him. Then she climbed the steps, listening as his faint whistling faded into the night. Tiptoeing across the hardwood floor, she eased the bedroom door closed, peeled off her clothes, then crawled beneath the covers. She closed her eyes as her body demanded escape from a hectic day.

I love you, Kyle Franklin, regardless of your feelings for me.

* * *

Two weeks later, Kyle powered down his cell phone before laying it on the dresser. If the caller didn't know the house phone number, they wouldn't reach him tonight. His time was better spent praying for the wisdom he desperately needed. Still ready for a family of his own, time spent with Sadie stopped him from rushing into a needless marriage. Why hurry? He had plenty of time to figure it out. Until then, he planned to pastor Kingdom Life Church. No more jumping ahead of the Father's plan. The fact that God never changed instilled confidence in His word.

Kyle sat on the loveseat, stretching out one leg across the cushion. He had a lot on his plate. Keeping his father's trusted advisors had been a brilliant move. They usually supplied him with workable solutions when needed. The new programs tested his abilities in multiple areas. He thought about the times he'd analyzed his father's decisions from the sidelines. Now, a trail of his own blunders kept him humble.

But there were a few success stories along the way, too. The midweek service began with a bang and increased in fervor. With new groups starting daily, the multipurpose center was packed with people five days a week. Each building was fully utilized and added to the church coffers instead of bleeding them dry. Like the daycare, the learning center was filled to capacity with a waiting list. And Sadie had jumped into the entertainment world with ease. The first author reading would be held tomorrow. Instead of going with a traditionally published author, Sadie had signed up a middle-aged lady who self-published her first romance novel last spring. Her explanation had board members scratching their heads.

"How can I ignore anyone who's stepping out on God's promises just like me? Pioneers must stick together," said Sadie, cajoling elders and deacons to promote her efforts. As one female elder told Kyle while leaving the meeting, "She's good."

And Sadie had made the perfect choice, it seemed. Tomorrow, the ecstatic author would read her first chapter to one hundred diners paying ten dollars each to hear it. She'd selected a grandmother who had been writing children books for two decades to headline the second event.

Five weeks ago, Sadie discovered a one-act play to produce by Christmas. Rehearsals were already underway. The rapid response to get the programs off the ground added to his dilemma. She was still too impulsive, as if trying to erase the past by overreaching.

And Kyle still didn't know why Sadie had come home when she did. No person just came to their senses without a catalyst. Did Lincoln cast her aside and she remembered her loved ones in Shiatown? Hitting the ground running meant nothing when she still refused to level with him. Why did she come home *now*? Returning to the people who loved her had always been an option she'd refused to take. Trauma issue aside, what situation had finally forced Sadie to act upon that knowledge?

Leanne came to mind while watching a couple strolling along the side-walk, holding hands. Before he left Glendale, she'd tried to extract a mar-riage proposal that he refused to give her. They hadn't spoken since he left Glendale over two months ago. But on his walk home from work, she'd called saying she was attending a conference in Washington, D.C. and had a stopover in Tulsa for Sunday afternoon. She wanted to see him and booked a room in a hotel near the airport to spend the night. The flight to Los Angeles departed at six Monday morning.

Why call two months after saying goodbye, unless she hoped to renew their friendship? Perhaps to take the relationship to a higher level of com-mitment than before. When he left Glendale, neither of them had actually said they loved spending time with the other. But they had both expressed regrets at being unable to see where the relationship might've led.

In one phone call, the woman in the recesses of his mind moved to the forefront of his thoughts. Front and center again, Leanne emerged bigger than life. However, his attraction to her had lessened after the heart-to-heart with Sadie. Yet Sadie's smooth transition into her old routine failed to win Kyle over completely. He refused to mend what was already severed. Freedom from her endless complications was too priceless to waste.

* * *

The next day, Sadie joined in the standing ovation lauded upon the brilliant author. Goose bumps rose on both of her arms. As people pushed forward to offer congratulations, she headed in the opposite direction. Halfway up the stairs, Sadie turned around as footsteps sounded behind her. Smiling when she saw Kyle, she leaned against the banister once she reached the landing. Her body surged with energy as he approached her.

"What's the verdict?" she asked.

"Perfection in every way. Why did you leave?"

"I want to enjoy each reading as a spectator. Now that it's over, the staff will meet in my office to hone next week's event." She touched his arm, batting her eyelids at him. "You were right. Cindy is perfect as my assistant. Her personality works well with Kate, Dee, and the others. She has a role in our first production."

Kyle laughed. "So I've heard several times."

"We have the perfect theater staff. Bringing Amy, Lenny, and George on board rounded us out."

"Doesn't Lenny teach English at one of the high schools?" He continued when she nodded, "I hear Kate and George fell in love with the whole process. I'm surprised Kate wanted another work relationship with her boss outside of the main job. It sounds like free advertising for the dinner theatre to me. How's the book coming along?"

Sadie moaned. "Glad you asked. How does penning scenes you know inside out become a chore?"

Kyle glanced at the people moving into the lobby area, then backed away from the landing. "If I recall correctly, you know the how and the when but not the why."

Sadie hesitated; his expression had instantly changed. Something significant had just transpired, but she had no idea what it was. It was sort of like getting a glimpse into his soul. *"If I recall correctly, you knew the how and the when but not the why."* Why do I feel like the remark is so important?

"You'll definitely need to figure out the whys before you can have the full story. Believe me, why is a crucial factor that people often overlook ... to their detriment."

Sadie stored that comment away for safekeeping as well. If he thought he was giving her a heads up about whatever he was thinking, he failed. She was never good at deciphering riddles. Maybe if she kept him talking ... "Do you mean the girls' motivations? I'd been thinking that, too. How about critiquing the first two chapters of my story tomorrow? I seldom write on Sundays, and your feedback will fine-tune my efforts for Monday."

"Drop it by the house later on and I'll read it tonight. I have an all-day engagement in Tulsa after service tomorrow."

With whom? Sadie wondered when Kyle walked away whistling.

* * *

The next afternoon after lunch, Sadie scoped out Kyle's house. Her patience paid off. Exactly thirty minutes later, he got into the car and drove off quickly. Who was he meeting in Tulsa? And why didn't they come to Shiatown to visit him at home? Sadie hated mysteries that she couldn't solve. Nonetheless, the day appeared no different than the previous Sundays before it. Kyle had delivered an excellent message about seeking God's presence throughout each day. Plus, he'd dropped off her manuscript before going to church that morning.

She closed the blinds to her bedroom window as the car rounded the corner. Too bad out of sight didn't mean out of mind. Sadie tossed earrings into her jewelry box. If he made subsequent trips to Tulsa this week, then Leanne must have flown into Tulsa today. For the most part, she understood how Kyle's mind worked. He would never hide a woman he dated in another city. Introducing Leanne to his mother would be a top priority. Settling in the living room, Sadie ran fingers through her hair.

I hate surprises and mysterious men who spring them. What's up with him?

* * *

Kyle added a point to Leanne's invisible scorecard when she stepped into view. Her face glowed as she spotted him standing next to the luggage carousel. Stepping lightly, she floated into the arms he hastily opened. Suddenly, her expectations weighed heavily upon him. The woman smiling up at him waited to be kissed, and Kyle involuntarily glanced around the area before brushing his lips against hers. People living in Shiatown virtually had him and Sadie planning their wedding ceremony. And Kyle left them to think whatever they pleased. Today, he planned to enjoy the company of a good friend dropping in for a visit.

She pointed out her suitcase, then hooked her arm through his as they moved away from the baggage area. A witty account of the D.C. conference entertained the couple until leaving the hotel to tour the city. Their easy conversation engaged Kyle throughout the evening. And the light dancing in her eyes conveyed she enjoyed their time together as much as he did.

Over dinner, Leanne unfolded a plan to spend a weekend in Oklahoma after attending a seminar in Houston later that month. Kyle agreed at once. An evening together would provide a pleasant escape from everyday life. He welcomed another visit until she added, "It's time I meet your mother and hear you preach at Kingdom Life Church."

Studying one another, they both silently acknowledged the truth. Her shrewd move placed the ball squarely in his court. And Kyle respected his delicate position. Putting stipulations on the visit he had just sanctioned might stifle the relationship and permanently undercut any romance left to pursue. But the Sadie debacle taught him a valuable lesson: Don't make unnecessary commitments. He and Leanne were both free agents and able to choose who they wanted to date.

Driving home jolted Kyle back into his everyday existence. Although pleasurable, the brief excursion with Leanne failed to whet his appetite for a more active role in her life; just as inhabiting Sadie's daily world didn't arouse any desire to deepen the relationship further.

Humming an old-style hymn, Kyle pulled into his driveway, turning off the ignition just as a light went out in Sadie's bedroom. Then he recalled a youthful Sadie had spied on him whenever possible.

* * *

Sadie tossed and turned throughout the night, tangling the bedcovers into a knotted mess. Finally throwing the bedding aside, she snuggled into her favorite seat. Jeanette had purchased the beloved rocking chair for her thirteenth birthday. Incredibly soothing, the gentle motion had pacified many sleepless nights since coming home.

Too often in Burgundy, she had lain awake until early morning, seeking an escape to a simpler place in time. To somewhere that didn't imprison her within innumerable bad decisions. Returning home was right. But the action emphasized the terrible injustice she'd inflicted upon herself before coming. In Burgundy, she'd convinced herself up was truly down without anyone to challenge her delusion. Not so in Shiatown. At home, no one left Sadie to her own devices.

Even though her father's immediate family had left town, aunts, uncles, cousins, and friends helped her stay grounded. The transition home pro-duced a miracle, settling Sadie onto the pathway to fulfilling her dreams. But sometimes the stench of Lincoln Miller sneaked into the comfortable life she was hoping to rebuild. And in those times, she softly cried until there were no more tears left to fall.

She was sure Kyle had spent the day with Leanne in Tulsa. The woman brought the fight into Sadie's backyard. Did she know about Kyle and Sadie's past? Was it possible for a man to love two women at the same time? How should she go forward? The wrong move could send him straight to Leanne. Then her campaign to win back Kyle might collapse without the ability to revive it. In the past, Sadie could read the man like a favorite book. But certain aspects of his personality had shifted over two years. Was it possible to be wiser yet distrust an ally simultaneously? It appeared so with Kyle, and maybe she deserved it.

But he was acting too laidback and carefree for Sadie's liking. For all appearances, Kyle Franklin was a man at peace with everyone in the world except for her. Did he still love her? Sadie's heart shouted the link was intact, however, he no longer considered loving her as a reason to accept her as his wife.

Sighing, Sadie rested her head on her shoulder. Every day God blessed her life in serious ways, keeping her alive and healthy. All the test results from the doctor's visit her first week home came back negative. No unwanted health issues had developed over her liaison with Lincoln or anything else.

Closing her eyes, she rocked until the sun rose in the eastern sky, signaling a brand new day of hope had dawned.

Chapter Twelve

Sadie hurried through the hallways on the way to Kyle's office. Closed-in passages were the perfect way to link structures together. The heated walkways sheltered her against the blustering wind pummeling large redbud trees situated in the square. She appreciated having access to each building without having to endure the harsh weather conditions outside. Sadie shivered despite the heat inside the building. Just looking at tree limbs flopping to and fro had her thanking God for the functional heating system.

Also, she prayed for God to soften Kyle's heart enough to approve a project he'd already rejected. Last Friday, he had nixed her plans to hold group sessions with teenagers in the learning center. She'd told him she would like to have closer interactions with teen girls for her book's characters. Sadie had requested to hold weekly talks with nine teenage girls ages fifteen through eighteen. She'd thought the proposal would receive a quick approval because teens already met in the multipurpose building on Wednesdays.

However, Kyle had refused to support the project in its original form. He cited multiple objections she had never considered. But to Sadie, his excessive caution impeded her progress. Over dinner that evening, she unloaded on her mother, who promptly took his side, saying securing the girls' privacy mattered more than using their responses to help write a novel.

During dessert, Jeanette advised Sadie to seek a less-invasive venture, and to let the girls and their parents know upfront that she was gathering information for a book. A meeting of the minds that incorporated the teens' viewpoints while rewarding their participation. Sadie went to bed that night praying for guidance instead of relegating the pet project to the abandoned file.

The next day, she and Cindy restructured the framework together. Both women agreed a direct but casual approach should suffice with the teens and their parents. Now her book would become a live production. The final proposal ensured no person could suffer manipulation for anyone else's personal gain.

So at a hastily called meeting Sadie, Cindy, and their five staffers incorporated the dinner theater angle. Then last night, she sat at Cindy's home until midnight tweaking the presentation she hoped Kyle might accept today. With his approval, she could send flyers to high schools and community centers in Shiatown and surrounding areas on Monday.

Sadie desperately needed to gather additional material for the book. The manuscript was almost finished, but now she needed to flesh out their characters better. Thus far, the girls were motiveless creatures who lacked the proper provocations for their actions. The missing ingredient hammered her thoughts until going to bed each night. She needed to determine who the girls were and what experiences had shaped their personalities and reinforced their beliefs.

Two months of observing teens undercover had produced uninspiring results. It didn't divulge enough material to define their behavior either good or bad. Hours spent with Amy showed times had changed considerably since Sadie had graduated from high school, so she knew she couldn't fall back on her own experience.

But her gung-ho spirit about sharing her plan with Kyle evaporated once she reached the fellowship hall. She hoped he would approve her plans this time. A quick glance out the window confirmed Kyle was still in the building. His car was parked in front of the church. Sometimes he attended meetings at other locations without her knowing about it. Hopefully he was inside his office and in an excellent mood. Then he might allow for the intensive preparations required to finish her book.

Sadie peeked into his office after a brief knock on the opened door. Kyle immediately ended the phone conversation as she entered the room. Was he talking to Leanne? Was the relationship not only alive but on target to steal Kyle away? Two months after coming home, he still bolstered the wall built up against her. Would he ever forgive the two years spent with Lincoln following the abuse?

"Hello, Kyle." Sadie stepped to the desk. "My newest baby is overhauled and ready to roll out. If you have free time, we can draw up a questionnaire for auditions next weekend." She hesitated when he sighed. "Did I choose the wrong time? If so, I can come back later."

Twirling a pen in his fingers, Kyle reached for the folder with his free hand. "Not for the right project. Let's hope this outline passes the Franklin test."

"I understood your concern about exploiting the girls' emotions. The staff developed a plan that will require their parents' consent up front, plus give the girls a personal stake in the outcome."

Kyle opened a writing tablet, glancing at Sadie. "A big agenda. Okay, let's hear it."

Sadie breathed deeply, then sat down, folding her arms on her chest. "We propose initiating two interactive classes per week."

"While beefing up the characters in your book based on information provided by the participants?" he asked.

Sadie rolled her eyes then stared at Kyle. "I'm neither sneaky nor underhanded. So no. Everyone will know the book is a work in progress."

"Glad to hear it. Please continue." He chuckled when her eyes narrowed.

"More teens may try out for roles by holding open auditions instead of pinpointing drama students." She hesitated when Kyle frowned. "In one day, the girls will read the dialogue for several characters. Then those teens selected will do role-playing for two hours on Wednesday evenings and receive drama training for five hours on Saturday mornings until rehearsals begin."

Kyle sat upright. "What rehearsals, Sadie? What are you talking about?"

"For my book," said Sadie, staring at him.

"Sadie—"

"Wait, Kyle, please let me finish. In a detailed letter and flyer, we'll disclose that the girls will audition for a four-act play. If successful, they will have drama classes two days a week for a work in progress. Then their hard labor will culminate in stage performances throughout the spring and summer."

Sadie paused as Kyle leaned back in the chair. At least he was listening without interrupting the flow. "I'm very excited about the prospects, Kyle. Rehearsals will begin once the book is self-published. What do you think?"

"That I need to hear more information," he said in a flat voice.

Sadie nodded her head then flashed him a smile. "It's almost too exhilarating to sit still, isn't it?" Instantly, her hands drew pictures in the air as she filled in the details. Finally exhausted, she slumped against the cushion, staring at him. Her heart warmed at the proud expression on his face.

"Miss Jeanette was right. You paint vivid word pictures. Make sure no one can duplicate your efforts."

"Don't worry. The exercises won't appear in my book. I plan to self-publish in early January, handing off the manuscript to a playwright to adapt the story into the play. Rehearsals will start in February. The play will debut the first Saturday in June."

She paused, tapping a finger against her lips. "Which reminds me. I've asked Aunt Yolanda to slot us four performances at her church in Naples, Florida, the third weekend in July. The person in charge of events penciled us in and will make the final decision after the play goes live."

Kyle slowly shook his head. "Now you're taking on responsibility for the safety of nine teenagers. Plus their traveling expenses and room and board."

Sadie slowly nodded. "That's just the East Coast. Our pastor should hook us up on the West Coast with performances at his old church."

"Sadie, you can't expect inexperienced teenagers to star in a four-act play with minimum preparation and then tour the country from coast-to-coast."

"It'll look awesome on their college applications," she said, beaming at him.

"Was that my stomach growling, or yours?" asked Kyle.

Her laughter tinkled into the air. "I think they're playing off one another like dueling banjos."

"Which happened to be a banjo and guitar." He grabbed his keys off the desk. "How about heading to The Teapot for dinner? My treat."

She was enthused by the unforeseen *date*, but Sadie tapered her reaction. Nodding, she picked up her organizer and headed toward the door in a sedate manner. But inside, she bubbled over with joy.

Turning off the light, Kyle walked out behind her. "Did you lock up at the learning center?"

"Yes. The last tutoring session ended before I left. I always travel through the hallways," said Sadie, trying not to smile.

Outside the building, high winds tossed unsecured items all over the place. High-tension power lines waved in the air as overhanging tree limbs whipped mercilessly against them. Shivering in the severe wind, Sadie hustled to the car. Hurrying to the driver's side, Kyle entered the vehicle then tweaked her nose, unlocking happy memories—for both of them, it seemed. He withdrew his hand and looked straight ahead, proving he regretted the intimate gesture.

Nevertheless, the ride to the restaurant was a blast from the past for Sadie. As usual, she adopted her normal demeanor, and this time, Kyle fell right into line with her. He even touched her cheek while waiting at a stoplight on the way. Better still, he took the scenic route to The Tea Pot, making the normally quick jaunt last more than twenty minutes.

After parking the car, the couple spotted Roland, Cindy, and Brian dining inside Bon Appetit. Glancing at one another, they headed toward the door. A full house greeted them. Sadie sat in the extra seat at the table, wondering when her brother planned to propose to Cindy, while Kyle searched the room for an available chair. Brian's antics always enthralled Sadie, who never spent leisure time with small children. Today she ogled as the child chewed one pea at a time. In fact, he engaged in an eating system unlike anything Sadie had ever seen. Even Kyle scooting a chair in between the two failed to disrupt her fascination with the boy.

Cindy followed Sadie's gaze then touched Roland's arm. All the adults smiled when Brian ate the last pea, grinned at his mother, then turned his plate until the mashed potatoes set directly in front of him. Unperturbed by the audience, he smacked his lips with the first bite, gobbled up the potatoes, then turned the plate around to the carrots.

Cindy glanced at Sadie. "He eats one item at a time, saving his favorite food for last. He'll finish up with the chicken leg."

"Don't look shocked," said Roland as Sadie's mouth hung open. "You always placed your food at twelve, three, six, and nine o'clock. And you refused to eat anything that touched something else on your plate."

Shaking her head vehemently, Sadie elbowed Kyle when he nodded.

"Miss Jeanette worked hard to keep juice off of Sadie's plate." Kyle rubbed his side when Sadie elbowed him again.

Cindy grinned at Sadie when two small girls playing in the kiddie center snared Sadie's attention. The noisy girls clapped their hands and yelled while playing bumper pool. The noise level in the restaurant steadily increased each time the door to the game center opened. "I'm surprised you and Kyle came to Bon Appetit. I'd thought both of you would prefer The Main Street Diner."

"We took a detour on our way to The Tea Pot once we spotted you guys in here," Kyle responded. "Sadie was filling me in about adapting her book into a play."

Cindy stared at Kyle. "And you agreed with the project, right?"

"Let's say for now I approve the basic concept with a few slight alterations."

Sadie frowned. "How do we gain your full support?"

"It's a tall order, Sadie. The trip must be prepaid four months in advance, with the dinner theater picking up the tab. No outside help or assistance from the mentoring program. The project will sink or swim under its own resources. A parent must accompany their daughter on the trip free of charge. The dinner theater must be able to pay their way. For now, completing those requirements works for me."

Roland glanced at Sadie and Cindy, who were both frowning at Kyle. "You two need to lose the outraged expressions. Those are reasonable stipulations. So far, no one has mentioned understudies. Each part will require a standby for home performances, as well as on the road—plus a parent when traveling."

Kyle turned to Sadie, shaking his head. "Ah, the expenses are escalating as we speak. We're looking at thousands of dollars to pull it off, and no monetary gain."

"The benefits justify the expense," said Sadie.

"You can't put a cost on goodwill," Cindy added.

Roland pushed his plate aside. "You're undertaking a tremendous responsibility that deserves lots of thought."

Sadie's gaze shot daggers at both men. "When did you and Kyle become such naysayers?" Disgusted, she glanced at Cindy. "I suppose they left their pioneering spirit in the previous year."

"Or the year before that one," said Cindy, poking Roland's chest.

Sadie's eyes widened when light sparkled from the diamond on Cindy's third finger. "Oh my goodness! It's official! You accepted the ring!" Glancing at Kyle, she jumped from her seat and rounded the table, grabbing Cindy's hand. "It looks gorgeous on your finger." She hugged her friend, kissed her brother's cheek, then sighed, staring off into space. With set features, Sadie tousled Brian's hair, circled the table, and stood beside Kyle. She sighed when he stared straight ahead, ignoring her altogether.

She touched his shoulder. "Roland and Cindy are getting married, Kyle." Then she watched as he skillfully de-escalated a potentially awkward situation. Without glancing her way, he shook hands with the couple and voiced his congratulations. But he paused as Brian swallowed the last chicken bite and yelled, "Yep, we're getting married!" Laughing, Sadie sat down, but she couldn't stop smiling. "When are you planning to spread the joy?"

"We're dropping by both houses tonight," said Cindy with a huge grin on her face.

Sadie was now working overtime to keep teardrops at bay. Although ecstatic for her brother and friend, their good news exposed the impasse between her and Kyle. Once destined to live a lifetime together, they currently appeared farther apart than ever.

She twiddled her thumbs on her lap. "I'm starving. We may as well eat here. Cindy, you can help me win Kyle over to our side."

"I'm game." Cindy laughed, wiggling her fingers at him.

Kyle's cell phone vibrated just as the server left the table with their order. It didn't take Sadie long to recognize that duty called. She waited until he replaced the cell phone into his pocket.

"What's going on?" she asked after several seconds had passed.

His head tilted a little as he smiled at her. "The answering service phoned. Mrs. Jenkins is feeling lonely and wants company this evening."

Sadie reached for her purse. "Should we head over there now?"

"No, we have time to eat, and I'll drop you off at home before heading her way. It won't be a long visit. I'm attending a junior high basketball game at eight."

Even though Kyle had declined her going with him, his pleased expression at her offer warmed her heart. "Oh, yeah, the Stewart kid is playing tonight." Sadie checked her watch. "It's five-thirty. Why don't we change our order to takeout and grab a meal for Mrs. Jenkins? She loves playing card games. She and I can play a few hands until you pick me up after the game is over. Or, I can have Mom or Amy stop by to get me."

"Asking your mom or Amy won't be necessary. I won't be gone long." He moved toward the server, standing at the counter.

"Kyle receives too many calls for his time," said Cindy, cleaning food from Brian's mouth and hands with a baby wipe. "Shouldn't Minister Dawkins or an elder or deacon handle senior visits?"

Sadie nodded. "In theory, yes. But the senior pastor must keep a flexible schedule."

"In your opinion, does a lonely old lady take precedence over a youngster playing his first basketball game?" asked Roland.

"In this instance, no. Mrs. Jenkins isn't sick. Which is why I offered to help out."

"Good answer," he said, then he glanced at Brian. The child was staring at children playing in the game center. Roland touched his shoulder, nodding that way. "Come on, slugger, a round of paddle ball is calling us."

Once the women were alone, Sadie outlined the conversation in Kyle's office, smiling when he returned to the table carrying a large paper sack.

"On second thought, your idea was terrific. Let's eat a meal with Mrs. Jenkins, and I'll leave you two playing cards."

Rising to her feet, Sadie hugged Cindy and said goodbye. The happiness on Cindy's face caused Sadie's own eyes to mist over. She wiped a fingertip across her eyelids. "When's the big day?"

Cindy nibbled her bottom lip. "Help me persuade your brother to get married on Christmas Eve."

"That's way too soon," said Kyle, "we'll talk later."

"And so will we," Sadie called over her shoulder as Kyle propelled her toward the door.

* * *

Kyle took a trip down memory lane on the way home that night, bringing up past adventures the second he drove away from the curb. Up until now, Sadie was the one who usually broached the topic. But tonight, it was all him, until he grew strangely silent. He started to speak twice, but stopped himself each time. Then he cleared his throat abruptly, switching the radio station from jazz to classical music. Sadie's lips quivered when Kyle cleared his throat again and lowered the volume on the radio. That time, she stared straight ahead, dreading what was coming next.

"Sadie ... Leanne is flying in on Thursday for a weekend visit."

She closed her eyes, then observed his reflection through the glass in the side window.

"Did you invite her?" she asked, bracing herself for the answer. Somehow, it mattered if Kyle had requested Leanne to come.

"All my friends have open invitations to visit whenever they choose."

"Did ... you ... invite ... her?" Sadie lowered her voice to a whisper as he studied the road ahead. "You know my feelings. They haven't changed. I love you more than ever." She paused, running fingers through her hair. "I want us to get married, Kyle, but I love you enough to walk away if Leanne is the woman you want."

Kyle immediately turned off the music. "I didn't invite her, Sadie, but it's okay with me if she visits."

Her body went numb. "Do you want to marry her?"

His fingertips drummed on the steering wheel like a man searching within his soul for answers he couldn't find. And Sadie almost yelled at him to just answer the question. Although she realized his silence shouted no, she knew Leanne was very much a contender in his mind. Thank God the woman was destined for Shiatown instead of visiting undercover in Tulsa. Sadie welcomed the chance to meet the woman claiming center stage in Kyle's heart.

* * *

Kyle said goodnight to Sadie and waited by the car until she closed her front door. Then he rushed inside his house to reassess the day in private. So intent on reaching his bedroom, he almost walked by Sarah as she appeared in the hallway.

"You're hurrying upstairs. Are you tired?" she asked, walking to the stairs.

"Never too tired for you, Mother." Looping her hand through his arm, mother and son scaled the steps together.

He kissed her cheek at the bedroom door, in a hurry to be alone. However, it seemed his mother had other ideas. With one look at her inquisitive features, Kyle abandoned any hopes of spending time by himself. Sarah was no longer able to wind down the day with his father. Evenings often found her left to her own devices.

He flashed her his widest grin. "You're in a bubbly mood tonight. You can't stop smiling. What happened?"

Her eyes twinkled as she smiled. "All mothers love to hear their children being bragged on. Harriet Jenkins called to thank me for raising such a thoughtful young man. And she was right. I won't keep you, dear. I know how much you love to reflect on the day before going to bed."

"Mrs. Jenkins enjoys gossiping. What did she say?" he asked with a wide grin.

Sarah laughed. "There's malicious gossip and rambling news. Harriet never speaks unkindly about any person. This evening, she raved about your bringing her favorite person for food and fun."

"She did enjoy herself. But I think Sadie tired her out tonight. It'll take her a month to recuperate."

"She still talks about how you and Sadie kept her company after Gary passed away five years ago."

"She liked that, huh?"

"She took great lengths to tell me about it before hanging up." Sarah stepped into her bedroom, then swung around, facing her son. "I'm curious, dear. Will Leanne broadcast that the two of you dated in Glendale, or is she discreet?"

Kyle cracked his knuckles, thinking about how to answer. "Good question," he finally said. "I have no idea. We hadn't communicated since she visited Tulsa, until she called the other day."

"Hmm. How much does she know about you and Sadie's relationship?"

He leaned against the wall, chuckling. "Nothing. Only Cindy knew anything about my private affairs while I lived in California, Mother."

Sarah moved into the hallway. "Dear, how does one contemplate marrying a woman yet hide relevant information from her?" She folded her arms. "Those are the things you discuss when seriously dating someone."

"We dated for three months," hedged Kyle.

Her eyebrows rose. "How many people have you dated since Sadie? Leanne is aware that you only dated her in Glendale. And you failed to bring her to Shiatown after she stopped over in Tulsa. A man who had seriously dated a lady would welcome her into his home."

"She'd already reserved a hotel room before contacting me." Kyle's eyes narrowed, seeing the humor in her gaze. "What are you laughing about?"

"The dysfunctional relationship you hope to keep hidden. Leanne made flight and hotel reservations without your knowledge. And you left her plans intact after finding out."

"Which tells you what?" he asked, laughing. "That I wanted to hide her away in Tulsa?"

"It tells me that three people are playing an integral game of wait and see."

Kyle shoved his hands into his pockets. With his mother, everything always came back to the girl next door. Would she ever accept his decision to move on with his life? Her conversations said no, but one could hope. "Sadie?" He chuckled when she nodded. "Now, how could I bring another woman into this house when my ex-fiancée lives next door?" he asked.

"That teasing voice doesn't fool me, son. Listen to yourself. You put off bringing home a woman you dated for three months so your ex-fiancée wouldn't get upset. Kyle, take your time with Leanne, even if you never marry Sadie."

"I plan to." He crossed the hallway to his bedroom, stopping in the doorway. Did his mother just accuse him of being shortsighted?

"Have you noticed the significant growth in Sadie's character?" she asked when he lingered in the doorway. "The hardships grew her up, allowing others to witness her inner strength. And she has plenty."

Kyle stared at the woman who refused to back down. He partially agreed with the glowing appraisal. Every day, Sadie blossomed into the woman he'd always envisioned in his heart. But there was something missing from the picture. She still hid the real person behind the self-sufficient image she projected. False gaiety masked the pain she endured inside. Too many unanswered questions still remained. Did she return of her own volition without a boot from Lincoln? Or did she head to Shiatown after he bolted the revolving door?

Sarah tapped a finger against her lips. "Your resistance to Sadie is gaining traction. She'll find inner peace even though she suffered a heart-wrenching experience."

Kyle couldn't whitewash Sadie's motives then or now. "It isn't an ouch contest. Pain is pain—it hurts." After Sarah shut her bedroom door, he threw his keys on the dresser without switching on the lamp. The moonlight proved sufficient for the man learning to see in shadows.

Chapter Thirteen

Matt's clapping hands resounded throughout the auditorium as Kate and Amy locked the outer doors. The tryouts were finally over. The last girls auditioning for Sadie's play left the auditorium exhausted. All day, sixty girls from Shiatown and neighboring communities competed for parts. The massive turnout prompted Sadie to call in additional volunteers from the learning center's staff. The church was obligated to guarantee each girl received a fair shot at the roles being offered. Although no one invited Kyle and Matt, both men had hung out in the theater seats since morning, observing the entire process in person.

Three times that day, beginning with breakfast, Hot Link City, Kizzie's Soups & Salads, and Fantasy Cupcakes donated enough food to fuel a small army. The swarming activity in the lobby had forced Sadie to station a man at the door with a simple assignment: not to allow anyone into the building except for the girls auditioning and their parents. Thank God, Dee had advised moving the reading to Sunday for that weekend.

The staff, drama team, volunteers, and a few onlookers, that now included Roland and Brian, waited as Jeanette and Sarah put out the final meal. Non-stop chatter swept the room while the group consumed deli sandwiches and a fresh green salad supplied by The Teapot. Stuffed and barely able to move, Sadie swallowed the last bite, vowing to fast until morning. But then Sarah presented banana pudding for dessert. Unbuckling her belt, Sadie filled her bowl to the rim like everyone else did.

After the hungry workers had demolished every morsel, Jeanette, Brian, Sarah, and the volunteers went home. That left the theater staff and drama team to select the perfect girls for each role. Sadie stared at the three men who refused to look her way. Then she glanced at Amy, who studied the interlopers with her head tilted to the side. "We're about to get started, guys," said Sadie when the men remained seated.

"Go right ahead," said Kyle. "We're doing good down here. Don't let us disturb you."

Kate glared at him. "Well, you won't if you run along. You've been here all day."

"This is my first behind-the-scenes peek inside a live production," said Matt. "I want to see how the full process evolves."

Dee jerked her head toward the door. "We understand, Matt. But it's getting late. I can fill you in later."

"Why, when he can watch a live account now?" asked Roland, frowning. "Why should he leave?"

Cindy turned around from stacking chairs against the wall as the director and his assistants looked from the women to the men. "Hey Roland, I thought you and Brian were playing miniature golf this evening?"

"Brian fell asleep, so Miss Jeanette took him to her house," said Kyle. He checked his watch. "It's getting late. We'd better get started."

The overly tired Sadie couldn't believe their attitudes. What gave them the right to horn in on her department's staff meeting? What if she and the staff made mistakes? This was the first real meeting with the drama team. But the next comment ended her annoyance somewhat.

"If I believe the program is on the right track, I'll talk it up at the business owner's breakfast," said Roland.

Lenny fired up his laptop. "We're in. You all can stay," he said, adjusting his glasses before setting them on the table.

George winked at Kate. "Sounds good. I'll second you each month, Roland."

Three hours later, eighteen girls were unanimously selected to star in the play. Overjoyed the auditions were over, Sadie noticed Kyle was grinning at her, and after a few seconds of thought, she knew why. The bullied mentoring student along with two bullies had made the final selection. All the girls would receive a call from Kate that night.

* * *

The following Monday, eighteen girls sat in a semicircle vying for Sadie's attention. She chatted with them until the staff walked on stage to join her. While most of the staff sat in chairs facing the girls, Cindy plunked down on the floor beside Sadie, wielding a stack of file folders she set to the side. Taking a seat beside Dee, Lenny started a question-and-answer session; the others made sure every girl participated in the back and forth. As expected, the seemingly random questions broke the ice in a hurry. The group no longer looked ill at ease but freely replied to the innocuous queries.

Moving them forward, Kate asked the parents, sitting offstage, to voice their concerns. And the teens became animated when Dee asked about their hobbies and study habits. Then George piped in with a simple question.

"You've committed to a nine-and-a-half-month production schedule that ends in August. Where do you see yourself once the program ends?"

Their responses increased Sadie's determination to make it a journey to remember. Each girl believed the project would change her life for the better. Several of them peered over the staff members' heads as footsteps sounded backstage. Sadie addressed the group as her sister sat on the floor next to Cindy.

"Everyone, meet Amy," she said, trying to keep from smiling. She was proud of her sister's involvement. Her coming on board made it a family affair. It pleased her that excitement covered the young woman's face.

"Hi, I was backstage finishing up a project, but I've been hearing the conversation," said Amy, removing a wad of gum from her mouth. "I'm eighteen, a freshman at Shiatown University, and Sadie's sister. *And* I'm the liaison between you and the staff." She got on her knees. "Beginning today, I promise to help you whenever possible. You saw them on Saturday, but you'll meet the drama team this Wednesday. Our director teaches drama at the university, and his assistant is the drama teacher at a local high school. The two coaches teach drama classes at a community center and will provide weekly training sessions on Saturdays." She scooted closer to the group, explaining the program's schedule.

Kyle strolled into the auditorium just as she finished speaking. Surprised that he came, Sadie happily called him up front, introducing him to the others. "Kyle Franklin is the senior pastor at Kingdom Life Church and backs our production efforts. In fact, Pastor Kyle gets one day off per week, and Saturday, he spent it with us, supporting the auditions."

Standing in front of the first row, Kyle acknowledged the teens and their parents. "You are a talented group. It's all about teamwork; each of us working together to accomplish our goal. We expect your best effort in exchange for our ongoing support. Let's do one another proud," said Kyle, smiling at the girls. Then he shook hands with their parents on his way down the aisle. He was there less than five minutes, yet after he left, expectancy surged through the air.

* * *

The next morning, Sadie flopped on her side as a distant noise penetrated through her sleep. Finding the buzzing alarm clock, she pushed the snooze button then turned in the opposite direction. But she immediately froze to the spot while pulling the cover over her head: Kyle had called last night, inviting her to breakfast this morning.

"Yes!" Out of bed in a flash, she glanced at the clock. "I'd better hurry." Throwing on a robe, she practically skipped into the hallway. *Good. Amy's still sleeping.* Just before entering the bathroom, her bedraggled sister appeared in the hall. "Hello, sleepyhead. I can't believe I beat you getting up this morning."

Amy's bottom lip protruded. "Let me go first. I'm meeting my counselor before class in ninety minutes."

"Sorry," she said, giddy with happiness. "I'm eating breakfast with Kyle in half an hour." She almost laughed out loud when Amy moaned loudly. "Believe me, little sister, this will be a beautiful day. Count on it."

Sadie walked into the bathroom as Amy pounded on Jeanette's bedroom door. Sadie poked her head into the hallway. "That's right, use Mom's bathroom. It's free. I heard her go downstairs a few minutes ago." She snapped the lock, bursting into laughter when a hard object hit the closed door. It felt wonderful living at home again.

* * *

Kyle was waiting in the car when she walked outside the house. Suddenly shy, she scooted into the passenger's seat, smiling at him. "No kiss?" he asked. "Come on, you used to lay one on me every time you got into my car."

Nostalgic again. That means something I won't like is coming. "Are you baiting me? And if you are, stop. I don't like it."

An eyebrow rose as he chuckled. "And all this time I thought you wanted us to get close and personal."

"Be serious, please." Sadie stared out the side window, ignoring his teasing.

Before turning into the restaurant parking lot, he waved at Cindy, who was tucking Brian into the car seat in Roland's truck. Her brother always dropped Brian off at the daycare before heading to his first job of the day.

In the restaurant, Kyle greeted everyone he passed by then headed to a secluded corner across the room. He took a menu from the server but gave his order without looking at it. He finally handed the menu to the man before he moved away.

"How did the meeting end yesterday?" he asked in a soft voice.

Sadie hoped that wasn't the real purpose of eating breakfast together. Kyle could've asked that question at the learning center. "On a high note, thank God." She slowly inhaled, wondering what was coming next.

Kyle looked around the room, seemingly gathering his thoughts. Then he focused on Sadie, a half-smile on his lips. "Lady, although you inspire me, I don't like seeing you locked within private thoughts when you think no one is watching."

Tears sprang to her eyes in an instant. The fact that he'd noticed something so personal pleased Sadie, but it made her unhappy, too. If he saw her inner struggles with the past, she hadn't sufficiently risen above the muck. "I put myself through unnecessary hardship, Kyle."

"But you grew up in the process. You've changed. Truly changed. Now, had you remained the same impetuous woman ..."

Sadie grasped his hands in hers. "God really blessed me. I'm not the same frightened person showing the world a confidence I never felt."

Kyle turned her hand over in his, squeezing her fingers. His gaze never left her face.

"You still hide within yourself, not allowing people to see the real Sadie. Your current challenges. Although your younger self was pretty spectacular, I appreciate the maturing woman even more."

Her pulse accelerated. Even though Kyle still questioned her stability, he was holding her hand in a public place. But how could he notice her vulnerability and withhold his love at the same time? What about Leanne's visit on Thursday? Sadie stiffened her lips to stop them from quivering.

"Sadie ... several times you've told me that you love me." He paused, looking up as Cindy set their meal to the side then walked away without making eye contact. Kyle watched her retreat. "I think little sisters are marvelous to have around, what about you?"

Sadie shook her head, laughing. "You might change your opinion if you'd seen Amy and me arguing over the bathroom earlier."

"I take it you won the argument since you left the house on time. Amy's car was still parked in the driveway."

She nodded, remembering her sister's temper tantrum. "Winning is a rare occurrence when battling Amy. Watching Roland rein her in improves my technique daily." She hesitated as moisture filled her eyes. "I've missed out on two precious years with my family and friends. I won't give up on us—unless you say that you refuse to marry me. Even then, I'll pray that God will soften your heart."

As her gaze locked with his, Sadie took an audible deep breath. The compassion flowing from his eyes spread warmth throughout her body. Sitting across from her was the man she fell in love with before learning to ride a bicycle. The man who saw into the depths of her soul from the moment they met.

He released her hand. "Nowadays, I live life one day at a time. Running ahead of the Holy Spirit's timing didn't work for us." He brushed a teardrop off her cheek. "I never stopped loving you, Sadie. Part of me wants you in my life more than ever." He raised up his hand when her lips trembled. "Don't think I'm unable to move beyond the relationship with Lincoln. My problem is with you." Kyle sipped his juice then set down the glass. "Why did you come home?"

The why question again. She'd thought about his reaction to the word since he'd harped on it at the first author read. Sadie still failed to grasp its significance to Kyle concerning herself. She spread her hands in supplication then dropped them on her lap. "My life is here."

"That's a simple answer to a complicated question," said Kyle. "Shiatown was your home the entire time you lived in Burgundy. Why did you come back in September?"

The food Sadie swallowed hit her stomach like a brick. Finally, she comprehended the intent behind the question. Her mother maintained that her coming home overrode the reason why she came. Sadie recalled her mother's exact words: "Honey, maturity allows us to make better choices."

However, Kyle wasn't a loving mother, but the man cast aside for the person who'd attacked her. Sadie had settled for her abuser even though Kyle loved her and treated her tenderly. Could that person agree with her mother's judgment? That it took courage to leave Burgundy and come back home whenever she came. Or would he assume Lincoln's dumping forced her to run away?

When she'd discovered that Kyle would relocate to Shiatown, it strengthened her hope to chart a new course. Sadie withstood the urge to make Lincoln pay for ruining her future. Instead, she turned to God, and Jesus brought her home. Far away from the damaging effects of physical and emotional abuse.

Could the man examining her reactions accept the simple truth? Sadie had always desired to come home, but she had never believed she had the ability to return until she did so. She watched the man quietly eating, knowing their relationship rested on her answer. This was hard.

"Lincoln brought another woman to my apartment the day I sent the flower to you and Miss Sarah." Picking up toast, Sadie broke off a piece, sipping orange juice to wash it down. "There was something special about that day. Like every component came together perfectly. You were burying Pastor Franklin. Miss Sarah was grieving about losing her husband. Also ..." Sadie paused, watching him slide the empty plate to the side. "Kyle, I knew you were moving back to Shiatown. So I wanted to come home too."

Sadie pushed hash browns across the plate then glanced at him. Her lips trembled as she tried to smile. "I know you believe I came home because Lincoln dumped me, but I didn't. He disrespected me many times before, and I remained with him."

"What else was different about that particular day?" he asked, watching her closely.

The alert expression on his face puzzled Sadie. The man analyzed each word she spoke as if dissecting her piece by piece. "Are you questioning my honesty?" she finally asked.

"No. You're speaking the truth as you see it. But it's all surface talk. You're not leveling with me."

Sadie abandoned the pretense of eating. "Why did you invite me to breakfast this morning? You could've interrogated me in your office."

Kyle shook his head. "This discussion was meant for a public arena, and you know it."

"Why?" asked Sadie, feeling confused. He was turning a simple discussion into an ordeal.

"Because I couldn't chance you running out of the building crying this time. You won't do that here."

"No, I won't," she said, trying to smile. "Kyle ... I hated existing instead of living, and I prayed God would give us a second chance. And He did. If we let him." Tears pooled in her eyes. "Until that day, I felt that Lincoln was my punishment for being stupid."

"You were never stupid, Sadie. Just overwhelmed with uncertainties. What opened your eyes to the truth?"

She sipped her water, taking as long as she could before speaking. "The showdown was building up for months. I didn't become fed up with life, only with him. It was a strange day. I opened the door for Lincoln and noticed a woman climbing the stairs behind him. No one spoke a word. He came into the house. He stared at me. I stared at him. I reopened the door, and he left. Two years of torture ended in less than three minutes. And I knew it was over. I was free to go home."

"Silent again, huh? I'm understanding Lincoln better. He quietly savors the win. Or ... when he expects to win. And since you left him this time, he lost."

"That's it!" she said, grabbing his hand. "Oh my goodness! I couldn't understand why he was passive aggressive. Lincoln only makes scenes when he feels intimidated. How did you know?"

"Men like him prey on insecure women. That was your past. Now it's time to live out your present, God's way."

She felt heaviness melt away. "See? We belong together." Her smile faltered somewhat when he failed to agree.

Kyle rose, looking at her half-full plate. "Your food is cold. We'll order a carryout meal at the counter."

Still trying to smile, she walked beside him. "How about admitting God made us for one another?"

"I can't," he said while his eyes filled with laughter. "God creates people for Himself."

"Stop teasing. I went to bed that night longing for home, and God gave me the story in a dream. You have to admit He's smoothing out those rocky roads for the book and play."

Kyle studied her with a blank face while walking to the counter. "Always seek God before plotting a course, Sadie."

"I have. All my paths lead to you through Jesus. The Holy Spirit will use our lives for God's glory. Wait and see. The Father has a plan that includes us working together."

Eyebrow raised, he spoke to the server. "One special to go."

Chapter Fourteen

Kyle raced down the highway in a hurry to reach the airport. A late meeting had spilled over into his travel time to Tulsa. He hated rushing and had prayed for a leisurely drive as he organized events for the next three days.

Too keyed up to finalize plans for Leanne's visit, he drummed his fingers on the steering wheel. So far, dinner tonight with his mother was the only engagement he'd arranged. His usual standbys, Cindy, Roland, Matt, and Dee, didn't prove acceptable options. Of course, Matt and Cindy had issued an invitation, but Kyle had the good sense to decline the offers.

Nevertheless, Kyle knew that for Cindy, the pendulum swung in Sadie's direction. It certainly did with him, until his mind faced reality. Sadie's ability to hide from herself and others bothered Kyle. The woman endured two nerve-wracking years without anyone around her recognizing it. From all accounts, the people in Burgundy considered her a happy, well-adjusted person.

The fact that she'd fooled so many people undermined his faith in her stability regarding himself. How could Sadie doubt his love, even with the trauma? A lack of insight into her reasoning stopped him from taking her back. But outside of her private life, she'd certainly matured in fundamental ways. She no longer sought validation from others to prove her self-worth. On a regular basis, she presented an account of her department's activities before the elder board with a confidence never demonstrated in the past.

Even Matt teased about the change, telling her, "I prefer the confident Sadie Cummings. Allow her to stick around for a while." But the offhand joke had brought tears to her startled eyes. Sadie wrapped her arms around Matt, putting her cheek on his chest. Then, smiling at Dee, she said, "You picked a winner, friend."

That one action had reminded him of the old Sadie and allowed happy memories to fill his thoughts. And there were plenty. Even when Kyle could've become angry with her rashness, he'd always laughed it away. He enjoyed helping her circumvent potential traps. Kyle had considered it all good because Sadie was a fascinating person. Time spent with her had filled him with purpose, pleasing him more than living a stress-free existence without her.

Approaching the airport terminal, he bypassed the parking lot, driving directly to the arriving passengers exit. In no time, he spotted Leanne waiting at the curb with her luggage beside her.

Kyle rolled to a stop in front of her. Springing from the car, he kissed her upturned lips before tucking her into the passenger's seat while apologizing. Her bag stowed in the trunk, he entered the highway heading to Shiatown. Turning off the radio, he listened to her describe a comedy routine she'd attended the night before. All the while, he reworked the strategy in his mind to acquaint Leanne to his new life. He glanced at her when she rested her head on his shoulder. Her eyes glowed as she smiled up at him.

"What can I look forward to this weekend? Did you set aside time for your visitor?"

His grip slacked on the steering wheel. "I'll spend most of my days with you." He glanced down at her. "You traveled fifteen hundred miles to see me, and I plan to enjoy your company."

"I came for us," said Leanne. "Kyle, where do we go from here? You were ready to settle down before you left Glendale. After leaving, something changed your attitude about us being together. What?" She set up straight, staring at him. "Why didn't you call me?"

Kyle lowered his speed, then moved into an inner lane, digesting her comment. "Taking on the new position required a different mindset, and God is building me up for the task." He glanced at her then focused on the road. "Self-will is an albatross I can't afford, Leanne. I want godly wisdom for my life. Over five hundred individuals trust me to hear from Him."

Leanne exhaled loudly. "What's different *now*? The first day we met you stated your destiny lay in pastoring your father's church."

"Did you believe me? You knew the church was located in Oklahoma."

She turned away, studying the countryside. "I realized you were never coming back to me when you said goodbye in September."

Kyle glanced at her. "Then why did you come?"

"To see if we can salvage our relationship. I don't want to lose you." Hesitating, she studied her fingers. She appeared off her game at the moment. He waited for her to speak.

She suddenly faced him. "I know you wanted us to get married while you lived in Glendale. Let's pursue that route."

"Impossible," said Kyle, acknowledging the truth to himself for the first time. "The adjustments I made in coming home put us light-years apart." He maneuvered the car into the exit lane. "I won't make any life-changing decisions in the foreseeable future."

"Are you saying I misinterpreted your intentions?" she asked.

"I'm saying we occupy two worlds that can't coincide."

"But we can live separately without it affecting our jobs. Or did I mistake your intentions when you requested a second date?"

Kyle disliked the battering back and forth. He preferred to solidify the friendship he now wanted instead of marriage. But first, Leanne needed to understand a marriage would never take place between them. "Pastoring Kingdom Life isn't a job, Leanne. It's my life. Serving as youth pastor under higher leadership doesn't compare with senior pastor responsibilities. Besides, I never denied I would return to Shiatown for good." Slowing down his speed, he made brief eye contact.

Anger leaped into her eyes. "Then why ask me out at all? Did you think I would walk away from the career I loved?"

"Deadlock." Kyle exited the highway. "Forgive me for miscalculating the situation. I hurt both of us in doing so."

Leanne clicked her fingernails together. "In other words, sit back, lady, and enjoy the scenery on the road leading nowhere."

Kyle pulled into the hotel parking lot in the heart of the downtown area. Turning off the engine, he stared straight ahead. "You called me two months after saying goodbye to renew a commitment I never made."

Leanne glared at him. "Lose the sarcasm, Kyle. You thought about us getting married. Somehow June turned the corner for you. The single lifestyle lost its appeal."

Opening the car door, he paused, gazing at her. "Go on."

"I guess the groomsman role in that friend's wedding ceremony started the slide. And then Cindy wowed your friend the first day they met. Admit the truth. Roland surrounds himself with available women, and you watched a seasoned player succumb without a fight. Their romance played out in real time. The man extended his one-week vacation to three to pursue a ready-made family."

Kyle chuckled. "I caught romance fever? Is that what you think?"

"For a lack of a better term, yes," she admitted, pursing her lips together.

"Then you own taking advantage of my weakened state?" he asked, grinning.

She glanced away from the steady gaze then faced him quickly. "You're quite the jokester today. You seldom teased in Glendale."

"Welcome to Shiatown." He winked at her shocked face before exiting the car.

* * *

Amy hurried from the window and ran up the stairs to the second floor. "She's here," she said, bursting into Sadie's bedroom without knocking. While Dee moved at a slower pace, she and Kate tripped over one another, racing to the window. Without moving the blinds aside, three pairs of eyes peered at the couple until Leanne and Kyle disappeared inside the house. But Sadie remained glued to the bed, too numb to move an inch.

The mystery lady was in his house. Eyes closed, she imagined Kyle introducing Leanne to the woman Sadie loved like a second mom. Would Sadie meet her before she left Shiatown? Did he purchase tickets for Saturday's author read? Her shoulders sagged. Kyle would never bring a date to an event she'd staged. Sunday-morning service loomed ahead. Leanne was probably thrilled about warning single females to stay away from Kyle. Sadie sighed.

Thanks for the heads-up, Kyle, but it still hurts. I don't know what to do at this point.

Sitting on the bed, Amy wrapped an arm around Sadie's shoulder. "Do you think Kyle will get upset if I drop by for a visit?" She laughed when three voices shouted, "Yes."

"Don't go near that house," said Sadie. "And do not allow anyone to see you peeking out the window."

Kate slipped on her sneakers, and Dee grabbed her jacket. "You're not moping around this house all evening," said Kate. "Let's go car shopping. Amy said you need a car so you can stop borrowing hers. Grab your coats, ladies; we'll wait for you in the car," said Kate, following Dee downstairs.

Sadie got up, but paused in the doorway. "Wait. I don't have down payment money."

"Nor did I," said Amy, pushing her out the door. "Mom let me take money from the trust fund the Grands set up."

Tears instantly flooded her eyes. Trust fund? It seemed her grandparents had forgotten about her while she lived in Burgundy. Sadie hesitated on the landing. "Mom didn't tell me you had a trust fund."

Amy skirted around her, descending the stairs. "I guess she forgot about it once you came home. Aunt Yolanda received the artwork, coins, and the condo in Belize. Except for Roland, the grandchildren received individual trust funds."

"Whoo! I thought they'd forgotten about me." Smiling, Sadie followed behind her sister. "I bet Nathan used a portion to open up a culinary school. Am I right?"

Amy removed their coats from the hall closet, passing Sadie's wrap to her. "It's still in the planning stage. Tiffany took her family on a cruise to Europe in August."

"Why did Mom keep it a secret from me?"

"So Lincoln couldn't swindle it away from you." Laughing, Amy wrapped a scarf around her neck, then peeked at her reflection in the hall mirror.

"I'll call them tonight," Sadie responded. Gliding outside, Sadie winced as the brisk wind stung her face. While Amy locked the door, she called over her shoulder, "I hope they won't think I'm an ingrate for not thanking them sooner."

"They can't. Grandfather decided to keep it a secret from you until you booted Lincoln."

Amy climbed into the back seat, laughing at Sadie's shocked expression.

* * *

The next day, when Sadie arrived for her shift at the bookstore, she set her purse behind the counter while Sarah checked out a lady purchasing a dictionary. She busied herself at an audio book display until the customer left the store. "Hello, Miss Sarah. Shouldn't you be at the nursing home? And where's Miss Michelle?"

"Sleeping late because I'm here," said Sarah, wiping a cloth across the counter. "On some days, both of us old ladies need a slower pace. This is one of those days, for Michelle, dear." The lines around her eyes crinkled when she smiled. "She'll be in later. So, another sellout crowd this Saturday?" she asked, storing her cloth and duster in the bottom drawer.

Sadie was so busy thinking of ways to bring up Kyle that she almost missed the question. "Absolutely. Miss Sarah," she said, warming to the topic, "is it the author reads or the exceptional dinner that draws our crowd? I can't decide why folks keep coming."

"More than likely, it's a combination of the two. Most people enjoy consistency and comfort. You provide both. Once the live productions begin in the evenings, consider switching the reads to afternoons and serve lunch."

Sadie's eyebrows rose. "Two shows in one day. I'd thought about doing that very thing. Won't people get tired of coming?"

Sarah shook her head. "More than likely, each event will attract a different crowd. But on some days, you might find a guest eating lunch and dinner with you."

"Thanks for the suggestion, Miss Sarah. I'll think about it. The author reads are a good thing. Everyone claims they're hearing about genres they'd never considered reading. But I wonder if Mom will provide a discount for lunch as well."

Sarah sat beside Sadie as she nibbled a thumbnail. "She will for you, dear. Jeanette has a thriving business. She's getting paid and receiving free advertising at the same time. Did you see Kyle at work? I believe he planned to be there part of the day."

"No, I was in the learning center all morning." Then she laughed, burying her face in her hands. "Yesterday, I invented a reason to go to his office today, but I changed my mind at the last minute. Did dinner go well with his lady friend?" she asked, fighting to keep from crossing her fingers that the meal bombed.

Sarah nodded. "Leanne is a pleasant enough person. And very knowledgeable about city planning. I believe her parents' consulting firm specializes in developing blighted areas. Kyle said her reliable contacts benefited the church while setting up the youth program."

Sadie slumped in the chair. "They'll be happy together? I'd hoped they would stop seeing one another."

"Successful marriages require two people who love one another enough to stick it out through the tough spots." She nodded at a tall woman and man trying to catch her attention. Touching Sadie's shoulder, Sarah followed the couple beckoning her from the non-fiction section.

Busy cataloging new books, Sadie looked at the door as three middle-aged women swept inside, chortling hilariously. One of them pointed to a young man eating a scone as he flipped through a magazine. That's what Sadie liked about the bookstore. Some customers came and left swiftly, while others began reading their purchases on the spot.

* * *

"Fancy meeting you here. Is the workday over?" Although the gray-haired lady spoke to Kyle, she stared at Leanne. "The Main Street Diner was packed as usual, so your uncle and I stopped by our second choice." Curious by nature, his mother's oldest sister quietly scrutinized his companion.

Kyle rose, hugging the woman who impatiently waited for an introduction. "Aunt Caroline, Leanne is a friend visiting from Glendale." He turned to the alert face eyeing the older lady. "This is my favorite aunt on both sides of the family."

"I hope he doesn't run into any more relatives," she told Leanne. "Then you would hear that statement repeated to five other women. Kyle, Cindy called the other day. I'm happy to hear she's settling down with such a fine young man." She paused, staring directly into his eyes.

"Where's my girl?" Aunt Caroline glanced at the man calling for her from the exit door. "It was nice meeting you," she told Leanne, turning away. Suddenly swinging around to face Kyle, she said, "Tell Sadie to call me tonight. I want her to set aside two tickets for the reading tomorrow."

"Too late," he said with a wide grin. "A sellout crowd for three consecutive weeks. We're on a roll."

"I see. Well, it's good for the church and author, but bad for Willie and me. I'll tell her Sunday to put aside two tickets for us each week." His uncle waved once she reached him at the exit, then glanced at their table while opening up the door for his wife.

Kyle watched their trek across the parking lot until losing sight of them. For two months, he'd traveled throughout the city rarely seeing anyone he knew, but he had run into practically everyone in the last two days. He noticed Leanne glaring at him. "You're bound to meet my entire family at this rate," he said, laughing.

She dropped her spoon onto the plate. "So, Roland proposed. I'm impressed. Few people can turn a three-week visit into a marriage proposal in just four months. She settled into small-city living fast." Her eyebrows arched as if asking a question.

Kyle sipped his drink. Her curiosity put him off. "She's engaged and very happy." Kyle set down the glass "It's a good match all around. The three of them were smitten at first sight." He paused as Leanne stared slightly over his head.

"Hello, Pastor Kyle. Who's your friend?" A lilting voice spoke beside him.

Kyle stared into the cold brown eyes of Kate's older sister. Turning around, he took in the table behind them where three women scowled at him. If looks were lethal, management would've called an ambulance by now. "Doesn't anyone eat at home anymore?" He stood, making introductions. "Leanne is a friend visiting from Glendale." A statement he'd repeated at least fifteen times that day alone. He turned to the woman whose set expression appeared more curious than angry. "I've known Tawanie since kindergarten."

Tawanie smiled engagingly. "Hi, Leanne! Kyle and I are old friends." Her gaze jerked to his when Leanne barely responded. Her expression softened. "Les took the kids to Bon Appetit for dinner, giving me an afternoon out with friends. I'd better get back to them. I'll see you at the read tomorrow."

"I'm sorry I'll miss you. I don't have tickets. It's a sellout crowd." Kyle chuckled, and Tawanie frowned at him.

"Imagine that," she said, studying the couple, and then she spoke to Leanne. "Blame your friend for missing the must-attend event of the week. Everyone hangs out with Sadie on Saturday evenings." She returned to her friends after giving Kyle the widest grin he'd ever seen.

As soon as she walked away, Leanne rose with her purse in her hand. "What's a read?" she asked through lips that barely moved.

Kyle explained the mechanisms behind the learning lab and dinner theater while paying, noting the setup with the restaurant to cater each affair. He agreed at once when she asked to look around the church complex. He found it odd, however, that she hadn't requested a guided tour while eating dinner at his house yesterday; it was next door, after all. On the way to the church, they passed by the diner. Slowing his speed, he pointed out the restaurant that almost spanned one full block. He then explained that Cindy and Brian lived in one side of the duplex next door to the building.

"I'd pictured a different establishment from what you said earlier," said Leanne, making a face at him. "This restaurant is close to downtown and in an upscale community. All neighborhoods should have numerous activities within walking distance of houses." Turning in her seat, she watched the building long after they'd passed it by. Silent for at least fifteen minutes, she stirred when Kyle turned into the church parking lot, surveying the complex, until the last building snared her attention.

"Let's begin at the building where the cars are parked." She glanced at her watch. "It's late. I thought everything closed down at four on Fridays."

"Apparently something's up tonight." Kyle crossed the pavement to the building situated slightly behind the others. After opening the door, he stepped aside, but Leanne grabbed his hand before strolling into the lobby.

Activity buzzed inside the lobby as workers scrutinized their handiwork. A Nativity scene dominated the southeast wall on the far side of the room. It showcased an open stable large enough to hold a manger, plus several striking cardboard images. The replica of baby Jesus held center stage with Mary and Joseph, and many farm animals gathered near the feeding trough. Four shepherds, one holding a lamb in his arms, peered inside the shed while camels carrying magi and their servants arrived from the east. Up above, angels were suspended in midair as a brilliant star shone luminous rays upon the stable.

"Take a look upstairs, pastor," said an excited man Kyle had never seen before. Wiping his hands on pants covered with glitter, the man pointed toward the west wing.

Secretly wondering how much the grand scheme cost the church, Kyle led the fascinated Leanne upstairs. He gaped in amazement on the landing. In the center of the room stood a gigantic Christmas tree adorned with blue and silver translucent ornaments. Sparkling crystal lights that wrapped around the base blinked on and off and covered it completely. Gifts of all sizes littered the floor underneath the branches.

And then a clanking noise in the distance quickly gained their attention. Kyle followed the sound until an overstuffed train rounded the tree's far side. Large freight cars hauled brightly wrapped packages within its spacious compartments.

Leanne pivoted, surveying the eye-catching design. "I'm impressed."

Crouching, she picked up a present, shaking it lightly. "This box has something in it." She shook a few more boxes then glanced at Kyle. "Is the church planning a huge Christmas party? I think there are about two hundred genuine presents here."

Kyle squeezed the back of his neck. How much did this wasteful extravagance set the church back? One look at the layout downstairs had placed dollar signs before his eyes. Was Kingdom Life in financial trouble from the expensive displays?

He gestured toward the stairs. "I must talk to Sadie."

Heads turned when they reached the main floor. Finished creating their masterpiece, people stood around eating snacks and talking.

A bearded man folded up a ladder just as they reached him. "Well, what do you think?"

Kyle patted the man's shoulder. "I'm speechless, Jim."

"Wait until you see the dining room," said his cousin, Rachel. She gazed at Leanne. "Hi, I'm Rachel. Aunt Sarah told us Kyle had a friend visiting from California."

Kyle grinned. At least one person could speak without mentioning Sadie's name.

Leanne pointed to the Nativity scene. "I've never seen two outstanding displays within one building. A lot of preparation went into each design."

"Check out the dining room. The theater staff finished setting it up an hour ago."

"Is it as exquisite as the displays here and upstairs?" asked Leanne.

Rachel nodded. "Sadie laid out the blueprint last month. She wanted the decorations completed before Thanksgiving."

Leanne glanced around the room. "You made it with time to spare."

"We put all of the pieces together today. Just in time for tomorrow's read. Are you coming?"

"No." Leanne looked at Kyle. "A sellout crowd. Your cousin failed to purchase tickets."

A knowing expression appeared on Rachel's face. "That's strange. He's attended every one since they started."

"Strange indeed." Leanne turned aside as laughter sounded behind the cracked-open door straight ahead. She looked at Kyle. "Dining room? Let's take a peek."

Kyle spoke to every person he passed on the way, only stopping when a man carrying a ladder drew up beside him.

"Thanksgiving's next week. The other displays must be completed by Wednesday. Your girl's cracking the whip today. This entire place is vintage Sadie all the way."

"It's a good job all around, Stan. Thanks for overseeing the projects."

Stan nodded. After looking at Leanne, he walked away.

Kyle took another glance around the lobby, then opened the door wider, peering into the room. He stepped aside for Leanne to enter in front of him.

"Sadie," she said, squinting at him. "I've heard that name several times since arriving yesterday. Now I get to meet this clever woman." Smiling, Leanne linked her arm through his.

Kyle stared at the woman gazing back at him before walking into the room.

Chapter Fifteen

A breathtaking winter wonderland greeted visitors at the door. Kyle almost shivered. Real evergreens scattered with fake snow decorated three corners. Glimmering crystals hung from trees, and frost glistened on Astroturf. On the north-end corner, behind the platform, ceiling lights reflected tree branches on a frozen pond as children made out of cardboard sat on a bench tying up their ice skates. The perfect backdrop for any author. The realistic display would captivate diners throughout the performance.

"I'd be enthralled by the beauty if I wasn't faint from the expense," Kyle spoke in a stage whisper.

The occupants at the center table turned around. Everyone glanced at Leanne before settling their gaze on Kyle.

Lenny put on his glasses. "Cost free to the church, I assure you. And that's a rarity these days."

"Hello, Leanne." Cindy rose to her feet, and moved toward them. "Did you check out the display upstairs?"

"Oh yeah. Are we having a Christmas party?" Kyle asked, his eyes on Sadie.

Dee nodded. "Children in the foster care system will tour the facility on Christmas Eve. Each child will select a gift from underneath the tree before leaving."

"So, what do you think?" asked Amy, her eyes searching his face.

"It's an incredible display on both floors. But I require a few more particulars before deciding." said Kyle, watching Sadie until Cindy intervened.

"Leanne, the learning center staffers and volunteers set up the displays upstairs and in the lobby. The theater staff tackled the reading room design. I work in both areas."

Leanne's eyes darted between Kate and Sadie, excluding the obviously pregnant, Dee. "The effect is quite astonishing. I like them all."

"Glad to hear it." Cindy gestured at the table. "Have you met our associate pastor, Matt Sweeney?"

Leanne nodded. "He dropped off a folder at Kyle's house yesterday."

"Good. Then from left to right ... Dee is Pastor Matt's wife. They're expecting their first child in March. Kate is an illustrator and designed the three displays. Amy, my future sister-in-law, is a college freshman and lives next door to Kyle. Lenny teaches high school English. George owns an advertising firm. Kate works for him. And Amy's sister, Sadie, is our fearless leader."

Leanne's gaze lingered on Sadie until Kyle pulled out a chair for her to sit down.

"Sadie, may I speak to you for a moment?" He pointed toward the door. "This won't take long," he told Leanne, moving away from the table.

Rising slowly to her feet, Sadie strolled over to Kyle, then suddenly spun around, wriggling her fingers at Amy, who visibly relaxed.

He glanced at the curious expressions around the table. "We'll speak in private a bit," he said, leading them out of the room. But he continued walking until they reached Sadie's office on the second floor. He sat in a chair in front of the desk, waiting for her to sit down.

"Lenny hinted that someone else bankrolled the decorations. Who?" he questioned as soon as she took her seat.

"Local businesses gave generously. And the community responded with free manpower. All the gifts were donated, Kyle. Plus, auxiliary clubs gift wrapped each one free of charge. Before you ask, the electric company promised a reduced rate for the season." Sadie made eye contact for the first time since leaving the dining room. "I had a difficult time convincing people to keep secrets from you."

"Too bad it doesn't prove hard enough for you. I won't dance around this one, Sadie. Stan implied you're not done. The learning center looks fantastic. What else needs to be added?"

For the first time since knowing her, she looked disgusted with him. Kyle understood the feeling, only he had a right to be upset.

"We're finished here," she finally said. "Our plans came together beautifully. Now the focus is on the other buildings and the grounds."

His eyebrow rose. "What is the cost, Sadie? How much goodwill did the business community extend?"

Sadie looked right through him. Evidently, some other matter occupied her thoughts. Blinking her eyes, she focused on him after he repeated the question. "There's enough money left over to decorate the other four lobbies. Plus the hallways, parking lot, and square. Also, we have a smaller Nativity scene for the altar."

"What did you promise them in turn for their generosity?" he asked, lowering his voice.

Squirming, Sadie ran fingers through her hair. "Every person involved will attend a private performance of *Salon Duty* before it opens. We'll stage two shows due to the tremendous support. Thursday and Friday before opening night. Another freebie provided by The Main Street Diner." She paused. "By the way, we're still set to open the Saturday before Christmas."

"How many children are you expecting?"

"Eighty-seven." She smiled, and her eyes twinkled. "This treat will include foster children in surrounding towns." Then she launched into the itinerary for the day. The gleam in her eyes enchanted him. Sadie was happy about the plans.

"When were you going to tell me about these engagements?" he asked.

Her face took on a gentle expression. "Kyle, you're always busy. I try to lighten your load any way possible."

"I know you do. Now is a good time to say thank you."

Her expression turned sardonic. Like she wondered why he was hassling her if he knew she wanted to help. But she kept the skepticism out of her voice. "The original plan was to *wow* you bright and early tomorrow morning. If you approved of the decorations here, I figured you'd come on board for the rest." She walked around the desk and stood watching him. "Stan and the staff from both departments were on standby. Your approval meant we would decorate the hallway and grounds before the reading tomorrow." She exhaled into her hands, then glanced at him. "It's late. And you left Leanne surrounded by my friends. Give me your verdict on Monday." Moving swiftly, she left the room, closing the door behind her.

Reopening the door, Kyle followed Sadie out the room, stopping next to the Christmas tree. He chuckled when the moving train prompted him to step aside. Shoving his hands into his pockets, Kyle surveyed the cavernous room again, viewing it from a neutral perspective. Filled with bookcases and room dividers placed far apart, the space provided privacy for tutoring students.

"I know you're still here, Sadie." He glanced under raised shelves, hoping to see her shoes. Giving up when she refused to reply, he said, "You did a superb job. Please continue with the decorations tomorrow. And plan to give the other departments the grand tour Monday morning. Stan said Thanksgiving Eve is the last day to complete the decorations." He turned around when laughter drifted up from downstairs. "We have three days to whip this place into shape."

* * *

Hiding behind bookcases, Sadie watched Kyle go down the stairs. Tiptoeing across the floor, she waited a few minutes before peeking over the banister. But instead of re-entering the dining room, he stood on the bottom step, his back against the railing, and softly whistled an old song they used to sing at camp.

He's troubled, and there's nothing I can do to help him this time. Leanne didn't mind him leaving her in a roomful of strangers. She knows I exist, but I saw the questions in her eyes. What did you tell her, Kyle?

Instantly, he glanced up at her, but Sadie refused to move away from the handrail. She had no reason to hide and nothing to be ashamed about. No woman could fight for her man if she ran away from the battle.

"I love you," she mouthed before he walked away.

* * *

That Sunday morning, Sadie's heart sank to her toes on the walk to church. Everyone's eyes seemed to follow her family's progress across the square. Unaware of the stares, her mother and sister were still laughing about Sadie burning their breakfast that morning. And then she spotted Roland and company waiting for them near the door. Maybe it meant people were gossiping about Kyle's visitor from California.

Looking straight ahead, she followed Jeanette into the sanctuary. But her skin prickled when she realized everyone was staring at her. "People are gawking, Mom," she said close to her mother's ear.

"Which has nothing to do with us. Ignore them." Jeanette made her way to the tenth row. She sat in the same chair every Sunday unless a newcomer beat her to it.

134

Cindy sat next to Jeanette, with Brian in between her and Roland. Taking a seat beside Sadie, Amy elbowed her in the side. "People are shocked. Everyone's dividing their attention between you and Leanne."

"Tell Amy not to point, Roland." Sighing, Sadie examined her shoes, wondering how her sister could act so happy when she was falling apart.

"It's pretty comical to watch. No one knows where to look," said Amy, giggling.

News traveled fast in a town with one hundred thousand residents. Did everyone hear about their pastor's visitor before coming? Several Cummings relatives that Sadie hadn't seen in church since she'd come back to Shiatown sat down in the row across the aisle. Each one caught her eye and sent her encouraging smiles.

Then her sister waved to a gray-bearded man seated at the end of the row. Amy elbowed her in the side again. "It's a full house today. The support team is out in force. Well, at least it got Uncle Jerry to church this morning." Still giggling, Amy covered her mouth with her hands when Roland frowned at her.

Sadie's shoulder muscles loosened once the music began playing. By the time Kyle took the podium, she was eager to hear the message. His sermons always strengthened her for the week that followed. Even though she couldn't figure out his reasoning concerning Leanne, the man heard from God on many occasions.

"Good morning, everyone," said Kyle. "In Mark chapter sixteen, verse fifteen through eighteen, Jesus told His disciples, 'As you go throughout the world, proclaim the good news to all creation. Whoever trusts and is immersed will be saved; whoever does not trust will be condemned. And these signs will accompany those who do trust: in my name they will drive out demons, speak with new tongues, not be injured if they handle snakes or drink poison, and heal the sick by laying hands on them.'

"The stone placed at Jesus's tomb signified his death. At birth, humanity became buried within the tomb of life. But once we receive Jesus as our Savior, we pass from that death to life. Then the journey begins. It's time to make Him the Lord and Master of our days. Being alive to God brings a new dimension to living.

"So let's roll away the stone that enslaves us to a master not our own and embrace the more abundant life our Savior came to bring. The Holy Spirit calls us to the Father morning, noon, and night. To praise Him in the promise of the morning. To inquire of Him in the warmth of the day. To talk to Him in the coolness of the evening. And to thank Him in the stillness of the night.

"Although believers walk through many trials, the Lord delivers us out of them all. Our mind should be on God, instead of on what the enemy is doing in the world. Let's live in His presence. His word fills us with courage whenever we obey His will and spend time with Him. The strength to live successful lives comes from focusing on Jesus. He keeps us in perfect peace when our minds stay on Him. Tunnel vision is a good thing if Jesus is at the end of the tunnel.

"Now, how do we keep our minds on the Son who saved us from the Father's wrath? It's simply by doing what He instructs us to do. We need to spend time with Him. Just as we would with anyone we enjoy being around. We cultivate a relationship with our Father by reading and obeying His word. By being still in His presence and giving him the first fruits of our days. When we obey God's known will, He keeps us in His perfect plan for our lives. Stop striving. Stop worrying. Stop wondering if we are pleasing Him. If we are observing His truths, we please Him. Jesus not only says, 'If you love me, you will obey my commands,' but empowers us to walk in obedience.

"Of ourselves we can do nothing, but we can do all things through Christ who strengthens us. The Holy Spirit enables us to obey Him. Let's start today by rolling away the stone to mediocre living which is servitude to an already defeated foe and to our own thinking. Beginning today, honor Jesus as Lord and Master. And never forget to whom we belong. In doing so, we'll pass from death to life. The more abundant life that Jesus came to bring moves us through life's milestones to reach real victory: the high calling of God in Christ Jesus."

Mist filled Sadie's eyes as Kyle handed over to Matt. Today he delivered a message aimed directly at himself. Miss Sarah was right. He penned his Sunday messages days in advance. He was troubled in the learning center Friday evening. But Leanne didn't spring an unexpected visit on Kyle. He allowed her to come. So what was his problem? Sadie turned around to see several pairs of eyes aimed at her back.

Okay, time to go home.

Once Matt ended the service, she quickly followed Amy into the aisle as her sister made small talk with everyone who engaged her. Then she sped across the lobby until a familiar voice called her name.

"Hey, roadrunner, slow down," said Dee in a lilting voice. "How about doing a big favor for me before you leave?"

"I'm trying to make a swift retreat," said Sadie, sidling up beside her friend. They both glanced at the entrance when Kate called Sadie from the front door. Dee laughed. "Great minds think alike," she said when Kate reached them.

"I went outside through the side exit when you called Sadie's name. Now Leanne thinks she was rushing out of the sanctuary to meet me instead of running away from her."

"She probably couldn't care less," said Sadie, running her fingers through her hair.

"She does!" Kate and Dee spoke at the same time.

"And she's staring at us. So let's make this discussion look real. Oh, I do have news. Matt's old teammate and his wife dropped by on their way to Houston last night with Lincoln Miller news."

"What's the word?" asked Kate, watching Sadie bite her bottom lip.

"He is in deep trouble. His teammates block for him just enough to win games. He takes a beating when the game is in the bag, never making it out of the backfield."

Sadie shrugged her shoulders, looking away. "He ticked off someone."

"Lots of people, from the sounds of it," said Kate. "Like quarterbacks, running backs need to keep their offensive line sweet."

"I'm surprised the coach allows such breaches on the field," Sadie said, facing them again.

"Why?" asked Kate. "He probably doesn't like Lincoln either."

"She's walking up behind you, Sadie. Get ready," said Dee, then she burst into laughter. "I can't believe we're acting like we did in high school."

Leanne stood at her elbow before Sadie could answer. "Hello, ladies. You all did a fantastic job decorating the grounds and hallway."

"Too bad you're leaving and can't view the lights after dark," said Kate, her eyes bright with laughter. "It looks pretty spectacular at night."

"I would've had Kyle drive by before dropping me off at the hotel if I'd known more decorations were underway."

Sadie grew weary of the conversation in a hurry. She surveyed the room while the others made small talk. The lobby was still quite full. And practically every eye was aimed in their direction. Sadie was always one of the first people to leave the building and had thought everyone else left quickly as well. Would these people ever go home? Surely their stomachs were growling for food by now.

Seconds later, Amy walked up with Cindy. "No one's leaving. I want them gone so I can deck out the church. I have plans for later."

Leanne coughed into her hand. "Sadie, may I speak to you in private for a moment?" She smiled at the others. "Yesterday, I missed an opportunity to talk with your leader."

Sadie nodded, and then said, yes, following behind her. But instead of stopping a few feet away as she'd expected, Leanne continued walking until they reached the hallway to the fellowship hall. Staring out the window, she gestured outside.

"The grounds look fabulous, Sadie. Your hard work paid off. I see that Kyle approved the work after all."

Sadie squinted at her. "Thank you. It was a labor of love. We all enjoyed it."

"I'm about to leave for the airport, but I'll get to know you better on my next visit." Leanne grinned mischievously. "I'm curious about your motives, Sadie. Your decorations mesmerized Kyle on Friday. Either you are a very clever lady or extremely guileless."

"Try unimpressed," said Sadie, backing up. "Forget about us meeting on your next visit. I spend my hang-out time with people who don't insult me. Enjoy the flight home."

Instantly, Kyle strolled up, stopping next to Leanne. "Ready to go?" He pointed to the side entrance. "It's a thirty-minute drive to the airport." When no one spoke, he studied Sadie's poker face, then turned to Leanne.

"Is everything all right?" he asked Leanne as Sadie looked on.

"I think Sadie is upset about something. She was about to run off when you arrived."

He studied Sadie. "Are you upset? You look amused."

"I'm fine, but I decided not to stick around while Leanne pondered whether I'm clever—or guileless." Sadie suddenly smiled, showing white, even teeth. "I answered truthfully. Maybe you can fill her in on the drive to Tulsa. Have fun."

Frown lines wrinkled Leanne's forehead. "I offered friendship, Sadie."

"Friendship? With me?" Sadie asked in disbelief. "Sorry to disappoint you, Leanne. I select my companions more carefully these days." Turning away, she retraced her steps across the lobby.

Jeanette and Sarah, along with Kyle's secretary, had joined the group in her absence. Laughing about something Kate was saying, the women grew silent once Sadie reached them. Then the older ladies, and Amy and Cindy, went into the sanctuary.

Lagging behind the others, Sadie gestured to her friends to slow down their steps. Once Kate and Dee stood beside her, she rolled her eyes and smiled.

"The woman has claws," she whispered, "the attack came out of nowhere."

Chapter Sixteen

"Who wouldn't feel frustrated?" asked Leanne. "I traveled fifteen hundred miles to seal a relationship you refuse to accept."

Her drawn features reminded Kyle of a person searching for a lost object. He inwardly recoiled from the emotion-driven scene. Leanne was a different woman outside of her comfort zone. She appeared determined to call the shots, expecting him to give in to her wishes. Her strong convictions might stimulate the right man. She projected a willingness to compromise that she probably didn't feel. Even though marriage was off the table, parting as friends remained a possibility.

Kyle opened the passenger door, but she refused to get into the car. Their discussion could've continued on the drive to the airport, but then she wouldn't be able to pace around him in circles.

"I know you wanted a lasting relationship," she continued. "What happened to us?"

"We're friends, Leanne. Dating allowed me to get to know you away from church."

She shook her head before he finished speaking. "Only because you wanted to deepen our involvement. You didn't date anyone before June." A light sprung into her eyes. "Wait. Did you break up with Sadie that month?"

He opened the car door wider. "Our engagement ended over two years ago. A mutual parting of ways."

"Engagement, Kyle? Really? Knowing that fact while we dated might've prevented this trip." Sliding into the car, she leaned her head against the headrest.

Sarah had told him the same thing a few weeks ago. Maybe he should've mentioned Sadie, but he didn't discuss her with many people. Perhaps

Leanne deserved an apology after all. She turned to him when he started the engine.

"I was already in love with you when you asked me out to dinner. You're the man I've waited for, Kyle."

His heart turned over while backing the car out of the parking space. "I've learned many lessons since coming home, Leanne. I asked you out because I enjoyed our time together. I didn't intend to mislead you."

She closed her eyelids then turned her face to the side window. "You never made love declarations, but you asked me out because you were ready to settle down. It was wrong to give off false impressions if that wasn't the case."

Kyle guided the car onto the highway. "People date to get to know one another, not to get married. Each person can pick someone to date and decline any offers."

"Are you rejecting the offer?" she asked.

"To propose on the drive to Tulsa?" he countered.

Leanne stared at him with half-closed eyes. "That's an adroit way of saying, I'll never marry you. Well, you can't get any more direct than that. Sadie's wormed her way back in."

"Leanne—"

"Earlier, I promised Minister and Mrs. Dawkins to attend a council meeting for their ward in February. I intend to keep my word."

"Give me a call. I'll pick you up at the airport. I want us to remain friends."

"Friends. Well, I expected much more." She sighed. "Is that why you accepted my visits?" She turned her face to the window again. "Wake me up when we reach the airport. Will I have to deal with a vendetta from Sadie on my return?"

"Look, Sadie and I are not the issue. My decisions are based on you and me. Besides, she's harmless and gets along with everybody."

* * *

Unable to rest, Sadie knocked on her mother's bedroom door, walking into the room without being invited. Jeanette lounged on a recliner with a book lying on her lap. She removed her glasses when Sadie came in. "Hi, honey. The author read yesterday was excellent. I may buy an adventure novel for the first time ever."

Sitting on the floor, Sadie laid her face on her mother's thigh. "Me too. Mom, folks are gossiping. They think Kyle flaunted Leanne at me."

Jeanette smoothed her fingers over Sadie's hair. "People will believe whatever they please. Let them keep their misconceptions." She placed the book on the side table. "Don't tell your personal business to onlookers. Few people need to know details."

"Even if an innocent man is receiving unjust criticism?" she asked, weighing her mother's comment.

"Honey, Kyle doesn't live inside a box. Since he brought Leanne to town, let him deal with the fallout from her visit."

Sadie placed her chin on Jeanette's knee. "It's wrong for people to accuse him of disrespecting me when I left him for another man over two years ago."

"That's the criticizers' problem, not yours. Unlike you, I'm interested in seeing how he manages this self-created trouble." She gingerly gripped Sadie's chin in her fingers. "Our families have seen enough drama to last us a lifetime. Rumors never go away. Don't feed the fire."

Sadie rose, wrapping her arms around her mother. "This is what I missed out on in Burgundy. Wise counsel from a woman who loves me." She kissed Jeanette's cheek, then smiled into her eyes. "I hear you, Mom. I'm listening to every word."

"Then discuss this situation with Kyle and Sarah. He's home. I heard him whistling before you knocked."

"I will feel better after clearing the air with him and Miss Sarah. I'll pop right over." Moving fast, she stopped in the doorway. "I love you so much. Thank you for loving me."

"Thank you for coming home where you belong. Go on next door. I'm sure they'll uphold my advice."

The pleasure on her mother's face delighted Sadie. They were a family again.

Kicking a stone across the lawn, she hurried onto the Franklins' porch. The sun's blazing rays brightened the afternoon and warmed her cheeks. Her spirits lifting, Sadie rang the doorbell, smiling.

Sarah opened the door wearing an apron. Her lips curved into a welcoming grin.

"Hello, Miss Sarah. I stopped by to discuss a problem. Is Kyle downstairs?"

"Come in." Sarah moved farther into the hallway. "He hides out in his bedroom on Sundays."

Sadie stepped into the house, closing the door behind her. "Good. First, I'd rather speak to you alone."

"Let's talk in the den," said Sarah. Leading the way to the room, she sat on the sofa. Kindness filled the eyes studying Sadie. Still grinning, Sarah patted the cushion beside her. After a quick glance at the doorway, Sadie sat next to her.

"Well, this discussion sounds serious. I hope everything is okay."

Sadie tried to smile, but suddenly remembered how she'd distanced herself from the lady who had never stopped loving her. Shaking her head, she scooted closer. "I'm praying. And God always answers prayers. Miss Sarah, I just finished talking to Mom about the rumors."

Sarah's eyes narrowed slightly. "And as you well know, Kyle doesn't bother with gossip, dear."

"But people are maligning his character. And it's all my fault."

Sarah grasped Sadie's hand in hers. "Gossipers do point fingers. It goes with the territory. But it's their problem, not yours."

Sadie looked down, then glanced up, smiling. "Mom said the same thing. But, I hate it when people reach the wrong conclusion."

Laugh lines crinkled around Sarah's eyes. "They usually do. And we both know that Kyle won't play ball with them. Let them have their heyday. The truth will reveal itself in the end."

"Although it's none of their business, I'll confess for Kyle. I owe him that much. Probably a lot more."

"You owe him love and respect, and you give him both. My son doesn't answer critics, Sadie. Don't do it on his behalf." Sarah smoothed the hair away from Sadie's face. "This issue must be handled by him. It's a rite of passage he has to meet." A light danced in her dark-brown eyes. "Now go upstairs and talk to Kyle."

Sadie headed for the door, then swung around and hugged Sarah, who was walking out of the room behind her. Resting her head on Sarah's shoulder, Sadie slowly pulled away.

"Miss Sarah, thank you for loving me even though I hurt your son terribly."

"I forgave you the moment Kyle told us you broke off the engagement. But remember this: Guard the entrance into your private life. Now, talk to Kyle."

Smiling broadly, Sarah swooshed Sadie upstairs.

Nostalgia overtook Sadie on the landing. She recalled many years of standing in that exact spot. But never wondering if Kyle wanted to see her. Although rekindling their relationship wasn't easy, patience preceded every unbreakable bond. Sighing, she announced her presence by beating the old rat-a-tat on various door panels.

"Sadie?" Kyle sounded surprised.

Holding her breath, she waited for the door to open, stepping back when movement sounded inside the room. Slightly cracking the door, Kyle stared at her.

Sadie beamed at him in spite of the slight. "You remembered my personal greeting!"

"It seems that we both did."

Feeling moisture seep into her eyes, she studied her shoes. "I loved the message this morning. They always take me through the week. May I come inside so we can talk?"

Kyle opened the door wider, then returned to the loveseat, removing the Bible and writing pad to the end table. Refusing to speak, he stared at her while massaging the bridge of his nose.

"Whenever you're ready," he said.

"Ooh, where to begin." She closed her eyes, then opened them quickly. "Kyle ... some people think you slighted me by bringing Leanne to town. I want to set the record straight."

"My friends won't pass judgment, so forget it."

Sadie grabbed hold of his thumb. "You're not a teenager daring adults to confront you, Kyle. Projecting the right image matters now."

"As it did in my teens. But I understand your concern." He turned her hand over in his palm. "I knew Leanne's visit might cause folks to wonder about us. But *I* needed her to come."

An invisible lump lodged itself in Sadie's throat. *He needed Leanne to come?*

"I won't hand-feed the rumor mill. And neither will you."

Sadie ran fingers through her hair. "Even if they're confused about our relationship?"

"Aren't we all? Please humor me, Sadie. Let it go."

"I won't reveal the entire story. Just enough to exonerate you."

"Really?" he asked.

The remark sounded sarcastic to Sadie, but compassion filled his eyes. Kyle was putting her reputation before his pride. It made her want to place him before herself.

"What will you say?" he continued when she didn't answer. "That even though Lincoln abused you, you chose him over me? Willingly staying with him for two years, refusing to come home during breaks and over the summer. And only returned to Shiatown after he brought another woman to your home."

A chill ran through Sadie's body. Did Kyle just tick off his own doubts? The reasons stopping him from letting her back into his life? He still didn't trust her or her motives.

"How far will you go? The tiniest crack in the door will create a landslide. No one deserves insight into matters that don't involve them."

Sadie laid her face on the armrest, covering her head with her arms. No tears rolled down her cheeks. Kyle didn't hate her. He despised the situation handed to him.

We—will—get—over—it—in—time. I'm certain God has a purpose and plan that can't be denied. Kyle admitted to loving me. Now he must learn to trust me.

Sadie calmed herself down when she heard pages rustling. Kyle resumed his Bible reading without asking her to leave. Perhaps having her around wasn't such a hardship for him after all. Sitting upright, she gazed at the man now staring at her. "Kyle, how do we move forward? What's next for us?"

"We both know that experiencing life one day at a time is the only way to live."

Her mind worked overtime, thinking of ways to make him talk about their future. Together. "Kyle, we've seen each other every day since September, and familiarity didn't bring contempt," she said, wondering how he would reply.

"Just like absence failed to make the heart grow fonder." He tilted her chin up when she lowered her eyes. "I don't want to injure you. Not ever. Do us both a favor, Sadie. Let it go."

She fought to keep her mouth from hanging open. Was he for real? Did he expect her to thumb her nose at God for the second time? Surely he didn't. "You mean just forget how much I love you? We were made to be together. You expect me to just walk away from what I know to be true?"

The wall came up even before he physically distanced himself from her. Kyle still expected her to explain behavior she might never be able to comprehend herself.

"Sadie, no more going around in circles. If God said it, He will bring it to pass." He ran a finger down her nose. "Consider Shiatown as the world. Enjoy it."

Her eyebrows rose. "Date other people? Won't that widen the gap even more?"

"If it does, we'll have the answer to our dilemma."

"But dating other men implies I have reservations concerning us. And I don't. I know where I belong." She felt as if her heart was breaking into tiny pieces. "If dating other women brings you home to me, have at it," she said. "But ... please. Don't make me wait too long. Okay?"

Laying his Bible on the end table, he stood, pulling up Sadie beside him. "Let's continue this discussion over a meal. The Main Street Diner?"

Anticipation relaxed her body. "It's always my first choice."

Sadie preceded Kyle out the room. Halfway down the stairs, she smiled up at him. "Is this our first date?"

* * *

On Thanksgiving Eve, Matt led the congregation around the church grounds in a long procession. The complex resembled a painting Sadie once saw in a Tulsa museum. Glittering lights illuminated each building, flashing multicolored crystals hung from the trees, and ground spike lights lit up the pathways.

After encircling the area, they marched into the sanctuary, touching pews as they circled the room. Then the group proceeded through the hallways, making a stop in each lobby, until leaving the building through the learning center's exit.

The prayer vigil culminated in the square, where Kyle stood in the center of the circle Matt formed. Calling Sarah to his side, he hugged her and kissed her cheek, then requested Minister and Mrs. Dawkins and Matt and Dee to join them. After that, all the elders and deacons stood in the circle with them.

"Our thanks to everyone attending the prayer fellowship," said Kyle. "Praying our way into Thanksgiving became a new tradition today. Let's spend the evening thanking Jesus for saving us from God's wrath. May our Father bless our lives for His glory."

"Pastor Kyle, the church and grounds are beautiful. Who did the decorations?" asked a man standing at the back of the crowd.

"Many people and businesses contributed to our blessing. On Sunday, we'll provide a benefactors list. Then the congregation can show its gratitude by blessing them back. Enjoy your Thanksgiving."

A buzz of conversations filtered throughout the crowd as everyone said goodbye. The prayer vigil marked the first time church members prayed together outside the building. Sadie liked the new tradition. Having a thankful spirit was the best way to kick off the holiday season. People who didn't attend Kingdom Life also joined them in prayer. Anyone using the facilities received a personal invitation to the Thanksgiving celebration.

One of the first people to leave, Sadie waved goodbye to her mother before following Sarah into her house. Earlier in the week, the three restaurant workers begged off cooking dinner tomorrow. The duty naturally fell on Sadie's and Sarah's shoulders. Not shirking their duties, Jeanette, Amy, and Cindy promised to prepare a scrumptious feast for Christmas at the Cummings's house.

Humming just like her son, Sarah busied herself about the kitchen, baking two huge pans of cornbread from scratch. Off and on, Sadie rambled about past holiday celebrations. The Cummingses and Franklins always celebrated major holidays together.

Happily dicing up a vegetable mixture to season the food, she stored it inside the refrigerator. They baked cakes and pies, giggling like school children. As always, the women worked well together, and the upcoming Christmas event topped the discussion.

While they slaved in the kitchen, Kyle hid inside the office, pretending to work at home. But Sadie knew watching the sports channel occupied the majority of his time. Laughing to herself, she spun around when he spoke to them from the doorway.

"I'm glad you're winding down." Kyle eyed the cakes waiting to be frosted. He winked at Sadie. "Mother, may I borrow your helper for an hour?"

Sarah glanced at Sadie. "If she wants to be borrowed. Is everything okay?"

"It will be." He chuckled when Sadie stared at him with one eye closed. "I need your assistance *again*. Les Sanderson called. Felecia's in labor. Her parents were already driving up from Lawton. We need to entertain three children until they arrive."

"Children ... thank God for Brian. Because of him, I feel comfortable around small children."

"I'll take over the four and six-year-old if you agree to help out. You can tackle the baby. Relax," he said when Sadie caught a thumbnail between her teeth. "She's fourteen months. You can handle her."

"So says you." Sadie washed her hands at the sink. Untying her apron, she covered up the cake plates. "Miss Sarah, the cakes will be cool enough to frost when I get back. Should I prepare both salads tonight?"

Sarah nodded. "I'll fix the trifle and cranberry sauce as well."

Sadie brushed past Kyle. "Come on, Pastor. A meal at Bon Appetit and games afterwards should suffice until their grandparents arrive."

* * *

At the restaurant, Kyle ordered the meal while Sadie entertained the children. After eating, they played endless games until the four-year-old girl spotted their grandparents outside the game center. The children squealed with excitement then ran to the door, hugging the middle-aged couple around the legs. Sadie and Kyle listened to the latest news concerning Felicia while he and the grandmother fastened the children into their car seats.

"Our deed is done. And quickly," said Sadie, waving goodbye.

She studied Kyle when he nodded his head instead of agreeing with her; she was unable to decipher his expression. It held the same look he'd always worn whenever Pastor Franklin denied him some treat he wanted when he was younger. Longing. Almost sadness.

She secretly observed him as he started the car and drove off the parking lot. But instead of going home, they visited a church member scheduled for surgery the next morning. Holding the patient's hand, Kyle prayed for healing. And Sadie hugged the man who thanked God for healing him before it happened. That was the life ordained for her. Ministry work with Kyle. Although the board and volunteers visited parishioners more than he did, he knew the circumstances affecting each member who attended the church.

Sadie glanced at him when he turned into the driveway. He wore the same pensive expression from earlier in the parking lot. And then she understood.

Kyle won't open up to me because I'm the problem.

Chapter Seventeen

On Thanksgiving Day, Sadie watched her sister open the door before the bell rang. Backing up, Amy ushered their brother and his future family inside the house.

"Finally, Roland. What took you guys so long?" Amy rolled her eyes at him, then her gaze settled on Brian. "Hey, little man." She scooped the child into her arms, hugging him tightly against her chest.

"Hi, Auntie Amy," Brian said, giggling into his hands.

Sadie's eyebrows rose. "Auntie Amy? He never calls me Auntie Sadie."

She followed the others into the living room where Kyle watched them from the recliner; amusement was etched into his tired features. Just like Pastor Franklin had, the man kept up an extraordinary pace. However, maybe because of it, his father died an early death.

Church members hounded Kyle all the time. Any person professing faith in God should rely on Him and not on other people. God called every Christian into ministry, but most individuals needed help themselves. *"Like you,"* a soft voice intruded on her thoughts. Properly chastised, Sadie tuned in to the conversation buzzing around her.

"Are you listening, Sadie?" asked Amy. "Why do folks raise topics without participating in the discussion?"

Chastened for the second time within thirty seconds, Sadie sat on the loveseat with her hands folded on her lap. "Sorry. Please, go on."

Her sister blinked rapidly at her, grinning. "Little children form habits quickly. I want him engrained in calling me Auntie before the wedding. Encourage him to call you Auntie Sadie. He loves it." Amy's eyes popped opened as Brian blew spit bubbles on her cheek. Laughing, she let him down, wiping her face with her hand. "He christened me." Stepping into the hallway, she grabbed her coat from the tree stand. "Come on, nephew, we're out of here."

Pulling up the zipper on her coat, she glanced at Cindy. "Call on the home phone if you need us. We're putting together a two-hundred-piece jigsaw puzzle in the guest bedroom. I'm working on his problem-solving skills."

"Wait a minute. Is my son involved in a school project?"

Amy nodded. "I'm teaching him how to coordinate his thoughts and actions. Having my own nephew kept me from borrowing a stranger."

"Your sister knows how to make her life easier," Cindy told Roland. "She can offer Sadie and me pointers."

Roland laughed. "Being a master puzzle solver taught her to simplify her days. May Brian follow in her footsteps." He hesitated, gazing at Sadie. "What's wrong, sis?" Roland asked as Amy and Brian left the house.

Sadie sighed to herself, noticing that Kyle stared at her through half-closed eyes. The man hadn't spoken directly to her all day. Working in the kitchen since morning, she'd only grabbed snippets of his lively debates with Amy.

A little consistency from you would improve my disposition, mister. Yesterday, you wanted my help. Today, you refuse to speak. Blowing hot and cold every day has got to stop.

She sighed out loud. "I love working puzzles. Too bad they don't help *me* coordinate my thoughts and actions."

Cindy gasped. "Don't ever say that again."

"Don't even think it," said Roland.

He sat beside Sadie on the loveseat, wrapping his arm around Cindy when she sat on his lap. "Don't underrate what you do, Sadie. Without prior experience, you started the learning center and dinner theater in one week. You're writing your first book. And you coordinated the Christmas decorations and gifts for foster children on Christmas Eve. What about the author reads? None of those programs materialized out of thin air. They are around because you breathed life into all of them."

"While working at the bookstore," Cindy added. "Stop working around the clock, lady. You're only one person. You can't tutor students morning and evening, plus work at the bookstore in the afternoon, and all the other not-so-little things you keep taking up. Stop it. Live like a normal person for a change."

Sadie heard their message loud and clear. She was exhausted, cranky, and about to plunge into a pity party. Up until early morning writing her book, she had only slept two hours before knocking on Sarah's door at nine. She smiled at the man who always encouraged her and the wonderful friend he was marrying. Sadie felt better now. At least two somebodies appreciated her efforts. She sought the eyes of the man who failed to chime in, then looked away.

"Thanks, you two," said Sadie, scooting forward. "I'm tired, but the whole process has truly blessed me. I meet new people every day."

"Then admit doing puzzles paid off in spades for both of my sisters."

A broad smile spread across her face. "I do. Group hug." Giggling, she wrapped her arms around her brother and Cindy.

* * *

An hour later, the doorbell sounded while Jeanette and Sarah placed warming trays on the buffet in the dining room. Then Sadie, carrying in the golden-brown turkey, set the platter on the center doily just as Amy and Brian walked into the house.

The group gathered around the table, holdings hands, but all eyes were on Sarah's sad face. This was her first Thanksgiving without William by her side after thirty-five years of holiday celebrations. Sadie's heart melted when her mother brushed her cheek against Sarah's shoulder. Long-term friendships provided comfort throughout a lifetime. Especially after burying a spouse. Thank God, He surrounded Sarah with family and friends.

Kyle winked at his mother before bowing his head. "Let's pray," he said, closing his eyes.

Once he finished praying, Sarah wiped a finger across both eyelids. "God is faithful. Each day, He gives us multiple blessings on top of salvation. Before eating dinner, let's tell one another what we're most thankful for this year."

"That's easy for me," said Jeanette. "Jesus brought my baby home where she belongs. He strengthened my friend through a tremendous loss and established her son at the church his parents founded together." She smiled at Roland. Standing beside Cindy, he held Brian in his arms. "My son met his soul mate. Her son adores him. And my youngest daughter lives a well-rounded life. What more could a mother want?"

Sadie was surprised when Roland spoke up next. He seldom volunteered himself without being asked.

"The pieces fell together this year. I'm celebrating Thanksgiving Day with my fiancée and future son. Plus, my family and friends will celebrate this holiday season with me. As always, Jesus hit a grand slam."

Her sister's sniffles caught Sadie's attention. For the first time since Sadie had come home, tears shone in the youthful eyes. The bubbly young woman never stayed thwarted longer than a moment.

"Ahem," said Amy, smiling at her sister. "My outlook on life improved when you came home, Sadie. Jesus shines through you to me. Don't hide away from everyone. God loves you."

A hush fell across the quiet room. No one spoke, including Sadie. How could she? Her sister had just singlehandedly released her from a bondage she'd never recognized. In a less-threatening takeover of her will, Kyle was molding her into his version of what her life should look like.

"Um, sorry to take so long; I'll end fast," said Amy. "Roland found Cindy and Brian. My mom's ecstatic, and Miss Sarah and Kyle are together again. Life is good."

Reaching behind her to the buffet table, Cindy snatched up a napkin, then gently blotted Amy's face. Amy instantly hugged her neck when she finished, then said, "I love you." The surprise in Cindy's eyes amazed Sadie. Kind people seldom expected to receive kindness in return for their own thoughtfulness.

"I'll go next," said Cindy. "My grandmother gladly took me in when my parents died. And then, I met the man who treated me like a sister before she passed away." She kissed Brian's cheek when he patted her face. "Brian and I love you, Kyle. God sent you fifteen hundred miles to bring us to Oklahoma. Then, He brought the love of my life across the country to meet us before we came."

She brushed Roland's cheek with her fingertips. "The Lewis family is engaged to a wonderful man. My fiancé taught his last boxing lesson last week." She looked at Jeanette. "No more head punches, Mom." Then she gazed at the boy in Roland's arm. "Tell us what you're happy about, Boo."

Brian stuck a finger into his mouth as if deep in thought. "Uh, my puzzle." The child opened his hands wide. "It's big!"

Sadie's heart tugged when a light gleamed in Kyle's eyes. He'd always loved family gatherings, and he was meant to have a large one of his own. In fact, he wanted six children just like his father had hoped to raise. He eyed his mother when she laughed. The dutiful son wanted to see Sarah happy.

Sadie smiled when Sarah winked at Kyle. What was his mother thinking?

"I'll go before Sadie and Kyle," she said. "This is a brand-new season in many ways. William is at home with the Lord. Kyle and Sadie moved back to Shiatown in the same month. And, Cindy found a good man to marry and the perfect father for her son." Laying her hands on the chair, she took a deep breath. Her eyes made contact with each person as she spoke. "This year, Jeanette, Amy, and I received an abundant answer to consistent prayers. God is good. Jesus is the gift that gives."

Even though Sadie closed her eyes after Sarah finished speaking, she sensed everyone was watching her. How like Kyle to make her go first. But, she wanted to share what the day meant to her. It meant a lot. She pointed to the food-laden buffet table. "Thank God for warming trays." Sadie laughed, and everyone joined in the laughter.

"Last Thanksgiving, I stayed in bed all day with my head buried beneath the covers. I came up for air when Mom called, wishing me a happy Thanksgiving. Sometime during the night, I heated a can of soup in a teapot, then went back to bed."

She licked her lips. "Yesterday, Miss Sarah and I baked desserts, fixed salads, and did food preparation for our meal today. This morning, I knocked on her door at nine ready to cook." Tears filled her eyes. "Only Jesus can accomplish the impossible. I thank God for loving me. And for surrounding me with people who love me and accept my love in return."

All eyes went to the man standing at the head seat. Sadie failed to discern his expression. He was no longer the friendly boy next door. Kyle had become a complicated man.

And although he spoke to everyone, his eyes never left her face. "I'm thankful the Holy Spirit is willing to direct our steps. It takes spiritual maturity to follow where He leads. I'm surrounded by the people I love. Thank you for loving me back." He sat down as a line formed at the buffet table.

Sadie whispered in Jeanette's ear. "That includes me."

"Words are meaningless without the actions to support them." With a pointed look at her oldest daughter, she stepped into line behind Sarah.

With her plate overflowing with food, Sadie ate her first Thanksgiving dinner in two years. She discovered she was half-starved, even though she'd snacked on food since morning. Every morsel tasted delicious. And she eagerly listened as Amy told them humorous tales from college.

No one left the table when the meal was over. Too full to eat dessert, they remained seated while Cindy relayed tales about the diner crowd. After that, amusing stories poured forth from every direction until Kyle excused himself to answer the house phone.

Sadie's heart plummeted when he came back to the dining room but stood in the doorway, studying Sarah. He spoke after he caught her attention. "Mother, there's a domestic disturbance brewing at the Sinclair home. I'll head over." He paused when Sadie scooted back her chair and then stood up, pushing her seat under the table. "Where are you going?" he asked when she headed toward him.

She paused in midstep, then planted her foot on the floor. "With you."

"Why do you want to go?" Kyle asked, moving closer.

That was a silly question. Why did he make an ordeal out of every little thing? "To help you, if needed. Why else would I tag along?"

Kyle looked at Jeanette. But the quiet woman sipped a glass of water, observing their interaction. He studied Sadie again. "Look, time is crucial. Please, sit down." He glanced at the buffet table. "Have some dessert."

"Don't placate me." Sadie hoped the anger she felt escaped everyone's notice. "Why did she call you and not the police? Her husband is a volatile man."

Kyle slid on his jacket while backing toward the door. "She's hoping it'll die out without bringing in the authorities."

Sadie reached out to him before he reached the doorway. "Don't go. Or at least let me go with you for support."

He pointed to the dessert table again. "Relax. I'll be back in a jiffy."

Cindy approached them at the door. "I agree that Sadie isn't the proper backup, but don't go alone. Call the police."

"OK, I won't go alone. Will you ride over with me, man?" he asked Roland. Kyle glanced from his mother to Sadie then back to his friend when he nodded. "I'll wait for you in the car," he said before leaving the room.

Roland's eyes met Jeanette's after standing. "This will be a quick trip," he told her. Tousling Brian's hair on the way to door, he kissed Cindy's parted lips when he reached her.

Cindy tugged his sleeve. "The police should be called." Her eyes full of tears, she looked questioningly at Jeanette.

Turning her face toward his, Roland brushed his thumb across her lips. "We'll be back soon." He left the house after waving goodbye to Brian.

Jeanette jumped to her feet, smiling at Cindy, who still stood beside Sadie. "They've been best friends for many years. Roland was going to go with him even before Kyle asked him. The asking was a formality for the rest of us."

Sarah joined her friend at the dining room door. "They're friends for life. Always there for one another. I trust the God who woke us up this morning to lie our heads down in peace tonight."

"Remember, little ears are listening. I don't want him to think anything is wrong," said Jeannette, nodding at Brian. "Come on, Brian. It's prayer time. We're going into the den to pray for a family named Sinclair."

Glancing over her shoulder at the younger women, Sarah followed behind her friend. "Cheer up, ladies. Father knows how to bring our men home safe from war."

Once Brian ran on ahead as if playing a game, Amy looped her hands through Sadie's and Cindy's arms. "It'll be fine," she said, propelling them into the den.

Chapter Eighteen

Kyle filled Roland in on the scenario the moment he entered the car. After that, he wondered about Sadie's strong reaction to his going. It was the first time; she'd failed to back down right away when he asked her to listen to reason. Then he thought about the Sinclair family's home life. They lived in a rural area outside of town. Changing lanes, he turned onto the highway, then set a steady pace.

A vibrating sound intruded into their thoughts moments later. Retrieving his cell phone, Roland read the text message. Grinning, he pushed the cell phone back into his pocket then glanced at Kyle.

"Cindy loves us despite our stubbornness."

"Glad she sent the message. It feels good knowing that you're loved and appreciated."

"I'm sure Sadie feels the same way," said Roland. "Stop stringing my sister along. Make a clean break if you don't want to marry her."

Kyle turned the music down low. "I told Sadie from the beginning I won't make hasty decisions concerning my future. And neither should she."

Roland snorted. "Asking her to date other men is nonsense. How could she after saying she loves you?"

"She did before," said Kyle, glancing at him.

Roland let out a deep breath. "Psychological trauma causes individuals to behave irrationally. Stop looking for loopholes. Leave Sadie alone if you don't want a personal relationship with her."

"Sadie went from me to Lincoln, now she wants to come back to me. Isn't it reasonable to want her to test the waters?"

"No. Why would she date other men when she's in love with you? If she did start dating, you could dismiss her claims that she loved you. Besides, you won't follow suit."

Kyle gripped the steering wheel tighter. "Leanne?"

"A nice lady, but not the woman for you, which is why you broke off communications with her once you moved back to Shiatown. My sister came home, man."

"After letting that slime touch her for two years." His body involuntarily shuddered. Grimacing, he glanced at his friend. Roland's cheek pulsated as he fought to control his temper.

"Traumatic stress is the culprit. Some people suffer from the affliction every day of their lives without detection," he finally said.

"How many kick their fiancés to the curb for an unsavory partner?"

"Probably more people than can be counted. The truth won't change to validate your behavior. Did you forget that psychological trauma can instantly alter normal behavior patterns?" Roland asked.

"So did the trauma of Lincoln calling it quits remind her that people in Shiatown loved her?"

"Her choices were less than rational, until deciding to come home. Now we know that shock can go undetected while ruining lives. Look, she revealed the whole story over two months ago. Forgive her instead of justifying your actions."

"You forgave Sasha without taking her back."

Roland chuckled. "How do you justify comparing a barracuda to a guppy?"

"Well, yeah. The premise is valid, though. Forgiving her doesn't mean I want her in my personal life."

"Admit you see Lincoln whenever you look at Sadie. I know I would," Roland said, looking straight ahead.

Kyle felt his shoulder muscles tighten before he responded. "I actually understand those initial mistakes after the abuse. But for two years?"

Roland cocked his head to the side as one eyebrow rose. "Sadie didn't recover quickly enough for you?"

Glowering at the man who never relented, Kyle exited the highway, lowering his speed on the bumpy road.

"It happens in many abuse cases," Roland continued. "Why should you make Sadie the one exception? After losing you, she strangely figured everything would be okay if he married her."

"Sadie didn't lose me, Roland. She threw me away."

"Because she thought you would leave her. If she thinks it's real, then it is. Her fragile mind failed to discern reality."

"Two long years, man," said Kyle, glancing at him. "And all the while the people around her thought she was fine."

"Some victims battle distress syndromes their entire life. Sadie thought you would leave her. She would've felt defeated if Lincoln had deserted her too. Her thinking was faulty but real to her."

"I don't blame Sadie for what happened to her. I don't even blame her for sending me packing. I'm having difficulty with the extended time frame after the fact."

"Suffering trauma at home in her formative years, plus watching her father get shot to death, probably aggravated the problem. It hindered the healing process."

"She's been through a lot," Kyle admitted. But she went two years without anyone knowing she was in serious trouble. She avoided the people who would've detected it. And that concerned him.

"I get it, man," said Roland. "You want guarantees that Sadie is a stable person. No one can see beyond the present moment. Look at her now."

"But will it last?" asked Kyle, hoping that it would.

"Trust me. It will." Roland grinned at him. "I understand how you feel about Lincoln, though. Looking at Brian every day reminds me Cindy had a physical relationship before meeting me."

Kyle laughed so hard the car almost veered into a ditch. "Those convictions might pass the morality test if I didn't know your lifestyle before you met her."

Roland joined in the laughter. "Don't we all desire better conduct from our loved ones?" His grin vanished just as quickly as it had come. He drummed two fingers on the dashboard. "Sadie is mending daily. Don't hinder her progress, Kyle. Don't keep stringing her along and then leave the family to pick up the pieces if she shatters."

The two men locked gazes until Kyle remembered he was driving. Of course his friend was right. Sadie had developed into an impressive lady. For the first time in her life, she seemed to feel secure inside and out. How protected would she feel if he refused to marry her in the end? Stronger than she'd ever been, Sadie could weather any storm, but rejection from him would wound her deeply. She'd already experienced enough turmoil to last a lifetime.

Kyle needed to move on if he wasn't going to marry her. The problem was his inability to completely let go if he wasn't. Nevertheless, he refused to embrace a woman he didn't entirely trust. Forget the "date other people" garbage. Neither of them would date anyone else unless the other one walked away for good. He failed to see why he'd made the suggestion only to then invite her to dinner on a whim last Sunday. It seemed that he and Sadie were stuck with each other for the foreseeable future.

Kyle pulled into the trailer park, stopping the car in front of the last single-wide trailer on the right. Dogs in the neighbor's yard began barking once the car doors swung open. Exiting the vehicle, the men stepped over toys strewn across the yard. A faint humming noise vibrated in the distance.

"Sinclair's watching us from the window," said Roland, knocking on the door.

* * *

Prayers in the Franklin home continued inside the den. Sadie sprawled in a recliner with her eyes closed, marveling that her mind was free from anxiety. Her thoughts had shifted since the men had left the house. In fact, Sarah's excellent suggestion had helped Sadie change focus. Now she wanted to put God first after hearing why everyone else was thankful.

She'd unknowingly lived for other people in the past. Earlier, Jeanette had told her, "Words are meaningless without the actions to support them." Until that moment, Sadie breathed, ate, thought, and dreamed Kyle Franklin. It would be rewarding to live for God for a change. She surveyed the room while praying quietly.

Brain lay napping on a pallet, clutching Floppy, a stuffed lamb he'd named after a Saturday morning puppet show on TV. Amy stretched out on the floor with her forehead on her arm. Cindy stared out the window, and Jeanette and Sarah sat next to one another on the sofa, praying audibly.

The duty-bound women had prayed for three hours nonstop. Nothing mattered more than praying for the Sinclair family's welfare. Every person deserved to live in a violence-free environment. No one could achieve their fullest potential within a battle zone. Plus, the women prayed for their men to return home safely.

The telephone rang just as the clock on the shelf chimed six. Jumping up, Amy quickly answered the call.

"Hello? Okay, Kyle, I'll put the phone on speaker."

Sadie set up straight, thanking God they'd called.

"Mother, Miss Jeanette, we're on our way home."

Sarah grinned. "Thank God. And all is well?"

"Absolutely. The Mrs. secretly called the police the moment we arrived. She was battered, as we'd suspected. Sinclair signed himself into a detox center after a lengthy discussion."

"He agreed to treatment?" asked Jeanette.

"The threat of going to jail made opting for medical treatment an easy choice," said Roland. "His wife refused to remain with him and was ready to press charges if necessary. Once he agreed to treatment, she placed the children into the already-packed car and drove off to her parents' home in Kansas."

Sadie brushed her fingers across her lips. What if their mother had left their father? Leaving Shiatown after the first incident had occurred? Where could she have gone? As an orphan, her father's family provided the only support system her mother had known.

"And Mr. Sinclair?" asked Sadie when no one else asked the question.

"The man is broken. His brothers followed the police to the rehab center. Roland and I visited with Sinclair after they assigned him to a room."

"How many children do they have?" asked Cindy.

"Four under ten. We just turned into the driveway," said Kyle, ending the call.

Amy sprinted to the door with a huge grin plastered on her face. She kissed their cheeks when they entered the house, then flopped into a chair by the window.

"How about that teamwork? You work, and we pray. I like those dynamics."

Everyone talking at once woke up Brian, who sat up rubbing his eyes. Seeing Roland and Cindy sitting together on the loveseat, the drowsy child stumbled across the floor, crawling onto her lap. He lay his head on Cindy's chest and his feet on Roland's thigh, sucking his thumb.

Sadie stopped herself from snapping a picture with her phone's camera. Why bother? The touching scene had already etched itself in her memory.

Sarah turned away from the happy family-to-be. "Kyle, please finish the story."

"In the end, the wife's smart thinking smoothed the path considerably. Something or other set him off last night, and she packed the trunk while he slept it off."

Roland chuckled. "Sometimes drunken stupors pay off for the other people involved. Since Pastor Franklin had reasoned with her husband in the past, she decided to give your son a shot with her husband long enough to make a getaway."

"Why did she call at all if she was leaving?" Amy scooted to the edge of her chair, holding her arms out to Brian.

Cindy set her son on his feet. "He might've harmed her if she'd tried to leave him."

"She planned to use me for cover," said Kyle. "Sneaking off with the children while he talked to me."

Sadie digested the alarming news. Mrs. Sinclair willingly placed Kyle in danger. Was that the reality of making house visits for ministers today?

Shocked, Sarah turned to Jeanette. "How selfish is that? The woman planned to leave my son with an irate husband while she ran off with the children. I'm glad she switched strategies."

"Me too," said Kyle. "She said *something* prompted her to call the police and his family the second we drove up. The rest is history."

"And a lesson well learned," said Roland. "While driving home, Kyle and I reached an agreement, Miss Sarah. On domestic issues, our pastor will either call the police to meet him there or decline the visit if the caller refuses to involve the police. So it's up to the caller whether he comes."

Concern left Sarah's face in a hurry. "God not only hears our prayers, He answers them. Sometimes, even before we pray."

"And sometimes, He takes forever to do it," Amy said, prompting a frown from Jeanette. "Well, He does."

Forgetting her problems with Kyle, Sadie silently thanked God for His goodness. No one lost their life or was critically injured during the disturbance. The Sinclair family would receive protection in Kansas from an unbalanced man. And hopefully, he would put effort into his own rehabilitation. Although separated, the Sinclair family was in a better place than they were before today. A miracle took place for Roland and Kyle. God-given strength surpassed anything humans could supply. She closed her eyes as warmth invaded her body.

I'm learning, Lord. It seems like a slow process, but I'm steadily growing up.

Then Cindy instructed Brian to find a toy to play with while Amy set up a board game she'd brought from home. Sadie watched as the child rummaged through a large tote bag. All eyes were on Brian except for Kyle's. He studied Sadie with half-closed eyes. And she recognized the expression in an instant. He was about to make a big decision that included her. Kyle hadn't mentioned Leanne to Sadie since taking her to the airport. But her presence lay heavily between them.

Time to go home.

Passing by the sofa, Sadie touched Jeanette's shoulder, strolled into the hallway, grabbed her wrap off the tree stand, then stood in the doorway, zipping up her coat. "I enjoyed myself, Miss Sarah. Thank you for a delightful two days of cooking and fun. Every detail exceeded my expectations." Sadie smiled when Jeanette winked at her. "I may come back later." Then she left the house after wriggling her fingers at Brian.

At home, Sadie accepted that bondage was stifling whatever form it took. It didn't matter who the captor was. And freedom from her mistakes made victory that much sweeter. No more crawling behind Kyle. If he wanted her, he knew where to find her. From now on, Sadie must manage her life better—even if it meant living without him.

In the downstairs powder room, she gazed at her reflection in the mirror. Smiling, she wrapped her arms around her body. "I love you, Sadie Mae. You're not a bad person after all."

And what better way to thank God than to work on the book He gave me.

Sadie raced up the steps with editing her manuscript uppermost in her mind. Sitting at the paper-scattered desk, she powered up the laptop, ticking off her to-do list. Her plate overflowed with multiple projects. It was surprising she'd managed time to write at all. Cindy and Roland were right. Sleep deprivation could only last so long.

In Burgundy, she'd often lain awake at night thinking of ways to get her life back. At home in Shiatown, she was consistently pounding out her story each night until just before daybreak. Without her noticing, the two part-time jobs had developed into a full-time career, overlapping one another. Yet working at the bookstore impacted her relationship with local writers and creative types. Everywhere creative people came out of the woodwork, and Sadie found she fit right in.

Her one-act play, *Salon Duty,* would premiere on schedule the Saturday before Christmas. And a special performance on the Thursday and Friday before the opening served as a thank you to contributors of the Christmas fund.

Bert Simpson, the drama teacher at Shiatown University, had had to bow out of the project for personal reasons. And his assistant agreed to take over the vacant position. Although Bert had been a fantastic director, Art's brilliant approach with the cast and crew astounded everyone involved in the project. Swapping directors midstream might've created chaos, but the rehearsals proceeded without disruption. The original plan had called for Bert to direct the one-act play on weekday evenings and Saturday afternoons while Art and his team coached the girls on Wednesday nights and Saturday mornings. Instead, Art served double duty after Bert's departure.

Good thing her relationship with him improved after the initial rocky start. Sadie laughed at the memory she'd since forgotten.

Now she and Art got along famously, settling into an easygoing friendship. She laughed again, recalling their first meeting. Art had pulled Sadie into a tight embrace after Bert introduced them. Only Sadie recoiled, telling him not to touch her without being invited. Stung by her reaction, he stepped back and kept apologizing.

Thankfully, Bert continued talking as if nothing had happened with Sadie, and Art was quick to follow his lead. Then, in no time, they moved on to form an exceptional working relationship. Over the weeks that followed, Art totally redeemed himself in her eyes. A clear-cut creative type, it seemed he was intuitive as well as gifted.

He invited her out for a snack when they locked up the building after rehearsals a few weeks later. In fact, her new buddy revealed his perceptive nature while eating burgers and drinking tea. Then, he admitted his sister had been abused, and he'd seen her respond as Sadie had reacted when crowded by strangers. Smiling, he apologized if his enthusiasm to greet her unlocked old wounds. After that, he switched topics, leaving Sadie feeling she might be able to trust him.

Now, she rotated her shoulders, preparing to edit the manuscript's second draft, but her mind drifted to the group's study sessions. The whole team had bonded quickly, blossoming into an extended family unit. Sadie still received requests from other teens seeking to join the crew.

Thanks to Amy's great idea, Sadie scheduled the first of three pajama parties for New Year's Eve. A perfect setup when considering *Pajama Party: The Story* was the name of her book. The empty duplex next door to Cindy and Brian proved an ideal location. The all-nighters perfectly set the stage for rehearsals scheduled to begin in late February.

It got even better. At Dee's suggestion, a different staff member brought a healthy snack to each Saturday session. And it was Kate's idea to reserve a private dining room at The Main Street Diner for lunch on Christmas Eve for the girls and their parents. Afterward, the teens would help distribute Christmas presents to the children at the learning center. Sadie appreciated their help.

Another unexpected bonus, with long-reaching effects that benefitted the entire team, came to mind. The youths adored Amy. Always a positive role model, her practical tips especially aided the troubled teens in the group. And the girls were a riot. Talk about blowing hot and cold. Frequently, one of them got angry during friendly discussions or burst into tears over nothing. But Amy had already given Sadie insight into their strange behavior at Burger Barn. Puberty! In all its erratic glory.

Sadie glanced at the clock on the nightstand. It was six forty-five. She would head back next door at eight.

Chapter Nineteen

Absorbed in editing the draft, it took several minutes for the voices talking downstairs to filter into her thoughts. Sadie squinted her eyes at the clock.

It's ten. I had wanted to eat dessert at the Franklins' house.

Scooting her chair back, she rose to her feet, bending from side to side as Amy poked her head into the room.

"You demand *me* to knock on *your* door before opening it," Sadie said to her.

"Do as I say and not as I do." Amy laughed when Sadie hurled a pillow at her. She caught it in one hand, tossing it onto the bed.

"Come down to the kitchen. Mom brought leftovers home. Including your delicious pineapple coconut cake."

"Can't beat me to the kitchen," said Sadie, sailing past Amy with a burst of energy. But she practically fell down the steps from giggling so hard.

Gaining on her, Amy pushed Sadie in the hallway, knocking her into the wall. "I won!" Panting from the exertion, her sister stood inside the kitchen. Her eyes shone brightly in the artificial lighting.

Sadie winced in pain and limped into the room. "She still cheats, Mom." She plopped into a chair. "She gets away with far too much in this house."

Jeanette set the microwaved meal on the table. "That's a weekly accusation I hear from all three siblings regarding each one."

Hunger pains gained her attention as she ignored her smirking sister. Then her mouth salivated at the feast Jeanette placed on the table. Plunging right in, Sadie savored every bite. The food not only smelled delicious, but it tasted better than the freshly cooked meal. She gulped down the marvelous-tasting punch her mother served at the diner: ginger ale mixed with apple and cherry juice. Sadie glanced up, still chewing when Amy spoke to her.

Her sister heaped giblet gravy over the turkey and dressing on her plate. "You know how to make an exit, Sadie. Kyle followed after you but only made it to our porch. He leaned against the railing for ten minutes before returning home."

Refusing to take the bait, Sadie tucked away the news to muse over later.

"Aren't you going to respond?" asked Amy, clearly puzzled when Sadie kept eating.

"I did, by moving on." Tears surged into her eyes. "Living on the fringes of Kyle's life is worse than praying for Lincoln to marry me."

Amy's fork clattered to the plate. "Why, Sadie? I don't understand."

"It's simple. I didn't want to marry Lincoln. But I do want to make a life with Kyle. It's been my most fervent dream since realizing we could get married. Even in Burgundy, I still wanted him."

"Is Kyle misbehaving? I know he loves you, Sadie."

"A lot has happened behind the scenes," said Jeanette. "But don't blame Kyle for all of their problems. His struggle isn't Sadie's choosing Lincoln over him. He understands abuse victims can identify with their abuser."

"Then what's his problem, Mom? I'm confused. He should make things easy for Sadie"

Looking at Sadie's tear-filled eyes, Jeanette moved swiftly, hugging her daughter in her arms until Sadie returned the embrace. Then she addressed Amy.

"Sweetheart, life isn't a romance novel where you meet a man, fall in love, and live happily ever after. Real life comes with real problems. Not manufactured friction to entice readers to buy your book. Sadie enjoyed a support system she turned her back on, rationalizing Lincoln's mistreatment until the showdown two years later. That is Kyle's dilemma. He views her actions as unstable and wonders what caused them. And whether they will occur again if provided the same stimuli once they marry."

"Why can't they work harder to heal the relationship?" asked Amy. "He knows about the trauma. They'll always regret giving up on each other."

"This is life, plain and simple, complete with all the warts that go with it. I look over the years and still wonder if some of the decisions I made were the correct choices. The obvious mistakes are glaring, while the others, not so much."

Sadie considered the discussion floating around her. Maybe coming to terms with life with or without Kyle was an ongoing process. She lost the exhilaration she'd felt just hours ago.

"Kyle still loves me, Mom. He admits it. And—sometimes—I feel his love emanating toward me. I'm willing to wait on Kyle. But I refuse to run after him anymore."

A look of agreement dotted Jeanette's features. "Dealing with strong-willed individuals is a chore. But putting up with a complacent attitude is harder. Life is complicated, honey."

Amy kicked Sadie's leg underneath the table when Sadie stacked her glass on her plate. "Don't go, Sadie. Talk to us awhile. How about this for a change in topic? Our mom has a not-so-secret admirer."

"Who?" Sadie stared at the blushing lady. Evidently, her self-absorption had hidden the romance. Jeanette was an attractive woman, but Sadie never contemplated her mother remarrying. Her father was the best husband in the world without the paranoia episodes. No other man could top his performance, ever. "I'm shocked, even though I knew this might happen someday. Do I know him?"

"Professor Blackburn arrived at the university the year you left for college. His wife died of cancer twelve years ago." Her eyes shining brightly, Amy could barely contain her enjoyment. "The man can't take his eyes off Mom. Grandmother commented on it several times before moving away."

"Are you interested, Mom?" Sadie sighed. "That blush says yes. When can I meet him?"

"He eats breakfast at the diner every morning, and lunch practically every afternoon." Amy cut a large slice of cake, then licked her fingers. "Mmm, it's scrumptious. Mom, force her to bake pineapple coconut cakes for the diner."

"And anger Sam by invading his domain?" asked Sadie. "You know he does all the baking by himself. Forget it. Eat breakfast with me in the morning, Amy. Think he'll show up the day after Thanksgiving?"

Laughing, she winked at Sadie. "Of course. Mom told him she was working tomorrow."

"He asked for my work schedule for the week." Jeanette pushed her chair back from the table. "Do not spread this drivel to your brother."

"Too late. He knows you and the professor make goo-goo eyes over the counter." Amy held her side, laughing as Jeanette cleared off the table. "I'll tell him Sadie's vetting the professor at breakfast tomorrow."

"Amy—"

"Mom, let Roland check out your man. He might pass with high marks." Sadie pointed a finger at her mother "If not, we move on. Okay? Amy, point him out while we eat."

"No need to. Just look for the man making goo-goo eyes at Mom."

"Enough teasing, you two. Sadie, I transferred funds to your checking account yesterday," said Jeanette, scraping the plates before stacking them in the dishwasher.

"Yes! I'll pick up the car tomorrow after breakfast."

"Don't go without your brother," said Jeanette. "Roland wants to accompany you to the car dealership."

"Ah, Roland cares. I like that. Sure he can come with us. Right, Amy?" Her eyes widened as she decided which dessert to eat. "Cut me a slice of sweet potato pie, Amy. I never ate my favorite dessert in Burgundy. Just looking at it brings back happy family memories."

She took a bite, savoring the only pie she had ever eaten.

Mmm, this is good. I wonder why Kyle came by without talking to me. Maybe love alone won't satisfy him. Time will show him that I handle catastrophes differently these days.

* * *

Kyle walked around the vehicle parked in front of the Cummings house. Someone bought a new car and Sadie was the only person who needed transportation. It wasn't parked here when he came home last night. Now Dee and Kate were at the party with him. So were Cindy and Roland. Who did the girl next door hang out with these days?

He'd expected to see her at the learning center Friday, even though it was officially closed. Yesterday had been an eye-opener for him in numerous ways. Sadie hadn't come to the learning center for the first time since it opened. Leanne claimed she missed Shiatown and could hardly wait until her visit in February. And his mother accused him of approaching the job like a businessperson rather than a pastor. Up until then, Kyle had thought he was doing a credible job on every front.

His eyes drifted to Sadie's bedroom window. Would she eat breakfast with him this morning if he asked her nicely? Or did she choose to continue her life without him? On the spur of the moment, he rang the doorbell, then shoved his hands into his pockets.

Sadie opened the door looking more beautiful than ever. His gaze traveled the length of her body as she watched him. Her toffee skin glowed in the sunlight this morning. An aura of innocence surrounded her as never before. The back of his hand stroked her cheek before he could stop the action. "Eat breakfast with me this morning."

"Why should I?" she asked in a toneless voice.

Her reply surprised him. His words had sounded like a caress to his ears, but they had clearly failed to move Sadie. Did she intend for him to jump through hoops going forward? After eating dinner together Sunday, he'd thought the two of them were closer than ever since she'd come home. Then Thursday, she ran out of his house as if spending the holiday together hadn't mattered at all.

Kyle moved closer until he stood right in front of her. "I prefer to sit across the table from you while eating breakfast this morning," he admitted.

Sadie studied him without blinking for a long moment. Conflicting emotions flickered across her face. Her gaze went from studying his features to surveying her shoes. He wondered why she refused to look at him. The one action pushed them farther apart.

Then sadness entered the eyes, searching his face. "Surely as a pastor you recognize you're treating two women poorly." Rolling her eyes, Sadie shut the door in his face.

No—she—didn't.

Kyle knocked on the door until she reopened it. He brushed past her into the foyer, glaring at her until she closed the door.

"What do you want, Kyle? Mom and Amy are still in their bedrooms. Today is the one morning they can sleep in. So don't disturb them."

He fought to slow down his breathing, not speaking until the anger lifted. "You shut the door in my face, Sadie." Taking deep breaths, Kyle shoved his hands into his pockets, glaring at the unrepentant face. "Why did you disrespect me?"

"Me? You ignore me on Thanksgiving Day and then expect congeniality two days later." She folded her arms, leaning on the door. "I left the playground behind when I left your house."

Anger rose within him again. If she had a problem with the way he treated her, this wasn't how to solve it. After all the grace he'd given to her, she owed it to him to talk it out, instead of drawing some arbitrary line then dare him to cross it. "Playground? I connected with you that day."

The surprised expression on her face calmed him down. Evidently, they'd both viewed the day from a different place.

"Like a stranger," said Sadie. "Speaking to everyone but me. And don't ever chastise me again about my time in Burgundy. Look at your performance in California."

Heat climbed up Kyle's neck until he felt as if he was on fire. Who was she to criticize his lifestyle? "What mistake did I make there?"

Eyes narrowed, she lessened the distance between them. "I was victimized in Missouri, mister. An unscrupulous man abused me and then traumatized my life for months afterward. But you entrapped a woman into dating you even though your heart belonged to someone else."

"You stayed in the relationship."

"And you began one with a woman you didn't love."

"Am I supposed to stay single because you jilted me?"

Sadie sat on the steps and buried her face in her hands. "Deep inside you knew something was wrong with me when you came to Burgundy. Twice you came. And twice you went home without me." She raised her head while tears streamed down her face. "Why? Because it was easier to leave me there than to help me."

Kyle squeezed into the space beside her. "Don't say that, Sadie." He attempted to enfold her within his arms.

She pushed him away. "Why not? It's true."

"It's only partially correct," said Jeanette from the upstairs landing.

Kyle looked up to see mother and daughter staring down at them. Jeanette held onto Amy's arm, keeping her youngest daughter from descending farther down the stairs. Amy seemed ready to throttle him.

"Honey, we all operated in blindness on this one. Only you and Lincoln knew what occurred in his room. Kyle didn't like the situation he left you in, but he didn't know the real story. He suspected something was wrong, but his hands were tied without your cooperation."

"I know. But I expected it to end once Kyle showed up."

His stomach muscles tightened when her lips trembled. "And it would have had I known the facts." Kyle tilted her face toward his. The hurt in her eyes hit his abdomen like a rock, although wisdom demanded he take his time with Sadie. Were his objections about her slow recovery valid in the circumstances?

"No one could help you without your assistance." Jeanette glanced at Amy when she whispered into her ear then walked into the bathroom. She refocused her attention back on Sadie and Kyle. "Do you believe any of us would've accepted your decisions if we had known the truth? You pleaded with me not to visit you anymore, politely asking me to leave whenever I showed up. And you refused your brother's visits after the first time he came.

"Honey, it's an unending list. Roland left Burgundy without you. Kate found a new roommate. Dee stopped hanging out. And Matt didn't ask his teammates to report what they witnessed to the authorities. And all because we were ignorant of the facts. We didn't know, and you were in no condition to tell us. We all blew the chance to rescue you. Please forgive us."

"I do, Mom. I shunned the people who loved me the most. The very thing Lincoln wanted me to do. The isolation crushed my will to fight."

"The administration dropped the ball when you stepped up in September," said Amy, reappearing beside her mother. Walking down the steps, she handed Sadie a tissue box. Then, glancing at Kyle, she sat on the step above Sadie, touching her shoulders.

"Honey, you know I confided in your grandparents and Aunt Yolanda," Jeanette said. "Well, your grandfather was livid. To appease Peter's anger, your Uncle Wes retained a lawyer on your behalf. He's in close contact with the school's attorneys."

Sadie rose, staring at her mother. Kyle stood slightly behind her, watching them all.

"The university placed Lincoln on probation. One more complaint and the man is history with full disclosure."

"Is that all he gets for assaulting Sadie?" asked Amy.

"He denied the accusation, sweetheart. It's your sister's word against his. The football players signed statements to give leverage to your sister's grievance. I'm afraid that's it unless she presses criminal charges against Lincoln." She looked at Sadie. "Your grandfather wants you to press those charges. But I convinced him to hold off talking to you until the new year. If you agree to go forward with a criminal charge, Margaret and he will lease a house in Burgundy during the trial."

Kyle kissed the top of Sadie's head when she sagged against him. Her body trembled until he folded her within his arms. Fear of going through the legal process without results might discourage any person. Especially if they shared a personal relationship with the abuser after the attack. The jury would probably share Kyle's reservations about her behavior, and he knew she was telling the truth.

"I can't do it, Mom. Please—tell grandfather—I just can't." Sadie took calming breaths before speaking again. "It's the one thing I hoped to avoid. At least the probation means the school didn't dismiss my allegation completely." She sighed then captured her bottom lip between her teeth, wringing her hands. Sighing louder this time, she cleared her throat. "I hope grandfather will understand my concerns."

"Peter won't take any legal action that might upset you. Margaret is on top of the situation. Your grandmother will intervene if needed."

"I'll call tonight. Mom, I thought the bad memories would stop when Roland brought me home. But different aspects keep cropping up."

"Sadie, look at me." Jeanette waited for her attention, rubbing her palms on the banister. "You are stronger than ever before. There are lessons to be learned in every trial. We grow from faith to faith by trusting God in each situation." Her voice lowered to a whisper. "Amy, come upstairs. Let's leave these two alone."

Kyle released his hold once Sadie's body relaxed against him, but she didn't move away. Instead, she turned around, placing her cheek on his chest. He wrapped his arms around her, pulling her closer. Intellectually, he knew the Sadie of today had matured beyond the alarming conduct of the past. She made better choices these days. Nevertheless, Sadie still refused to face difficulties head on. She needed to address problems instead of hoping they would go away.

Kyle rested his mouth against her hair. "Sadie, eat breakfast with me at my house so we can talk in private." He realized she'd erected a barrier against him since Thursday. Was she trying to downplay his importance in her life? Her body stiffened against him.

"What will we talk about?" Sadie mumbled into his chest, clearly considering her best interest before agreeing to come.

Reluctantly, Kyle held her at arm's length. "Us. I'll tell you where I am these days, and you can do likewise."

"Why now?"

"Honestly?" Kyle asked. "My father often said that I made rash decisions when it came to you." He hesitated when her lips quivered. "He loved you immensely, Sadie. However, he believed we should date other people to see where our hearts truly lie."

Turning away, she chewed on a fingernail. "I'd always thought your father believed that God cares about who we marry. Didn't he believe that God destined us for one another?"

Kyle walked around her, wanting to see her face before continuing. "You know, he preached those beliefs from the pulpit on many occasions—that God cares about every aspect of our life. Where we go to school, who we are to marry, and how we raise our children. But also to obey Him and not run ahead of His plan."

Sadie closed her eyes for what seemed like an eternity. Problems blindsided her from all directions. Studying her troubled features, Kyle felt an urgency to share his feelings. Did she still want a future with him?

Her mother's timely intervention had salvaged the morning for them. Still, he understood what Miss Jeanette didn't say with words. He and her friends in Burgundy withheld information that neither she nor Roland possessed about the goings on at the university. Perhaps her daughter suffered needlessly because the people in the know withheld the facts.

Miss Jeanette would've initially approached Sadie differently had she known about Lincoln's character. Then Sadie would've cracked as she'd always done in heart-to-heart discussions with her mother. Too late, Kyle envisioned Miss Jeanette filing a police report and dealing with Sadie's emotional trauma, Roland putting Lincoln on notice, and Sadie's grandparents leasing a home in Burgundy to support their granddaughter. And then Matt could've convinced his teammates to file a report to the authorities. Kyle owed Sadie an enormous debt for not digging deeper into her relationship with Lincoln.

"Sadie, I let you down when it counted the most in more ways than you probably imagine. Forgive me for failing you."

Teardrops glistened in her eyes as she smiled sadly. "Give me an hour to come over for breakfast. I want to talk to Mom and Amy before I go. But our discussion has to be honest, Kyle. I need clarity about our relationship."

He left the Cummings home wondering if they would understand each other over breakfast.

* * *

Sadie smiled at Kyle when he pulled out the chair for her to sit down, thankful they would eat in the kitchen. The cozy room supplied the intimacy she preferred at the moment. She laid a napkin across her lap while he set the meal on the table.

"Where's Miss Sarah?" she asked, wanting to bring them together with talk if nothing else.

"Taking an early nap in her bedroom. She had eaten breakfast before I left home this morning."

"Then I won't disturb her."

Her stomach gurgled when he uncovered the serving dish. It was now after eleven, and Kyle had cooked lunch instead of the usual breakfast meal. Smiling, she scooped piles of the mixture onto her plate. Kyle made the best fried rice in the world.

She poured apple juice into glasses after he said grace, wondering when the conversation would begin. And the wait wasn't long. Kyle set down the glass after taking a few swallows.

"Sadie, I want us to date without obligations on either side."

She squashed her enthusiasm, not wanting to raise false hopes. "Meaning?" she asked without looking at him.

"I can't insist you date other men or me. But seeing other people will be good for us."

It seemed that dating other men would become a recurring theme until she agreed. "In other words, you plan to continue seeing Leanne?"

"No, that's over. But if another woman catches my attention ..."

Leanne was history. Sadie smiled for the first time that morning. "How long is this experiment to last?"

Light twinkled in his eyes. The rascal was enjoying himself.

"Until one of us ends the arrangement." Suddenly, his expression turned serious. "I'm taking the chance you might find a better prospect than me."

"I'm not wishy-washy, Kyle. Either you're saying that God changes his mind or that we didn't hear Him correctly in the beginning."

"Neither. I love you and believe you love me. Sadie, a lot of living went on during our separation. We failed to grow together as a couple should. I dated Leanne, but you've never gotten to know another man in a healthy dating way."

178

Oh my goodness! Kyle doesn't count Lincoln against me. He chose Leanne, but I had Lincoln by default. "You were never far from my thoughts," Sadie admitted. "Never." *Lincoln often threatened to remove you from my mind. But I resisted. And images of your tenderness created an oasis in my heart.*

Kyle appeared to read her thoughts. "We have numerous fond memories. But those happy thoughts won't sustain our future. Exploring other opportunities won't short-circuit what's meant to happen." He hesitated when she frowned at him. "Our lives gel together at the moment. But two years is a long time without personal contact. You can't balance two years against two months."

She looked away from the attentive eyes studying her reaction. "Kyle—"

"We can't take up where we left off before Lincoln," he interrupted. "We're no longer the same people, Sadie. Too much has changed. For both of us."

Why argue with the truth? They both had changed. And maybe not all for the better. "In your office, you claimed we left off with my choosing another man over you."

"Not realizing you were traumatized when the decision was made."

Sadie's breath caught in her throat. She felt lightheaded. Was it a breakthrough at last? But a real step forward came without an escape clause written into it. Still, his heart had softened somewhat.

"Then you believe those decisions were reached in anguish?" she asked.

"Absolutely. God delivers His children even if it's two years later."

Sadie marveled at the sincerity on his face. At last, they were communicating and not talking *at* one another. Would he answer a few questions or shut down altogether? She sighed. *Here goes nothing.* "What problem do you have with me? I know something is bothering you, Kyle. What is it?"

Chapter Twenty

"When you're in love with a man, you confide in him, Sadie. You trust and depend on him. You did none of those things with me. You expected help while obstructing the assistance you sought." He hesitated when she rested her elbows on the table. "And, I left you with a man I disliked on sight," he added. "You were distraught. I should've booted Lincoln out and talked to you alone. I accepted your decision instead of fighting for you with more than words."

Her mother's remark on Thanksgiving jumped into her mind. *Words are meaningless without the actions to support them.*

"What does our behavior mean to you?" she asked in a whisper.

"We had a flawed relationship in the past. Taking our time will allow us to view each other as the individual we desire a future with and not as a lifeline to happiness."

Sadie glanced at the thumbs twiddling on her lap. Art Conley had offered friendship. Last week, he'd suggested they attend theater conferences in other states.

"Will it be fair to date a man if I already love you?"

"Not man, men. The point is to see what personality types you like. Dating is getting to know a person better and doesn't imply marriage in the future."

Sadie shook her head. "I don't want to know any men better." She brushed her knee against his. "You're seeking a guarantee that we'll live happily ever after before committing. I already know we will."

"You mean that we'll absolutely have a successful marriage, and not that we can make it work?"

"*Can* make it work? *Can* is for people who didn't receive a mandate from God. I did, even if you didn't."

Kyle grinned. "Then all I can say is Lord help my unbelief. I won't commit to any woman until I've exhausted every possibility with you."

"You're hedging, Kyle. God remains faithful to His purpose and plans. He hasn't placed a desire to see other men in my heart. Date other women if you must. But I reserve the right to date only you." Smiling, Sadie played footsy with him underneath the table. "Lincoln was a misstep. I won't stray from His design ever again. But thank you for giving me a second chance. I won't let us down."

Kyle appeared deep in thought as he picked up his fork. The discussion over, Sadie delved into the cold yet delicious food. Uncovering the serving bowl for a second helping, Sadie found the food much warmer.

She understood his push to date other people. They both dropped the ball in Burgundy and took two years to pick it back up. Kyle simply didn't understand her slow recovery and his refusal to assist her with it. Sadie didn't either. She'd tied his hands, and he'd refused to untie them. Maybe slowing down the pace was the best solution.

The peaceful mood in the kitchen fueled her appetite, and Sadie practically inhaled her meal. Fully stuffed, she pushed her plate aside. Draining her apple juice, she smiled at Kyle when he glanced at her.

"I hear Leanne is Oklahoma-bound in February. The Dawkinses are ecstatic about the help she promised."

"Leanne is a professional. She'll come prepared to tackle city council."

"Will she be nicer on her return?" asked Sadie, not really caring how the woman acted. The fact that Kyle was no longer interested in Leanne sufficed for her.

Kyle chuckled. "Of course. The last time Leanne visited you revealed a conversation that was intended to remain private. It's a potent weapon and a definite deterrent to behaving badly."

Sadie burst into laughter. "I'm always willing to lend a hand where needed." Sobering quickly, she studied Kyle. "People are watching every step we take. The congregation will discard your messages from the pulpit if you don't set the right example outside of church. Perception is everything in the end. People normally believe what they hear, yet sometimes disregard that as well."

"Sadie, pastoring Kingdom Life Church is a tremendous responsibility I wholly accepted. I intend to grow on the job. A firm foundation is the only ground to build on in every arena in life."

Sadie sighed loudly then gazed at Kyle. "I'm glad you agreed to officially date me."

"Officially?" asked Kyle, raising an eyebrow.

The laughter in his eyes excited Sadie. He appeared actively engaged in their courtship now. "We've been dating since October, even though you failed to acknowledge it," said Sadie, grinning. "Stop laughing. It's true." She waited until he sipped his juice. "Still, making it official will make losing you harder to accept, if it comes to that."

He reached across the table, gripping her hands. "For both of us, Sadie. We failed the test two years ago. I think we both had misconceptions concerning one another. Let's pray we fully commit the second time around."

"I will never stop loving you," said Sadie. "I'll always want you by my side."

Kyle's steady gazed pierced her heart as if he stared into her soul. Then Sadie made peace with the private battle warring within him.

* * *

As Christmas loomed ahead, the succeeding days passed in a blur. Although her life surged along the same pathway as before, Sadie gained insight into her befuddled state with Lincoln. Kyle's abhorrence of sexual sins had plunged her into a deep depression. She had blamed herself for going into Lincoln's room that night.

But she daily reminded herself that all of that was in the past. Now it was time to live in the present. The present she hoped to share with Kyle. And Sadie loved dating him now more than she ever had before. He was attentive, thoughtful, and made her feel special. His kisses still tingled all the way to her toes. Energy spread throughout her body every time he touched her. She felt connected to Kyle even without the honeymoon experience.

Both of them had matured in substantial ways since their last meeting in Burgundy. Getting to know the full-grown man provided her with endless pleasure. And the astounded gaze he directed at her proved that he concurred in regards to herself.

At the bookstore one day, Sarah spoke candidly to Sadie about Sadie and Kyle's relationship, saying, "Maybe God sent you both away to give you a better understanding and respect for one another."

Sadie had quietly listened, but her heart agreed wholeheartedly with his mother's assessment. If she and Kyle continued to mature together, they would become the wife and husband that they were meant to be.

* * *

Tired after another long day, Sadie partially closed the blinds then slid underneath the covers. Instead of falling asleep, she thought about Christmas Eve. Just three days away, the events promised to test her endurance more than previous projects had. But Sadie still believed they could host a luncheon with the girls and their parents, then follow up with the gala for foster children that afternoon. The groundsmen and maintenance crew had already completed their tasks, the lobbies and hallways were refreshed and ready for visitors, and fifty people from the church had volunteered to host the children's party.

A satisfied Sadie twiddled her toes beneath the covers. Saturday's opening night for *Salon Duty* had been a smash, matching the successful response to Thursday and Friday's pre-performances. Since the debut surpassed expectations, the staff added Sunday afternoon to the schedule and then secured six additional shows until the end of February. Now the rush was on to secure another play posthaste.

But how could Art coach the girls, direct *Salon Duty*, and start rehearsals for another play while working his job that paid the bills? Thus far, the cast and crew volunteered their time for the experience factor alone. Yet, Art often joked about quitting his job to work full time in theater. Would Kyle give him a full-time job? That's where the church was headed if all continued to go as Sadie expected. Now the author readings were in the afternoons. The first afternoon read and evening drama had boasted a sellout crowd.

She snuggled under the quilt when she heard Amy come home. Her sister worked hard and played even harder. Home life meant everything to Sadie. Untold blessings had manifested just from living in Shiatown. She felt a part of everyone's life just like she had before leaving for college, from sharing in Dee's pregnancy to watching love develop between Kate and George. Kate said dating her boss brought unforeseen difficulties into the relationship. Especially since they also worked as part of the theater staff. It was too easy to take one another for granted. Plus, they failed to set boundaries in the mul-

184

tiple hats they wore together. It was the same lesson that Sadie was learning with Kyle.

Also, a certain Professor Blackburn and her mother began dating this month. Sadie never believed Jeanette might fall in love with another man, but Henry's superb treatment of her mother earned Sadie's respect in a hurry. He appeared to be a family man and was hoping for his two children to relocate their families to Shiatown someday.

And no one could forget the wedding ceremony set for March. Cindy chose Amy as her maid of honor, and Sadie and Kate as bridesmaids. The pregnant Dee had refused to walk down the aisle with her stomach leading the way. Since Roland wouldn't get married on Christmas Eve, tying the knot in March allowed Amy to babysit Brian while she was on spring break. The honeymooners planned to vacation in Belize for a week.

Sadie cast a blurry gaze on the clock. Every day she had too much to do and not enough time to do it. Her desk at the learning center was covered with work. Eating lunch with Kate and Dee tomorrow should lessen the stress a little. Her lips curved into a smile as she drifted to sleep.

* * *

"Thank you," said Dee when the server set their plates on the table. She continued speaking once he moved away. "Hey, Matt's and my decision isn't debatable." She pointed a fork at Sadie. "Stop quibbling. You are godmother number one, and Kate will be godmother number two. End of discussion." Dee shifted her position on the cushion, seeking comfort for her protruding stomach. Squirming again, she rotated her shoulders. "Matt wants four children. But after this first pregnancy, one seems like an adequate number to me." Her eyes sparkled at Kate. "Don't keep secrets. How's the romance going between you and George? Set a date yet?"

"No, it's too soon to think about marriage," said Kate. Then she stared at Sadie, who was quietly eating hash browns. "Can you believe her?"

Sadie nodded, sipping pineapple juice. "It sounded like a Kate-directed question to me."

Kate grinned. "Since we're talking about new relationships, what's up with you and Art? The man is always staring at you."

"He's an asset to the theater," said Sadie, cutting her sausage patty into strips. "We share a common interest, theater. Did you ask George about taking you on as a partner in the company?"

Kate wiped a napkin across her lips. "It's much too soon for that development as well. I'm searching for the right moment."

"What's holding up the engagement?" Dee paused when the server laid the check on the table. "I'm jealous of your freedom. It's time to settle down."

Kate's face glowed, and she couldn't stop smiling. "I love my life. And I like that George sees me as both capable and lovely. We work and play well together." She nibbled a piece of toast. "And so do Sadie and Kyle."

Dee nodded. "It's definitely heating up again, Sadie."

"Yeah, it is … but … The working part is great, but it's frustrating that Kyle draws a line on everything else."

"This far and no farther? Not allowing the relationship to grow?" asked Kate, brushing crumbs from her fingers.

Sadie's shoulders sagged. "Exactly. Just when I think we're making progress, he redraws the line, pushing it farther away."

"But it's getting better," said Kate. "Kyle loves you, Sadie. I see the look in his eyes when he watches you when you're not looking at him."

"And he's happy," Dee added. "Kyle is a loner who is beginning to enjoy other people more."

"I know he likes to be alone a lot, so I try not to crowd him. Only, I want to see him after work, too. Kate and George make it look easy even though working together makes dating more difficult."

"Difficult but doable, Sadie, for both of us," said Kate.

Sadie nodded, switching her gaze to Dee. "Deanna, I love being with you and Matt. You're both so happy that it feeds my hope for Kyle and me."

"And Kyle's hope, too," said Dee. "He's happier than ever since coming home. Remember how the old Kyle used every trick he could think of to get his way?" She laughed as Sadie shook her head no.

"You're the only one who doesn't," said Kate.

Dee nodded, grinning. "Now he remains pleasant even when he loses an argument. I can only fault him for taking up with Leanne."

Kate frowned. "Now if only little miss almost perfect would stay in California."

"I think she still calls Kyle," said Sadie. "Leanne will probably plan another event in Shiatown when she comes in February. She's in for the long haul, ladies, but so am I." Sadie drained the glass, laughing as juice trickled over her lip. She rose, wiping her mouth with a napkin. "Christmas Eve is two days away. See you in the war room, ladies."

Waving her fingers at her friends, she strolled to the checkout counter. Fatigue covered Sadie like mist before reaching the cheerful woman at the cash register.

* * *

The day before Christmas Eve saw vehicles lined up along the three-mile shopping strip in the heart of the city. Unimaginative city planners had inflicted the town with multiple retail stores and restaurants on one central street. Even Kyle would've foreseen the congestion created during rush hour and shopping holidays. And those scenarios combined had deadlocked the atrocious traffic for over twenty minutes. Thank God he wasn't in a hurry to make an appointment and was only frustrated with the delay.

Kyle surveyed the stalled cars waiting to continue their journey. But he thought about how quickly situations could change in less than twenty-four hours. Yesterday, he'd accepted an unexpected speaking engagement at Hope in His Word Church. His old employer requested him to lead a panel on rebuilding cities for God's glory. Speaking at the two-day conference the second week in January fitted into his schedule. Kyle had welcomed the opportunity, until Leanne called with a dinner invitation from her mother. The request took him by surprise. He'd never talked to her parents outside of church while living in Glendale. An invitation after he'd moved fifteen hundred miles away from the state—and had stopped dating her—had vexed him.

He declined the offer even though Leanne explained it was a thank you for Sarah's superb hospitality to her. But he'd stuck to his original decision. It was over. And instead of bowing out gracefully, she appeared to dig in deeper. Perhaps the Sadie factor triggered her competitive nature. Whatever the motive, Leanne resisted being relegated to the friendship file. It was an unintended consequence for the man who streamlined his life whenever possible. Still, the delicate situation caused him to tread lightly. Kyle liked Leanne. Why cast her away if retaining friendship was an option?

"Get a grip, man. Why do you insist on staying friends with a woman who wants to marry you? Guilt only goes so far. And you have nothing to feel guilty about. Let her go."

Kyle chuckled, switching on the radio. "Now I'm talking to myself."

He turned down a side road that led past The Main Street Diner and pulled into a parking spot in front of Cindy's duplex. She was off from the learning center this week except for the Christmas party Wednesday. But normally, Roland dropped off Brian at the daycare center in the morning while Cindy walked to the diner next door. Then Cindy worked at the learning center in the afternoon, and Roland took them home in the evenings. Too tired to cook from juggling two jobs, they often ate dinner at Bon Appetit. Overworked all of her adult life, she might opt for the job of homemaker once married. But lately, she worked more in the office than on the floor at the restaurant.

The door opened before Kyle rang the doorbell. "Welcome, stranger. It's about time you visited me without an invitation." She hugged him around the neck, then sauntered into the living room, leaving Kyle to close the door. She was curled up on the couch with a throw wrapped around her shoulders when he entered the room.

Kyle sat on the loveseat. "Are you cold?" he asked when she drew the wrap around her neck.

She shook her head, giggling. "My sweetie bought it for me last weekend. It's so soft and cuddly. I like rubbing my face in it."

"Like Linus and his blanket. Are you going to keep working after the wedding?"

"At my mother-in-law's restaurant and the church you pastor? Of course. Four hours at Main Street and four hours at Kingdom Life. It will be easier once I buy a car. Then Brian and I can go home at five instead of waiting for Roland to pick us up." She hesitated, tucking her feet underneath her. "You look worried. What's troubling you? Lay it on me."

Kyle burrowed into the cushion, stretching out his legs. Then he launched into the conversations with his old pastor in California and with Leanne. He grinned when the alert listener threw aside Roland's present.

"Your thoughts?" asked Kyle, steepling his fingers underneath his chin.

"Uhh ... you do realize that spreading your love around causes complications, right?" she asked, laughing.

"You sound like I have a bevy of women hanging on my arm."

"Not a bevy, two." Cindy held up two fingers. "For a pastor, two is one too many."

Amusement relaxed his features. "So pastors are never to marry? Or do you suggest we skip dating altogether and walk down the aisle on a whim?"

"Personally, I recommend they consider practical candidates ... which eliminates Leanne."

Cracking his knuckles, Kyle stared at her. "It's over with Leanne. She's a lovely lady but wrong for me. I erred in asking her out."

"Quite often I hear you say dating engages a person on deeper levels. I knew Leanne was nice and selfish without you going on a date."

"Selfish? Let's concede she's incredibly focused."

"Yeah, on herself and her agenda." Her lips stretched into a grin. "Those qualities might work for an apathetic man."

Kyle glanced at the fireplace. Pine fragrance scented the room while flames licked against the screen. The crackling fire reminded him of family values, representing the individual touches that turned a house into a home. He glanced away, then leaned forward, studying her. "Her projects assist numerous people each year."

"But only include her pet causes."

"She loves me," he said in a low voice.

"How long will you play her game? You already ended the relationship for the second time. Walk away now. Leanne won't give up until you make her do so."

Kyle laughed. "Do I dish out advice this easily?"

"It comes with your job description. Your parents worked hand in hand for years, Kyle. Sadie understands the role of a pastor's wife and embraces it. She's willing to work by your side."

"She knows the drill. Sadie's lived around my family since birth."

"She loves the job, the church, and the people you serve. But she loves you most of all. I didn't know her before Burgundy, but I believe God handpicked her for the position, grooming her for the winding path through multiple hardships in Burgundy."

One eyebrow rose. "God directed those foolish decisions in Burgundy?"

"No, but He'll use each one for His glory and the good of people everywhere. Admit your mishandling of Leanne resembles Sadie's mistakes in Burgundy. And no one traumatized you." She lowered her voice. "And by the way, Art Conley is laying on the charm with Sadie whenever possible."

Chapter Twenty-One

For the first time in recent history, Christmas Eve fell on a balmy day. The Cummings siblings had never experienced such weather during the winter season. Today began the family celebration that spanned two days. Roland would sleep in his old room that night, something he hadn't done since moving into his grandparent's house in May. And Cindy and Brian were staying overnight next door. Weeks ago, Amy had invited the Franklins over for a special pre-Christmas celebration at seven.

Contentment flowed inside the living room. Jeanette reclined with her feet up while her children prepared the house for company. Sadie set out presents underneath the newly decorated tree. Roland built a roaring fire in the fireplace. And Amy strategically hung icicles on ivy spread about the room. Then she hung an enormous bunch of mistletoe on the doorframe. "Too bad I forgot to invite a couple of fellows over for a visit."

Sadie giggled at the thunderous expression on Roland's face. "Careful, little sister. You're stirring up trouble."

"I see your point." Amy flicked some mistletoe with her fingertip. "Asking the day after Thanksgiving next year will ensure a greater turnout." She burst into laughter when Roland noisily placed the fireplace poker in its stand.

Closing her eyes, Jeanette set the rocker to a slower pace. "Amy, quit teasing your brother. I expect two peaceful days of bliss, beginning this second."

"Sorry, Mom." Climbing down the ladder, Amy hugged Roland around the waist, brushing her face against his chest when he kissed the top of her head. "Are we keeping Brian's gifts here or sending them next door?"

"Next door," said Sadie. "Cindy will call Roland once Brian wakes up in the morning. Then they can open up his presents as a family."

"Humph, that sounds like a Sadie idea to me. I want him to open up our gifts over here so I can watch."

"I had a little input," admitted Sadie, placing another gift on the tree skirt.

"How big is a little?" Amy asked, frowning at her. She turned away then spun around again.

Sadie's stomach muscles tightened when Amy looked at her with a strange expression then glanced at Jeanette. Her sister had given her that same speculative look all day. As if she waited to receive Sadie's confidence on a matter. And then she understood. Something had happened, and Amy didn't know how to break the news. She set the packages aside. "Tell me, Amy. What's wrong?"

Amy sat on the floor beside her. "I overheard Minister Dawkins congratulate Kyle on his first speaking engagement."

"Yes!" Sadie jumped to her feet, wrapping her arms around her body. Giggling, she gazed at the serene woman, surveying her reaction.

"It's beginning, Mom."

Jeanette nodded. "God answers prayers in His timing, honey."

Smiling, Sadie envisioned traveling around the country with Kyle. She nudged Amy with her stockinged feet. "Where's he going? Hope I can go with him."

"Glendale, California."

Sadie's mouth dropped open. Getting a break in his old girlfriend's hometown only occurred in nightmares. What persuaded him to accept a speaking engagement where Leanne lived? Who initiated the conference? Stop playing into her hands, Kyle. Sadie gazed at Amy's sympathetic features. "Hope in His Word Outreach?" Her shoulders drooped as her sister nodded. Why would he accept an invitation to speak at her church? "It was very busy today. I guess Kyle planned to tell me tonight."

Amy stood up, clutching Sadie's arm. "I overheard their discussion two days ago."

It seemed the world collapsed around Sadie. Her earlier joy fled. The successful luncheon with the teens and their parents and the Christmas party for foster children couldn't sustain one personal defeat. For two whole days the man she exclusively dated had hidden an important secret from her. What other pivotal news was he withholding? She wavered at her brother's stern expression.

"Did you know about this?" Sadie asked him.

Roland folded his arms on his chest. "Cindy told me last night. It was Kyle's place to tell you."

"How about you, Mom?"

Jeanette brought the chair to a standstill. "Sarah mentioned it the other day."

Sadie glanced at Roland again. "So much for his telling me."

"So Kyle mentioned the situation to his mother and Cindy. Is requesting advice a female prerogative?" Roland leaned his arm on the mantel. "Or do males have the right to seek wise counsel as well?"

Tears sparkled in Sadie's eyes as she tried to keep from crying. "The entire family knew before me and then chose to keep me in the dark. Why did you choose Kyle over me?"

"That statement is way too dramatic," said Jeanette. "No one picks sides in this family, but if so, we'll always fall on yours."

Sadie shook her head, backing up against the ladder. Amy shrieked when it wobbled. Stepping in front of the Christmas tree, she steadied the shaky legs to stop it from toppling over. But Sadie ignored the incident and tapped a finger on her chest. "I'm dramatic when Kyle confided in everyone but me?"

"Seriously, you're upset because he spared your mind from unnecessary clutter?" asked Jeanette. "He let you manage two massive undertakings stress-free today."

"Glendale, Mom?" Sadie threw up her hands in the air.

"Stop seeing Kyle if you can't trust him to travel alone." She paused when tears fell from Sadie's eyes. "Kyle was trying to be supportive of your projects, honey. Either you believe he broke it off with Leanne or you don't trust him. Stop dating him if it's the latter."

Sadie brushed tears away. "It always falls back to me."

"Geez," said Amy. "That's because you have a starring role in the drama. But I think it's almost over. Think about it this way. You're in the third act of a four-act play." She burst into laughter, then covered her mouth with her fingers. "But act four is coming soon to a theater near you."

Sadie sniffled. "That isn't helpful, Amy."

Roland's eyes narrowed. "Sis, that martyr attitude is a sure recipe for failure. If you want to lose Kyle, keep traveling on that road of helplessness. Stop gripping what you can't hold, and release what you can't lose. The man loves you."

Sadie laid her head on his shoulder, drying her eyes with a tissue. "Take the mystery out of that riddle, please."

"Every person will try to escape a choke hold. You want marriage. Let him find his way back to you."

She leaned her whole weight against his frame. Listening to reasonable viewpoints released her frustration. Her family knew Kyle well. Their opinions amounted to more than taking a shot in the dark.

"Mom, this is what I missed out on in Burgundy. I'm confident that Miss Sarah and Cindy set Kyle straight as well."

Jeanette rocked the chair in a soothing motion. "I trust that they did."

Sadie sighed loudly, wiping the teardrops away. "Come on, Amy. I'll help you prepare a fabulous meal."

* * *

Ten minutes before seven the doorbell rang. Brian's "hello" reverberated throughout the house as the doorbell continued to sound. Untying her apron, Sadie sauntered down the hallway, peeking into the living room. "Good. Roland stashed the toys out of sight," Sadie mumbled on her way to the door. She opened it wide, then stepped aside.

"We're here!" Brian's finger still pushed the button.

"Stop, Boo." Cindy set the child on his feet. "The noise sounds much louder inside the house."

Sadie stood aside while their neighbors trooped inside the doorway.

"Look, Mommy, more gifts!" He sprinted into the living room, jumping up and down in front of the tree, giggling loudly. Then, clapping his hands together, he plopped on the floor, fingering the packages.

Staring at Sadie, Kyle shut the door once Sarah and Cindy followed behind Brian. "Who told you?" He brushed his fingers over her cheek when she squinted her eyes at him.

Without speaking, Sadie sat on the stairs, patting the place beside her. "We must reach a consensus, Kyle. Stop shielding me. I can handle bad news, plus take care of my responsibilities."

Kyle laid his forehead against hers. Brushing his lips across her mouth, he cuddled her in his arms. "I wanted the luncheon and tour to be over before we talked."

"I understand ..." She paused, searching for the right words. "Let *me* decide how much information I can handle. I've never spun out of control when told bad news."

"Slow down, Sadie. Too much is on your plate. You need adequate time to rest just like everyone else. You can't eliminate the past by overextending in the present."

"You think I'm unstable? Well, interacting with me on an adult level will banish those fears." She leaned her back against his chest. "Am I going to California with you? And yes, I wanted to go with you before knowing where you were going."

She felt laughter rumbling through his body as he squeezed her against him.

"Take your time," said Sadie. "We need to communicate and not talk *at* one another."

Kyle rested his chin on her hair. "You would want to accompany me no matter where I traveled. I know that." He squeezed her gently. "For many reasons, I need to go alone."

Sadie accepted his decision although an image of Leanne's smug face infiltrated her mind. "Have you heard from Leanne?"

"Her mother invited me to dinner, but I declined the offer."

He chuckled when she kneeled in front of him, wagging her little finger beneath his nose, bending it up and down. Her body shook as she tried to keep from laughing. "You won't let her lure you into the spider web? Come on, pinky promise."

Chuckling, Kyle hooked his finger onto hers, brushing her lips with a kiss. He pulled her closer, then kissed her again.

"What, no mistletoe?" Her sister sat on the step where Sadie knelt.

"Amy!" said Sadie, laughing up at Kyle.

"Exactly. Get it into gear, you two. This evening is for the little tyke." The happiness in her eyes didn't fit the sarcastic remark. She rose to her feet and strolled into the living room, waving a Children's Illustrated Bible in the air.

Sadie smiled at Kyle. "See? Unlike Leanne, people can be focused and sweet simultaneously. Amy pulls it off daily."

Kyle's lips brushed her forehead as he stood, pulling Sadie up with him. "It's over and never should've begun. My heart was with you the entire time. But I wronged Leanne in the process."

Sadie shook her head. "I loved your sermon two weeks ago. The one where you told us not to let the enemy fill our thoughts with false guilt. That God wants us to make the appropriate restitution if any is required and then let Him direct our path."

A glow highlighted his features as he shifted on his feet. The warmth in his gaze drew her like a moth to a flame.

"Thanks, Sadie. It's good to know at least one person is being fed on Sundays."

"You speak His words to my heart each time, Kyle. Yet, I do realize they're easier to express than to live out."

Arms wrapped around each other, the couple settled onto the floor beside the fireplace. Still nestled in his embrace, Sadie stretched out her legs, leaning her back against him. She clapped her hands with a big smile on her face. The evening was turning out to be as magnificent as the afternoon. "Before we get started, thanks to everyone for helping today," said Sadie. "Thank God it's over until next year."

Sarah's overly bright eyes were filled with tears, but the huge grin on her face proved she was very happy. "I loved this day. Providing foster children with gifts and snacks fulfilled a lifelong vision. William always desired to bless forgotten children. Like King David supplied material for Solomon to build the temple. This generation will take up the mantle of William's God-given dreams."

Jeanette studied the younger faces. "Can you imagine the progress once the grands and greats get established? Let's make tonight special for Brian."

Amy passed the Bible to Cindy, who handed it to Roland. And then a broad grin spread across Cindy's lips.

"Good news, family," Cindy said, making eye contact with everyone. "A certain gentleman in California sent my attorney notarized consent for stepparent adoption papers. I received them today." Cindy smiled at Roland. "I called the office just before Roland picked us up. Ready, babe?"

On cue, Roland's rich tone read the Christmas story as retold in Luke's gospel. Snuggling against Kyle, Sadie lost herself in the written account of Jesus's birth. She refused to let her mind revisit previous Christmases spent alone in Burgundy.

* * *

The next morning, Sadie and Roland cut across the grass to the Franklins' house at six thirty. An excited Brian had awakened at six, eager to go downstairs. Kyle opened the front door before they reached the porch. Inside,

Cindy walked down the stairs with Brian. And Sarah removed an empty plate and glass from the end table in the foyer.

Sadie pointed to the empty tray. "Look, Brian! Santa Claus ate the goodies you left for him."

The boy pulled on his mother's sleeve. "He did! Santa was hungry. He ate a big piece of cake and lots of milk."

Sadie sidled up next to Kyle. "Did you enjoy the late-night snack?" she whispered.

"I went back for seconds," he said, laughing.

Once Brian stepped off the stairs, he headed straight to the toys laid out in front of the tree in the den. He grinned at Roland.

"I got my bike! Look at all my toys!"

After that happy observation, the little boy ran from toy to toy without spending much time with any of them. He frequently looked at Roland and Kyle, keeping track of the toy-assembly progress. Sadie counted four boxes of toys needing assembly.

Sarah glanced at the child who was busy unwrapping another gift. "Have fun, Brian. I'm going back to bed." Then she smiled at Sadie before leaving the room.

"I'll prepare breakfast," said Cindy, stopping in the doorway. "Are you eating with us, Sadie?"

She shook her head, happy to watch the activity from her perch on the couch. Her thoughts filled with foster children within their community. They were happy yesterday but how would the rest of their lives play out? What else could the church do to help them throughout the year? How could Kingdom Life keep their numbers from increasing inside the community?

Maybe the church could adopt a less exuberant celebration for major holidays. Also, they could provide breakfast on Christmas morning instead of celebrating the day before. Actors could perform the Christmas story while the children enjoyed a meal. Then each child would leave with presents after viewing a live production.

Kyle would grumble at the suggestion but might agree if she supplied a workable outline. Typically, his practicality restructured her plans anyway.

She studied the men working side-by-side like mirror images. Kyle whistled softly while assembling a gigantic rocking horse, and Roland hummed her favorite Christmas hymn as he connected a game center together.

Sighing, she glanced at the numerous toys scattered across the floor. No wonder Roland had hitched a trailer to the truck. Both families went overboard buying toys that year. Some children received an abundance of love and goodwill, while others often went to bed hungry and feeling alone.

The older foster teens approached adulthood and would soon be on their own. A long time ago, her mother explained the fear of growing older. She had known the orphanage would boot her out of the house two weeks after turning eighteen. Sadie closed her eyes. How could they make a lasting difference in the lives of children who deserved better treatment?

A whirling noise captured her attention. Looking up, Sadie ducked just as a remote-controlled helicopter spun in a circle over her head. The mischievous little boy giggled uncontrollably. Brian had received too many toys. It seemed no one had practiced restraint with shopping for him this Christmas. Even Sadie had purchased four gifts, including a full-scale remote control train set.

She stood to her feet, stepping around discarded toys strewn across the floor. "I'm leaving. See you all later." After saying goodbye to Cindy, Sadie scurried across the lawn, praying for a scheme to rectify the children's problem. Jeanette left the kitchen as she walked into the house.

"Hi, Mom. You're up early."

"Just checking on the diner. It's a full house, and it's only seven thirty. But we're still closing the doors at noon."

"Were you nervous about how many people would show up? I expected a crowd."

Jeanette exhaled through clenched lips. "The demand has always been there. Only your grandmother never opened the restaurant on Thanksgiving or Christmas Day." Tiny lines around her eyes crinkled when she smiled. "The Teapot is full, too. The college students should spend time with their families instead of congregating together."

"Maybe they're too stubborn to go home. Or don't have a home to return to for holidays." She paused when her mother nodded. "It's a good thing Bon Appetit and Burger Barn are closed. I don't think enough workers volunteered to cover all four restaurants."

Jeanette stood on the bottom step leading upstairs. "They didn't." She yawned, covering her mouth with her hand. "I feel like I'm sleep walking. Thank God we prepped the food last night. Cindy's coming over at ten;

Roland and Kyle will entertain Brian until dinner." Her eyes shone brightly. "I like that my family is growing."

Then Sadie unveiled her plan to incorporate foster children into the Kingdom Life Church family.

Jeanette studied Sadie as she spoke. "Simplicity and repetition are the keys here. First, introduce the youths to the Wednesday evening programs. You never know what might develop through close contact with other children and their families." She grimaced at the clock. "I'm going back to bed."

Laughing at her mother's hasty retreat, Sadie began preparations to surprise Jeanette and Amy with breakfast in bed.

Chapter Twenty-Two

Sadie refused to hide as Kyle peered at her through the bedroom window. She smilingly waved him off even though she wanted him to stay home. Her forehead pressed against the glass; she followed his progress until the vehicle turned the corner a block away.

His flight should arrive in Los Angeles in seven hours. Kyle didn't expect to see Leanne before tomorrow. Did reality speak, or was it wishful thinking on his part?

In Kyle's mind, all personal dealings with Leanne had halted on the drive to Shiatown in November. They were friends, and nothing more. But Leanne struck Sadie as a woman who liked to run the show, and did not respond well to resistance. Hopefully, she would single out another man and leave Kyle alone. But Sadie wouldn't clear the field for another player, and neither would Leanne. The Dawkinses expected her to attend the city council meeting in February, and Sadie knew Leanne would come.

On a high note, Kyle had approved the idea to pick up foster children on Wednesday evenings and Sunday mornings. He'd appropriated funds a week ago to buy three fifteen-passenger vans. Enough volunteers had signed up for van-driving duty to warrant the purchases. But was Kyle as astute in his personal life as he was in pastoring the church? What could be wiser than marrying her? Weariness engulfed Sadie in an instant. Closing her eyelids, she laid her face against the cold glass, distrusting the quiet before the storm.

* * *

That night, she fell into bed too tired to think, yet she repeatedly glanced at the clock while falling in and out of sleep. At midnight, she turned onto her back, sighing. Kyle's plane touched down an hour ago.

Wide awake, she considered the days they'd spent together since he'd agreed to date her. Especially Christmas Day. He'd lavished so much love on Sadie that Amy figured he'd proposed before the night ended. But Sadie knew he was far from asking her to marry him again. Groaning, she thrashed about the bed, finally pummeling her pillows into submission. Then she tossed and turned until daybreak.

* * *

Kyle shook hands with the attendees the next day as they left the building. He'd stood on his feet since nine that morning. Now he wanted nothing more than to take a nap at the hotel until the evening service began. But the previous night, his old boss had revealed other plans. Several small meetings were set up for them both to attend after lunch. At least the discourse in the first session was well received.

After shaking the last hand, he stiffened when soft fingers caressed his upper arm. Leanne stood beside him, with her parents standing inches behind her. Kyle steadied himself for the unwelcomed exchange that was sure to follow. His desire was to part on friendly terms. A candid discussion was long overdue, but it seemed a private conversation wouldn't be happening, at least for now. Still, the ambitious lady gained his attention as intended.

"Let's eat lunch together," said Leanne, smiling engagingly. "Your ideas regarding open speech in public arenas truly inspired us."

"As it did for everyone listening." His gray-haired old boss walked up behind Kyle. "Sorry to pre-empt your plans, lovely lady, but I lined up back-to-back meetings for this young man." He checked his watch. "We have time for a quick lunch in my office before the first one begins."

"Pastor—" Leanne pouted prettily.

Pastor Tibbs glanced at her parents' sober faces. "Getting the right individuals together requires lots of planning. The schedule can't be changed on short notice."

Mrs. Robertson stepped forward, speaking directly to Pastor Tibbs. "I invited Kyle to dinner tomorrow, but he's flying out right after the meeting. So Herbert thought we could steal him away for an impromptu lunch."

Kyle wondered how the senior pastor would handle their dissent. The man had to stand his ground without offending three staunch financial supporters. While growing up, he'd witnessed many pastors fold under the friendly reminder that their contributions paid the bills. In this instance, integrity won out over financial gain. The wise man restated the previous schedule was going forward as planned.

Then Leanne concentrated on Kyle. "You'll be tired and hungry later on. How about a quiet meal at the hotel after the last meeting?"

"I'm sure to be hungry by then." Kyle glanced at her parents' speculative eyes. "Lorraine, Herbert," he said, shaking their hands. Then he followed Pastor Tibbs down the passageway to his office.

* * *

Over dinner that evening, Leanne struck the perfect note, keeping the dialog on neutral topics during the meal. The woman was an expert at luring in the unsuspecting. That one attribute likely contributed to her great impact as a community consultant. But Leanne was more than just a keen strategist. She truly desired to alleviate suffering for people on multiple levels. Kyle liked that about her.

He also enjoyed her ability to divert a conversation to wherever she chose. Plus, he approved of her sophisticated dress style. Heads turned in appreciation every place she went. One time he questioned why she never wore casual clothing. Her simple explanation had surprised him. She said, "In my world, indirect marketing garners unparalleled results. First impressions can set the pace of endless negotiations. Subtle influences with the proper props may seal the deal before the talks begin."

Leanne was a pro. That fact alone should've stopped him from asking her for a date. And although it was hindsight, the knowledge would help him properly deal with her going forward. Past blunders didn't just disappear. Sometimes there was a price to pay for making wrong choices. Sadie immediately came to mind. Dating mattered in getting to know a person better. Hindsight again.

Exhausted, Kyle checked his watch. The conversation was on the road to nowhere. It was time to redirect the dialogue away from insignificant matters. "So you have a teeming client base begging your attention," said Kyle when Leanne paused. Her tinkling laughter was pleasing to his tired ears.

A light twinkled in her eyes. "Don't worry. I'm visiting you in February."

One eyebrow rose as he set down his glass. "Me or the Dawkinses?"

Leanne pushed back on the cushion, staring at him. "I'm well aware the invitation came from the Dawkinses. Do you want me to stay home, Kyle?"

"It wasn't my invitation, so that makes my opinion irrelevant."

An alert expression crossed her features. "You know what I mean. Would you rather I stay in California?"

Kyle appreciated the direct question. He studied the tense woman staring at him. Redefining the relationship was harder than he'd imagined. "If the visit is for any reason other than advising the Dawkinses, staying home might benefit you more."

"I'm out of the running?" Leanne asked.

She actually appeared stunned. As if the concept had never crossed her mind before. "Life isn't a competition, Leanne. We had this conversation in November while I drove you to the airport."

Her expression became less friendly. Anger flashed in her eyes. "Admit you're back with Sadie."

"Our relationship is about you and me. No one else."

Leanne bridged her fingers together, then rested her chin on them. "Forget the mutual parting of ways nonsense. Who broke off the relationship, Kyle?"

He leaned forward, choosing his words carefully. "I don't discuss you with Sadie."

"Kyle Franklin is a fair man who takes life seriously. You walked away from me twice and still have difficulty sending me packing for good. And that man would never break it off with his fiancée. Sadie bailed on you."

Kyle chuckled, slowly shaking his head. "How about discussing you and me?"

Leanne grinned. "Did my comment hit too close to home? Did your childhood sweetheart fall in love with another man at college?"

Kyle grinned at her overconfident demeanor. "Not even close," he said, shaking his head. "That's why you and I never had a chance. We're worlds apart when it comes to civility. Look, you were a helper from the beginning. Thank you for the friendship."

"Don't go there," said Leanne, her eyes flashing fire. "The man who asked me out in June had commitment on his mind. You purposely left the door open for our relationship to continue the day you relocated to Shiatown."

"I disliked long-distance relationships then, and I like them even less now," said Kyle. "Let's move on."

"But you were on board with me moving to Oklahoma at the time."

"That possibility was never broached as a topic by either of us."

"Because I didn't allow the conversation to go there. But I missed you after you left and thought living in Shiatown might be doable after all." She glanced away as if reality had finally dawned. "But Sadie returned home while I was deciding. We might be married if I'd agreed to relocate before you left Glendale."

Kyle signaled the waiter. "No one knows if someone they're dating will end up as a marriage partner."

"Then why did you ask me out nineteen months after meeting me? You didn't date anyone else during that time."

The waiter held out the check for Kyle's signature. Kyle turned to Leanne once the man moved away. "As a pastor, I feel it inappropriate to juggle multiple women." His own words shocked him. He thought about asking Sadie to date other men and telling her that he would date other women. On Thanksgiving Day, Roland had said that Kyle wouldn't date other women. And in his mind he had agreed. But later … He focused on Leanne when she continued speaking.

"You have to date in order to choose a wife. You're a single man."

"And wise enough to understand a marriage between us wouldn't work."

"We can make this relationship work, Kyle," Leanne said, stopping short of pleading. "Love conquers all, or so they say. And you're the ideal man for me." She smiled at him. "You are kind and considerate to everyone. Even one of those qualities is hard to find in most people."

"Leanne, you'll make the perfect wife for the right man. We both deserve mates willing to make sacrifices to benefit the marriage. Where we live isn't the only issue."

Her eyes glazed over. "In other words, I won't do for a pastor's wife?"

"Nor I as a community organizer's husband. Stalemate. We can't win in a marriage together."

"So Sadie wins? At least the good people in Shiatown will be happy." She shuffled in her seat. "Kyle, you were happy in Glendale."

"But I'm happier at home. For me, all roads lead to Shiatown, and that isn't your destination."

"What do you see in store for me?" The wide-eyed stare dared him to suggest meeting another man.

Kyle grinned. "Success in all your endeavors."

Sighing, she closed her eyes, then studied him again. "Just not with you?"

"Never with me. Our lifestyles are too different. A fact I should have recognized before asking you to dinner. Blame me for sending us both down a rabbit hole." The conversation was a difficult one for Kyle. He resisted grabbing her hand. "Please accept my apologies. It's over, Leanne."

The tears glistening in her eyes never fell. Silently, she stared at him. And then her gaze roved over his upper body before returning to his face. The action appeared to etch an image of Kyle into her mind. Closing her eyes, she breathed deeply; then she headed for the exit. "I won't waste my breath asking you not to escort me to the car," she said when Kyle appeared beside her.

Neither one spoke as they walked across the parking lot. At the car, she turned to Kyle, and her unhappy expression sent a muscle spasm through his abdomen.

She gazed at him after sliding inside the vehicle. "I'll explain to Mother you won't have time for dinner tomorrow. I know you said that you wouldn't come, but we'd hoped to change your mind. Will you pick me up at the airport next month?"

He nodded. "I keep my promises."

"Are you and Sadie an item again?" She turned the key in the ignition, waiting for the reply.

"We're dating."

"For the right couple, that's enough." Flinching, she shifted the car into gear and drove away.

Standing with his hands in his pockets, Kyle watched Leanne drive out of his life. There was no going back to the woman he gave away for the third time.

* * *

Saturday evening, Sadie sat in her office while *Salon Duty* entertained another sold-out crowd in the theater. Sighing loudly, she checked the clock on the wall again. Kyle's flight landed at the Tulsa airport two hours ago. Sadie shuffled papers around the desktop, resisting the temptation to check the arrivals online. She picked up a pen, then tossed it aside.

A simple phone call while he was away might've curbed her anxieties. Kyle should've known better. Just what did the man say to couples when one took the other for granted? That was the problem in a nutshell. Kyle considered her to be a date. Not a person requiring details concerning his private life. The clock chimed out the hour. Ten o'clock, and all wasn't well.

At least the theater crowd was exiting the building. Sadie expected Cindy to deliver a full report any moment. Cindy had given up her role to the understudy two weeks into rehearsals. The working mother refused to take any more time away from a son who spent his weekdays at the daycare center.

I may as well freshen up in case a few stragglers knock on my door.

Sadie almost fainted as she peered into the powder-room mirror. She looked terrible. Like she hadn't slept in days. Appearing in public looking unkempt bothered her. She scrubbed her face, applied makeup, and brushed her tangled hair.

The office door opened while Sadie stowed away her beauty supplies in the vanity drawer.

"Be right with you, Cindy. Take a seat. We're destined to work seven-day weeks if Kyle doesn't hire theater staff soon. Did the cast receive another standing ovation tonight?" she asked, strolling into the room. And then her heart rose into her throat. Kyle sat in the chair in front of her desk, grinning at her. Sadie darted across the room and sat on his lap. And then she kissed his cheek, laying her face against his neck. She smiled once she felt his breath blowing in her hair.

Kyle set her upright, chuckling. "I liked that reaction. But tone down the affection in public places," he reminded her.

"No," said Sadie, hugging him again. "This is my office."

"Located inside a public place." He shook his head when she placed a kiss on his cheek.

"If people knock first they won't receive the shock that Sadie and Kyle kiss and hug like many dating couples."

"Always keep them guessing." He rubbed his cheek against hers when she frowned. "I agree with your earlier remark. We'll discuss permanent staffing once Cindy arrives."

"Permanent staffing? As in, we're going to hire full-time help? Come on, give me a hint. Please," she wheedled as he shook his head. When he just looked at her, smiling, Sadie pulled away, examining his features. Kyle was exhausted yet still sought her out tonight. "Tell me about the conference. Was it open to the church community or denomination specific?"

Laying his head on hers, he gave her a play-by-play of events until the door swung open ten minutes later. Cindy barged into the office and grinned when she spotted Kyle. She hugged his neck then sat in the chair beside them.

"Welcome home," said Cindy, tucking one leg beneath her.

Kyle nudged Sadie. "See what I mean?"

Her eyes darted between them. "What? Did I intrude on a private discussion?"

Sadie shrugged her shoulders. "Mi casa es su casa. Kyle doesn't want affection from me in public."

Cindy stared at Kyle. "This is Sadie's private office."

"My point exactly. You entered the room without knocking."

"I never knock. I don't mind seeing Sadie sit on your lap in her office or any place."

"Thanks for the support, friend." Sadie said. "He liked my greeting even if he won't admit it." She elbowed him in the ribs. "Didn't you?"

Kyle laughed. "We're friends for life."

Suddenly, Sadie pulled away, hurrying to her chair. Sitting down, she glanced at Cindy's knowing face and then at Kyle's baffled expression. "Kyle has learning center news to discuss before we go."

Cindy poked Kyle in the chest with a finger. "Hurry up with the news. Sadie and I are going to a prayer vigil until one. Roland has Brian for the night. I'm sleeping at your house." She glanced at Sadie. "Art said he'll see you later."

Kyle sat on the edge of the desk. "We're posting several positions for the learning center next week. We're hiring Sadie full time, but Mother wants her at the bookstore one day a week. She's retiring next year and wants Sadie able to run it on her own. So, no more tutoring, or weekends, Sadie. Administration duties only from nine to five. Work out something with Mother about the bookstore." He made eye contact with her before switching to Cindy. "We're hiring Cindy part time from one to five, weekdays only."

Kyle rose, stretching his muscles. "I'm tired of sitting down. Here's the remaining schedule. On Monday, my cousin Bridget will take on receptionist duties from five until closing. I want the doors locked at nine on weekdays. We'll still shut down at four on Fridays. No more working after hours for either of you."

"What about theater staff?" asked Sadie, pleased with the shortened workweek.

"Caretakers will occupy the church apartment beginning tomorrow. They'll work at the learning center Saturdays and Sundays and wherever needed. They'll open each building in the morning, turn on heat or air conditioning as needed, securing everything back in the evening. Steven West and his wife, Phyllis, are perfect for the job. Next week, we'll hire dinner theater staffers for Saturdays and Sundays." He looked at Sadie. "I'm negotiating a contract with Art Conley."

"For a full-time position?" Sadie smiled when Kyle nodded. "It's the perfect arrangement."

Chapter Twenty-Three

Life became easier once Sadie stopped tutoring students, and the dinner the-ater hired a dedicated staff. She had self-published her first novel, *Pajama Party: The Story*, a week ago. Several of Sarah's colleagues were selling it at their retail and online locations along with other well-known retailers. Sadie had submitted the final draft to an editor in December, and she didn't have to search long before locating a top-notch editor who provided more than a simple copyedit. Sadie learned more about writing a book during the editing process than in all of her previous writing classes. Loving the entire process, new books sprang to mind every day. Too bad none of them came with a complete storyline attached.

Still happiness overtook her despite the trial of loving a cautious man. Five months after she'd come home, Kyle still moseyed down the pathway to marriage, reluctant to commit to a future together. Even in his partial state of denial, the man made her feel special as well as protected. He was attentive on top of his hectic schedule. No wonder Leanne still had difficulty moving on.

Sadie headed to the window when a car door shut. Staying back until they reached the porch, she glimpsed Leanne's backside as she stepped into the house. Was this truly only a visit to assist the Dawkinses? Or was she still pursuing Kyle? Only time revealed hidden agendas. How long could ten days feel like?

* * *

"Too long," said Sadie, sitting in the rocking chair.

Leanne traveled all over Shiatown, hiring taxicabs as if they came cheap. Sadie spotted her on numerous occasions. And gossipers revealed the men loved the knowledgeable woman with the sociable smile.

On the Wednesday after her arrival, Leanne and Mrs. Dawkins visited the study group in the learning center. Sadie relaxed when the cordial exchange turned into an enlightening discussion. No jabs, jeers or catty remarks dotted the conversation like at their last meeting in November. Instead, the chatty woman supplied several relevant ideas to the youths before departing.

The following afternoon, Sadie ran into her in the hallway connecting the daycare to the multipurpose center. Alone this time, the women spent a few minutes making small talk before Leanne entered the daycare facility. Then there was the time she saw Kyle and Leanne going into The Main Street Diner as she turned into the parking lot. They were sitting with the Dawkinses on the far side of the restaurant as she left with a takeout sandwich. After wriggling her fingers at them, Sadie hurried off to the bookstore.

But before going to bed that night, she received numerous reports that Leanne inquired about her personal life whenever possible. It seemed she used her free time to check out Sadie instead of visiting Shiatown's west-side district. Would the chatter reach Kyle, isolated at the church? The best scenario let him deal with the troublesome woman by himself with Sadie nowhere in sight.

* * *

The next day, Sadie peered around the bookcase in the learning center as high heels clicked across the tile floor. Only this time, the visitor didn't call out for assistance but browsed through the curriculums posted on the board. Crawling silently across the cool floor, Sadie slipped inside her office, gently closing the door behind her. And then she raced to the powder room.

Easing its door shut, Sadie studied her tired reflection in the mirror. Too many long days at the bookstore and learning center had been coupled with nightly writing sprees.

Well, I'll get through it. Of course, Leanne resembles a fashionable business woman. But catching me at my worst seems to be her favorite pastime. Why can't Kyle see the mischief behind the confident facade? Is it real? Or do I only hate being upstaged on every level?

Leanne sat upright in a chair facing the desk when Sadie reentered the room. The cool, unfriendly gaze bore into Sadie. Plus, the award-winning smile that bowled men over was missing this time. Standing beside the desk, she tapped her fingertips on the desktop.

"Hi, Leanne. Did you stop by for a tour of the center?"

Leanne pointed to Sadie's chair. "A chitchat. Take a seat."

Smiling, Sadie tilted her head to the side. "That's my line. How may I help you?"

Evidently, her reply surprised the other woman. Instead of speaking, she adjusted her position, and then sat ramrod straight. "You're not going to make this a friendly conversation, are you?"

"Did you imagine that I would?"

"Yes, if you truly have Kyle's best interest at heart."

"Whew." Sadie grinned. "Thank God I don't answer to you." *Her claws are showing; so much for our little chitchat. I guess I should be thankful Leanne isn't holding a drink or I would be sopping wet.* She shivered as if she could feel the chill coursing through her body.

"Then who do you answer to, Sadie?"

No longer amused, Sadie sat down, folding her hands on the desk. "Stop playing with me. Why did you come?"

Suppressed laughter shone from Leanne's eyes. "Let Kyle go. He'll never achieve his best potential with you. He's an innovative thinker. The agenda established at Kingdom Life Church should be implemented in churches worldwide. Doesn't scripture teach us to put our lamps on the stand to shine?"

"To attract people to Jesus and not to ourselves." *She can't seriously be quoting scripture to justify her own plans.*

"That type of limited thinking will stymie his drive. This facility can be a prototype for churches worldwide." Leanne's expression softened as if Sadie were in need of guidance.

"No, it doesn't stymie him," said Sadie, shaking her head. "It protects Kyle on the road to his destiny. And only if he follows God's will, which may not include expansion."

"Does His will include Kyle marrying you?"

She nodded, tired of playing games. *Time to leave, Ms. Robertson; the countdown has begun.*

Leanne tugged on her ear for a moment, then lowered her hands to her lap. "Sadie, there's nothing whimsical about you. And your methods are far from haphazard. You designed a solid game plan."

Although her body quivered on the inside, Sadie's smile deepened. "I'm in step with God's plans for both Kyle and me."

Leanne scooted to the edge of the chair. "More in tune than the man himself?"

"Of course not. Kyle and I are in sync. He genuinely likes you. Everyone tells me you're a nice lady." Sadie sighed. Leanne's startled expression surprised her.

Then Leanne studied the ceiling, her hands gripping the armrest. Finally, she stared at Sadie. "Is that a recommendation?"

"I'm afraid not. You're the wrong woman for Kyle." She studied the woman scowling at her. Sadie understood why Kyle liked her. But she didn't back off if she wanted something. And she appeared quite determined to acquire Kyle against his will.

Outwardly fuming, Leanne pushed her chair away from the desk. "So say you."

"I think that pronouncement goes higher than me."

Leanne rose, placing her hands flat on the desk. "So you know God's heart as well?"

"About this, I do. Every pastor needs a wife who doesn't operate on the peripheral of obedience."

"You doubt my salvation?" Leanne asked, pointing to herself.

Sadie squinted at the ruffled woman. "Only God knows the heart. I question your commitment to the call He gave to the man you won't let go."

Her eyes half-closed, Leanne chuckled. "You think I'm desperate? Okay, I'll bite. Why do you distrust my dedication?"

Sadie laughed. "You expect me to help you trap the man I plan to marry?"

The speculative look in Leanne's eyes almost unnerved her. Sadie imagined wheels spinning inside the woman's head. And then her mood altered. Sympathy entered her gaze. Did she see Sadie as a misguided bumpkin? They might've viewed one another objectively under different circumstances.

"What will you do if I relocate to Shiatown, Sadie?"

"Thank you for giving Kyle another person from Glendale to attend our wedding—"

"Look, missy, I know what no one else in this town appears to understand. You broke off the engagement to Kyle."

Sadie giggled. "Pure speculation. You know nothing about me or our engagement."

Cold eyes stared at Sadie. "I will uncover the truth."

Sadie nearly gasped as spasms shook her stomach. No woman had ever engaged her in a battle of wills before. Her whole body overreacted to the intense confrontation. She breathed deeply, eager for a reprieve. Finally feeling calmer, she hoped her smiling face radiated confidence.

"Good luck with that. The Holy Spirit doesn't gossip, and Kyle will never tell." She turned on the computer. "Happy scavenger hunting. Please close the door behind you."

Sadie sprawled in the chair the second Leanne left the office. She laid her head on the desk once the heels ceased clicking on the steps. Going to the window, Sadie observed Leanne walking across the square. Probably on the way to Miss Sarah's house.

Leanne will never be happy living in a small southwestern city. Why not lay her cards on the table? Only then would Kyle forget about keeping the woman as a friend.

* * *

Thirty minutes later, Kyle opened the office door just as Sadie knocked. Stepping aside, he ushered her into the room. His back against the door, he kissed her forehead.

"I'm glad you're here. Great minds think alike."

He's glad to see me in spite of his venom-dripping friend. "Leaving? I'm heading to the bookstore. I'll walk you to the car."

Kyle captured her hands in his. "I was headed that way to beg a dinner date tonight. What brought you over?"

"Missing you. I just wanted to say hello," she said.

"So, eating breakfast together every other morning doesn't count?"

She shook her head. "Not when I want to eat lunch and dinner with you too."

"You give good answers," he said, chuckling. "How about adding a movie to dinner tonight, if you're free?"

"Perfect. I'm in the mood for a romantic comedy."

"Thinking about us?" He chuckled again. "You choose. I like your choices."

"You said great minds think alike."

Kyle winked at her. "Since I hear that opportunity isn't a lengthy visitor, I'd better ask now. Eat dinner with me tomorrow too."

Grabbing his tie, Sadie pulled him closer, brushing her lips against his. "Just don't skip our breakfast in the morning."

"It's a done deal. Pick you up at six."

* * *

Sadie walked home alone after church the following Sunday. The message had hit her hard as if it was directed solely at her. "The Art of Friendship" touched her in significant ways and unlocked several recurring questions, especially the one that troubled her the most. Even though Kyle never looked her way, his voice massaged her soul.

"What is the significance of friendships in the Christian life?" he asked from the podium. "Jesus's ministry laid the foundation for confidence in everyday living. Throughout the Gospels, we find that Jesus taught the masses, worked with the seventy, and unveiled secrets to the twelve. He revealed deeper truths to the three and often prayed alone to the Father while still finding time to dine with Martha, Mary, and Lazarus. Let's use His examples as our guide.

"As we all well know; the Christian lifestyle can appear just as precarious as that of the nonbeliever. Even though in principle we no longer partake in this world's system, we often operate in the same darkness as the world we live in. And how we handle other people reveals if we adopt worldly views instead of using biblical concepts.

"Many times, we choose our companions out of preprogrammed emotions rather than godly beliefs. In other words, we can and sometimes do select our relationships through impure motives."

As she recalled the sermon, Sadie suddenly broke into a jog, almost tripping over uneven ground. For some unknown reason, Art Conley popped into her mind again. An image of the man haunted her throughout the sermon. Maybe seeing Leanne sitting with the Dawkins family had ruined her morning. Eight days down and only two days to go. Panting, she rushed up the steps to her porch just as the cell phone vibrated in her purse.

Stunned by the caller's identity, Sadie slowly answered. "Hi, I was just thinking about you. Is anything wrong?"

Art sighed loudly. "Why do you ask that same question each time I call?" He continued without waiting for an answer. "At church this morning, a buddy gave me tickets to the ballet in Oklahoma City. Care to join me?"

Sadie froze. The phone call right after her earlier thoughts was uncanny. Was she supposed to go with him? She thought about Kyle's message "The Art of Friendship." Did Art need a friend?

"Hold on. It's freezing outside." She rushed into the house and glanced around the foyer as if wisdom hid itself within the woodwork. Then she closed her eyes, sliding into a sitting position on the bottom step.

"Sadie? Are you still there?"

"I'm here. It's a two-hour drive." She hesitated, cringing. "What time does the program start?"

"At four. We can grab a bite to eat and be on our way in ninety minutes."

"I—can—meet you there." Sadie closed her eyes as sweat dripped from her forehead.

"Why? We can ride up together—unless you don't want to be alone with me?"

How could she reply with what she was thinking? *You're right, I don't. Not trapped in a car with you for two claustrophobic hours each way.* She couldn't relinquish her control as if it meant nothing. Easy prey. That's what she would be if she rode in the car with him. Sadie pushed her breath through pursed lips. She was afraid. They had each driven their cars when she and Art ate at Burger Barn. Her heart palpitated at the thought of making another bad decision. The side effects continued long after the event ended.

"Sadie, are you there?"

Breathing deeply, she patted fingers on her lips. "I'm thinking, Art. Please bear with me a minute."

"And I'm thinking of ways to ease your mind. I feel your apprehension through the airwaves."

I'm acting silly. Art Conley is light-years away from Lincoln Miller.

Sadie laid her face on her lap, then sat up straight. "I would love to go. Dinner at The Main Street Diner?"

"My exact thought. I'll pick you up in thirty minutes. We'll have fun."

Sadie laid her head against the wall, still clutching the cell phone as if it was a lifeline when Jeanette touched her knee.

"You look dazed, honey. What happened?" Jeanette touched her hand to Sadie's forehead.

Then Amy removed the cell phone from her sister's fingers. "Who were you talking to?" She glanced at Sadie while scrolling through the call log.

Sadie rose, wiping her hands on her dress. "Sorry, sorry. I didn't hear you come in." Tilting her head to the side, she hesitated. "Mom, Art Conley repeatedly came to mind during Kyle's message this morning. He called before I made it home. A friend gave him tickets to the ballet in Oklahoma City. He's picking me up in," she looked her watch, "twenty minutes."

"And?" asked Jeanette when Sadie hesitated.

"I'm afraid to go with him."

Jeanette wrapped her arms around Sadie's shoulders. "Why?" she asked when Sadie laid her head against hers.

"I'm antsy about being inside a car with a man I hardly know for two hours. Each way, Mom. It'll be dark by the time we leave Oklahoma City."

"What do you think may happen? That he may harm you?" Jeanette hugged Sadie, kissing her cheek when she nodded. "You can't hide away from men because of Lincoln. Sure, there are predators out there, but you have to live, Sadie, and not in fear."

Still holding the cell phone, Amy moved closer to Sadie. "I scrutinize any man asking me out after your experience. But Art is cool. I like him. He won't harm you. What do you think, Mom?"

"Sadie has to follow her heart on this one, sweetheart. I won't cast a vote either way."

"I'm behaving foolishly." Sadie laid her head on Jeanette's shoulder then pulled Amy closer. "Art won't hurt me. He thinks I was attacked like his sister. He told me the awful story one day. It hit too close to home." She glanced at Jeanette. "Mom, the fear came out of nowhere. All of a sudden I was terrified."

"Maybe Roland can get tickets for him and Cindy to go with you and Art," said Amy, handing Sadie the cell phone. "I'll babysit Brian."

Hope rose inside Sadie, then faded. "I can't disrupt their day because I'm afraid. I'll go. I just hope this isn't another disastrous decision that I'm making."

Jeanette brushed Sadie's hair away from her face. "I don't believe it is. But being cautious is always advisable, honey."

"I'll change clothes quickly. Come on, Amy." Sadie ran up the stairs before she could change her mind.

In the bedroom, she kicked off her shoes, then placed them on the shoe rack. "What should I wear?"

Amy walked into the room, going straight to the closet. "For your first date, it has to be something special."

Sadie chewed a thumbnail, frowning. "Friends don't date, Amy. And that's all we are."

Jeanette spoke from the doorway. "He'll see it as a date if he likes you that way. And if that bothers you, stay home."

"I thought I'd jumped the final hurdle when I ran upstairs," Sadie said. "I'm game if Art just needs a friend." Smiling, she threw up her hands. "We'll talk it out over lunch at the diner."

Sadie sat ready in the living room when Amy opened the door to Art. The man immediately broke the ice by handing Sadie a beautiful bouquet of pansies. Sniffing the delightful blooms, she placed the vase on the mantel in the living room. Moving away, she suddenly spun around, taking another sniff.

Laughter twinkled in Art's eyes. Clearly careful not to touch her, he stood back, letting Sadie walk out the door first. While strolling to the car, he entertained her with tales about children who disrupted church service; first by playing, and then by whining after being reprimanded. Her tension lessening, Sadie settled into the car, glancing at the Franklins' house once Art shut the door. A smile lit her lips as Kyle watched her from the window. About to wave, Sadie quickly looked away when the unsmiling man shut the blinds abruptly.

And that was just the tip of Sadie's problems. Maybe The Main Street Diner was the wrong restaurant for a meal. The diner overflowed with the crowd from Kingdom Life Church. Their censorious gazes bore into her back the entire time she ate. No one seemed as startled as the Dawkinses, who were sitting at a corner table with Leanne. Then a shadow crossed over her plate. Sadie glanced up smiling as Kyle's young cousin stood beside the table, smacking on chewing gum.

"Where's Kyle?" she asked. "You two are usually joined at the hip."

Sadie laughed. "He clears everything off his plate after services on Sunday. I'll tell him I saw you. See you next week," she said as the teenager walked away.

She frowned when Art laughed. "What's funny?"

"You are the center of attention. Kyle will hear disjointed details before you arrive home tonight."

"Kyle received the same treatment in November over Leanne. And there she sits, eating lunch with the Dawkinses. Folks were alarmed about nothing."

Shrewd eyes observed Sadie. "Explain the relationship with Kyle. Most people say you were childhood sweethearts but broke off the engagement when he moved to California."

"I believe in miracles. We're finding our way back to one another." She smiled, gazing at him. "You do understand, right?"

"Until a ring adorns that lovely finger, you're free to date other men." Art relented when Sadie blinked at him. "Don't be alarmed by the truth. You're a charming lady and right for the perfect man who may or may not be Kyle."

He glanced across the room, and then his troubled gaze sought hers. "If you didn't know, I've lived a cautious if worldly life, Sadie. And I waited until the age of twenty-six to do the unthinkable."

"What?" Sadie's mind went into overdrive. The sadness in his eyes overwhelmed her.

Wistfulness entered into the watchful eyes. "I fell in love with a woman way too young for me. Except for saying, 'hi' and 'bye,' she happily dismisses me."

Reaching across the table, Sadie touched his hand. "How young is too young? Surely not jailbait?"

He laughed, shaking his head. "No, no. But she is beautiful and very innocent in spirit. She views life as an adventure. And she's busily enjoying every second of it without me."

"There's still hope if she hasn't rejected you outright," she said encouragingly.

"Regrettably, she doesn't consider me at all. But she was instrumental in leading me back to Christ. I'm a changed man. Too bad I squandered my time living in disobedience. I sorely mismanaged my young-adult years."

Sadie sighed loudly. "Me too. But we're on track for the long haul." She gave him a wide grin. "Art, thanks for sharing a little of your life with me."

He reached for the check while standing. "It's getting late. We'd better head out."

Peace of mind fled as Sadie slinked out of the restaurant, trying to disappear. She felt the angry stares follow her steps as she walked out the door and even onto the parking lot. Out of sight inside the car, her shoulder muscles began to gradually relax. In November, poor Kyle had suffered through the same agonizing inspection she'd just gone through. Everyone knew that she and Kyle were dating again. Did they think her stupid enough to cheat on him in public? And some of these people knew Art personally. They should know that the two of them could only be friends.

* * *

Later that night, Sadie stretched out on the sofa in the family room watching classic movies with her mother. The fear over being harmed had left during her lunch with Art. She enjoyed a marvelous time and considered him a safe person to hang around.

His unfulfilled longing for his soul mate won Sadie over completely. She liked him. He displayed his incredible charm at will, it seemed. The lady he loved didn't stand a chance. The ingenious man would woo her to his side before long. All evening she'd considered attending those workshops with him out of town. Amy was right. Art was cool.

Chapter Twenty-Four

The next day, Sadie walked around the counter when a group of women bustled into the bookstore talking nonstop. "Yeah," said the plump lady with salt-and-pepper hair. "They say his car hydroplaned going ninety miles per hour on slick pavement."

Another animated woman chimed in. "One news account claimed he's paralyzed for life. What a dismal end to such a bright career."

A tall, slim, motherly type pulled a book from the shelf. "You can bet Burgundy University plopped down a hefty bundle investing in his future."

Stunned, Sadie hurried over to the bookshelf, eavesdropping on their conversation. Her hands shook so much that several books dropped to the floor practically at their feet. The booming noise startled the women, who rushed to assist her.

"Dear, you went to Burgundy University," said the only woman Sadie recognized. "Did you hear about the tragedy? Somehow the news was out a week after the accident occurred."

She took a deep breath before speaking. "No, I didn't. What happened?"

The smaller woman answered. "Lincoln Miller was paralyzed from the waist down in a car accident. The university is coordinating with the family to airlift him home to Seattle."

"No, I didn't hear anything about the crash," she said in a low voice. "Please hold him up in prayer."

Sadie hurried back to the counter and sat at the computer, skimming the headlines. And there it was in black and white. Burgundy University's all-star running back severed his spinal cord a week ago. He was seen racing at high speeds in the early-morning hours. One spectator, a truck driver heading to Nevada, claimed the young man was being chased by another vehicle that got away.

Oh God, no.

Sadie leaned her head on the keyboard. How did the school manage to keep it a secret for a week? She'd never foreseen that type of destruction in his future. Who chased after Lincoln? He must have feared for his life to speed on slick roads. Of course they got away; troublemakers often did. Could someone hate him enough to kill him? Or did they want to talk to him and he panicked? Either way, the outcome was horrendous.

She grimaced, acknowledging what she had to do. And then her mind wavered back and forth. The waging battle tore her apart until she reached a final decision. She must see Lincoln. The man didn't possess one real friend. Just hangers-on determined to link themselves to his success story. Once the chatter died out, they would abandon him for the next sensation.

Sadie made small talk with customers then laid her forehead on the counter after they left the store. When would the hospital transfer Lincoln to a rehab center in Seattle?

Lord, when should I go? How much time do I have before leaving?

When her mother found out, she spent fifteen minutes over the phone buoying Sadie's spirit. Nevertheless, guilt hammered away at Sadie after Jeanette ended the call. Lincoln had almost died, and she had never prayed for his salvation. Each selfish word she had prayed assaulted her ears. *God, make him treat me better. Make him marry me as quickly as possible. Let us live a harmonious life together.*

Plus ... she hated him. She closed her eyes against the self-incrimination. Then she glanced across the room when the little bell over the door jingled. The pent-up pressure slowly seeped away. Kyle stood in the doorway, smiling at her until he reached the counter. Her knees melted just looking at him. Several people had called her, but her sweetie came in the flesh. Who couldn't love such a thoughtful man?

He brushed a finger beneath her chin. "How's Sadie?"

Her soft laughter filled the room. "Better now. Be careful. Someone might see our coziness through the window and mistake us for a couple."

He laughed softly. His eyes never left hers. Hypnotized by the pull of his charm, Sadie tilted her head to the side. The compassionate gaze filled all the hurting places inside her heart. Sadness had fled the moment she saw him standing in the doorway. He came to her just as she would go to him. She hadn't seen Kyle since he saw her sitting in Art's car on Sunday. Acting as one during adversities meant they belonged together forever.

"What's on the agenda?" he asked.

"Heading to Burgundy is my only option, but I don't know when I should make the trip. Timing means everything under the circumstances. His entourage will visit him until the novelty runs out. I must time my visit between their losing interest and the hospital airlifting him home." Sadie moaned inside when his eyebrow rose. What was wrong with her reasoning this time?

"If you insist on going, it must be before the hospital transfers him to another facility. It doesn't matter if he has a visitor when you arrive."

Sadie thought his remark was strange under the circumstances. "*If* I go? I don't have a choice."

"We always have other alternatives whether we use them or not," said Kyle, studying her reaction.

Sadie glanced away from his scrutiny. Guilt consumed her. Visiting Lincoln might satisfy the remorse she felt. He could've died without her praying for him, for his salvation, and ... while she still hated him for almost ruining her life. He'd lost everything that mattered to him the most, while she gained strength day by day.

"Lincoln treated me horribly." Closing her eyes, she breathed deeply, then sighed. "The man is friendless, Kyle. He's all alone. The university probably can't wait to see the back of him."

Kyle ran a finger down her nose. "Don't turn a good deed into an ordeal, Sadie. As Jesus told Judas, 'go quickly.'"

"Really?" She snapped her fingers. "Just like that. After preaching every Sunday for us to pray before making decisions, you want me to dash to Missouri today?"

"Tomorrow," said Kyle, clasping both of her hands to his chest. "Don't hem and haw over this trip. Since you're determined to visit Lincoln, leave in the morning and come home quickly. What are you thinking?" he asked, tweaking her nose when her eyes narrowed.

"That Lincoln isn't a likable person. His talent opened doors his personality would have nailed shut."

He kissed the top of her head, his lips lingering a moment before he spoke. "Letting go entails giving it to God. All of it." Suddenly he separated himself. "What time are you leaving in the morning?" he asked, opening the door.

Sadie backed up against the counter. "Kyle, I didn't agree to travel tomorrow. I have too many loose ends to tie up first."

She smacked the countertop with her palm when Kyle winked at her, closing the door behind him. Lately, he strived to have his way about everything—and in every way possible.

* * *

The next morning, Sadie almost knocked the alarm clock off of the nightstand when it buzzed. Rolling over, she gritted her teeth in the darkened room. She hated ultimatums, and Kyle loved to dish them out. Last night, he played an endless game of one-upmanship until she accepted his opinion. And he was right. She was a hostage to her decision to go until she actually made the trip. At least she recognized sound advice when she heard it. Even the smallest decision could produce terrible results if it was the wrong choice.

Fully dressed and psyching herself up for the lonely five-hour drive, she shut the front door behind her. She had been surprised that her mother didn't offer to travel with her. It was cold, dark, and dreary. She felt neglected, even though making the journey was her own brilliant idea. Feeling forgotten, her annoyance increased with each step she took. All the while, she wished she was lying beneath the covers in her warm bed.

An engine started as she strolled across the grass. Mired in self-pity, Sadie jumped in alarm. Focusing past the headlights, she saw Kyle watching her from the car parked at the curb. *Where is he going so early? Prayer doesn't start until six, and he never drives if just going next door.*

* * *

Kyle let down the window after Sadie ignored the silent message. "Come on, get in. I'm driving you to Burgundy."

She rolled her eyes, ignoring him, and slid into her car.

"Either we ride there together, or I'll escort you there and back." He drummed his fingers on the dashboard when she laid her forehead on the steering wheel.

Sadie deserved the apology he planned to give her on the road. Last night, his abruptness went over the top. But her stubborn streak had really irked him. He shouldn't have to coerce her into doing the right thing. She never drove long distances, and the weather forecasts in both Oklahoma and Missouri were dismal. Sadie was a horrible driver. Her mind was on everything except the road in front of her. Stress and deplorable weather conditions

226

were a dangerous combination for the best driver. Why couldn't she just accept his help without quibbling?

Perhaps he should've explained that he'd planned to drive while at the bookstore, or at least when they'd talked last night. Although Sadie continually tried his patience, this current problem was solely his fault. For five months he'd complained about her rash decisions, and then he became angry when she rejected his suggestion, because he said so.

Still, Sadie exasperated him. Adept at running the learning center, the choices she made in her private life still concerned Kyle. Like going out with Art Conley without letting him know beforehand. She always rejected his advice. Kyle advised her to date multiple men instead of concentrating on one individual. He shook his head, chuckling. A just comeuppance. Sadie had followed his advice to the letter. She dated both him and Art. Two men.

However, the woman didn't drive well on dry ground, so how could he let her travel to Burgundy by herself in bad weather, braving the lion's den alone. Here they were again. No way to move forward unless one of them gave in. And Kyle refused to be the one to buckle every time.

Suddenly, Sadie left her car and slid into the passenger's seat beside him. She stared into the dark sky until he apologized to her.

"Forgive me, Sadie. I urge you to always pray first, then expect you to take my advice without hearing from God." Her expression softened when she looked at him. The quick smile appeased the ache of irritating her needlessly. "You're a competent woman and don't require anyone to spoon-feed you. Thanks for taking my help. Lincoln's accident would've unnerved anyone, including me."

When Sadie nodded, Kyle pulled away from the curb, hating to see her upset. But he secretly loved how her bottom lip quivered whenever she tried to tame her emotions.

She tapped him on the shoulder before they reached the highway. "My mom knew you were driving me this morning."

"How do you know?" he asked when she smiled at him.

"She stayed in bed instead of driving to Burgundy with me. Her signature move, by the way, is supporting her children in everything." She rested her head against the headrest. "Thanks for driving, Kyle. I didn't sleep well last night. Too busy beating up myself for not praying for Lincoln before the fact." She paused, staring out the window. "Not once did I pray for his salvation. No prayers were made for his sake, only for mine."

Sadie held her head back a little, then cleared her throat several times. "And he … ceased to exist once—I … closed the door on him. I hated him, Kyle. I wanted him out of my mind as well. He'd forced himself on me too long."

Every muscle in Kyle's abdomen twisted into tight knots. Heat creeping up his neck threatened to set him ablaze. Slowing his speed, he tapped his fingers on the steering wheel. He wanted her free from Lincoln's hold.

"Even though I tossed and turned all night, I came to terms with the relationship at last," she continued. "That night with Lincoln had devastated me far too long. Thank God, He set me free from my folly. I forgave myself. I'm rebuilding my life on top of those bad experiences."

Redirecting the conversation, Kyle led them down memory lane. They spent the trip reminiscing about the good times they'd shared together. And then Sadie recounted the highlights from her first two years in college. When she finished, she closed her eyes, reclined the seat, and left Kyle to reflect on the present difficulties.

Leanne had exploded when he told her the Dawkinses would take her to the airport that afternoon. The reality of the situation had failed to rank with her. Sadie needed to make the journey today, and he refused to let her drive to Burgundy without him. Who knew how Lincoln might react in light of the circumstances.

He thought of Art Conley and Sadie together, knowing she would've chosen to help Kyle instead of doing a favor for Art. Cindy had warned him that Art was interested in Sadie. *Why hadn't she opened up to him that she and Art were dating?* His mind returned to the reason for the trip as he turned into the hospital's parking lot.

Lincoln's room was across the hallway from the nurse's station, and Sadie turned to Kyle before reaching the door, saying, "I'll go in alone in case he acts out. Football was Lincoln's life, and he may become irate. Without it, he won't think he has anything left to validate himself. Lincoln could barely read, Kyle." She shrugged her shoulders. "He was overbearing and crude, but what did that matter? He possessed tremendous athletic ability."

About to insist that he accompany her, Kyle shoved his hands into his pockets. Of course she was right. The man would probably think they'd come to gloat over his misfortune. Being paralyzed from the waist down would be devastating to any person, but especially to a man who centered his life on the use of his legs.

"Okay, have at it." Kyle jerked his head toward the door. And then he smiled. "Hey, I'm very proud of your tenacity."

The sudden light in Sadie's eyes almost caused him to wrap his arms around her and pull her closer. Instead, he winked and blew her a kiss. His outward affection seemed to reduce her weariness. Smiling, she laughed softly. The tinkling sound acted as a balm, spreading healing to his flagging spirit. The answering wink made him chuckle as she sauntered into the room.

Seconds later, Kyle stood beside the door. True to form, Lincoln replied to Sadie's cheerful greeting with a stinging jab. "I see you heard about my accident and came crawling back to me. You probably think that you can have me to yourself now." The guttural laughter revealed the intense emotional pain inside of him.

"I came to pray for you, Lincoln."

"Pray for me? Don't you know how to pray at home? No, you're just like everyone else, coming to smirk at the cripple. What good will your prayers do anyway? They couldn't save you from me. I took what I wanted, stayed as long as I wanted to stay, and left when I wanted to leave. Thanks for coming, though. We're just alike. Alone. Nobody wants a loser breathing the same air."

Kyle strolled into the room, gazing at Sadie. Smiling, he reached out his hand. "Come on, sweet pea. We're done here. It's time to go home."

Sadie's eyes popped wide open. Kyle hadn't referred to her by that nickname since she'd turned eighteen. And the shock on Lincoln's face might've been comical if he wasn't handicapped for life. Not a nice man on any day, the debilitating condition emphasized his belligerence.

Instead of moving toward Kyle, Sadie turned back to the man hurling abuse at her. She was totally detached, seeing Lincoln for what he was: A paper tiger that had held her captive; sidetracking her destiny to satisfy his urges. She was mistaken earlier. Here and now, it was finally over. The last stronghold broke, setting her completely free from the stifling bondage. Overcoming her past, she was free to find fulfillment in future challenges.

"Goodbye, Lincoln. I wish you God's best."

Sadie backed away then strolled to Kyle's side. Kyle drew her close when she reached him, kissing her cheek while Lincoln yelled curses at them. As they walked out of the door, a male nurse hurried into the room, rushing to his patient's side.

Sighing, Sadie glanced over her shoulder at the man shouting obscenities at their backs. Heading to the elevator, Kyle was shocked at how many individuals gawked as if Sadie and he were an entertainment act. A few even snickered in their faces. Insecure people sometimes sought solace in other people's pain.

Ignoring their mockery, Sadie drew up to the nurse's station. "Please overlook your patient's temper tantrums. Playing football was his life. He's hiding behind the arrogance and hateful comments." A smile curved on her lips. "Excuse his lack of manners and help him anyway. Many people are praying for his recovery."

Backing up, she waved and walked away, leaving quite a few people with shamed expressions.

Neither Sadie nor Kyle mentioned Lincoln on the drive home. They concentrated on church business until the car rolled into Shiatown a few minutes before five. Kyle pulled into Sadie's driveway, glad they'd made the journey together.

Instead of getting out of the car, Sadie stared at her house. Then her sad eyes studied his face. "Thank you for being there for me *again*. Believe me, I plan to be there for you going forward." Tears entered her eyes. "All this time I thought you'd failed me, Kyle." She paused, staring at him. "But now I see that I let you down as well. I opened the door for Leanne, and you let her come in. And believe me, that mistake will never be repeated."

Sadie kissed his cheek, her lips lingering a few seconds, then she hopped from the car before poking her head back inside. "I hope the meeting goes well this evening. I'm praying for you."

Kyle watched her traipse up the steps. He understood how a devastated Sadie had completely mismanaged Lincoln. The attack added to her already low self-esteem. Once she entered the house, his mind shifted to the meeting he'd scheduled across town several weeks ago. While backing out of the space, he noticed Cindy stood on his porch, waving her hands. When he stopped the car, she dashed to the door he opened, slipping inside.

Shivering, she rubbed her hands up and down her arms. "How did the visit go with Lincoln?"

"As well as could be expected, but much prayer is needed. The man has a gigantic mountain to climb without the promise of recovering. It's an atrocious prospect to face even when surrounded by family and friends." Kyle glanced at the envelope Cindy removed from her pocket. Her solemn expression told the story.

"It's from Leanne," said Cindy, before she hopped from the car and sprinted into the house.

Relief flooded his body as he put the letter on the dashboard then sped across town. Leanne's flight would arrive in Los Angeles at eleven his time. Kyle planned to give her a call at midnight, verifying she reached her home safely.

* * *

Two hours later, he unlocked the office door at church, scanning the appointment book before sitting at the desk. His secretary had scheduled a meeting with a couple having marital problems tomorrow. Some parishioners thought his acquiring a wife might lend validity to his marriage counseling. Chucking, Kyle attacked the work piled in his inbox. The letter from Leanne still lay on the dashboard of his car.

Chapter Twenty-Five

Kyle sat outside on the deck in the wintry night, opening the letter from Leanne. His vision adjusted to the night light, illuminating the page.

Kyle,

Yes, I was angry when you handed me off to the Dawkinses. Did my reaction surprise you? I bet you're overwhelmingly relieved at the moment. Now I can't interrupt Sadie's relentless pursuit to win you over.

I know friends and family believe you wronged Sadie by moving to California. Of course, my subsequent visit incited that mistaken notion. And for some reason, you accept the blame for the breakup. Only, somehow, the girl next door did you a great injustice, whether you admit it or not.

Several people in Shiatown told me that Sadie has always loved you, as if our prior relationship meant nothing special. And maybe it didn't mean much to you, because once I arrived, our relationship disintegrated before my eyes.

This was my last scheduled visit to Shiatown. It would have been wonderful to spend the remaining afternoon alone with you. Kyle, you and I boast a mutual appreciation of forging ahead despite the pitfalls encountered in life. I grew to love the man pursuing his God-given destiny against all odds.

When you're ready for an adult relationship full of love and sincerity, call me. I'll be waiting.

Leanne

Leanne appeared determined to rekindle the relationship without his co-operation. A movement by the door caught his eye. Wrapped in a bright-red parka, his mother stomped her feet on the wooden deck, practically jumping up and down to keep warm.

"Is there any reason we're stuck outside in freezing temperature instead of drinking hot apple cider inside the den?" she asked when she caught his eye.

"No, ma'am," said Kyle, following her into the den.

Two steaming mugs and a plate of oatmeal raisin cookies had been placed on the sofa table ahead of time. Sarah sat down, asking him to sit beside her. She sipped her drink, flinching when the hot brew singed her tongue. After several silent minutes, she sat down the mug.

"What's troubling you, son? Were you numbed to the stinging cold outside?"

"A little," he said, shaking his head. "Mother, Leanne left a note for me with Cindy. She is ... a persistent woman." Kyle had given up hope of keeping on friendly terms with Leanne. He'd thought that goal had already been accomplished on his trip to Glendale. But in one day, he rediscovered the power of Sadie's hopes for their future and the strength of Leanne's determination to marry him.

Wise eyes bored into his.

"We both know what you would tell any person with the same issue; break off all communication. So do it," she said when he grinned. "Do you feel guilty?"

"Actually, I don't. I like adding to people's lives, not subtracting from them. I thought we could remain on friendly terms. But her actions killed that hope."

"Kyle, place each lady into the proper slot, and leave her there."

"I have. Well, at least concerning Leanne. I thought I would fall in love with her. But it never happened. And then Sadie moved back to Shiatown. Yet, I now know that our relationship wasn't an airtight love match like I'd thought. Father had recognized that truth from the beginning."

Shifting position, Sarah set her cup on a marble coaster. And he could tell by the silence that she weighed her words before speaking. Finally, she focused on him. The hand that touched her lips trembled. She closed her eyes then studied him again. "Kyle, the mistakes we make can impact lives for years to come. I had a closet filled with skeletons before marrying William. But your father never regretted forgiving my misjudgments."

Kyle rested his feet on the ottoman. His parents had alluded to having a rocky start and several years of discord before their marriage truly worked. And only once had Kyle learned an inkling of the problem. It happened during his sophomore year in college. His father had wanted him to spend the summer with a pastor friend living in Sweden. He told his wife that separating Kyle from Sadie would give him exposure to a variety of women. Plus, Sadie would have an opportunity to interact with other young men.

Sarah immediately exploded, accusing her husband of seeing her in Sadie and himself in Kyle. She said they should pray and trust God instead of manipulating situations to their liking. He guessed she planned to let him in on their problems tonight.

She wiped her hand across her eyes. "Dear, this is by far the second-most-difficult conversation of my life. Of course, the first one was with your father." Sarah gazed at him through mist-filled eyes. "Sadie and I have a lot in common. She lived next door to you, and I lived across the street from William. He and I were smitten from the first time we met and only dated each other. William had joined the army and was stationed in South Korea for two years before I graduated from high school."

Sarah wrung her hands on her lap, an action he'd never seen her do before. "We planned to marry when your father was discharged. But five months before he came home, I slept with another man." Her voice faltered when Kyle glanced away. "On Thursdays, a group of co-workers regularly went to a lounge after work. One of the men took me home afterward, making a detour to his apartment. I slept with him that night."

She sighed loudly. Tears clouded her eyes at the memory. "The next day, he invited me out to dinner. I guess he figured I was on board for an endless fling. Needless to say, he hounded me relentlessly, threatening to tell co-workers if I didn't agree to see him again. I avoided him, Kyle."

She paused, breathing deeply. Her unfocused eyes stared into space. "I'd left William's letters on the credenza at work. I used to read them over and over throughout the day. Well, this man stole one without my knowledge. After work one day I sat on a bench, waiting for the bus, when he pulled up to the stop. I ignored him, until he held up an envelope. I knew it was your father's letter. My heart almost ceased beating. I can still hear the snickering when I got into the car, reaching for my letter. He handed it over without any hassle, but he told me he'd copied down the address. I asked why, even though I knew the answer. Blackmail is ugly, and trapping a person into having sex with you is an egregious wrong. Two wine highballs had ruined my life.”

Shocked, Kyle stared at Sarah, not believing his ears. Could the Franklins’ tower of strength once been so blatantly gullible? “It would’ve been simpler to confess to Dad. Why did you let him extort you, Mother?”

Her regretful eyes studied him. “I was twenty-one-years-old and not as worldly as I’d imagined. I didn’t want William to hear about it that way. We needed to talk in person.”

“So you continued cheating on Dad to confess to him face-to-face?”

“I know it was a stupid decision, but the circumstances confounded me. I didn’t know what else to do.”

Kyle barely kept himself from shaking his head in disbelief. How could anyone be that naïve? “Why didn’t you confide in someone wise enough to give sound advice?”

“I didn’t want anyone else to know what I had done. I knew once William left South Korea this man could no longer contact him. So, I stood him up after William arrived in the states. Then all I had to do was open up to William after he came home.” She tried to smile at Kyle, but it failed. “I quickly found out it was a ridiculous plan. I avoided being alone with the man at work, until one day he cornered me at the water fountain. Then I discovered that he was separated from his wife and had three children. He threatened to tell William I’d had a five-month affair with a married man.”

Kyle groaned silently. “You stayed in the relationship after my father came home.”

Sarah nodded, laying her head on his shoulder. “I’d planned to leave on my honeymoon and never return to Shiatown again. It was another ludicrous idea that I’d thought would work. But somehow the news about the wedding had leaked out. He showed up at our reception and unloaded everything to William. Needless to say, the honeymoon never happened. Your father left as planned. And I returned to my parent’s house with none of the guests the wiser. I flew to California the night before William was due to return home. It took all morning to convince him to take a chance on me. Yet, he did.” Sarah brushed away the tears. “A year later, I discovered a pelvic inflammatory disease had caused infertility. But after twelve years of marriage, God finally gave us a miracle named Kyle Michael Franklin. I truly felt forgiven the moment I held you in my arms.”

Kyle wrapped his arms around his mother. The woman's love for him was boundless. She willingly risked losing his respect to help him come to terms with his life. Only his father and the stranger in question could have recounted the events; she didn't have to tell him. His father had been buried five months ago, taking the story about Sarah's indiscretion with him. Resurrecting her painful past taught her son a much-needed lesson in showing mercy.

Sarah dried her red-tinged eyes. "It's hard to believe that at one time I was extremely vulnerable. Strong-armed by another individual's self-will."

"But look at you now," he said, hoping the pride he felt at her humbleness soaked through her shame. "No one knowing you today would ever believe how green you once were. Mother, you made a lot of rash decisions."

"I behaved foolishly. And the only trauma I'd received was self-inflicted. Sometimes I'm still disgusted by my mistakes. Yet those humongous errors enabled me to help numerous people throughout the years. Sexual sins physically tie you to another person. Thank God you were taught better than I. Still, your father might have gone overboard in schooling you about the fallout." She brought his hands to her lips as tears streamed down her cheeks. "Don't ever forget godly wisdom is gained by living out biblical principles. Don't lock up your life playing it safe."

Kyle wrapped his arm around her shoulder, and mother and son sat quietly together on the sofa. His father took his wife back while he was on a honeymoon she should've shared with him—even after hearing at his wedding reception that his bride had just ended a five-month affair with a married man.

His father was right about sexual sins, but the personal letdown had intensified the belief. William had wanted to spare Kyle and others from the heart-wrenching experience that he'd suffered through. His father was from a large family, and he'd wanted to raise six children. That one dream was terminated because his wife had engaged in a relationship with someone else. No wonder his father had poured himself into his only son.

William had lived with the aftereffects of his wife's poor choices the rest of his life. Only the couple's love for one another had fortified their marriage. Whatever happened to the other man? Did he still live in Shiatown? Did Kyle know him? Thank God he was born twelve years later, or his father might've died doubting his parentage.

An explosive beginning evolved into a solid marriage many years before his father's death. Thirty-five years later, Kyle recognized his father had made a wise decision in keeping Sarah as his wife. His mother's admission gave him hope for a relationship with Sadie. Too bad he'd already pushed her into dating Art Conley.

He checked his watch, surprised Sadie hadn't called. Her car being outside meant nothing. She could've gone out with Art. Glancing at the woman with her eyes closed, he shook her gently. Leanne should be in California by now. Time to make the call.

Standing, he reached out a hand to Sarah. Her troubled face wounded him. Pulling her to her feet, he hugged her, pressing his cheek to her forehead. God had blessed him with two remarkable parents. Kyle could only hope that he and his wife would bring strength into their family circle. Happiness rose inside him just looking at Sarah. She was an outstanding woman that repeatedly gave herself to others.

Kyle led her up the stairs. "I love you, Mother. You've been a godly example for me all my life."

After saying goodnight, he closed his bedroom door, strolling to the window once a shutting car door sounded outdoors. Popping his knuckles, he observed Sadie and Art trudge up the porch steps to her house until the couple was out of sight. He checked the clock on the nightstand when Art failed to return to his car. It was after midnight, past the time for chitchat in the living room after an evening out. Also, it was time to call Leanne. An hour later, Kyle readjusted his pillow when Art's car drove away from the curb.

* * *

The next morning, Sadie packed a breakfast fit for a king into an insulated carrier. It was a good thing she only had to lug her bundle down the street to the fellowship hall. Early-morning prayer would've ended by the time she arrived at Kyle's office. Hopefully he didn't have an appointment scheduled before nine.

Pouring tea into an insulated bottle, she wondered how the talk with Leanne had gone last night. That Kyle had called the woman before going to bed was a given. He never mentioned her reaction to his not taking her to the airport on the drive to Missouri. Or who drove her to Tulsa on his behalf.

Surely he didn't ask Roland to make the trip. But her brother would've done the favor if he was available.

Sadie grinned when her stomach gurgled in response to the delicious aroma wafting from the bag. Buttermilk pancakes, crispy bacon, fried eggs, and fried potatoes and onions seasoned with fresh garlic and parsley. A proper thank-you breakfast for setting aside his appointments to drive her to Burgundy yesterday. She was pleased that he went with her on the visit. Seeing Lincoln in such a broken state had unnerved her. It was a blessing that she hadn't faced the angry man alone. The cruelty spewing from his mouth, plus his physical condition, might've thrown her emotions off balance for weeks.

Her only option was to use the knowledge gained for future trials and to build upon each success story. Triumphant lifestyles were lived in the present—no more existing in past regrets or future dreams. She'd come a long way, but the journey had just begun.

Kyle's secretary laughed when Sadie trudged past her office hauling a warming carrier, insulated bottle, plus a sack bulging with decorative items. Tapping the door with the toe of her shoe, she pushed inside the room before Kyle acknowledged her presence.

"Good morning. I hope you haven't eaten breakfast yet." Sadie made a beeline to the love seat. After setting out her masterpiece on the sofa table, she turned around, frowning at the man watching her from his desk. Kyle failed to greet her when she walked into his office. Something had upset him since he'd dropped her off at home the day before. Sadie tapped the cushion beside her. "Come and eat breakfast with me. It's my thank-you gift for your support yesterday."

He slowly approached the couch then sat beside Sadie, staring at her. "You have smudges beneath your eyes. What time did you go to bed last night?"

"Late. I left Cindy's house right before midnight. We went over the rollout for *Pajama Party: The Story* with Art. Rehearsals will begin next Saturday for five hours, and then two hours on weekdays until opening night. The girls are ready to roll." Squirming, she scooted forward. "Kyle, how involved do you think I should get with the rehearsals? I avoided the rehearsals for the first two plays, but Kate attended most of them. She loves working in theater."

Kyle heaped food onto his plate. "Do authors typically take an active role?"

"It depends on the author and director. Art's encouraging me to do so." Her forehead wrinkled under the uncertainty. Instantly, she smiled at him. "Good news. Kate plans to market the book for free."

"That is good news. Doesn't George's advertising firm cater to the pharmaceutical and food industries?"

"Yep. Now he wants them to branch out and try their hand at book promotion, using me as a guinea pig."

"It can't hurt. Their advertising firm already operates at the top of their field."

"Uh-huh. My thoughts exactly. Their help is a dream come true." Setting down her cup, Sadie piled a forkful of potatoes into her mouth. "Mmm. This tastes fantastic." She immediately picked up a strip of bacon. Kyle was hardly cooperating with her. How badly did the call with Leanne go last night?

His eyes narrowed as if reading her thoughts. "I noticed Art dropping you off at home after midnight."

"You did?" she asked, smiling. "We would've stopped by if I had known you were awake. I wanted your opinion on attending a workshop with Art next week in Chicago. Cindy wants to go, but Roland is attending a banquet that Saturday evening. Of course, he offered to invite a friend in her place, but Cindy nixed that idea."

"Is it a weekend trip?" he asked when she continued eating.

She nodded, munching on potatoes. "We can leave Friday evening and return Saturday night. Do you think it's a sound investment of time and money?"

Kyle popped his knuckles while considering the question. "That depends on your reason for going."

The implied accusation irritated Sadie. She set down her cup, splashing liquid. "What other reason could I have other than gaining knowledge?"

"A personal interest in the man going with you?" he countered.

"My personal interest is reserved for you. Besides, mister, don't forget you begged me to date other men."

"And don't you forget about arithmetic 101. Art is one man."

"Oh," said Sadie, damping down her anger, "so in other words, you'd prefer me to have the female equivalent to a harem?"

Chuckling, Kyle sipped his tea. "That word is antiquated."

"But the concept is still alive within your thinking." Sadie settled against the cushion. "Make up your mind. Either you want me with other men or you don't."

Chapter Twenty-Six

"The purpose of the exercise was to open you up to a variety of personalities. That way, you'd know what type of man you wanted."

She scooted farther away from him. "It's possible to know your favorite food without pigging out at a smorgasbord. I decided years ago. How about you?"

Standing, he walked over to the desk, picked up a file folder, then returned to her side. "What about Conley?"

Sadie accepted the folder and peered inside before responding. Speechless, she gazed at Kyle. He'd already lined up four workshops for her and a guest to attend at the church's expense. Eyes opened wide, she hugged his neck, laughing. "You were going with me!"

"Sorry to disappoint you," he said. "But I thought it would be a nice trip for you and Amy."

"I'll tell Art about the seminars you already approved. He can accompany us to one of those conferences if he wants." Tears misted in Sadie's eyes. *He made real sacrifices for her on every level. Always thinking about what was best for her. How could she not love him?*

Sadie clasped his hands. "You're a kind man, Kyle. I want to be there for you, too."

Kyle reversed the hold on her fingers. "You are. Explain the relationship with Conley."

Sadie immediately launched into her mindset during Sunday's sermon. How she'd received several images of Art while Kyle spoke. And how he had called with a ballet invitation in Oklahoma City on her way home from church. Then she explained his heart belonged to a young woman who treated him in an offhand manner.

"Amy?" Kyle asked when she finished speaking.

Sadie gasped. "Amy is only eighteen. He can't be in love with my baby sister."

"Younger sister. Amy is no longer a baby. He described her to perfection. Beautiful and very innocent. She views life as an adventure—and is busily enjoying every second of it. Alone. Amy prefers it that way for now."

Sadie crossed her fingers. "Art doesn't stand a chance with her?"

"No man does at this point. Amy isn't looking for love. She enjoys life on her terms."

"Are you sure?" Sadie sighed loudly when he nodded. "Good. I like Art, but he lived without restraints. That makes him the wrong man for Amy."

Kyle chuckled. "You stated he's attending church and repented for past sins. What else can the man do?"

"Twenty-six years running away from God versus three months of obedience. You do the math."

"Come on. Allow Art the opportunity to grow."

"I have. Just not with Amy. Let him pick on someone else's sister." Sadie bent over laughing when Kyle shook his head. "I need to see a positive track record before signing on, if Amy's interested. Let's see how far he's matured after she graduates from college."

Kyle kissed her cheek before clearing off the table. He repacked the carrier and stowed the insulated bottle in the sack before rejoining her on the couch.

"How about us? Is the experiment over?" asked Sadie, crossing her fingers in front of her face.

"Quit doing that," said Kyle, unlocking her fingers.

"Is the experiment over?" Sadie asked, smiling. *Just say yes, Kyle, so we can move on.*

His steady gaze held mixed emotions until he clasped her hands again. "Did it ever begin? Can we make it work under normal circumstances, Sadie? We do an excellent job in crisis mode."

Sadie groaned. "What do you mean?" When did his excessive caution develop? Kyle was ruining the high point of their getting back together.

"I understand your feelings, Sadie. But we spent two years apart and can't rely on what we knew about each other. Who are we now? You're less impulsive than in the past, finish what you start, and don't mind listening to advice."

Good. Kyle noticed her outlook had matured. "What's the downside?" she asked, pondering what he said.

"Trying to reclaim the two years you consider lost instead of living one day at a time. God meets us where we are, and our obedience plants us on His pathway for our lives. Stop running on your own steam, Sadie. The Father supplies wisdom when we ask for it."

Sadie closed her eyes, then opened them wide. "Have you asked for wisdom concerning us?"

"I'm crawling along until He points the way forward."

His solemn expression showed his sincerity. She realized Kyle wanted a lifetime with her as well. But he would walk away from the relationship if he deemed it necessary.

"See, I've changed too," continued Kyle. "Nowadays, I'm more interested in pleasing God than myself. I get stumped just like everyone else. My desire is to keep it real. No more confusing anyone with false impressions. Do no harm is a hard motto to live out."

"Are you rescinding the 'date other men' requirement?" she asked.

"Of course. I want unlimited access to you," he admitted, grinning.

"It's called marriage," said Sadie. "Commitment is an honorable word. Stop belittling our bond. It's real and not an illusion."

His expression lightened then turned serious again. "Admit we fell in love with an image we created ourselves."

Sadie tilted her head to the side, acknowledging the truth. She fell in love with a knight in shining armor and then discovered a real man lived inside the shell. And Kyle realized his perfect partner was an insecure woman afraid to face life head-on.

"Does our car have enough fuel for the journey, Sadie. Or are we driving on fumes?" He touched a finger to her mouth when her lips parted. "We owe it to ourselves and each other to take our time."

Either Kyle had changed in meaningful ways, or there were aspects of him she never knew. His waiting on God, when his heart wooed him to succumb to her dreams, boded well for both their futures.

He kissed the tip of her nose. "I only ask that you don't keep any secrets from me. In the past, we both failed on that score."

"But not anymore. At least where I'm concerned. You're going to get tired of hearing what makes Sadie Cummings tick."

He shook his head. "You're a special lady. I want to know everything about you."

For the first time in two years, Sadie felt that her life was on the right track. Every obstacle she met turned into a stepping stone to the next level. Perhaps her change of focus left her free to be herself. And she was finally discovering who she truly was.

Straightforward directions had her racing toward the prize with more confidence than she'd ever known. Still high on her wish list was raising a family with Kyle. But out of nowhere, following Jesus's pathway for her had gained importance. Sadie strove hard to understand His purpose during each developmental phase she faced.

Before going to bed one night, she sat in her rocking chair, thinking about her next move. *Pajama Party: The Story* was self-published with the marketing turned over to Kate. Now Sadie felt free to pursue whatever God had in store for her. Play rehearsals started last Saturday, and the handpicked teen cast exceeded expectations.

Kyle had rightly cautioned against exploiting the girls in any manner, and Sadie desired each one to adapt godly principles into their daily lives. She loved those girls and invested considerable time to support them.

Hopefully the time spent at the learning center would direct their paths for years to come. How wonderful if they left high school equipped to tackle college or whatever avenues they chose to pursue. Each girl held such solid convictions about herself. Strong personalities prevailed within the group at large.

Her closeness allowed Sadie to observe them through times of happiness and when they were hurting. Her opinions about their character fluctuated on any given day. One fact never changed: None of the eighteen followed anyone at random. In fact, she and Kyle often discussed how individuals who appeared to be followers were selective in who they followed. It seemed they never followed anyone to places they had no wish to go or engaged in events they had no wish to join.

A few days prior, Kyle had confessed to an ongoing fascination with the discovery from a biblical viewpoint that followers were more selective than he'd thought. He felt that God led him to scriptural references that matured his perspective on the topic. But instead of sharing the revelation with her, he'd stated it was a continuing study that touched him personally. And Sadie experienced a first with Kyle. She respected his privacy and dropped the subject.

Smiling, she rocked the chair in a soothing motion. Sharing other people's lives had increased her awareness of right and wrong thinking within herself. A sea of change from the previous two years of wallowing in self-pity.

Life tripped happily along for the people closest to her as well. Henry Blackburn had become a permanent fixture for Sunday dinner. Roland, Cindy, and Brian frequently joined in the meal with them. Discussions usually revolved around Roland and Cindy's wedding, which would take place on Saturday.

They, along with Sadie, usually dined at the Franklin home on Friday evenings. Then she and Kyle spent the rest of the evening and most of Saturday together. It was always an enjoyable end to a hectic workweek, even though they spent Sunday after services apart.

Kyle even requested that she sit next to Sarah on Sunday mornings in honor of their relationship. And Sadie was happy to do so. On the first Sunday, with Sadie next to his mother, Kyle left the podium after the message and stood in front of her, holding out his hand. Sadie blushed when murmurs instantly surfaced throughout the sanctuary. Grasping onto his fingers, she meekly followed him down the aisle into the lobby, where she and Kyle greeted parishioners leaving the building.

At her mother's insistence, Sadie spent most evenings at The Main Street Diner learning the ropes. Jeanette wanted her children able to manage operations years before her retirement, even though the responsibility to manage it day-to-day would rest on Amy. And as a business major and finance minor, her sister eagerly looked forward to the task.

Due to deliver any moment, Dee spent most days at home, except for attending play rehearsals Wednesdays and Saturdays, along with church on Sundays. These days, she used her free time to keep redecorating the nursery. Newly engaged, Kate and George visited his grandparents in Arkansas two weeks ago, setting their wedding date for mid-September.

Matt told them one day that the hospital transferred Lincoln to a rehab center in Seattle just days after Sadie had visited him. Listening to Kyle had worked out well for Sadie. That last meeting with Lincoln had cut the final cord between them.

It reminded her of another assumption Kyle had gotten correct. They both *had* changed a lot since ending their engagement. Surely the man had never been as bossy as he was now. He'd chuckled when she brought it up while eating dinner one evening, but it was true. Kyle had a particular way he wanted things done and didn't mind telling everyone about it. Also, he had tremendous insight on human nature and didn't shy away from giving his opinion. He normally made good choices, though. So far, his handling of Leanne had been one of the few exceptions.

On the downside, while Sadie freely shared her life with Kyle as he'd requested, he still sometimes seemed clearly bothered by a matter he failed to discuss openly. And even though she remained silent, it put her off balance whenever it happened. Kyle had sufficiently dealt with the earlier obstacle of Lincoln. Now he replaced it with another complication he hid away from her.

Sadie ceased rocking, planting her feet firmly on the floor. Mind made up, she slid beneath the covers, turning off the lamp.

I want answers, Kyle. Tomorrow, you play by your rules.

* * *

Hands shoved into his pockets, Kyle stood next to the railing, softly whistling a favorite tune. While stars twinkled high in the moonless night, a crisp breeze kept his mind alert. The neighborhood was quiet except for the occasional barking dog. However, the serenity of the moment escaped his notice. Kyle was troubled. The man who prized clear direction recoiled from the lack of clarity. Timing mattered to God, and Kyle wanted to hit the bull's-eye in every arena of his life.

Over two years ago, he learned the hard realities of charting his own course. Now, would indecision cause him to miss out on what God had always planned? Was he exercising prudence or experiencing cold feet?

Last June, he thought his future might be with Leanne. Only his father's sudden death banished that careless idea. And then, eight months later, he and Sadie were hoping to build their lives together for the future. Might the second time around be the catalyst that brings his personal life into focus?

Last spring, loneliness pressed him into taking up with the wrong woman. He had to get it right. Making another mistake would harm Sadie and him in the end.

The next evening, Sadie sat inside her car waiting for Kyle. Her fingers on the car horn kept the beat with the tune she sang. The flat tone had her giggling in between the words. Busy surveying the Franklin house, she jumped when a knock pounded on the glass beside her.

Quickly removing her hands, Sadie let down the window, smiling sheepishly at the elderly lady staring at her. Maybe she'd made more racket than she'd supposed. And then her mouth hung open in amazement at the colorful outfit her neighbor wore. The widow living two doors down the street was dressed in mismatched clothes. She wore an orange hooded coat, purple hat, red gloves, and a pea-green scarf wrapped around her neck.

Instead of showing anger, amused brown eyes glittered at Sadie. "He knows you're waiting for him, sweetie. Since the entire neighborhood is aware, I can't imagine how it could escape his notice."

"I'm sorry, Mrs. Perkins." Sadie hung her head out the window, speaking to her neighbor as she retreated. "Please forgive me. I promise it won't happen again." Trying hard not to laugh, a repentant Sadie resumed singing without the car horn ensemble.

On her porch, the gray-haired lady pointed to the man approaching the car on the passenger's side. Then she waved at Sadie before closing the front door behind her.

Kyle slid in beside Sadie, kissing her lips. "What a way to begin an evening out. Shame on you for bringing a senior out into the bitter cold."

"Very funny, mister. It's fifty-five degrees outside. The warmest day this month." Sadie glanced at him, giggling. "I was biding my time while you kept me waiting."

Kyle sighed. "Minister Dawkins called. Wendy Kirkland's grandmother tumbled down the stairs, breaking her hip. The ambulance is taking her to the hospital. He's thirty minutes away from Shiatown, so we'll stop by on our way to dinner."

Nodding, Sadie started the car, pulling away from the curb. "How did it happen?"

"A grandchild left a ball on the steps. Thankfully, she was over halfway down the stairs before tripping."

"Should we skip dinner out and cook a meal at home later on?"

He shook his head. "The Dawkinses are on their way."

* * *

The parking lot was full at the restaurant when they arrived an hour later; that didn't bode well for the half-starving couple. Tonight was the debut of The Hidden Corner, the newest and last edition to The Main Street Diner's sub-eateries. To Sadie, feeling faint from hunger, it took ages to secure a table. But finally, she sat in the chair Kyle pulled out for her in an intimate alcove tucked away in a corner.

A proud Sadie gazed about her after the server took their order. The restaurant looked incredible. A romantic atmosphere saturated the wine cellar-like setting. Jeanette combined two rear meeting rooms into one space. Multiple groups of three small columns added privacy while low-key lighting and candles created a cozy ambiance.

An outer door had been added, which gave the occupants direct access from the parking lot, and tinted windows adorned the back wall. Twenty tables strategically situated around the room were fully occupied tonight. Good thing the server took their orders swiftly. She and Kyle had waited forty minutes for a table, and people still poured into the foyer.

Pleased with the turnout, she thought about ways to keep customers from waiting so long before being seated. "Kyle, maybe we should take reservations for The Hidden Corner on weekends."

"An excellent idea. This place is a hit. Who suggested the concept and thought of hiring a jazz pianist?" he asked, surveying the room.

"The whole idea came from Roland. He and Cindy convinced Mom to give it a go." Smiling, she waved when a cousin passed by their table. "The pianist is an acquaintance he ran into with hungry mouths to feed. This is the perfect part-time job for him. He'll spend three hours a day on weekends honing his craft. Hopefully this job will lead to other gigs."

"Then he can quit the day job?"

"Exactly. Miracles still happen. Look at us."

Kyle's eyes roved over her face until he focused on her lips. "If you were sitting closer, I would kiss you."

As if floating on air, she immediately kneeled beside him and raised her face toward his. Without hesitation, Kyle cupped her cheeks in his hands. Unblinking eyes gazed into hers as he lowered his mouth to her lips. A shiver spread through Sadie's body. All he'd done was brush his lips across hers, but she felt an explosion go off inside her. He willingly showed her affection inside a crowded restaurant. Keeping the contact alive, Kyle held onto her hand until she sat back down.

Sadie reached for his other hand, unable to sit still. "I have a question for you, Kyle. Do you ..." She paused, licked her lips, then shifted in the chair. "Kyle, do you think about Lincoln when we kiss?"

He released her fingers; leaning across the table, he caressed her cheek. "I only think about Lincoln when I'm praying for him. He's at home with his family and hopefully rehabilitating. People triumph over physical limitations every day."

Her hand covered his, and she smiled when his eyes blazed with light. "Something is troubling you, Kyle. What's keeping you from fully committing to us?"

"Nothing." Without breaking eye contact, he reached into his jacket pocket. "There is a concern that I can't pinpoint. But the problem is mine to solve and not yours."

Sadie stared in astonishment as Kyle pulled a ring box from his pocket. Tears blurred her vision when he placed an engagement ring on her finger. "Oh, Kyle!" It was the ring she'd fallen in love with over five years ago.

One Saturday afternoon, during her senior year in high school, Sadie had accompanied Kyle to purchase a birthday present for Sarah. His mother favored a certain jewelry retailer, and his father frequently bought her little trinkets from the store. Sarah owned several antique charm bracelets, so Kyle wanted to add another keepsake to her collection. Before leaving the store, Sadie had spotted the engagement ring that now glittered on her finger. She had fallen in love with the ring she couldn't take her eyes off of now.

Unwanted memories quickly flooded into her mind. When did Kyle make the purchase? The expensive ring was priced outside the college student's ability to pay. According to Miss Sarah, he'd planned to give her the ring on her next visit home over two years ago. Did the store owner give him a payment plan for three years? If so, he'd worked hard to buy a ring that lay useless until tonight.

Tears filled her eyes. "It's as lovely as ever. When did you buy it?"

The flicker in his eyes drew her closer. "The day you told me that you'd fallen in love with it. I went back to the store after dropping you off at home."

Her emotions spiraled out of control; Sadie stared at the patient man gazing at her. Teardrops rolled down her cheeks.

"Kyle, you slaved for three years to pay for a ring that you were unable to give to me." Sniffling, she glanced downward. "And then you kept it tucked away for over two years just to offer it to me tonight." Even though Sadie suffered greatly during his absence, Kyle endured the pain of her decisions in untold ways. Yet, he still loved her. "I'm so sorry, Kyle. Please forgive me." How could she rise above the hurt she'd dealt the man?

"Don't dwell on the past. This ring represents our present and future." He paused until she looked at him again. Then he winked at her, smiling. "I've always loved you, Sadie. And I'm happier than I've ever been in my life. Even before we broke up." He hesitated, squeezing her fingers. "Please marry me. We'll blend our lives together for the rest of our days."

Jumping from her seat, Sadie hugged his neck, her cheek flat against his. She closed her eyes when Kyle wrapped his arms around her, laying his face on her hair. At the moment, she couldn't have cared less if the other patrons watched the emotional reunion. The man Sadie loved cherished her just as much as she treasured him. Her fingers drying her cheeks, she studied his features, loving each one.

"I love you so much it hurts." Breathing deeply, Sadie braved a smile and brushed tears from her face. "Do you foresee any particular trouble on our horizon?"

The grin on his face never wavered. "Of course there will be problems to overcome. And we'll overcome them. I just don't want to lose myself in you and sideline my purpose."

Sadie hiccupped, then giggled, touching her fingers to her lips. "I'm confident that won't happen to either of us. You wouldn't have proposed if that had been a possibility. Will you promise to tell me when you discover what's bothering you about our relationship?"

Nodding, Kyle kissed her knuckles before releasing her hand. "I'm here for the long-haul, sweet pea. You have my promise to be honest with you at all times. Sadie, I won't keep you in the dark about anything ever again."

"I'll confide in you, too. About everything."

Chapter Twenty-Seven

On Monday, Sadie drove behind Amy, who led the way to Cindy's bachelorette party. Last Saturday, the day after Kyle proposed, he and Roland moved Cindy and Brian to his and Sarah's house. The family from Florida arrived in Shiatown later that evening. And Tiffany and Nathan's families always occupied both sides of the duplex while in town. Her grandparents, along with her aunt and uncle, were staying with Roland.

All the plans were set up weeks ago. The reception would be held in the fellowship hall immediately following the wedding. Unfortunately, neither best man Kyle nor groomsman Matt could officiate their friend's big day. So Minister Dawkins had willingly stepped in to perform the ceremony.

Cindy, who rode in the car with Amy, took the week off from work to plow through the preparations. And after the final dress fitting that evening, the bridal party and Dee met up with guests to celebrate by restaurant hopping.

Pulling into the parking lot at the first stop with Kate and Dee, Sadie hurried out of the car, anticipating a terrific time while making the rounds that evening: hors d'oeuvres at The Teapot, dinner at Taylor and Company, and dessert at The Ice Cream Machine. The noisy entourage spanned the generations. Her grandmother, mother, aunt, cousin, Miss Sarah, Mrs. Dawkins, and Nathan's wife, Ruby.

At each location the women talked endlessly about the wedding. The bride-to-be's actions were hilarious and kept everyone laughing. Too stressed for even her extremely laid-back nature, Cindy was overreacting to the smallest detail they discussed.

"Thank God you and Roland can only get married once," said Amy, drizzling ketchup over french fries. "I wonder what time the men will stumble home tonight?"

"Don't get me started." Dee glanced at the others. "What was Matt thinking, traveling to Tulsa without us?"

Kate laughed. "Having a night out on the town with his buddies."

Sadie joined in the laughter with the other ladies, but she secretly fumed. When Matt heard about their outing, he remembered an old teammate's offer to celebrate at his nightclub in Tulsa. It was a ridiculous idea even if the club would be closed to outsiders. None of the men going drank alcohol, except for wine, most of them didn't drink at all. Nonetheless, each man invited was gung-ho about going. That evening, the women pigged out on a food blitz in Shiatown, while the men traveled forty miles for a private party.

Frowning openly, Sadie dove into a bowl piled high with her favorite ice cream, chocolate ripple. *Mmm, this is delicious.*

She looked up when her Aunt Yolanda hugged her. The Cummingses were a loving family, and so were their friends. The camaraderie around the table represented life at its fullest. Watching her grandmother's happy face brought a smile to Sadie's lips. In perfect health, the gray-haired lady was the life of the celebration that night.

Although having a good time, both Tiffany and Ruby rose to leave once the last dessert disappeared.

Tiffany hugged Cindy. "Time to collect the little ones from the babysitter. This is my idea of a bachelorette party. Welcome to the family, Cindy. I'm glad my cousin found you."

"Roland picked a keeper. Welcome aboard," Ruby added before walking away.

As if on cue, Aunt Yolanda scooted back her chair. "I agree. You'll make the perfect wife for my only nephew," she said, helping Margaret stand.

Her grandmother rose, still holding Jeanette's hand, forcing her daughter-in-law to stand up, too. On her feet, she turned to Cindy. "God blessed my grandson when he met you." Margaret closed her eyes for a moment. Roland looked exactly like his father. No doubt an image of her only son had entered her mind before pausing. She squeezed Jeanette's hand. "Mutual love and respect is important in marriages. You and Roland have both."

Cindy dotted a napkin across her face as tears trailed down her cheeks. "I'm getting married Saturday to an awesome man *and* his remarkable family. Six months ago, Brian and I came to Shiatown without being invited to come. But Mom and Kyle accepted us into their family, and so did the Cummingses. We found our place. It feels like the whole town took us in on sight."

"You'll cross another milestone Saturday," said Jeanette. "Enjoy the week alone with your husband. Your family will be waiting for you two to return."

"Whoa!" Dee rubbed her stomach. "This little one had better wait until after the ceremony. I don't want to miss the wedding of the year." She glanced at Kate, grinning. "Oops! The first wedding of the year. Did I say it right this time?"

Kate nodded. "Your apology is accepted."

Laughing, Kate and Sadie scooted back chairs, helping Dee to stand.

* * *

Saturday morning arrived with Sadie floating through the day happier than ever. The wedding went off without a hitch. As the reception came to an end, guests surrounded the happy couple about to make their getaway. Single females pressed forward until Cindy tossed the bouquet over her shoulder. And the shameless Amy almost bowled over several people in her zeal to catch it. Unembarrassed, she glanced around the room, clutching the flowers to her chest.

Sadie froze as her sister's eyes met Art's alert gaze before Amy quickly turned away. Did Kyle guess right? And was Amy interested in the older man? Perhaps she should wait a few days before mentioning it to her.

Ten minutes later, Kyle piled the couple into the vehicle for the trip to Tulsa while onlookers waved goodbye in the parking lot. Amy had swooped Brian off to the game center at Bon Appetit right before the couple left. Jeanette thought it might be too hard on the child if his mother left the reception without him. But for Sadie, saying goodbye to Cindy and Roland at the airport culminated a blissful day.

Flying to Central America after getting married had become a Cummings family tradition. Sadie's parents, aunt, and both cousins had honeymooned there as well. She and Kyle were next. The family condo always welcomed its visitors as if they'd come home.

* * *

Unwilling to wait until a decent hour, the newest member of the Sweeney clan kicked it into high gear bright and early Sunday morning. At four thirty-five, Sadie's cell phone rang, jarring her awake from a pleasant dream. Groaning loudly, she flopped onto her side as her fingers scrambled across the nightstand, trying to stifle the noise. But her hearing adjusted in an instant to the panting voice.

"Wake up," Dee whispered. "We're driving to the hospital now. Kate's picking you up in thirty minutes. Oh, God, not another one!" And then the phone went dead.

"Oh my goodness." She jumped out the bed, sliding her feet into slippers. "Dee's in labor!" Sadie shouted in the hallway before dashing into the bathroom. Dressing quickly, she ran outside just as Kate drew up to the curb.

Seven hours later, Samantha Michelle Sweeney, weighing eight pounds and six ounces, debuted at Hope Memorial Hospital.

* * *

After that delightful beginning of the week, the next five days passed by in a blur of activity. Breakfast at The Main Street Diner every other morning with Kyle was followed by endless pursuits throughout the day. Between the regular daily bustle, Sadie squeezed in visits to Dee and little Sami. Plus, Jeanette decided to pre-spring clean the house before the weekend began. All the while, Sadie prepared for her book read just two weeks away.

Pajama Party: The Story hit the market with multiple sales due to purchases by family and friends across the country. Now the real test would come once those avenues were drained. Hopefully Kate's marketing technique would increase sales beyond the friendly-purchase buyers.

And Sadie finally decided to skip play practices except on Wednesday evenings. The director and his team could apply their craft without her peeping over their shoulders. Plus, it would make attending the dress rehearsal that much sweeter.

* * *

She and Kyle gave Amy a break from babysitting over the weekend, taking Brian along for the ride when they dropped off the bride's new car at the airport on Saturday. It was only forty miles away from Shiatown, but it was the longest distance she'd ever driven without stopping. She was so nervous about driving on the highway for more than ten miles that the short drive exhausted Sadie. Then she remembered the five-hour trip she had planned to make by herself last month. It was a good thing she had listened to reason.

At the airport, she parked the car in the extended-parking lot, stashing the exit ticket inside the glove compartment. She was happy to slide into the seat beside Kyle. She had driven enough for one day. The next stop was

Tulsa's zoo. Brian loved it, and he spent most of the afternoon begging for endless train rides and drinks. Then they rode the carousel with him several times while he alternated between riding the elephant and the giraffe.

Having been stuck inside a building all week, Sadie enjoyed the freedom of walking around the grounds for hours. Until she ate so much junk food with Brian and Kyle that it ruined her day. Too late, she remembered why she seldom ate snacks, except for ice cream, but by then her stomach had already rebelled. By the time they stopped at the petting zoo, she was ready to leave. As she reclined in the passenger's seat and rubbed her stomach, Kyle and Brian sang camp songs the entire trip to Shiatown.

After pulling into the driveway, Kyle kissed her goodbye at the door, then waited for Brian and her to go inside. He was on his way to play softball at the park with his friends. Sadie walked into the house, wondering how he would be able to run around a ball field all evening. She and Brian were too tired to do anything except sleep. Sadie took one look at the sleepy boy and relinquished on the nightly bath. After tucking him into bed, she left the door ajar and settled into the living room, waiting for the newlyweds to return.

She woke up when the front door opened, and then she stumbled into the hall just as Cindy and Roland breezed into the house that night.

"You look done in, sis. Where's Amy?" asked Roland, climbing the stairs.

"I'm exhausted. Your son wore me out today. Kyle and I took Brian to the zoo this afternoon. Plus, Mom made us clean the entire house this week. Amy's hanging out with friends."

"She probably needed a break," said Cindy, laughing. Then she filled Sadie in on the vacation while they waited for Roland to get Brian.

As she spoke, Sadie's mind filled with thoughts of her and Kyle honeymooning there this June, a year after they should've gotten married. She'd held off from discussing a wedding date with him, wanting him to broach the subject first. But, he took too long.

"You're next. Wait until you show Kyle Belize," Cindy whispered when Roland came downstairs, carrying Brian over his shoulder. Then, waving goodbye at the door, she followed her husband and son outside.

Sadie dragged her tired body up the steps after locking the door behind them. Kyle's car was parked in the driveway. She liked the way he still made time for his friends even after spending the day with her and Brian. Tomorrow, he would spend the day in his room praying and studying scripture.

She slid under the cover then turned off the light. It was the first time she'd fallen asleep before her mother and sister had even come home.

* * *

Turning over in bed, Sadie stretched her limbs beneath the covers, yawning. Suddenly, her eyes sprung open, and she stared at the redbud tree across the street. Tiny reddish blooms covered it in brilliant flowery splendor. Blinking rapidly, she clapped her hands, then immediately sat up in bed. Sunlight blazed through the glass, and birds chirped on tree branches outside the window.

Usually, the birds had stopped singing once the sun blazed high in the eastern sky. But not today. That morning, the continuous serenade tweeted her awake on the first day of spring.

It was Kyle's first baby dedication as well. Dee and Matt opted to have little Sami christened seven days after her birth while relatives were visiting Oklahoma from out of town.

It was fantastic that her own goddaughter would receive the special honor that morning. It was hard to imagine that Kyle had spent six months pastoring over five hundred people without one wedding ceremony or baby dedication to officiate. Cindy and Roland's marriage didn't count. Sighing softly, Sadie wrapped her arms around her body.

We're perfect together. Lots of firsts will dot our future. Today is just the beginning of more to come.

Hopping out of bed, she opened the window, staring outside. A light breeze filled the air with the fragrance of fresh flowers. There were numerous gardens in their neighborhood, and Sadie closed her eyes, inhaling deeply. It was a marvelous way to begin the morning.

The closing front door across the driveway instantly gained her attention. Smiling, Sadie waved when Kyle glanced up, spotting her at the window. He blew her a kiss, and she mouthed the words, "I love you" before he continued down the street. Her gaze followed his progress across the square until he disappeared into the fellowship hall.

Hearing a noise in the hallway, Sadie quickly snatched her clothes from the rocking chair. Racing from the room, she managed to beat a surprised Amy into the bathroom. Swiftly shutting the door, she secured the lock, then leaned her back against it while her sister pounded it with her fist.

After dressing, Sadie whipped up a quick breakfast as an olive branch to Amy. The table was set and the food was piping hot when her sibling stepped inside the kitchen. Without speaking, the younger woman sat down at the table and lifted the top on the warming tray. While sniffing the enticing aroma, her eyebrows raised.

She stared at Sadie without a smile. "Some peace offering."

Unperturbed, Sadie set a pitcher of fresh-squeezed orange juice on the table. "What's wrong? I cooked sausage, bacon, toast, and hash browns. Your favorites. Plus, scrambled eggs, even though Mom and I like fried eggs better."

Mischief sparkled in Amy's eyes. "You made toast. I woke up craving buttermilk pancakes."

Sadie laughed, scooping hash browns onto a plate. "Talk about ungracious attitudes. Enjoy your meal, ingrate."

Amy glanced at Jeanette, taking the seat across from Sadie. "Mom, we need another bathroom in this house. Lately, Sadie insists on showering first every morning."

"That's because *you* insist on placing lit candles around the tub and then bathing for an hour." She burst into laughter. "Or do you soak thirty minutes, then lotion up the other thirty?"

"You run over me in the hallway, and then have the audacity to mock my beauty regimen?" Amy studied Sadie's calm expression. "What are you fixing for dinner today?"

"Nice try. Guilt only goes so far. It's your Sunday to cook. Don't forget, Kyle and Miss Sarah are joining us. Along with Brian, Cindy, and Roland." Smiling to herself, Sadie ticked names off on her fingers. She glanced at Jeanette. "And ... Henry Blackburn."

Ignoring the comment, Jeanette checked the clock on the wall. "The food is delicious, Sadie. Next Sunday, Amy will treat us to that pancake breakfast she's whining about." She glanced at her youngest daughter. "Sweetheart, give us a replay of your week while we eat."

Immediately, Amy launched into snippets of her week. As always, the freshman's witty remarks made them laugh until Jeanette noticed the time.

"Come on; we're running late." Rising from the chair, she grabbed her purse from the counter and headed for the front door.

Once outside, Sadie waved to people, turning into the parking lot as she and her family strolled across the square. Driving down from Tulsa, Dee's grandparents pulled into a parking space across the lot, and three cars parked close by. It seemed that baby dedications still mattered to many people, including the elder Gibsons.

Sadie kissed her mother's cheek inside the sanctuary when Jeanette stopped beside her favorite row. Strolling to her seat, she hugged Sarah, then spoke to Dee, sitting behind her. Even though every chair was filled, Kyle had vowed not to initiate another service. In a board meeting, he'd entertained setting up a monitor in the largest conference room, saying, "securing fifty additional chairs will provide sufficient overflow for gatherings like special dedications. We're here to build God's kingdom and not our own."

Watching ushers place additional chairs in the back, she looked up when the ministry team took the platform. Minister Dawkins continued to his seat, but Kyle and Matt stood together at the podium, chatting. Finished talking, Kyle nodded at Sadie before requesting Dee and the Gibson and Sweeney families to come forward.

At least thirty people surged to the front and stood on both sides of the podium. Once there, the proud mother handed Sami to Sadie. Then the godfather, Matt's older brother, Gentry, gathered beside her and the sleeping baby.

No one in the sanctuary spoke a word as a hush announced the seriousness of the occasion. The ceremony proceeded smoothly until Kyle's body gave a slight jerk while blessing Sami. Next, his eyes opened wide, and his hand shook before he mastered control over his body.

Trembling, Sadie practically wobbled on her feet. Had she imagined what just happened? Although no one else seemed to notice, she saw Matt staring at Kyle. Something was wrong. Her mind filled with questions that couldn't be asked until much later.

However, she faithfully watched his every movement, almost missing her cue as the dedication flawlessly continued. Once the ceremony ended, Sadie handed her precious godchild to Dee and sat down beside Sarah, praying her fiancé wasn't ill. Maybe he shouldn't have gone to the park yesterday.

Throughout praise and worship, her gaze was glued to Kyle. His head lowered, he sat motionless in between Matt and Minister Dawkins. But right before the choir finished singing, Kyle lifted his hand in praise to God, and then her mood lightened.

Matt went to the podium to read the announcements as the choir left the platform, thanking the congregation for praying for his daughter. Once he returned to his chair, a revived Kyle stepped to the podium, smiling freely. Instead of speaking, he cleared his throat, then chuckled. The rich tone resonated within Sadie's heart.

"March has been an incredible month for me. How about you?" He paused, actually waiting for replies.

Sadie glanced around when several voices concurred. Although silent, many heads nodded in agreement.

"Besides the baby dedication, today marks another first occurrence for your pastor. I'm abandoning my text to tell you what the Holy Spirit dropped into my spirit ten minutes ago." He glanced at Sami still asleep in her mother's arms, and then at Sadie. "How many of you personally know Sadie Cummings?" Kyle pointed to her. "She stands beside me at the door after services each Sunday."

Eyes open wide, she glanced at the woman sitting next to her. Sarah smiled then stared inquisitively at her son. Glancing behind her, Sadie's body shook when Jeanette, her head tilted to the side, watched Kyle.

I'm with you, Mom. Where is Kyle going with this?

Completely at ease, Kyle tapped his fingers on the podium, surveying the people sitting in front of him. Then, grabbing the microphone off the stand, he moved closer to the platform's edge. "Most of you sat through my father's teachings for many years before his death in September. In fact, over three hundred of you watched as my life progressed from birth until today. But how many people can say you truly know me? Who I am? What I believe? And how I behave behind closed doors? Until twenty minutes ago even, I couldn't truthfully answer two of those questions myself."

Hesitating, he pointed to Sadie. "Two weeks ago, I proposed to this lovely lady, *again*. And although she said yes for the second time, the occasion marked the first time that I really wanted to marry her." He paused when several gasps sounded around the room. "Now, don't get me wrong, I wanted to marry her the first time I proposed. But not the essence of who she was, but the person I'd envisioned her to be."

Sadie chewed on a thumbnail when Kyle glanced at her. Still on the platform, he moved directly in front of her chair.

"My twenty-year-old self expected my eighteen-year-old fiancée to become the perfect woman. Yet, I was an imperfect man. How many of you know those types of miracles don't happen overnight? The Father conforms us to Jesus's image as we trust in His goodness. It's all about relationships.

So, after seeming devotion, Sadie and I called it quits. That is, until we both relocated to Shiatown. Until then, I'd last laid eyes on her the day before I flew to California. God taught me a valuable lesson once I arrived home. The purpose for our lives didn't change while we were apart."

Tears misted Sadie's eyes as Kyle's gaze held hers. "Facing off two years later, we loved each other as much as ever. We'd fallen in love at first sight. Practically in our diapers." He paused when people laughed. "Yeah, I know. Our minds never wavered, even through puberty."

Folding her hands on her lap, Sadie mouthed the words, "I love you" when he paused. Then she twiddled her thumbs after he told the congregation that she'd just said she loved him.

Kyle continued when people finished oohing and aahing over her response. "Being around her again, I became very confused. What had happened to the match everyone, including me, had thought was made in heaven? Some time ago, my fiancée set off a bombshell inside my mind with one simple question: Why do people labeled as followers fail to follow everyone they meet? In fact, they shun certain dynamic personalities for others not so dramatic." He shrugged his shoulders. "Why does this strange happening occur? The person who follows individuals making wrong decisions could have opted to mimic a person making good ones. And vice versa."

Smiling, he glanced at Sadie. "You see, from the beginning, both Sadie and I believed God had a purpose for our lives that included one another as husband and wife. What sidetracked two people in love into following alternate paths for more than two years? Once we relocated, Sadie got on track quickly. Unlike your pastor, she'd repented before coming home."

Abruptly, he turned away, returning to the podium. "The answer to those questions evaded me too long. But sit tight. My mind opened up to God's word this morning." He glanced at his watch. "Here we go."

Chapter Twenty-Eight

"We all know the scripture Matthew seven, thirteen through fourteen, 'Go in through the narrow gate; for the gate that leads to destruction is wide and the road broad, and many travel it; but it is a narrow gate and a hard road that leads to life, and only a few find it.'

"Scripture is infallible. But what constitutes sound doctrine? Do we recognize truth when we hear it? Or do we hold on to beliefs that diminish our trust in God? Growing up in church didn't destine me to obey God or discern truth from error. Only meditating on His word and fellowship with Him will give us the wisdom we need to live godly lives.

"The Holy Spirit is faithful to guide us, exposing our attitudes and motives when we trust Him. But truth can become muddled within our hidden motivations and private agendas. Yet scripture has drawn a fine line we should never cross. And in second Kings, chapter sixteen, the life of King Ahaz gives us a vivid reminder. He ruled over Judah when the kings of Syria and the Northern Kingdom of Israel declared war on the nation of Judah. In fear, King Ahaz asked the Assyrian king to save the land from captivity."

Kyle paused, surveying the room. "Sound familiar? Instead of crying out to God for protection, King Ahaz turned to the world for help. The Assyrian king agreed, saving Judah from destruction. And then, King Ahaz traveled to Damascus to meet his deliverer. While there, he saw an altar he liked and sent a model of it back to Uriah the priest in Judah to duplicate.

"Once he returned home, he hurried to see the altar. Still admiring it, he declared that all sacrifices be made on the new altar. But he would retain the bronze altar for prayer and finding out what God wanted him to do. Thus, we have a divided heart. Two altars served by the same king."

He stepped away from the podium. "I'll ask you the same question Jesus asked me a week ago. How many altars do you serve?" With a wide stance, he gazed at the congregation. "Do you see the pattern? Sin escalates like yeast. Not trusting God, King Ahaz turned to the world for help. Instead of repenting, he went into enemy territory. Instead of repenting, he brought the world into his house. At any time, he could've abandoned the road to destruction. But he failed to judge himself.

"Indulging the moment, King Ahaz moved aside an altar designed by God, for God's own purposes. Anyone serving more than one altar will accept teachings that hit either one. People embrace ideas and notions that are palatable to their belief system. It doesn't matter if we consume an appetizer, side dish, main course, or dessert. Error is error. And like yeast, it permeates everything it touches.

"Spiritual maturity protect us. One day, out of nowhere, the Holy Spirit spoke to my heart, saying, 'If you want to eat the good of the land, you must first live in the good of My word.' That wasn't a new concept for me. For years I've understood that my obedience and fellowship serves me. Saying yes to His rule and Lordship will provide the fellowship I crave. Nevertheless, I almost sidelined my own destiny, turning my back on God's plan for me.

"I should have known better. In my freshman year of college, I stopped fighting against God's authority in the areas where I recognized my failings. But what about those areas lying beneath my radar?"

Moving across the platform, Kyle stopped in front of Sadie. Chuckling, he pointed at her when she frowned at him. "How many of you know that I'm in big trouble? My fiancée is not a happy camper at the moment." Smiling, he saluted her then strolled to center stage. "A curious thing happened last month that snared my attention. Sadie actually accused me of becoming bossy since we parted."

He nodded when people laughed. "Exactly. When have I not wanted my own way? Look at the implication, though. Sadie picked up on several character flaws after time away from me. Until then, she'd considered my failings normal behavior and accepted them without complaints."

Kyle moved to the platform's edge. "Since coming home, God reminded me there isn't a place called arrival in Christ. The Father wants to transform us into the image of Jesus. And it is ongoing work. Obedience, fellowship, meditating on scripture are valuable tools and will accelerate spiritual growth as we pursue God's purpose for our lives. Remember, obedience releases His anointing, and His anointing breaks those yokes of bondages that hold us hostage.

"Our Lord Jesus had the Holy Spirit without measure. He walked in perfect obedience to the Father. He only said what He heard His Father say. He only did what He saw His Father do. No one else can truthfully make the same claim. We grow from faith to faith."

After studying the congregation, Kyle nodded, then moved to the podium, replacing the microphone. "Matt." Descending the stairs, he stood in the aisle, facing Sadie.

At once, Sadie realized what had been bothering Kyle. Standing up slowly, she scrutinized him a moment before strolling toward him. She could barely stop smiling when he held out his hand.

She clutched it quickly, whispering into his ear as they walked down the aisle. "I noticed your reaction to christening Sami, and I watched you during praise and worship. You've been troubled about our having children together. Thinking my time with Lincoln might have stolen our family away from us. Why would you think that could happen?"

With her face downward, she kept in step with him, knowing he wouldn't reply until they were alone.

Kyle released her hand at the front door, stroking the back of his fingers over her cheek. "The thought hit me during the baby dedication but had probably been buried in my subconscious since our trip to Burgundy. I had a frank discussion with a trusted advisor that evening. And the topic came up during the conversation, but not concerning us. It was based on a situation that had happened to another young couple years ago." He hesitated. "You're not disappointed in me?"

"How could I be anything but proud of you, Kyle? Your message ignited a living hope within me before you finished speaking. And when you held out your hand to me, I realized you accepted me without proof of my fertility. That you actually trust that we will learn how to weather the storms we'll face in life together. What erased the concern?"

"Right thinking. Life won't give you any guarantees that I can father children, yet you agreed to marry me."

"Adoption?"

"Foster children need good homes, too. That option is worth consideration even if we do have children together." He paused when she giggled. "Why are you so happy, sweet pea?"

"On my first day at home, Mom told me she'd scheduled a full physical for me the following week. She literally forced me into her doctor's office."

Sadie smiled into his eyes, squeezing his fingers. "All the tests came back negative. I believe we will have children of our own, Kyle. I'm trusting God that there isn't anything physically wrong with either of us."

His lips murmured against her hair as the choir finished the last song. "You're the love of my life, Sadie Mae. Thank God He's faithful even when I stumble. I have thoughts of a June wedding. How about you?"

Sadie's eyes glistened with tears as she nodded. "I'll never stop loving you, Kyle."

Sighing, she stepped beside the man who cherished her more than ever. She and her lifelong love had finally come home *together*.

A Note From E. C. Jackson

"The Write Way: A Real Slice of Life" is the slogan on my website and Facebook author page. If every person reading my book feels connected to the characters, my job is done.

A Living Hope is my second book and has been another labor of love. I hope you enjoyed Sadie and Kyle's story just as much as I enjoyed sharing it with you.

Stay tuned for the spin-off young adult novel *Pajama Party: The Story* and Book Three of the hope-themed series; both books are coming soon.

Continue reading for an excerpt and book blurb from the hope-themed series' first book, *A Gateway to Hope*.

If you liked reading this novel, please leave a review on the site of the retailer of your choice.

Thank you for your time!

If you enjoyed reading *A Living Hope*, please check out the first book in the standalone hope-themed series.

A Gateway to Hope

Twenty-one-year-old Neka is a bit of an introvert, she also happens to be stunningly beautiful. When she discovers her friend James is about to be dumped, she sees the perfect opportunity to escape from her quiet life. Can she summon the courage to leave it all behind?

James Copley comes from a ruthless family. It's rubbed off. Years ago, he disengaged from his brother's smear campaign, but now his father has offered him an ultimatum, "Get married or lose your seat at the table." Plotting to stamp his design on the family business, he proposes to a woman, even though he doesn't love her. But his carefully laid plans start to unravel when she leaves him on the day she's due to meet his family. Could years of planning his comeback vanish with her departure?

A possible solution comes in an unexpected form: Neka. She's not only a friend, but the daughter of his benefactor. And she's right there, offering to support him. But will her support stretch to marriage? He attempts to win her over to his plan but collides with her powerful father who wants to leverage the situation for his own gain.

In their fight for survival and love, they are forced to face some uncomfortable truths. Can they overcome thwarted dreams and missed chances to find true love, or does forcing destiny's hand only lead to misery?

Excerpt

Nikhol Lacey stepped into the muted glow from the wall sconce above the door, grabbed her luggage from the porch, and hurried down the stairs. The path lights cast a shining arc across the yard. Pine scented the air, and fresh-cut grass clung to her sandals.

She sidestepped debris along the footpath to avoid snapping any twigs. To anyone looking, the maneuverings would have resembled a child's game of hopscotch. It seemed like ages had passed, but at last she reached her destination. Lips curving into a fleeting smile, she placed her cases at the cab driver's feet.

After shaking her hand, he lifted the bags. His raspy voice broke the silence. "Good morning ..."

"Call me Neka."

She scooted into the car and eased the door shut behind her. But she froze in place when the noisy driver stomped every twig she had missed and slammed the trunk. Her gaze swept over the second-floor windows. The house remained dark inside.

Good. No signs of movement.

Neka lay back on the cushion but bolted upright when the driver sped away, crunching loose twigs scattered across the road.

She brushed her fingers over her neck and chest and then clung to the front of her T-shirt. Familiar landmarks silhouetted against the dusky morning. She sighed, touching the window as her home faded into the receding darkness.

Regret surfaced. Would her family understand her leaving home without notice? Massaging her right earlobe, she laid her head against the seat.

James needed her. She was the only person able to help him. Finally, someone she cared about required assistance that only she could provide. Tears blurred her vision at the admission that she often felt unneeded. Self-revelation came at a price. Closing her eyes, Neka laid her face into the palms of her hand.

She was committed. It was too late to turn back now.

Lord, help me.

* * *

James Copley stood half hidden in the shadows outside the Tulsa airport terminal. He contemplated the disruption to his plans, sighing as he shoved the cell phone into his pocket. Through the window, he watched a stooped man swishing a mop over the lobby floor.

He jerked around and frowned when a car pulled up to the curb behind him. The taxi dropped off an older man in plaid shorts, who hurried into the building without noticing James's six-foot frame standing to the side.

The stillness shifted. Red and orange lights streaked a pattern across the eastern sky. Dawn hovered on the horizon as the night subsided into a brand-new day.

The quiet June morning sprang alive. Steady streams of cars carrying a bevy of people rolled down the street. A white four-wheel-drive SUV pulled to a stop in the no-park zone. A gray-haired lady dropped off a family of five, and they hugged their farewells. When the SUV drove away, it was replaced by a black sedan. A jean-clad man exited the passenger's seat, laughing as he waved good-bye. Vehicles continued replacing each other in fast succession.

The touching scenarios highlighted his fiancée's absence. Did Teri over-sleep or have a car accident on the way to meet him? He rejected those ideas, struggling to remember her travel plans. Had she mentioned who would bring her to the airport? Or had he assumed she'd order a cab as he'd done?

Leaving the milling people, he searched for a secluded corner. The spot he chose placed him closer to the curb, though he remained a great length away from the cars. James was a master planner and detested surprises he didn't spring. Not that he willfully devised sneak attacks behind anyone's back. He just worked overtime to ensure no one else affected him with their unpredictability.

A no-show Teri Campbell dealt a harsh blow to plans he'd thought he'd carved in stone. His mind replayed the strategy he'd conceived four weeks ago. Jaw muscles pulsated as he clenched his teeth and bit down hard. An old sinking feeling rose at an alarming rate and failed to retreat when ordered.

Get a grip, man. You can do this. James was no longer the thirteen-year-old boy with lofty ideas.

He glanced at the clock in the lobby and shook his head. Six o'clock. Their flight would depart in ninety minutes. The cell phone had made it halfway out of his pocket before he realized and pushed it back into place. Knowledge of Teri's scheming nature stopped him from calling her.

Why now? Like most people, he hated fighting a hidden foe. No one could adequately prepare for an unknown assault. Without sufficient warning he was just an unarmed soldier in the midst of battle.

As he forced his back against a pillar, James cringed at the thought of abandoning his plan. A sudden chill struck him, as if a northern wind swirled around him. He willed his mind to focus and weigh the situation. The unfurling trouble begged a response, but the wishy-washy brigade held no sway over him. Once he reached a decision, he stayed the course.

Frowning, he stepped forward to reaffirm his resolve. In spite of Teri's absence, his plans would proceed without another hitch. Snags to his plans didn't matter. After living six years on the periphery of his family, James craved their acceptance more than ever. His life was spartan and geared to obtain his primary goal—running the family company. He closed his eyes but failed to block out the memory: days and nights occupied with endless planning, strenuous labor, and not enough rest in between.

But those times were gone forever. Years of hard work with minimal play had paid off. It was time to return home and prove to his folks that life existed after mistakes and bad decisions.

He relaxed his knotted shoulders. He hadn't spent half a decade spinning a web to see it dissipate without ensnaring its prey because of one little snag. This trip was crucial. A lifetime of professional achievements depended on its outcome. He narrowed his eyes as he considered Teri's inflexibility when they'd spoken yesterday. She'd refused to share a cab with him this morning.

The laughter in her voice when he'd tried to change her mind had riled him. "Believe me, James. Nothing could stop me from meeting you tomorrow. Count on me showing up. I'm coming."

Those words hadn't sounded ominous when spoken last night, but now ...

He ran his hand over the concrete pillar. "Not today, Lord. Not after I gave in to Father's demands."

A maroon sedan swept up to the curb. Teri alighted from the vehicle—sans luggage.

James steeled himself. The woman who'd accepted his proposal four weeks ago glanced around as if admiring the scenery. Her slow gait indicated she expected him to meet her halfway.

Forget that idea. That contradicted the way he'd play her game.

His tensions diminished as she approached. Many years battling his older brothers had taught him that remaining calm despite provocation usually won the victory. She hoped to toy with his emotions. Stiffening, he widened his stance, holding his position until she reached him.

Teri's lips curved into a welcoming grin. "Hello, handsome."

When James remained silent, her ready smile vanished. It seemed she'd lost composure after he failed to respond to her tease. Her glance flickered over to people yelling good-bye a few feet away, and keys jangled in her hand.

Eyebrow raised, he centered in on the restless movements. Teri brushed a bright-copper hair from her face. Nodding, she studied his features as if seeking out weaknesses.

A slight smile touched his lips at the war of wills.

Her tenacity amazed him. She read him well. Instead of being icy, her blue eyes flashed fire.

"When does your flight leave?" Teri pursed her lips whenever she wanted to drive home a particular point. It removed any thought of convincing her of the immediacy of the situation. "You can lower that one eyebrow. I'm not going with you to St. Louis."

Though Teri appeared to brace for an angry outburst, she couldn't keep the smirk off her face. She rubbed her chin, peeking over her shoulder to where the sedan had once idled at the curb.

In one smooth movement, James gently gripped her arm, pulling the un-resisting Teri closer. His gaze never left her face.

"So this is the real James Copley." Locking gazes with him, a thin bead of sweat dotted the skin above her lips. "I thought this engagement secured our future. Yet you refuse to talk to me."

"Why should that matter when you disrupted our arrangement at the last moment?"

"I agreed to marry you in good faith. It would be good for both of us." Tossing her curly hair over her shoulders, she laughed. "But you sabotaged our engagement from the start. Twice my friends spotted you around town with Cynthia Ward."

The jealous act caught him off guard. She was acting like a scorned woman instead of someone who'd traded herself for personal gain. He knew her real motive for agreeing to marry him. At another time, her Oscar-winning performance might've entertained him. But he didn't have time to be amused. The clock in the lobby showed he had less than ninety minutes before the flight left.

Teri tossed her hair again, gathering steam.

"We shared two wonderful years together. But Cynthia Ward? For four weeks you claimed you needed me to secure your place in the family business. You should've concentrated on me. Okay, I get it. Women fall all over themselves to please you." She jerked her hand from his grasp. Sneering, she leaned closer. "Where's that winsome smile now?"

James shook his head, looking at the cabs dropping off passengers. "So, unfounded rumors made you destroy our arrangement. You just brushed me off without notice. What about those two wonderful years you just raved about? Your response to your friends' accusations says it all."

"Why did you take her out?"

He laughed. "That question's a little late. I promised to escort her to three events *before* we got engaged."

Moving nearer, her perfume saturated the air. Her quiet appeal might have weakened a lesser man.

"You could have told me about the previous arrangements. Instead, you allowed me to stew in everyone else's version."

James stepped backward. "I can only fix problems I know exist."

Teri's body went limp until she plastered herself against him.

"I blew it, huh? I guess my emotions went into overdrive." She glanced away, shaking her head. "I let a job promotion replace my desire for us to marry. At the time, it seemed simple—career increased, so James Copley must decrease."

She fingered his collar, letting her thumb brush along his neck.

You can buy *A Gateway to Hope* from your favourite retailer.

More information:
ecjacksonauthor.wordpress.com/books/a-gateway-to-hope/

About the Author

E. C. Jackson began her writing career with the full-length play *Pajama Party*. For three and a half years she published the *Confidence in Life* newsletter for Alpha Production Ministries, in addition to writing tracts and devotionals. Teaching a women's Bible study at her church for eleven years led naturally to her current endeavor, writing inspirational romance novels. Her mission: spiritual maturity in the body of Christ through fiction.